THE GLIMPSES OF THE MOON

THE GLIMPSES
OF THE MOON

Edmund Crispin

FELONY & MAYHEM PRESS • NEW YORK

All the characters and events portrayed in this work are fictitious.

THE GLIMPSES OF THE MOON

A Felony & Mayhem mystery

PRINTING HISTORY
First U.K. edition (Victor Gollancz): 1977
First U.S. edition (Walker): 1977
Felony & Mayhem edition: 2012

ISBN: 978-1-937384-03-6

Manufactured in the United States of America

Printed on 100% recycled paper

Library of Congress Cataloging-in-Publication Data

Crispin, Edmund, 1921-1978.
  The glimpses of the moon / Edmund Crispin. -- Felony & Mayhem ed.
    p. cm.
  ISBN 978-1-937384-03-6 (alk. paper)
  1. Fen, Gervase (Fictitious character)--Fiction. 2. English teachers--
  Fiction. 3. Oxford (England)--Fiction. I. Title.
  PR6025.O46G57 2012
  823'.912--dc23
                              2012008843

CONTENTS

The icon above says you're holding a copy of a book in the Felony & Mayhem "Vintage" category. These books were originally published prior to about 1965, and feature the kind of twisty, ingenious puzzles beloved by fans of Agatha Christie and John Dickson Carr. If you enjoy this book, you may well like other "Vintage" titles from Felony & Mayhem Press.

———◦◦◦———

For more about these books, and other Felony & Mayhem titles, or to place an order, please visit our website at:

www.FelonyAndMayhem.com

or contact us at:

Felony and Mayhem Press
156 Waverly Place
New York, NY 10014

Other "Vintage" titles from

FELONY&MAYHEM

MARGERY ALLINGHAM
The Crime at Black Dudley
Mystery Mile
Look to the Lady
Police at the Funeral
Sweet Danger
Death of a Ghost
Flowers for the Judge
Dancers in Mourning
The Case of the Late Pig
The Fashion in Shrouds
Traitor's Purse
Pearls Before Swine
More Work for the Undertaker
The Tiger in the Smoke
The Beckoning Lady
Hide My Eyes
The China Governess
The Mind Readers
Cargo of Eagles
Black Plumes

ANTHONY BERKELEY
The Poisoned Chocolates Case

EDMUND CRISPIN
The Case of the Gilded Fly
Holy Disorders
The Moving Toyshop
Swan Song
Love Lies Bleeding
Buried for Pleasure
Sudden Vengeance
The Long Divorce

ELIZABETH DALY
Murders in Volume 2
Evidence of Things Seen
Nothing Can Rescue Me
Arrow Pointing Nowhere
The Book of the Dead
Any Shape or Form
Somewhere in the House

NGAIO MARSH
A Man Lay Dead
The Nursing Home Murders
Death in Ecstasy
Vintage Murder

THE GLIMPSES OF THE MOON

For Ann

CHAPTER ONE

Reminiscences of Old Gobbo

There's humour, which for chearful Friends we got, And for the thinking Party there's a Plot.

Thomas Betterton, or Anne Bracegirdle, or William Congreve, or Anonymous: from the prologue to Congreve's *Love For Love.*

"**T**HAT'S ANOTHER OF THEM, don't you know," said the Major. As some people can sense the presence of a cat in the room, so the Major could sense a journalist, or at any rate claimed he could. "Really, it's too bad. How long is it since Routh was murdered?"

"Eight weeks, I suppose."

"Eight weeks at least. And yet here are reporters still rooting round the place like...like pigs in Périgord. What the devil do they expect to find, after all this time?"

"I don't believe that's a journalist," said Fen. He ate the last of his veal-and-ham pie—conventionally insipid stuff with which, however, The Stanbury Arms served Bengal Club mango chutney in mitigation—and drank some beer. "Of course that's not a journalist, Major. You've got journalists on the brain."

The subject of their discussion, who had come into the bar only a minute previously, was a harmless-looking man in early middle age with scanty hair and a round, clean-shaven, yellowish face. His eyebrows were thick and smudged, as if laid on with a palette-knife, and he wore a dark townsman's suit. As he paid for his drink he eyed Fen and the Major speculatively, and after a moment, glass in hand, came across to speak to them.

"Excuse me," he said. "I'm a journalist." Fen gave a snort of exasperation. "Padmore's my name," the newcomer went on, with diminished confidence. "J. G. Padmore. I wonder if I might join you?" He peered anxiously at them out of moist brown eyes.

"Sit down, my dear fellow, sit down, do," said the Major cordially. Whatever his other faults, he never let his prejudices debase his manners. "I'm the Major, and this is Professor Gervase Fen, from Oxford."

"How do you do?" said Fen. "I'm sorry I made that noise. It was the Major I was irritated with, not you."

"Yes, I do irritate people, I'm afraid," said the Major, pleased at Fen's tribute. "I talk too much, for one thing. Yes, well now, as I was saying, Fen is a Professor, and from Oxford. He's staying down here for part of his sabbatical, to write a book. It's to be about the modern novel. The post-war novel, that is. The post-war British novel." He seemed to feel that Padmore's vocation necessitated filling him in on all this detail before anything further could be allowed to occur.

"Burgess, Anthony," Fen instanced helpfully. "Amis, Kingsley. Lessing, Doris, Howard, E. J., Drabble, Margaret… Brooke-Rose, Christine."

"Hysteron proteron," said the Major.

"I don't know Hysteron's work," said Padmore. "But the others, of course, are all very—are all very—"

"Well and fine," the Major suggested.

"But as you'll have gathered, I'm still only at the card-indexing stage." And not mad-keen to be forging forward from it, either, Fen's tone implied. He frowned. "Major," he said, "do tell that dog of yours to stop sniffing at my head."

Padmore, who could see Fen's head but no dog anywhere near it, looked round him a shade wildly. He relaxed, however, partially, on catching sight of a small black whippet, skeletal like an advertisement for some animal Oxfam, which was investigating a sack dumped in a corner by the bar counter.

"He's only sniffing," said the Major. "He won't try and worry it out, don't you know, not the way Sal would." Sal was the Major's other pet, an inexhaustibly strident cocker bitch loved by no one but her owner.

"It's a pig's head, for brawn," Fen explained to Padmore. "A present."

"From a Mrs Clotworthy," said the Major, the informative urge still fermenting in him. "A butcher's widow, just turned seventy-five. She lives here in Burraford in a cottage."

"Oh, good," said Padmore vaguely. "How do you do?" he said. Then, "Well, if you're sure I'm not interrupting anything..."

By this time, regardless of whether they were sure or not, he had sat down on a narrow old black-painted bench fixed to the wall beside their table. There were several such benches in the bar-room—memorials to a centuries-extinct clientèle of pin-buttocks—but otherwise the furniture was all modern, from the oak counter with its mirror-backed shelves to the green glass-topped tables and the matching vinyl-covered chairs grouped round them. Isobel Jones, the landlord's wife, hummed quietly to herself as she polished glasses. By the fireplace, an ancient man with no collar on sat motionless as a reptile, the breath moaning in his nose like wind up a chimney. Fred, the whippet, had abandoned Fen's sack with a heavy sigh and lain down; he was now alternately licking his forepaws and gazing lachrymosely at the Major. For a pub at 11.30 on a sunny Saturday morning it was not a large complement, but there was good reason for this: nearly all the able-bodied local men who would normally have been present had been dragooned by the Rector into putting up stalls and marquees for the Autumn Church Fête to be held that afternoon in the grounds of Aller House.

Padmore, having inoffensively siphoned some of his ale-froth in under an extruded upper lip, put his glass on the table in a decisive manner, by way of indicating that he was now, so to speak, open for business. "It's about Routh," he said. "And, of course, Hagberd."

Since this news came as no surprise either to Fen or to the Major, they said nothing, but merely nodded at him slowly in unison, like a pair of china mandarins. "You see, I'm writing a book too," said Padmore. "I too am writing a book. About the case." They nodded again. Suddenly a new thought seemed to strike Padmore. "No, I'm not," he said.

Fen looked at him in perplexity. "You're *not* writing a book?"

"I mean, not now."

"Started it and then gave it up," the Major suggested. "Pity. Would have been just the job, if you'll forgive my saying so."

"I mean, as a matter of fact it's finished."

"Good gracious, my dear fellow, you have been quick," said the Major admiringly. "Only eight weeks since the thing happened, and you've done a book about it already."

"You've got to be quick nowadays, with murders," said Padmore. "Otherwise someone else who's interested gets the jump on you and takes half your sales away. I've been worrying about that, I can tell you. 'Is someone going to get the jump on *me*?' I ask myself. 'Or have I been lucky —am I in fact leading the field?'"

"Yes, yes, my dear chap, of course you're leading it."

"And I can only answer, 'I don't know. I can't know'."

"No, now you come to point it out, naturally you can't."

"All I can do is to rush into print as fast as possible, and hope for the best. But it's not right."

"Not right at all," said the Major. "Dreadful thing to be forced to do."

"I mean, the draft of my book isn't right," said Padmore testily. "That is, re-reading it, I don't find that the two men, Hagberd and Routh, *emerge* vividly enough. They don't start out at one from the page."

"I should hope not," said the Major. "A very nasty experience, that'd be. No, no, my dear fellow, I know what you mean. I was only trying to make a joke."

"Not properly rounded," said Padmore. He paused in momentary confusion as his eye lit on a photograph of a scrawny fashion model in a newspaper which lay on the bench beside him. Then, recovering, "So I thought I'd give myself a few days longer," he said, "and come down here again, talk to some of the people who knew them, and try to visualise them more distinctly." Put like that, the project sounded at once tedious and insubstantial, like ectoplasm at a seance. "And then do a certain amount of rewriting, I suppose," he concluded unenthusiastically.

"No use looking at me, I'm afraid," said Fen. "I didn't get here till a week after it happened. Try the Major. He knew them."

But the Major regretfully shook his head. "Only to pass the time of the day with, don't you know. And I should think you'll find it's the same with most people. Horrible man, Routh. And Hagberd, mad as a hatter, poor chap. So of course there was no one at all close to either of them—not that I'm aware of, anyway."

"Hagberd definitely struck you as insane, did he?" said Padmore earnestly. "Even beforehand?"

"Lord, yes, he'd been like it for months," said the Major. "Ask anyone. It was all that work he did."

"But what I can't understand is, why nobody took any action about it, if they realised he was dangerous."

"But, my dear fellow, that's just what none of us did realise. He could be very fierce, of course, especially against Routh and Mrs Leeper-Foxe, but then, who wouldn't be? Besides," said the Major with an air of great reasonableness, "everyone who lives in the countryside's a bit touched, one way or another. If we all started trying to have each other certified there'd be nobody left."

"So in fact, the murder came as a complete surprise?"

"We-ll…" The Major took an interval for consideration, passing the side of his right index finger along his narrow black

moustache. "Yes and no. All that hacking and hewing afterwards, don't you know—somehow *that* fitted in with Hagberd
all right. What didn't seem to fit in was the killing itself."

Padmore reached for his glass. "To Hagberd, the dead
flesh was dead flesh: nothing more," he intoned. Evidently he
was now quoting from his book. "In the abusing of it," he went
on, "the abusing of the dead flesh, that is, there could consequently be no true harm. Pain, not death, was the enemy." Fen
and the Major made simultaneous mental notes, reducing the
book's potential sales by two. "Is that right, would you say?"
asked Padmore, relapsing into the language of everyday life.
"Right more or less?"

"Quite right, my dear fellow, absolutely right," the Major
agreed. "And very...very forcefully put. Yes. The only thing is—
if you don't mind my mentioning it—that I don't exactly see
the point of putting it at all, forcefully or any other way. I mean,
although it's true that we all thought Hagberd was harmless, he
wasn't was he? He just ignored our ideas on the subject, and
went ahead and murdered awful Routh anyway."

And it was at this point that a new voice struck into the
conversation: the voice of the ancient man by the fireplace.

"Er never," it said.

The ancient man was called Gobbo.

That, at least, was how he was universally addressed; his
real name, Gorley or Gorman or some such thing, had been
in disuse for so long that by now he had probably forgotten it
himself. As to 'Gobbo', that was a Gothicism (nothing to do
with Shakespeare) bestowed round about the time of the relief
of Ladysmith owing to the young Gorman's (or Godwit's) habit
of hawking and spitting with an amplitude considered excessive
even in those relatively coarse-grained days. Gobbo no longer
hawked or spat, his third wife having with some effort cured
him of these obnoxious practices; but the nickname was by that

time ineluctable (the third wife's reward, on sinking exhausted into the grave, had been to have 'Agnes Lucy Gobbo' carved on her tombstone by a monumental mason labouring under a misapprehension), and had remained. For the rest, like many native Devonians off the beaten tourist track, Gobbo gave the impression of having been left over unaltered from a very early novel by Eden Phillpotts. He cackled pruriently at references to love or courtship. He cadged drinks. He reminisced, racily if not particularly engrossingly, about a boyhood whose chief amusements had apparently been poaching and voyeurism. He proffered recipes for long life. In winter, The Stanbury Arms gave him a free pint of bitter each day, for looking after the fire. Sometimes he would remember to do this. Grunting feebly from the exertion, he would throw on to the fire a great log, which would dislodge another great log, which would tumble out and roll, burning fiercely, to the centre of the room.

"Er never," Gobbo now repeated.

Padmore, who had opened his mouth to reply to the Major, slowly shut it again. He and the Major swivelled to face Gobbo, like gun-turrets on a man-of-war in a *Look at Life* at the pictures. Fen meditatively spooned a selected piece of Bengal Club out of the jar and ate it in his fingers on its own.

The Major said, "Who never what, Gobbo?"

"Er never killed en."

"Hagberd never killed Routh? But, my dear fellow, that's nonsense. We know he did."

"Giddout," said Gobbo.

This, if inexplicit, nevertheless had a punctuating effect, so that the Major felt obliged to pause for a moment or two before pursuing the argument. Then he said, "But why, Gobbo? The police were satisfied, more or less. What makes you think they were wrong?"

Gobbo moved his jaws silently. He was considering. Presently, "I'll tell 'ee fer why," he said.

Gilded and warmed by the steady October sunlight, they waited as patiently as possible for Gobbo to go on. Isobel Jones had disappeared into a back room, from which clinkings and bumpings indicated that she was shifting crates of bottles about. The whippet Fred, tiring of the companionship of Fen's sack, had rejoined the humans and was nudging, with his nose, the rubber tip of the propped-up walking-stick which the Major carried for his arthritis. Like most dogs, Fred detested pubs, and knocking the Major's stick over was one of his regular methods of giving notice that in his opinion the time had come for departure.

The silence extended itself.

Fen wiped his fingers on his handkerchief and lit a cigarette.

At last, abruptly, Gobbo spoke.

"I'll tell 'ee fer why," he said.

The Major's stick fell with a clatter to the floor. "Yes, well, my dear fellow, get on and tell us, then," said the Major, retrieving the stick with the dexterity of long practice.

Again Gobbo's jaws moved, this time with a stridulating noise. He was summoning up saliva, presumably with a view to further speech. Again they waited. But when after a suspenseful interval no further speech had in fact occurred, it suddenly became evident to them all that Gobbo's mind had unhitched itself from the topic, and was drifting rapidly out to sea. "Quick! Catch him!" said Padmore agitatedly, and, "Gobbo!" the Major rapped out in an army voice. "Answer the question, please!"

Luckily Gobbo had never been in the forces, so this worked. "Ur," he said. The current had reversed course, and he was coming back inshore again. "Ur. Ur, ur." All at once a spasm of energy seized him. "Er never," he began recapitulating, *doppio movimento, accelerando.* "Er never killed en. And I'll tell 'ee fer why. Cuz," he coda-ed triumphantly, *allegro assai,* "I wer' talkin' to en."

Padmore stared at him. "Talking to Hagberd?"

"Ehss."

"When?"

"Ehss."

"Concentrate, Gobbo," said the Major severely. "You were talking to Hagberd *when*?"

"Ehss."

"*Concentrate.* You're trying to tell us that you were talking to Hagberd at the time when he was supposed to be killing Routh?"

"Ehss."

"And you're quite sure you know when that was? I mean, the date, and time of day?"

"Mazed as a brish, er wer'."

"Yes, yes, my dear chap, we know all that. What I'm asking is, when was it?"

Gobbo once more fell silent; but this time, perceptibly, it was because he was giving the matter in hand his full attention. "Twenty-second," he presently announced, with decision.

"August the twenty-second...well, that's right enough," said the Major, whose voice was by now back in mufti. "That's right enough."

"Monday," Gobbo elaborated, flushed with his success.

"Yes, that's right too. It was a Monday. And the time?"

"Ar pars seven, when I leaves."

"You're not saying you were talking to Hagberd at half past seven *here*?"

"Ehss."

"But my dear fellow, you can't have been. People would have seen you both."

"Us wer' out under tree."

"Oh...They shove him out of here at half past seven every evening," the Major muttered explanatorily to Padmore, whose eyes were already glazed with the effort to understand, "because otherwise the woman who gets him his supper won't wait. But there's a seat round the trunk of the old elm outside, and he sits down and has a rest there on the way home...So you talked to Hagberd that evening under the tree?"

"Ehss."

"Do try and be a bit more garrulous, my dear fellow, can't you?" said the Major plaintively. "At this rate we shall be here till next week. You talked to Hagberd that evening—right. Now, what did you talk about?"

"Ehss."

"'Yes' isn't a proper answer, Gobbo."

"Ehss."

"No, it's not. I'll put the question another way. What did *Hagberd* talk about?"

Gobbo, clearly on the point of reiterating his monosyllable, at the last moment thought better of it and substituted something else instead. He said, "Said er wer' crook wi' a sheila."

This unlikely-sounding string of vocables had a temporarily stunning effect, not because of its content, but because to listen to, it seemed at first to make no sense at all. After a few moments, however, Fen nodded in sudden comprehension. "Hagberd was an Australian, wasn't he?" he said. "So he was annoyed with a girl, or upset about one."

"What girl, Gobbo?" said the Major.

"Er didn' arf create."

"The girl did?" said Padmore, baffled.

"'Er' means 'he', my dear chap," the Major told him. "In this context, anyway."

"In *this* context," said Padmore heavily. "Yes. I see. But anyway, what girl? This is the first I've heard of there being a woman in the case—I mean, apart from Mrs Leeper-Foxe and the Bust child."

"I don't think Hagberd would have referred to Mrs Leeper-Foxe as a sheila," said the Major. "Sheila's a more or less complimentary word, isn't it?" He returned to the attack. "Now listen, Gobbo. You say Hagberd was going on about a sheila. What sheila?"

"Doan know no Sheilas," Gobbo retorted firmly, as if he were being accused of something. "Furrin sort of a name," he offered, supplementing entertainment with instruction.

"Let's try another tack, then," said the Major. "Gobbo, you know *where* Routh was murdered, do you?"

"Ehss."

"Well, where?"

"Bawdeys Meadow."

"And how far away from here is that?"

Gobbo ruminated. "Better nor tew mile," he eventually said. A joke occurred to him. "So be they abbn' move' en," he added, cawing with laughter.

"Yes, well, my dear fellow, don't you see, if Hagberd was two miles away from here murdering Routh, you couldn't have been talking to him under the tree, could you?"

"Ehss."

"No, you couldn't, Gobbo."

"So be," said Gobbo happily, "they abbn' move' en—abbn' move' en, see? Abbn'," he croaked on a note of deep self-satisfaction, "move' en."

"That's right," said Fen.

"But he *can't* have been talking to him," said Padmore irritably. "He's thinking of the wrong day." He addressed himself to Gobbo direct. "You *can't* have been talking to Hagberd that evening. Or anyway, not at the time you say you were."

Gobbo gave a dignified sniff. "'Tes trew, after that," he said. "So be 'ee doan believe ut, ask en up over," he went on, jerking his head in the direction of the ceiling. "Er sees all, knows all."

These indications, which seemed to Padmore to add up to God, were more mundanely interpreted by the Major. "Jack Jones?" he said. He meant The Stanbury Arms's landlord, a pronounced ergophobe of thirty-eight who spent almost all of his time upstairs in bed. "But if he'd seen you, he'd have been bound to mention it, I'd have thought."

"But it's all nonsense," said Padmore. "It *must* be all nonsense."

"Still, think what a scoop you'll have, my dear chap, if it turns out that Hagberd didn't murder Routh after all."

"I don't *want* a scoop. I just want not to have to write seventy-five thousand words all over again."

"Someone ought to have a word with Jack Jones about it, though," said Fen.

"But it's all nonsense."

"Oh, come now, my dear fellow," said the Major, "we can't just drop the matter at this stage, can we?"

"But if there was anything in it, this Jack Jones or whoever you're talking about would have said. You said so yourself."

"Yes, but he may know something he doesn't know he knows. Fen, my dear fellow, don't you think it possible that Jack Jones knows something he doesn't know he knows?"

"Quite possible, I'd say."

"Well then, so we must dig it out," said the Major, as though Jack Jones were a challenging deposit of mineral-bearing clay. "Let's ask Isobel if we can go and see Jack now, shall we?"

"Now?" said Padmore.

"Yes, why not?"

And Padmore sighed. "Oh, all right," he said resignedly. "It's a wild-goose chase, obviously—or at least, I hope it is. But all right."

So they got to their feet—the Major effortfully, because of his arthritic hip—and went across to the bar-counter. Fred, who had sprung up with a yelp of gladness on seeing them begin to move, subsided again despairingly as soon as their direction became apparent. With the suddenness character-istic of old age, Gobbo had fallen fast asleep; his mouth hung open, displaying ochrous leathery gums and a pink tongue. Isobel Jones, summoned from the room at the back, said Yes, of course, her husband would be delighted to see them.

"Just a mo' and I'll let him know you're corning," she said, "so he can straighten himself up. Not that he isn't very clean and neat always, but he likes to make a special effort when people visit him." Picking up a broomstick, she thumped lightly with its handle on the ceiling; and after a short interval an answering thump came from above.

"There you are, then," said Isobel, nodding brightly at them.

"Away do go," said Fen.

Jack Jones's avocation—doing absolutely nothing, cleanly, healthily and inexpensively—had defied rational expectation by making him happy—though there had been, of course, difficulties, such as any true pioneering scheme must encounter as a matter of course, at least in its earlier stages. In Jack Jones's case, the chief of these had been a woman doctor in Glazebridge, who three years previously had taken it into her head to try and get his license for The Stanbury Arms withdrawn, on the grounds that the landlord's systematic physical inanimation must mirror a deep-seated psychic disturbance, liable to result in neglect of the lavatories, watering of the whisky, a colour bar and many other similar anti-social catastrophes; and although the Glazebridge magistrates, who disliked the woman doctor, had collaborated with the Glazebridge police in blocking this pragmatical nonsense, the woman doctor was still about, and Jack Jones consequently went (or to be more accurate, lay) in constant fear of the assault's being renewed. As a result, once yearly he would constrain himself to a fever of activity, getting up, dressing and having himself driven into Glazebridge, all in order to attend Brewster Sessions personally and make sure that his livelihood was not again meddlesomely being put at risk. As he himself was the first to admit, these expeditions were purely superstitious, since licensees are always notified well in advance if any objection to them is going to be made; but he would have been incapable of neglecting them, in spite of the dreadful exertions they dictated, however hard he tried.

In all other respects, however, his existence was a sunny one. At nights he slept with Isobel in the bedroom at the back. In the mornings, after exercising on a rowing-machine and taking a bath, he moved into another bed in the living-room at the front, so placed that he could look out of the window over the car-park, and watch people's comings and goings during opening hours. As to Isobel, far from resenting this regimen, she enjoyed running the pub single-handed, and was delighted that her husband had had the chance to settle down to a way of life which suited him so definitely. What a piece of luck it had been (she often said), that Pools win which had made it possible for them to buy the Arms! But for that, poor Jack would probably have been forced to stay on in Dagenham for years and years and years more, going out to that nasty motor factory five days a week or more.

A thin, spruce man with horn-rimmed glasses which looked too large for him, Jack Jones greeted the committee from the bar with his usual sociable warmth. "How do you do?" said Padmore, on being introduced. "You're on the mend, I hope." So then Fen and the Major had to explain that their host was not an invalid, but merely had a settled disrelish for being up and about.

"It's back-to-the-womb, so they tell me," said Jack Jones, giving the tidily tucked placental sheets an approving pat. "I'm emotionally immature—can't bear the thought of having to face up to life's problems. Well, it *is* nice to see you all," he said with evident sincerity. "I *am* pleased."

They said that they were pleased, too, and the Major explained why they had come.

"Well, I don't know," said Jack Jones, frowning slightly. "It's a bit difficult. I do remember that evening, of course, because the police questioned everyone in the neighbourhood about it—even," he said in gentle wonderment, "me. So of course, that way it got fixed in my mind. And I can tell you one thing—Gobbo certainly did leave here that evening bang on time. I know because I looked at my watch because the afternoon seemed to have gone by in a flash, and I could hardly believe it was so late. And he did have his sit-down as usual under the old elm. But as to whether he talked to anyone, I can't be sure. Because, look."

With deliberation, so as to avoid punishing his muscles needlessly, Jack Jones elevated himself an inch or two against the pillows. He pointed out of the window. Clustering round the bedhead, Fen and Padmore and the Major gazed intelligently in the direction indicated. There, sure enough, was the elm-tree, with the bench fixed round its bole. There too was the battered grey Morris 1000 which Padmore had hired in Glazebridge to take him round the neighbourhood. And there too was a much newer, larger, shinier saloon, whimsically disfigured by the words AVGAS WILL TRAVEL painted along its side. Hundreds of unidentifiable small birds sat in rows on the telephone wires, pecking sedulously at their armpits. A light breeze blew. In the centre of the lane beyond the car-park a couched cat was having a choking fit, trying to bring up a fur-ball.

"Because, look," said Jack Jones. "From where I am"—and his inflection made it clear that where he was could be taken for all practical purposes as immutable—"from where I am you can see the tree. Bend closer." They bent closer. "You can see the tree—only not, of course," said Jack Jones, "if there's anything in front of it."

The Major straightened up rather abruptly. "Yes, quite so, my dear fellow," he said. "One very seldom can see anything if there's anything in front of it. Not properly, anyway. So there was something in front of it that evening, was there? A car, I suppose. But in that case, from up here, couldn't you even so have seen if—"

"No, because it was a horse-box," Jack Jones said. "One of Clarence Tully's. I've told him he can leave them here any time he wants, and that evening he did, and that's what cut off my view of the old elm."

"So actually, you couldn't even see Gobbo?"

"Oh yes, I could see *Gobbo*. Well, part of him."

"Well then, couldn't you see if he was talking to anyone?"

"No, I couldn't, I'm afraid. Anyone he was talking to would've been hidden completely by the horse-box."

"Yes, quite, but what I mean is, you could see he was talking to *someone*, couldn't you? You could see his mouth move and so forth."

"No."

"But, my dear chap, why ever not?"

"Because it was only Gobbo's back part I could see. I couldn't see his face at all."

"Well," said Fen, "but what about when Gobbo left, to go on home?"

"I wasn't here, I'm afraid. I'd got up to go to the toilet. And then when I came back, Gobbo had left...I'm sorry," said Jack Jones sadly, "but there it is."

"As a matter of interest, though," said Fen, "when you came back, was there anyone in the car-park at all?"

"No, no one. Nothing except for the horse-box. Mondays are always quiet. No, the only other—Wait, though!" said Jack Jones in sudden excitement. "Wait! The Rector!"

"The Rector, my dear fellow? What about him?"

"He passed!"

"Passed? Where? When?"

"Just before I went to the toilet, it was," said Jack Jones, gratified at having at last found something positive to tell them. "Coming up along the lane fast, the Rector was—you know, with that bandy-legged stride of his—and he scowled up that path that leads back to Mrs Clotworthy's cottage, and then when he got opposite the old elm he scowled at Gobbo too."

"Scowled?" said Padmore in some surprise. He evidently had no idea that Burraford's Rector, a naturally splenic man, was apt to be irked by the mere sight of a parishioner, no matter how harmlessly occupied. "Scowled. I see. Yes. And what did he do then?"

"Went on past."

"But if Hagberd had been there, talking to Gobbo, then he must have seen him, mustn't he?"

"No. Not if Hagberd was round at the back of the old elm. Because look at how thick that trunk is."

"Yes, I see that, but—but— Look, let's put it this way. Was Gobbo facing right?"

"No, left."

"I'll try again. What I meant was, was Gobbo facing the right way to have been talking to Hagberd if Hagberd was at the back of the elm?"

"Oh, that. Yes. Sure he was."

"We'll have to ask the Rector," said the Major. "There's nothing else for it."

"But if he'd seen Hagberd talking to Gobbo, he'd be bound to have told the police."

"Yes, my dear fellow, but as we were saying before, if Gobbo was seen talking to *someone*, that would verify his story at least to *that* extent. We've got to go on inquiring, it seems to me, so long as there's anything left to inquire about. Jack, don't you agree?"

"Gracious, yes, Major. It's all very interesting—quite an excitement. I'm only sorry I can't help you more over it myself, but it was that rhubarb Isobel gave me for lunch that day."

CHAPTER TWO

Alps on Alps Arise

*Though we write "parson" differently, yet 'tis but "person"...and
'tis in Latin* persona, *and* personatus *is a parsonage.*

John Selden: *Table-Talk.*

So THEY LEFT JACK JONES and went back downstairs to the bar, which by now was beginning to fill up a bit. Gobbo was still asleep—bent forward at an alarming-looking angle, as though putting his head down to ward off a faint—and Padmore, who wanted to ask him more questions, said that it would be only humane to wake him, and set him upright again. But the Major disagreed. They had much better see the Rector first, he said, and then if necessary refer the matter back to Gobbo later. As to Gobbo's posture, he often slept that way, and it seemed if anything to do him good, possibly by easing the pressure of his heart on his diaphragm, or vice versa. This transferable-vote hypothesis having subdued Padmore temporarily, they retrieved the whippet Fred, and Fen's sack, and went out into Indian summer.

The small birds had all disappeared, no doubt on the first leg of a migration, and so had the cat. From the kennels of the

Glazebridge and District Harriers, three quarters of a mile away, came a clamour of hounds, at this distance uncannily suggestive of the bawlings of football fans attending a match. Suddenly there was a muffled explosion, and the near-side rear tyre of Padmore's hired car subsided to a rubber pancake.

"*Now* look what's happened," said Padmore.

But the Major said that he was supposed to walk anyway, for the benefit of his arthritis, so after Padmore had stared fixedly at the car for several moments, the expedition to the Rector set off on foot. Waving goodbye to Jack Jones at his window, it turned left along the lane in the direction of Aller and Glazebridge—past the church with its tall tower ("Popish", was the Rector's opinion of church towers) and ring of seven bells ("Popish"); past the Old Parsonage, where Mrs Leeper-Foxe had had her dreadful experience while eating breakfast; and so, after a couple of hundred yards, out of Burraford into what once, before the Central Electricity Generating Board got at it, had been open country.

Power-lines marched and countermarched, criss-crossing one another at all angles, like files of army motor-cyclists giving a display at a tattoo; it was to Burraford, for preference, that the Board brought distinguished foreign visitors when it wanted to exhibit its method of never using one pylon where three would do as well. Underneath the Board's jumble of ironmongery there were, however, fields, hedges, trees, brooks, footpaths and farm animals. To your right, on a reasonably clear day, you could see part of the south-eastern escarpment of the moor. To your left you could see the eighteenth-century façade of Aller House. Ahead—about a mile ahead, where the lane sloped upwards to a series of narrow bends and the hedges changed to high stone walls and embankments—you could see Aller hamlet. Here the Rector lived, and here Fen had rented a cottage for the three months of his stay. If you carried on beyond Aller, for five miles or so, you arrived eventually at Glazebridge, the small but affluent market town which was the centre of the district.

Owing to the Major's hip, progress was slow; but Fen's sack weighed heavy enough to make him glad to amble, and Padmore was clearly not athletic at the best of times. They met, and were greeted by, a steady trickle of people coming away from the preparations for the Church Fête. Pattering along a yard or two ahead of them, Fred frequently turned his head to make sure they were still there. He seemed to be afraid that if he relaxed his vigilance at all, a pub would spring up magically by the roadside, and suck the Major in.

Padmore gave an account of himself.

He was not, it appeared, properly speaking a crime reporter at all. In reality he was an expert on African affairs, and had returned from the dark continent three months previously with the cheerless distinction of having been expelled from more emergent black nations, more expeditiously, than any other journalist of any nationality whatever. Even Ould Daddah and Dr. Hastings Banda had expelled him, he said— the latter inadvertently, under the impression that he was a Chinese.

"Underdeveloped countries with overdeveloped suscepti- bilities," said Padmore sourly.

There had been no question, he went on, of his trying to knock African aspirations; on the contrary, he sympathised with them. Simply, he had had a run of exceptionally bad luck. He would send off a cable censuring some dissident General at the exact moment when the General's minions were successfully gunning down the palace guards, the Deputy Postmaster and the doorman at the television studios. Or he would praise the enlightened policies of a Minister already on his way to be sequestrated or hanged. Or he would commend the up-to-date safety precautions at an oil refinery which the next day would go up in flames, with fearsome loss of life. As a result of all this, eventually his paper, the *Gazette*, tiring of running indignant news items about their special correspondent's various expulsions, had called him back to London, a call he had answered as soon as he could get out of the Zambian prison where he had been put because of an article drawing the world's attention to how well President Kaunda was always dressed (this had been interpreted as imputing conspicuous waste in high places). The *Gazette* people had been very nice about it, Padmore said. They hadn't at all blamed him. There had been no question of not keeping him on the strength. Nevertheless, no one had been able to find anything much for him to do until the night when Chief Detective Superintendent Mashman had given a party to celebrate his retirement after thirty years in the Force. All four of the *Gazette*'s senior crime staff had gone to this, and on their way back from it had driven rapidly into the back of a Bird's Eye Frozen Foods lorry and been removed to hospital. So when the sensational news of Routh's murder had come in, the following morning, Padmore had been assigned to cover the story; not (as he admitted) because he had any special qualifications for doing so, but because his mooning about the office was beginning to get on everyone's nerves.

"I expect you'll find you've seen much worse things in Africa," his Editor had said.

"So I came down to Glazebridge and stayed for a week at the Seven Tuns," said Padmore, "and that was when I got the idea of ...why are we speeding up all of a sudden?"

The Major explained that they were speeding up because they were about to pass the Pisser.

Padmore said, "I see."

"Listen," said the Major. "It's making its noise again."

There certainly was a noise going on, Padmore realised, and a disquieting one at that. It was being produced by a large, old-fashioned pylon set close against the left-hand side of the lane; and it was owing to the basic character of this noise, the Major explained, that this pylon which issued it was known throughout the neighbourhood as the Pisser (even intensely respectable elderly ladies, the Major truthfully claimed, would ring one another up and say, "It's such a lovely afternoon, why don't we meet at the gate by the Pisser

and go for a walk over Worthington's Steep?"). Long familiarity with the Pisser had not, however, bred contempt for
it. On the contrary, it was universally felt that one of these
days the Pisser's noise would end in a detonation, so that it
would release the cables it supported, and these would fall
on, and electrocute, anyone who happened to be in the lane
at the point over which they passed. Complaints about the
menace of the Pisser had at first been pooh-poohed by the
electricity people, the more so as its activity was intermittent,
so that the first draft of investigating engineers had found
it as quiet as an oyster, and had gone away full of indignation at having their valuable time taken up with false alarms.
But then, months later, the Pisser had chanced to be overheard by a high official of the Board picnicking near by with
his wife and children; the attitude of authority had consequently undergone an abrupt change, and the Pisser was
now frequently visited by technicians in helicopters or vans,
hoping to catch it making its noise and to decide what was
causing it. In the second part of their programme they had
so far been unsuccessful, since the Pisser's noise had not only
survived two complete ovehauls, but had actually intensified
both in volume and in oftenness. For this reason everyone
still stepped out smartly when in its vicinity, sometimes even
breaking into an agitated trot.

By the time Padmore had been told about the Pisser's
ways they were safely past it, but as the Major was out of breath
from talking and hurrying at the same time, they stopped for a
brief rest where a horse was peering at them over the hedge.

"You awful animal, you," the Major said to it.

"Is it in poor condition?" Padmore asked.

"No, no, my dear fellow, it's just an ordinary healthy horse,"
the Major assured him. The horse rolled its eyes at them,
revolving its ears on its skull. "Horrible treacherous brutes," the
Major said. "Nip you in two at the neck as soon as look at you."

As if to confirm this, the horse bared large discoloured
teeth and seized hold of an ash shoot, backing away in an unsuc-

cessful attempt to tug the shoot loose from its moorings in the hedge. "But I thought you'd been in the cavalry," Fen said to the Major as they walked on. "Before it was mechanised, I mean."

"Quite right, my dear fellow. Twenty years of it, I had, in India."

"But didn't that get you used to horses?"

"No, the reverse," said the Major. "The more I saw of horses, the more *un*used to them I got. I was drunk for a week," he confided, "celebrating the day they took them all away. Because after they'd gone, don't you know, I couldn't have a fall."

"You mean you'd had a lot of falls."

"No, none. I *never* had a fall, not even when I was learning to ride, as a child. Well, you can see what that implied. Theory of Probability and so forth," said the Major, jouncing along briskly with the aid of his stick. "The longer I went on without having a fall, the more likely it became that I *would* have one. In the end it got a bit unnerving, because every time I got on a horse, the chances were about a billion to one against my *not* having a fall. I won through, though," he said proudly. "I survived. No fall. I'm here to tell the tale. Padmore, do you ride?"

Padmore said not.

"Don't ever be tempted to try," said the Major. "Not unless you fancy sitting astride a mobile double bed with ten homicidal lunatics carrying it."

On their left they passed the straight stony cart-track, with wire fencing on either side, which led to the grounds of Aller House; through the trees and the massed pylons they caught glimpses of the Church Fête stalls and marquees. Then on their right, coming round a bend into Aller hamlet, they passed the lane leading up to Broderick Thouless's bungalow, to Youing's pig farm, and to the Dickinsons' cottage which Fen was occupying.

Finally, round a second bend, they arrived at the Rector's house, a huge, lowering mid-Victorian erection in a comfortably large garden.

The Rector's house was called Y WURRY.

The Rector's family had lived in Aller continuously ever since one of his remoter forebears had fled to Devon to avoid being burned to death for Protestantism under Bloody Mary. Confirmed demolishers and rebuilders, they had put up house after house after house on the same site, a habit which had kept its impetus till the 1860s, when the Rector's great-grandfather had invested the family fortune in a Tavistock arsenic mine, and lost the lot. Not that the Burges were impoverished, exactly, even then. Though one of their dominant genes caused them to regard houses as infinitely expendable, another had made them very tenacious of other kinds of property, so that in the course of five centuries they had accumulated a staggering quantity of furniture, pictures, porcelain, silver, books, brocades and so forth, much of it rubbish, but some of it extremely valuable; and despite the fact that a great deal of this had been sold off during the last hundred years, enough still remained to fill three of the five attic rooms where once the damp souls of housemaids had despondently sprouted (thirty-five miles to the nearest Music Hall).

To do the Rector justice, Y WURRY hadn't been his idea. Up to 1937 the place hadn't been called anything in particular; but then in that year the Rector had gone off to India to preach better behaviour to the polyandrous Todas, and had decided on a furnished let during his absence, to help top up the Church funds. Not realising what they were letting themselves in for, a trusting couple from Hinchley Wood had taken on the lease on the agent's say-so. The wife, normally a stoical woman, had burst into tears ten minutes after entering the front door, but since they weren't specially well off, and couldn't afford to compound for the rent, they had had to make the best of it. It was not, they wrote to friends, that there was anything definite they could complain about. It just wasn't home-y, that was all. ("Great big rooms with pointy sort of windows," the wife wrote, more tears splodging on to the page, "and all heavy dark furniture not like our nice Civil Service Stores and all heavy drapes dust traps and I'll swear there are mice or even rats! though Roland says don't be silly as we've put down cheese and no one's eaten it.") Eventually they had taken to living almost entirely in the kitchen. The wooden name-sign on the gate had been the last despairing bleat on Roland's slughorn in face of the Dark Tower; after that they had abandoned the attempt to humanise their surroundings and had instead anaesthetised themselves by constantly going into Glazebridge to the cinema, where they often saw the same programme three days running, worsening their condition, as they stared at the screen, by getting diarrhoea from eating too much ice-cream.

The Rector, returning from India, had been surprised to find his property baptised in his absence, but, not being a man very sensitive to literary nuances, had done nothing about the sign until many years later, when the Major had filled a conversational gap by suggesting that not worrying was probably a Popish practice, and so *ipso facto* unfit to be continuously recommended on the gates of proper Christian people of any sort, let alone proper Christian clerics. Though temperamentally little subject to anxiety himself, the Rector, struck by this notion, had at once gone to work on the nuts and bolts which held the sign to the massive wrought-iron curlicues of his great-grandfather's gate. When these resisted him—being by now rusted tight —he had seized a hatchet and dealt the sign itself a heavy blow diagonally across the middle, and would certainly have gone on to reduce it to splinters but for being interrupted by a parishioner in trouble. Later, after he had given the parishioner a lot of money and no advice, it had occurred to him that since many undeniable Protestants, such as Jesus of Nazareth, had advised against worrying, the Major must have been speaking frivolously; so that apart from a sermon against frivolity the following Sunday, with special reference to the Major (lightly camouflaged as "a certain retired military person"), he had expelled the matter of the sign from his mind, and it had stayed expelled.

When the party from The Stanbury Arms arrived at the Rector's gate they saw a grey Mini neatly parked outside it.

Visitor.

They went on in nevertheless.

The Rector's acreage was planted to a disconcerting extent simply with hedges—huge, unkempt, dusty, spider-haunted walls of lonicera and laurel and yew; making your way among them, you felt that you were in a giant's knot-garden, or a maze. And that Fen and Padmore and Fred and the Major were going to have to make their way among at least some of them was at once obvious. From somewhere out of doors over to their right, the Rector's voice, which even when imparting confidences could be heard fields away, was being raised in wrath.

"*I* don't care," it was saying. "*I* don't care. For all *I* care, the population of Plymouth can light its houses with tallow dips. Pylon, indeed. You're not putting any pylon in *my* paddock, and that's flat. And I'll tell you another thing."

Guided partly by this uproar and partly by the Major, who professed to know his bearings, they plunged into the greenery, and so presently reached the source of the disturbance, which proved to be an overgrown circular grass clearing with an ancient sundial in the middle and hedges all round. With force rather than finesse, the Rector was in process of trimming these hedges, which as a result were beginning to look like a sort of cubist switchback. He had got down from his step-ladder and was waving his shears threateningly at a terrified little man in grey.

"Ha!" said the Rector.

If you took the Rector from the top downwards, the first thing you saw was iron-grey hair thatching a high, noble forehead. Below this point, however, matters deteriorated abruptly. No doubt about it, the Rector's actual *face* was simian—so that the overall effect was as if Jekyll had got stuck half-way in the course of switching himself to Hyde. The clothes were a crumpled, laurel-spattered clerical black, with dog-collar and with outsize cracked black shoes. Despite bow legs, the height was six foot three, and the frame was formidable. "I'm not," the Rector had once complacently remarked, "the type of thing you want to meet unexpectedly on a dark night."

The Major said, "Morning, Rector. This is Padmore, who's here on a visit."

"How do," said the Rector. "Morning, Fen. What's that you've got in that sack?"

"It's a pig's head. Mrs Clotworthy's birthday pig's head, actually. I picked it up from her porch this morning. She gave it me because I'm an M.A."

"Poor woman's obviously getting a bit gaga," said the Rector. "Ah well, we all come to it, if we live long enough. I don't imagine *I* shall, mind, but most of us do."

The terrified little man in grey said, "I'm from Sweb."

"How do you do?" said Padmore. "From *where*?" he asked.

"Acronym," said the Major. "Stands for South Western Electricity Board. They think that if they call themselves Sweb, don't you know, it'll make people look on them as friends." He shook his head sadly at the thought of so much innocence exposed in a harsh world, like babies on rocks outside Sparta.

"Damn the man if he doesn't want to put up a pylon in my paddock," said the Rector.

"They want to put up pylons everywhere," said Fen.

"Every effort is made to safeguard the amenities," the man from Sweb said in a high, tremulous voice. "*Every* effort."

"I can safeguard my amenities without any help from you, thanks very much," said the Rector. "You go and safeguard someone else's amenities. Oh, and by the way, now I come to think of it, since you're in the neighbourhood you can look in at the Church Fête this afternoon. Do you a world of good."

The man from Sweb smirked wretchedly. He was neat as a hen-bird, all in grey except for shoes and tie. Despite the warmth of the day he wore an overcoat and a homburg hat with a diminutive turned-up brim. His face was round and pink, a uniform clear pink like the inside of a young cat's mouth; his eyes were blue and protruding. He was clean-shaven. His little pot-belly kept his overcoat buttons occupied without straining them too noticeably.

"Church Fête? I—I'm not religious, I'm afraid," he managed to get out.

"If you're not religious, you do well to be afraid," said the Rector. "However, we've no objection to taking money from the heathen, I'm glad to be able to say. If you can't get to the Fête, you can make your contribution to me personally, now."

"I—I'm afraid that at the moment it's not—not quite convenient to—to—"

"Tight-fisted as well as a heathen," the Rector commented. "Well now, I hope you're quite clear in your mind about this pylon proposal. I reject it."

"Y-you understand that we have p-powers to obtain a c-c-c-compulsory order," the man from Sweb trepidantly squeaked.

"Don't you try threatening me, my man," said the Rector, almost kindly. "I've made my decision, and that's the end of that. So now be off with you." He frowned slightly, apparently feeling that this peremptoriness ought in Christian charity to be softened a little, perhaps with a touch of light humour. "Be off with you," he amended, "or I'll chop off your feet with these shears, and leave you to run away on your bleeding stumps."

At this, the man from Sweb gave a small, moaning cry, turned from them and stumbled out of the clearing. Diminishingly they heard him blundering into shrubs and hedges as he tried to find his way back to the gate.

"Uncivil sort of a fellow," the Rector remarked. "Didn't even have the elementary courtesy to say goodbye. Well now, what can I do for you lot?"

They told him.

"Gobbo!" the Rector exclaimed. "Yes, certainly I saw *Gobbo* that evening, the evening Routh was knocked off. Why shouldn't I have seen him?"

"No reason at all, my dear chap," the Major agreed. "But if I may say so, you seem to have rather missed the point. The question is, did you see Hagberd as well?"

"No, because he was off somewhere else, murdering Routh."

"Yes, but Gobbo says he *wasn't*."

"Ah," said the Rector magnanimously, "I see what you mean now. You didn't make yourself at all clear at first, chorusing at me all together like that. Did I see Hagberd with Gobbo, you're asking."

"Yes."

"No."

"He wasn't there?"

"He may have been *there*," the Rector admitted. "All I'm saying is that I didn't *see* him. Couldn't have done, not if he'd been behind the horsebox or the elm."

"It's all a lot of nonsense," said Padmore.

"Gobbo *was talking*, mind you," the Rector said.

"He was?"

"Yes. Might have been just to himself, though. Or he might even," the Rector added doubtfully, "have been saying a prayer...Actually, don't pay too much attention to that," he advised them, though none of them was in fact paying it any attention at all. "Me being a clergyman, my mind tends to run on prayer."

"Jack Jones said," said Fen, "that just before you got to the pub, you looked along the path that leads to Mrs Clotworthy's cottage and scowled at somebody."

"Scowled?" said the Rector, scowling. "I never scowl. And anyway, I don't remember that I—"

But then he did remember. Flicking his horny fingers with a noise like a fire-cracker, he said, "Yes, I do, though. It was Youings."

"Who's Youings?" Padmore anxiously demanded.

"A pig farmer, my dear fellow." The Major began absently scratching Fred's back with the rubber tip of his stick. "Lives just up the road."

"He was coming away from Mrs Clotworthy's," said the Rector. "Or perhaps he was just taking the short cut through from Chapel Lane."

"Youings," Padmore muttered. He seemed depressed at this fresh addition to the *dramatis personae* accreting round Gobbo's troublesome disclosures. "Youings, Youings. Youings."

The Major said, "Did Youings follow you past the pub, Rector?"

"Don't know," said the Rector. "Could have done. You'll have to ask him."

"House that Jack built," said Fen.

"Well, I'm going back to talk to Gobbo again," said Padmore. "He's the mainspring."

"Rusty old mainspring," said the Rector. "And if you take my advice, you'll take no notice of all this gammon he's been spouting." (*"Right,"* said Padmore.) "Amuse yourselves with it, by all means," said the Rector, as though offering them a valuable indult. "Don't take it seriously, that's all." To Padmore he said, "By the way, don't forget to come to the Fête, will you? All the fun of the fair. Yes, and while you're there don't forget to see the Botticelli."

"The Botticelli?" said Padmore faintly.

"Well, of course, it isn't a Botticelli really," said the Rector. "Awful great nineteenth-century daub actually, size of a barn door. Assumption of the B.V.M. or some such thing. Popish. Still, the Misses Bale imagine it's a Botticelli, so they get upset if enough people don't go and see it. You pay five bob and go in alone and sit in front of it and meditate on it for ten minutes."

"Do you?" said Padmore helplessly.

"Yes, because that's what the Misses Bale's mother used to make their father do. Terrible woman. I don't believe she believed it was a Botticelli at all, but she always told her daughters it was, and now they can't get the idea out of their heads. Nice women otherwise, mind you, do a lot of work for the Church."

"The Botticelli is School of Burne-Jones," said the Major. "And he's getting to be quite sought-after nowadays. There was a programme about him the other night on the telly."

"Telly, telly, telly, telly," said the Rector, as if calling a cat. "All you ever think about is telly."

"I don't watch much except for the commercials," said the Major meekly. "And then it's only for the jingles."

This was true. Though a skilled water-colourist and a voracious reader, the Major had suffered all his life from tone-deafness, and so had had no comprehension whatever of music until ITV had come along, reducing the art to such brevity, and such absolute banality, that even the Major had found himself able to grasp it.

"The hands that wash dishes can be soft as your face," he suddenly sang at the Rector in a loud, crackling falsetto, "with mild green Fairy Liquid...Liquid, Liquid," he sang. "I like that melodic turn, or whatever you call it, on 'Liquid'. Very affecting."

"It's your wits it's affecting, if you ask me," said the Rector. "I suppose you haven't been eating properly again. He doesn't eat properly," he reported to Padmore.

"Ah," said Padmore, pretending to have had a suspicion confirmed.

"You'd better stay to lunch," the Rector told the Major. "Liver and bacon today, fill you up with vitamin B."

"Good," said the Major. He liked eating with the Rector, who not only had a first-rate cook but also declined to allow conversation during meals. Explaining this policy to his Bishop, who had been about to dine with him during the course of a visitation, "What is the good," the Rector had said, "of God

giving us delicious-tasting foods, if every time we lift a forkful
to our mouths we have to break off to cope with the inane prat-
tlings of our guests?" (The Bishop, though he prided himself
on his conversational skill, had taken this very well, on the
whole. In any case he found the Rector much less of a burden
than the incumbents of some other parishes in his diocese,
who were given to composing pop masses, selling Coca-Cola in
the vestry, blessing motor-cycles and other similar unedifying
practices, thereby offending such congregations as they had
without permanently, or even temporarily, recruiting anyone
new.)

"A Dettol home is a happy home," the Major sang.

"Can't ask you other two," said the Rector, "because there's
not enough." Padmore uttered a single disclamatory vocable
which would no doubt have blossomed into a full-length
previous engagement if the Rector had given it the least chance.
"And now I must get on with these hedges," the Rector said.
"Major, you can stand by and pick up the bits."

On their way out, Fen and Padmore lost themselves,
coming out on to the Rector's front path considerably nearer to
his shallow front porch than to his gate. In the porch they saw
grey-clad buttocks bent as if for a caning, their owner peering
anxiously in through the letter-box.

"So there we are," said the man from Sweb, straightening
at their approach. "Has it gone in, or hasn't it?" he added, in
the bright, uncommitted fashion of a television question-master
offering alternatives in a quiz.

The Major having been left behind with Fred, and
Padmore being still half stunned by the complexities of English
rural life, Fen felt that it was up to him to take the lead. "What
is it," he asked, "that may or may not have gone in?"

"The Compulsory Service Order." The man from Sweb
sighed, with every evidence of genuine regret. "We *ask* people

to co-operate, of course, but if they won't, then there's nothing else for it."

"But couldn't you save time and trouble by compelling everyone to co-operate straight away?"

"Oh, no," said the man from Sweb, shocked. "That'd be dictatorship, wouldn't it? Sweb wouldn't do anything like that. Dear me, no...The only thing was, I didn't feel the Rector was in quite the right mood for me to give him the order personally, so now I've put it in the letterbox."

"Let's hope so."

"Of course I have." The man from Sweb re-buttoned his grey overcoat efficiently across his middle. "Well, I must be away, away, away. Anyone for a lift?"

But there was no one for a lift, since Fen lived close by, and Padmore was heading back to Burraford to have another go at Gobbo, whereas the men from Sweb's headquarters were in Glazebridge, in the opposite direction.

Though lunch was still pending, the man from Sweb puristically said "Good afternoon," and trotted off to his Mini.

"Ought to have remembered to tell him to get his people to do something about that pylon," said Padmore, on whom the Pisser had made its usual abiding first impression. "You'll have a word with this Youings, then?"

Fen said that if possible he would. He still, however, lacked any real interest in the Routh-Hagberd horrors, and off-hand, considered it unlikely that Gobbo's reminiscences, even if correct, were going to make any serious difference to anyone so long as they remained so feebly supported.

"That tyre," said Padmore sadly. "I'm going to have to change that wheel."

Fen walked with him for fifty yards, back towards Burraford, and parted from him at the entrance to the Thouless-Youings-Dickinson lane. They had arranged to meet again later on, at the Church Fête.

"Watneys brings us all together," Fen heard the Major singing in the distance. "What we want is Watneys."

CHAPTER THREE

Youings: A Rebuttal

> Various the roads of life; in one
> All terminate, one lonely way
> We go; and "Is he gone?"
> Is all our best friends say.

Walter Savage Landor: *Wisdom of Life and Death.*

As HE WALKED up the lane, towards Youings's pig farm and his own cottage, Fen heard more music.

To be accurate, what he heard was not so much music as sounds. The sounds were being produced by Broderick Thouless, on the piano in the hut in his garden where he worked.

Film-music composers are just as liable to type-casting as actors and actresses. Chance pitchforks them into working on a picture which turns out specially successful, and subsequently, regardless of whether they have contributed anything ponderable to the picture's success or not, producers go on for years and years mechanically re-hiring them for further pictures of the same kind, with the result that one spends his working life in a perpetual seascape, another writing wah-wahs on trumpet parts for people surfacing in mud-baths into which they have comically fallen, a third assembling electronic beeps for nude love scenes, and so on.

For more than a decade now, Broderick Thouless had resentfully specialised in monsters.

For him, type-casting had set in with a highbrow horror film called *Bone Orchard*, a Shepperton prestige production which against all probability had made a profit of over a quarter of a million pounds. By nature and inclination a gentle romantic composer whose idiom would have been judged moderately progressive by Saint-Saëns or Chaminade, Thouless had launched himself at the task of manufacturing the *Bone Orchard* score like a berserker rabbit trying to topple a tiger, and by over-compensating for his instinctive mellifluousness had managed to wring such hideous noises from his orchestra that he was at once assumed to have a particular flair for dissonance, if not a positive love of it. Ever since then he had accordingly found himself occupied three or four times a year with stakes driven through hearts, foot-loose mummies, giant centipedes aswarm in the Palace of Westminster and other such grim eventualities, a programme which had earned him quite a lot of money without, however, doing anything to enliven an already somewhat morose, complaining temperament. A bachelor of forty-six, he existed in an aura of inveterate despondency, lamenting his wasted life, various real or imagined defects in the luxurious large bungalow he had built himself, the slugs among his peas, his receding hair-line, taxes, the impossibility of getting decent bread delivered, the Rector, jet aircraft, the deterioration in the taste of Plymouth Gin ("It's a grain spirit now, you see") and a whole manifest of aches and pains, some of them notional, others the inevitable consequence of smoking too much, a sedentary life, mild obesity, not being young any longer. In spite of his tales of woe he was quite well liked in the neighbourhood, possibly because his depressive phases were relieved on occasion by manic ones, during which he could be amusing company. His single state was accounted for locally by the theory that on his visits to film studios he seduced starlets, a breed which no one realised had long since become extinct.

The monster music suddenly transformed itself into the last two phrases of *Pop Goes the Weasel*, then ceased altogether. Thouless appeared in the doorway of his hut, caught sight of Fen over the hedge, and waved.

"Come in and have a drink," he called. "The recording isn't till Monday week, and the only section I've got left to do is where they fail to destroy it with an H-bomb.

"Though why they want music over that, God alone knows," he went on, crossing to the hedge. He was short and plump, with untidy hair and horn-rimmed bifocals, and like most men who have spared themselves the strain of supporting a wife and family, looked younger than his age. "The effects track's going to be so noisy that no one'll hear a note of *that* section, I can tell you. Still, good for one's performing rights, I suppose, that's if they leave it in, which they probably won't. And performing rights aren't what they used to be, anyway. Do you know how many cinemas close down in this country every year? It runs into hundreds. I'm in a dying industry except for the telly stuff, and the pop boys have taken over all that, Grainer and that lot. I ought to try and strike out on a new line, but I'm not young enough, haven't got the adaptability any longer. In the end I expect I shall have to sell the bungalow, and even then I shan't get anything like what I paid for it, particularly if you include those fantastic fees the architect and the quantity surveyor mulcted me for, and the money I had to spend making the garden."

Fen said that he was sorry, he couldn't stop for a drink at the moment.

Thouless nodded gloomily, a cram-full pin-cushion for life's darts into which, unbelievably, yet another spicule has successfully been inserted. He peered at Fen's sack.

"That your pig's head?" he inquired, and when Fen had agreed that it was, "Brawn, I never liked brawn. Try not to salt it too much, or it'll be like getting a wave in your mouth when you're bathing. I must go and find myself some lunch, if there's anything in the house worth eating. Do look in and see me sometime, no one ever seems to visit me nowadays. You going to the Fête this afternoon?"

"Oh yes, I think so."

"Radio Three gave rain," said Thouless. Suddenly he produced from his trousers pocket a fistful of crumpled pound notes, which he thrust at Fen across the hedge. "I wonder if you'd mind buying something for me. At the Fête, I mean."

"Aren't you going yourself?"

"Yes, but I can't possibly buy *this*. It's my scores for *The Mincer People*. I gave them with a lot of other junk to be sold on the Rectory Stall."

"And now you want them back?"

"Good God, no. It's just that no one in his senses is going to offer a penny for them, so if they're left over they'll be a sort of embarrassment, or at least, so I suppose."

"Not to the Rector, surely."

"Not, admittedly, to the Rector, but it won't be him, it'll be poor old Miss Endacott, who's so shy of people, she practically faints away whenever she catches sight of anybody. I'm sure she'd rather hang herself than face bringing the scores back to me, so you see, they've got to be disposed of somehow."

"I wouldn't mind buying them myself," Fen said.

"You would, you know," said Thouless, all at once speaking quite cheerfully. Consideration of *The Mincer People* had improved his emotional tone, so that he was now veering towards one of his unpredictable fits of euphoria. "Terrible stuff, you're never *heard* such a noise. There was one bit of kiss music, for a marvel, but by the time I got to it I'd done so many murders that it sounded exactly like another one. *Derngh!*" he exclaimed in his nose, imitating sforzato stopped horns. "And then *erk, skerk*," he added, possibly attempting to convey ponticello strings. "And then there was one part where I got Jimmy to put the xylophone down on its side and play tremolandos on the resonators—unspeakable, that was. I can't remember anything nastier I've done except for those sickening wailing violin harmonics in *Thing of Things*."

"All right, I'll buy the scores for you, then," said Fen compliantly.

"Thanks. And now I think I'd better go indoors and turn out a spot of relief music before I eat," Thouless said. Relief music was his anodyne for the X-pictures, the example in hand at the moment being settings of poems from *A Child's Garden of Verses*. "How's your health these days?" he added, as if Fen had applied to him for life insurance. "Good?"

"Yes, very good, thanks. Yours?"

"Indifferent," said Thouless. "Still, I suppose I've been worse, even if I can't remember when. See you this afternoon, then."

"See you this afternoon," Fen agreed, and went on up the lane until he came to Youings's well-kept pig farm.

❀ ❀ ❀

In the yard beside the house, Youings was hobnobbing with a gigantic brood sow. A massive, fresh-faced, blond man of about forty, he was bent over double, addressing the sow practically nose to nose.

"'Ullo, my dear," he was saying to it tenderly in his mild Devon accent. "'Ow *are* you, then—WILF? You funny little thing, you." The great creature grunted and swayed in satisfaction, its dugs wobbling like mottled blancmanges.

"Wilfreda, is it?" said Fen. He had become accustomed, by now, to the fact that west-country sows often bore the same sort of names as the higher-born women in Thomas Hardy; for example, there was another of Youings's which was called Eusalie. "Nice animal," Fen added with fake judiciousness.

"Ah, morning, Professor," said Youings, undoubling himself. "Yes, proper little wildego, this one." He meant harum-scarum, a description which seemed inapposite unless, as the reiterated 'little' suggested, he still thought of Wilfreda as a piglet.

"Cobby," Fen remarked, using a Devon word for well-knit, compact. This too was on the face of it inapposite, but since animal breeders have different standards of animal beauty from those of mere lookers-on, in practice it went down very well. There were some, said Youings, who in their ignorance of pigs would maintain that Wilfreda had too much fat on her, was flabby even. Wrong. Wilfreda was in actual fact as lean as a healthy sow could be, and Fen had shown great, though only-to-be-expected, acuity in noting her leanness.

"That Mother Clotworthy's head, then?" asked Youings, innocently inquisitive, nodding at Fen's sack. Fen nodded back, reflecting that his brawn project seemed to have become established in Burraford and district as a sort of Forthcoming Event, on a par with the Meet at The Stanbury Arms next Saturday, or the Amateur Dramatics in the Church Hall the Saturday after. True, the circumstances which had given rise to it were slightly unusual, even for the countryside. Mrs Clotworthy being popular with her friends and neighbours, they had clubbed together to offer her a seventy-fifth birthday treat, envisaging something in the nature of a day trip to Guernsey by boat; when consulted, however, Mrs Clotworthy had affirmed unhesitantly that what she would really like best would be to cut up a nice pig, and the money subscribed had therefore been diverted to buying one for her. At this point, Fen had become involved in the matter. Mrs Clotworthy's late husband, the butcher, had often spoken to her of how much he regretted not being an M.A., and when Mrs Clotworthy heard that Fen was one, and that he had been complaining about the quality of some brawn he had bought at the pork butcher's in Glazebridge, she insisted on presenting him not only with a recipe for homemade brawn but also with the head of her birthday pig, to make the brawn with.

"Mind and salt en well," Youings advised.

Fen said that he would be sure and do that.

"One of mine, that were," said Youings. He gazed sentimentally at the sack. "Pretty little girl, were Tabitha, pink as a rose."

Bypassing this valediction, Fen embarked on an account of Gobbo's reminiscences, and Jack Jones's, and the Rector's.

Towards the end of it, Youings's wife Ortrud appeared at the side door of the house, carrying a paper bag. An Amazonian woman almost as tall as her husband, she had great physical strength and an emphatic, Junoesque figure. ("Those bosoms, don't you know," the Major had once pronounced, more in amazement than in admiration. "Prodigious things—dazzling—flesh-bulbs.") Her inexpressive nordic head combined dark eyebrows with cheese-coloured hair put together in a complicated bun at the back, like pallid worms transfixed in mid-orgy.

"*Zu mir, Liebchen*," she said, evidently addressing Wilfreda. "*Konditoreisachen*." She paid no attention to Fen, the ordinary civilities of life being unknown to her.

Wilfreda stopped swaying from side to side and began swaying from back to front instead. In this way she developed enough forward momentum to be able to get her trotters on the move. Wheeling, she lumbered over to Ortrud and was fed with handful after handful of yellow boiled sweets out of the paper bag. Against the resultant background of scrunching and snorting Fen finished his recital, while Youings stood frowning concentratedly.

Then Youings spoke. He did this in low tones, presumably in order to avoid scarifying his wife's sensibilities by refer-ence to the macabre events of eight weeks previously. Since Wilfreda's eating made a perfect acoustic baffle, and Ortrud was practically out of earshot anyway, it was an unnecessary precaution. Because of it, however, and because he was sunk in the ninth beatitude of expecting nothing, Fen failed at first to grasp what was being said to him, and had to ask for a repeti-tion. Getting it, he sharpened to attention. For what Youings was asserting amounted to an unqualified denial of everything Gobbo had asserted. In short, wherever else Hagberd might have been at the time when Routh was getting himself brained in the copse at Bawdeys Meadow, he hadn't, Youings assured Fen, been talking to Gobbo outside The Stanbury Arms.

It worked out this way. Taking the short cut through Mrs Clotworthy's garden from Chapel Street, where he had been delivering a home-cured ham at the village shop, Youings had seen the Rector stalking past along the lane towards the Arms, and had followed him at a distance of some thirty yards, arriving at Gobbo, the elm and the horse-box just as the Rector was vanishing round the lane's first bend. By this time Gobbo had lurched to his feet and was setting off home to his supper, mumbling tetchily and scratching his bottom as if, said Youings, "a load of old fleas was eating at him". And quite definitely Hagberd hadn't been there. Youings knew this because he had paused to inspect the horse-box, a new double-axle Rice which Clarence Tully had just bought; and Hagberd couldn't possibly have been lurking in or behind that, or behind the elm, or anywhere else in the car-park. He couldn't have nipped into the pub unobserved, since there had been three people drinking in there as well as Isobel Jones serving. He couldn't have crossed the lane unobserved, even if there had been anything but a blank wall for him to cross to. And finally, he couldn't have got round to the side or back of the pub without shinning up another wall or breaking down a locked door in it, which was about as likely, Youings gave Fen to understand, as that he'd flown up into the air and perched himself on a twig. Besides, said Youings reasonably, why *should* Hagberd have done any of these things? Granted, he'd been a bit mazed up top, but only, when you got down to it, about work and animals and Routh and Mrs Leeper-Foxe. And anyway, he hadn't been the skulking sort—quite the opposite, in fact.

Fen pointed out that if Hagberd had murdered Routh, he'd skulked when it came to the Bust child.

"Didn't want to frighten en, simly," Youings surmised.

All this, taken in conjunction with the others' testimony, seemed decisive enough, and Fen wondered why now, for the first time, he was perversely inclined to believe that there might have been something in what Gobbo had said. He kept this thought private, however, thanking Youings with the air of one whose skein of string has been obligingly untangled by a passer-by less ham-handed than himself. Simultaneously, Ortrud Youings shovelled the last of the boiled sweets into

Wilfreda, dropped the empty paper bag on to the ground, and turned to go back into the house.

"*Mittagessen gleich*," she called to Youings over her shoulder. In spite of fifteen years' residence in England, she still never used English when German would do, or even when it wouldn't.

"Dinner, that means," Youings translated. "Proper little cook, my Ortrud." He gazed wistfully after her as her bun, broad back, muscular buttocks and long legs disappeared from view through the side door.

And apart from her quite liking the pigs, Ortrud Youings's cooking—Fen reflected as he went on up the lane—was about the best that anyone ever seemed able to find to say about her. "Oh, my dear soul! That Ortrud, er leads en a turrable dance," Mrs Clotworthy had confided to Fen on one occasion, discussion of brawn and M.A.s having temporarily palled—a statement which had been confirmed, with trimmings, by everyone Fen had talked to on the subject except Thouless, whose preoccupation with his own sorrows made it difficult for him to keep track of anyone else's. Youings had met Ortrud while doing his military service with the B.A.O.R. A willing horse, he had been led up the bridal-path only to discover that in addition to having been married for his money (he owned a small amount of investment capital as well as the pig farm) he had saddled himself with a nymphomaniac of a peculiarly tiresome kind. It was bad enough that Ortrud kept having affairs. What made it even worse was that instead of going off with the current favourite, as any other wife would have done, she invited him, if single, to live in Youings's house, and it was Youings who went off, making do for weeks at a time in a flatlet over Clarence Tully's stables and commuting daily in order to look after the pigs. Yet through all these frequent intermissions of misery, Youings's devotion had remained unshaken. It had even grown. Grieving, he doted more and more. The local women, offended at the waste of a perfectly workable husband, were inclined to be censorious about Youings's apparently limitless tolerance, but the men, in between suggesting that Ortrud, if not divorced, ought at any rate to be beaten—an enterprise few of them would have cared to attempt themselves—were more sentimental, an exception being the Major.

"Poor silly fellow's no better than a muffin," the Major said of Youings, sternly.

Unfortunate Gobbo, discredited by a muffin.

All the same, Fen was now beginning to ask himself if there hadn't been more to Routh's murder than the bizarre details that had met the eye.

The Dickinsons' cottage which Fen had rented had originally been two eighteenth-century semi-detacheds, housing farm labourers; but recently the two had been knocked into one, with the addition of a bathroom at the top of one of the two narrow, precipitous flights of stairs, and of a scullery at the back, so that where the peasantry had once banged their heads rushing out of doors to the earth-closet, the professional classes now banged theirs on their way to do the washing-up. (After two such experiences, Fen had taken to stooping whenever he went through any of the cottage's doorways, even though all but the one between the kitchen and the scullery were quite high enough to allow him passage upright.) To the outer side wall of the cottage, near the modern garage, clung a garden telephone bell—a clapper set between two enormous mammiform metal domes, their overall effect, through weathering, suggesting some fertility goddess dug up at Benin and rejected as worthless on account of the black bakelite box inscrutably attached to it just above the navel. Downstairs consisted of the scullery, the big kitchen with its Rayburn, and a pleasantly furnished living-room with an upright piano on which Fen played hymn tunes, bits of *Don Giovanni*, and *A Little Sea Picture* by Alec Rowley, which he had learned at the age of eight and for some not easily analysable reason had been unable to forget; upstairs there were three bedrooms as well as the bath. A good small garden surrounded three sides of the cottage, petering out at the back in a neglected half acre of grass, shrubs, trees and what seemed to be rabbit tracks. This part (the Dickinsons had encouragingly told Fen, prior to departing for Canada, where they were now touring around music-examining for the Associated Board)—this part of the estate provided an excellent close approach to the cottage for burglars, who would also be helped by the fact that any ground-floor window would swing open at once if a midge collided with it, even glancingly.

Fen's cleaning was done for him three mornings a week by Mrs Bragg, a big, hennaed woman who shrieked with happy laughter all the time. He cooked, if you could call it that, for himself.

Trudging up the drive, an access constructed of sharp, ankle-turning rocks lightly filigreed with mud, Fen was displeased to see that Ellis the tortoise, who had gone into hibernation ten days previously, had changed his negligible mind and re-emerged, presumably because of the continuing summery weather. He had also been capsized by a dog—or else, as was quite conceivable if you knew him at all, had somehow managed to get himself wrong way up unaided—and was lying on his back on the lawn, head retracted, feet waving slowly about in the air in what Fen took to be extreme agitation. Restoring him to normal, Fen circled the lawn picking petals from late pansies to feed him with. Ellis was specially fond of pansy petals, but like other foods, they unfortunately had to be pre-masticated for him. He was undershot, his biting surfaces nowhere near in alignment; left to his own devices, he bolted things and became, according to the Dickinsons, ill. Fen was not so fond of pansy petals. No matter what their original colour, they came out of his mouth black, in the form of tidy, shreddy pellets; they also left him feeling as if his teeth had been sprayed with a particularly odious cheap face-powder. Frowning, Fen conscientiously mumbled pansy petals between tongue and soft palate until Ellis gave signs of being sated. Then he went indoors to rinse his mouth, while Ellis set out on one of his trips to the wall at the lawn's end, a favourite destination which yet never failed to amaze and terrify him by its impermeability when he arrived at it.

Fen would get on with the brawn that very evening, he thought. Meanwhile, the interior of the small refrigerator being almost entirely filled with shin of beef, he left the pig's-head sack beside it, adopted his Quasimodo crouch and ducked successfully back into the kitchen. Here he paused by the mirror, from which, not unexpectedly, his own face looked out at him. In the fifteen years since his last appearance, he seemed to have changed very little. Peering at his image now, he saw the same tall lean body, the same ruddy, scrubbed-looking, clean-shaven face, the same blue eyes, the same brown hair ineffectually plastered down with water, so that it stood up in a spike at the crown of his head. Somewhere or other he still had his extraordinary hat. Good. At this rate, he felt, he might even live to see the day when novelists described their characters by some other device than that of manoeuvring them into examining themselves in mirrors.

His entry into the living-room shook the ancient floor-boards and disturbed a mixed pile of Duffy, Powell and Naipaul, which collapsed in several different directions simultaneously. Other postwar British novelists, in other piles, held firm. On the chesterfield the second of Fen's animal responsibilities, a marmalade tom-cat called Stripey, lay heavily asleep. Stripey had returned earlier that morning exhausted after one of his three-day forays among the district females, expeditions which he seemed to Fen to tackle less for pleasure than because of some vague, oppressive sense of social responsibility, like a repentant long-term convict volunteering for medical experimentation. He was archetypically male, at once coarse, bumptious and pathetic.

Fen sat down beside him, letting his eyes wander over Snow, Mortimer, Manning, Fielding, Murdoch, Golding, Mittelholzer. He let them wander away again. Instead of criticising other people's novels, he would write one himself. It would be entitled *A Manx Ca.*

Now all that remained was to think of something for it to be about.

The veal-and-ham pie at The Stanbury Arms had been because of having missed breakfast. Digesting, it was deterring Fen from lunch. He decided to do without lunch, a policy he would regret round about mid-afternoon. He felt like a hero continually arriving a good deal too late to save a succession of women in distress.

The Fête didn't open till 2.30.

Stripey slumbered on, resting his gonads so as to be fit for another public-spirited bout of propagation when darkness fell. With a sigh, Fen reached over the arm of the chesterfield and picked up a bundle of *The Western Morning News*, ten days' issues which had been lent him by the Major, but so far had remained unread. The fact was that Routh's murder, though admittedly *outré*, had somehow failed to snare Fen's interest. It had snared the Major's. When Fen had first moved into the Dickinsons' cottage, the Major, an early acquaintance, had talked about the murder often and at length, giving many minutiae which even as good a paper as *The Western Morning News* obviously hadn't the space to take cognisance of. But although the Major's extensive local colour had registered in Fen's retentive mind, he hadn't, up to now, felt any urge to disinter it and pick it over. Up to now, Routh's murder simply hadn't seemed to him mysterious enough to be genuinely interesting.

Was it, in fact, mysterious even after Gobbo?

Necessary to find out.

While Stripey twitched in his sleep and Ellis crept on towards the dry-stone edge of the world, Fen settled down to read what *The Western Morning News* had to tell him, supplementing its facts with the details supplied by the Major.

CHAPTER FOUR

Prompt Hand and Headpiece Sever

I believe the right question to ask...is simply this: Was it done with enjoyment—was the carver happy while he was about it?

John Ruskin: *The Seven Lamps of Architecture.*

HIS PARENTS DYING when he was three, Hagberd was brought up in a Kalgoorlie orphanage which also acted as trustee for the small amount of money his father had left him. This money he spent, as soon as he was twenty-one, on four hundred acres inland from Esperance, on a herd of Herefords to graze them, and, as more or less of an afterthought, on a pre-fabricated shack for himself to live in. He had always got on well with animals, and the beef production thereabouts was at the time inconsiderable.

Other factors were not. With the Western Australia irrigation scheme still several years in the future, Hagberd found it desperately hard to water his cattle, even, let alone the pastures which kept them fed. Again, Australia lacks coprophages. Enormous expanses of it have none at all. The industrious beetles which elsewhere gobble up cow-pats as if they were coffee meringues have to be imported, and even then are liable to pine. Consequently, the cow-pats poison not only the grass they lie on, but also a quite extensive area round them.

With more money Hagberd might have survived—money for wells and ditches and an ingenious but expensive mechanical stand-in for the dung-beetles called McGlashan's Chemical Foraging Facility. With more money he could also have hired an assistant or two, instead of trying to do everything himself. But there was no more money to be had. After three years he abandoned the unequal struggle, sold the land and the herd for what they would fetch, and worked his passage to England.

It was reasonable that he should be temporarily disenchanted with farming. What was not so reasonable was that a man deeply in love with hard work should take employment in a Midlands boiler factory. Flabbergasted to find that his fellow-workers knocked off every day at an hour when the edge of his own appetite for toil was still completely undulled, Hagberd had at first expostulated and then, when that had no effect, taken to staying on after hours in order to sweep up cigarette butts in the yards, mend the wire of the car-park fence, disinfect lavatories, whiten doorsteps and clean windows. Once, at 10.30 p.m., he was discovered polishing the floor of the Personnel Director's office, which by some mischance had been left unlocked. Five weeks and six strikes after his arrival, he was sacked. As far as the shop stewards were concerned, he might have lasted longer than that: his passion for work being clearly pathological, they bore him no resentment, and in any case he supplied a valuable pretext, Union-approved, for downing tools. The management, however, saw matters otherwise: there were enough pretexts for strikes already, without adding Hagberd to the list. From his office window the Managing Director watched the final departure, recoiling when Hagberd spat on the windscreen of the directorial Rolls Royce (but this, it turned out, was only in order to wash a bird-dropping off it), ringing frantically for his secretary when Hagberd paused to weed a large geranium bed near the main gate, and at length heaving a groan of relief as the lean, gangling figure disappeared into the traffic and the industrial murk.

Temporarily at a loss, Hagberd now decided to make a pious pilgrimage to Plymouth, where in 1809 an ancestor of his, a naval rating, had been hanged on Devonport dock for trying to push his Captain overboard instead of getting on with manning his gun against the French. So he came to Devon. And so, his thoughts turning again to farms and all the delightful beasts they supported, he in due course came to be employed in Burraford by Routh, with consequences which were to prove disastrous for them both.

Hagberd not only was an Australian cattleman, he looked like one. He was sinewy, lanky, long-armed, easy-striding. He wore broad-brimmed hats. His weather-beaten face was a yard of muddy pump-water, his nose a beak. He had small, intensely blue eyes, set very close together. His ears stood out like jug-handles. Routh was physically his antithesis—short, pulpy and white-skinned, with a compressed sort of face, the little ears and nose seeming as if tight-laced by invisible Sellotape.

And Routh was Hagberd's antithesis not only in the physical sense.

Routh was a very bad farmer. And when he thought it safe, he was deliberately cruel to animals.

Routh liked hearing an animal scream.

Stalking about Routh's farm from before dawn to beyond dusk, doing the work of three men, Hagberd was at first unaware of this; and when his suspicions did eventually stir, he found it practically impossible to credit them. How *could* anyone want to give pain to an animal? No sentimentalist, Hagberd knew that rearing animals once in a while inflicts pain unavoidably. No vegetarian, he knew that the terminal few minutes in the slaughterhouse often inflict fear. But so long as animals were alive, surely nothing within reason could be too good for them, could it?

The turning-point came when Hagberd discovered not only that Routh's visits to Longhempston, twenty miles away, were for the purpose of watching hare-coursing, but also that Routh had been a prime mover in getting this baneful recreation locally revived. There had been other things—among them, a Leghorn with both legs broken, a ewe in milk with a long strip of her wool and hide torn away, a starving mongrel stray with its ribs trodden in—but these might, after all, have been due to accidents or to predators. The hare-coursing was something else. Learning of it, Hagberd started keeping an eye on his soft-spoken employer, and so one day came on him enjoying himself privately with a two-months-old kitten.

Hagberd dealt with him thoroughly, left him lying in the muck of the yard, and went off to notify the R.S.P.C.A., taking the dying kitten along for evidence. But Routh had snipped and ripped with precaution. A fox, he said: undoubtedly the kitten had been mauled by a fox. The vet had reluctantly agreed that it just conceivably could have been, and the Society had equally reluctantly decided not to attempt to prosecute. Routh said that he should hope not. Here was he examining the poor little thing to see if anything could be done for it, and all of a sudden here had been Hagberd, snarling and lashing out with his fists like a maniac. He, Routh, wouldn't take any action over the assault, he selflessly said, since Hagberd clearly wasn't right in the head. Not taking any action, he added (but only to himself), would also help to quash the likelihood of there being any really thorough-going investigation of the stimulating ways in which he chose to spend some of his spare time.

Hagberd left Routh, and went to work for Clarence Tully.

On a bleak morning of early February, the Major, out for a walk, watched Hagberd teaching a baby lamb to skip. Uttering strange antipodean yelps of encouragement, Hagberd was repeatedly jumping into the air, his great wellingtons crashing down again into the icy slush, while the lamb watched him in timid fascination. By the time the Major hobbled back that way, ten minutes later, the lamb had caught on.

"Look at that, then!" Hagberd called triumphantly. "Bucking like a brumby!" And the Major, though he frowned momentarily at this distasteful mention of horses, had to admit that it was a pleasant sight.

"Heinz Spaghetti makes a meal taste great," he sang, getting a curt but friendly nod from Hagberd, who, prevented by his incessant labours from ever watching television, simply assumed that this familiar neighbour had all of a sudden gone harmlessly mad.

Though Hagberd was very content with his job with Clarence Tully, his animus against Routh remained unabated. If anything, feeding on the fact that he was no longer in a good position to know what Routh was up to, and so he came to imagine more horrors than there actually were (Routh's deviation being perfectly controllable—like most such things—he was taking care to control it for the time being, as a matter of self-preservation). There was also Mrs Leeper-Foxe. A widow, Mrs Leeper-Foxe had been endowed by her late husband with a fat income from factory farms, and though too fastidious to have anything directly to do with them herself, undeniably was battening on de-beaked chickens, calves with induced anaemia and pinioned necks, pigs tearing each others' tails off in desperation at being unable to move, and other such martyrs to the British craving for ever greater quantities of ever more and more tasteless, un-nutritious, hormone-adulterated meat. Compounding her heinousness, Mrs Leeper-Foxe associated with Routh. As a matter of fact they were thrown together willy-nilly because no one else would associate with either of them.

"I don't approve of speaking ill of people," the Rector said. "On the other hand, if you didn't speak ill of Routh, you'd never be able to mention him at all." He added that Mrs Leeper-Foxe probably had several good qualities, though none of them had so far claimed his own attention, either directly or by hearsay.

Invited by Mrs Leeper-Foxe to take sherry with her, Routh put on his best blue suit and tugged his forelock, making it clear how honoured he was that she should deign to be gracious to a lowly creature like himself; his financial state was precarious, and he probably had vague hopes of persuading her to underwrite him in some way. As to her, she wallowed in Routh's respectfulness like a hippopotamus in a mud-bank. The unspeakable fawning on the ineffable, they sat together in what Mrs Leeper-Foxe called the withdrawing-room of the Old Rectory—which she had bought three years previously, and had had redecorated at considerable expense—sipping Oloroso from minute glasses and deploring antiphonally the decay of the class structure. Not that Mrs Leeper-Foxe was in Burraford often or for long. She had two other houses; and in any case, being lazy as well as a donkey, she was deterred from frequent visiting by the mysterious unavailability of adequate domestic help.

"Routh and Mrs Leeper-Foxe are soul-mates," said the Major.

"Hogwash."

"Routh and Mrs Leeper-Foxe are *Wahlverwandtschaften*."

"You should spend less time reading Goethe, Major, and more reading the Bible."

"I read the Vulgate," said the Major, who did nothing of the kind.

"Old Red Socks'll get you in the end, you'll see. And you won't be able to say I didn't warn you, will you?"

"No," the Major agreed, "I certainly shan't be able to say that, shall I?"

Meanwhile, unfortunate Hagberd got madder and madder.

The grass grew and was cut (Hagberd previously grabbing up all discoverable hen-pheasants and transferring them with their broods, in Booth's Gin cartons borrowed from Isobel Jones, to safer places). The corn ripened, the cows mooed, a fresh line of pylons sprouted in the only combe hitherto unaffected, the Dickinsons started packing for Canada, and three miles from Routh's farm a puppy was found suffocated to death, after long and interesting struggles, in a sealed polythene bag. On Monday, August 22nd, the Bust girl went to a school-friend's home for tea, and overstayed her time.

This was bad, being certain to result in much energetic slapping of wrists, calves and bottom.

The Bust girl's parents offered the rare spectacle of a married couple neither complementary nor opposite, but identical—identical, that is, in everything except sex and appearance. In conversation they quite often actually chorused, without any sort of pre-arrangement, and in matters of discipline they were equally unanimous. The Bust children were pitied, however, less because of their parents' simultaneous walloping fits, which though frequent were short-lived, than because of their parents' joint sense of humour, which was almost unbelievably imbecile in character. In the Michael Innes phrase, the Busts were not people with whom a joke readily loses its first freshness. Fourteen years after the birth of their daughter Anna May, they could still reduce each other to tears of helpless laughter merely by mentioning her by her full name; and they thought it a masterstroke to have followed up their initial inanity by calling their son John Will.

"Lucky for them they didn't come to me for the christenings," said the Rector, "or I'd have held their silly heads down in the font till they drowned."

But it was, of course, the punitive rather than the humorous aspect of Anna May's parents which chiefly occupied her mind as she hurried, towards 7.30 p.m. that Monday, along the little-used lane which flanked Bawdeys Meadow to the north. As she explained later to the police, she was quite sure about the time because her watch was a good one and she had had plenty of reason (she dolefully added) to keep looking at it.

Most of Bawdeys Meadow is open pasture; at one corner of it, however, there survives an ancient, ugly copse, relic of one of the insanely finicking property deals which have been the recreation of farmers from time immemorial. The trees grow thickly there; though not in fact dead, they are dead-seeming. Litter strews the spongy ground—not picnickers' litter, but the litter of people who, with disagreeable things to get rid of, have found a conformably disagreeable spot in which to dispose of them—and light filters only sparsely through the tangle of crooked, mossy boughs. A high, neglected hedge hides the copse from the lane, except at one point where a sagging gate gives access.

That particular Monday evening was chilly and overcast: the weather had made a false dusk two hours in advance of the true one. Hurrying along towards home and retribution, the backs of her plump legs tingling in anticipation, Anna May was only very vaguely aware of the two voices muttering together somewhere on the other side of the hedge. She had other, more pressing things to think about.

But then, with terrifying suddenness, one of the voices skirled upwards to a mindless squawk of pure dread.

The sound of the blow was followed by a crashing in the underbrush, approaching rapidly. Still moving forward automatically, Anna May arrived at the copse gate just as Routh staggered into view out of the trees.

His caved-in right temple, as yet scarcely masked by bleeding, showed like a hollow punched in a ball of white plasticine. Groping mindlessly for support, he reeled and fell; Anna May heard the small detonation of his arm snapping under him. Abruptly the blood gushed, first from his mouth and then from his ruined brain. He twitched three times, very violently, before finally lying still.

Afterwards, Anna May remembered that there had been a sound of someone else moving, and that the sound ceased when she happened to scuff her shoe in the grit at the lane's edge. But at the time she was thinking in terms of accident, not of assault, and in any case the spectacle of Routh had shocked her into temporary unawareness of everything else. With considerable courage she walked forward and stood over him. She had done well in school at First Aid, and after all, this sort of thing was what First Aid was *for*, so perhaps—

She bent to feel for his pulse: nothing. Watched for his breathing: and nothing. Wild thoughts of attempting the Kiss of Life flitted through her mind. But if there was bad brain damage, the Kiss of Life wouldn't do any good, would it? Besides, she didn't believe she could possibly force herself to try it. Not possibly. It would mean letting her hair fall on to that congealing horror, and pinching the squat white nose shut, and feeling inside the mouth to make sure the tongue didn't fall back and block the air passages. No, not *possibly*. Besides—

From behind the screen of crippled trees, someone who was looking on suddenly uncontrollably giggled.

As the new pattern slipped clear and complete into her understanding, like a replacement transparency in an epidiascope, Anna May turned and ran, heart racing, throat dry, rubber soles throwing up little spurts of white dust as they flip-flopped frantically on tarmac worn smooth and slippery with age. Nearest, as it happened, was her own home, and when it came in sight she slowed a little, looking back.

No one.

Puffing up the path and through the front door, Anna May found herself instantly in the middle of a whirlwind of flailing palms; her parents were particularly incensed with her that evening—her being so late having delayed the start of an outing of their own—and the few disjointed words she managed to blurt into the hubbub were interpreted by them as an ill-judged attempt to tell them about something she had been watching on television. Bawling in unison, they condemned her supperless to bed. And for the time being Anna May didn't persist. In her present confused state she obscurely felt that it might be safer to keep quiet. Mr Routh was dead all right—nothing anyone could do for him now. Also, he was good riddance to bad rubbish. Let him lie, while she latched her bedroom window and locked her bedroom door and sat down to think things out calmly.

By the following morning she had done this—and more importantly, by then her parents had become relatively approachable again. Expecting more slapping when she repeated her story, Anna May instead found herself fallen on with loud protestations of affectionate anxiety. She must see a doctor, see the police, eat another piece of toast and marmalade, be given a bicycle. The senior Busts then rushed off together to Bawdeys Meadow.

But the body had been found earlier on.

When they saw what had been done to it, both the Busts fainted.

The body had been found round about 6.30 a.m., eleven hours after death, by a farm labourer called Prance who was passing Bawdeys Meadow on his way to work. It had been moved from the copse to the meadow proper, and Prance, glimpsing it through a hole in the hedge, had climbed up on to the bank to get a better view of it.

Fortunately Prance was an extremely phlegmatic man.

The meadow here sloped down to the hedge quite steeply, so that the effect of what Prance saw was that of a five-piece infant's jigsaw puzzle assembled with the usual infant incompetence on a tilted green-baize table. In death, Routh was divided. Moreover, although in death, as in life, his trunk remained central to his anatomy, other parts of him had been re-dealt. Briefly, both his legs and both his arms had been first cut off, and then, in relation to the rest of him, swapped: his thighs now sprouted from his shoulders (the toes of his shoes pointing up-hill), while his arms—neatly disposed in parallel, with the palms of the hands flat on the grass—appeared to be attached to either side of his groin.

Having examined this composition impassively for some seconds, Prance made a provisional identification from the clothes, and then went off to the nearest telephone box to ring Constable Luckraft's cottage in Burraford. The identification had to be provisional, since the head, though like the limbs it had been severed from the trunk, was nowhere visible.

Luckraft got out his motor-cycle and came at once. He stood guard while Prance trudged once again to the telephone box, this time to notify the police station in Glazebridge. Luckraft dealt with the Busts, listened to their story, promised them that Anna May's evidence should be heard at an early opportunity, and shooed them off home. He wandered about a bit, and presently, a few yards inside the copse, came on what appeared to be—and indeed was—the weapon with which the murder had been done.

Detective-Inspector Widger and Detective-Constable Rankine arrived by car. They hadn't hurried themselves: Prance, in a fit of bucolic mischief-making, had given the Duty Sergeant at Glazebridge full details of the discovery, thereby ensuring that his call would be treated as an egregiously puerile hoax. Now Widger stared at the remains dazedly while questioning Luckraft, who in due course conducted the party into the copse to look at the heavy wrench which lay there, its business end slightly stained with what was presumably Routh's blood.

"*That's* not been lying there for weeks on end," said Detective-Constable Rankine. "You can tell it hasn't, simply by looking at it." No fact or inference, however obvious, really existed for Rankine until he had put it into words.

Widger said, "Let's hope we can trace the owner."

"*And* it's heavy enough to have done the job. One good whack with that, just one, and *pfft*, you're dead."

Luckraft said that he thought the owner of the wrench was probably him, Luckraft.

"Yours, Luckraft?" said Widger, flustered. "What on earth makes you think that?"

"It's missing, sir, from the tool-kit on my bike. I just looked."

"Good heavens, man, don't you keep your tool-kit locked?"

Luckraft pointed out that the tool-kits on police motor-cycles were not equipped with locks.

"Well, but how long has it been missing?"

Luckraft said that the wrench could have been missing for as long as eight days; it was eight days, anyway, since he had had occasion to open the kit. He added that of course he was round and about the district quite a lot, and often had to leave the bike temporarily unattended, for instance when visiting people in their houses.

"So that what we have here looks very much like a case of premeditation," said Rankine. "Someone sees this bike—unattended, as has been remarked. He says to himself, 'Now, this bike has a tool-kit, and in the tool-kit will be a stout wrench.' He glances around him to find out if he is observed."

"If it is mine, sir," said Luckraft, "there'll be my initials scratched on the other side."

"I see. May I ask if you always scratch your initials on police property?"

"Yes, sir. Always. Because otherwise it gets nicked. By my fellow-officers, I mean."

"I see. Well, we're not going to touch the wrench yet awhile. You yourself haven't touched it, I hope?"

"Certainly not, sir."

"Bringing us back full circle," said Rankine, "to the central puzzle in this affair: where is the deceased's head? Several possibilities suggest themselves. The head may be buried somewhere quite close by. Or it may have been taken away. Or it—"

"Be quiet, Rankine," said Widger. "Get to a telephone and ring County—urgent. And ring Dr Mason—urgent." With obvious reluctance Rankine took himself off, on foot, while Widger climbed into the police car and drove away in the opposite direction, for a preliminary talk with Anna May. Luckraft remained on guard, keeping at bay the sightseers who now began to trickle along in response to the Bust parents' agitated gossiping. One enterprising middle-aged lady, a Mrs Jewell, climbed a near-by tree in order to get a proper look, but almost at once was taken dizzy and fell to the ground, fortunately suffering nothing worse than a few scratches and bruises in the process. After that, by bawling angrily from his post at the copse gateway, Luckraft managed to prevent all further tree-climbing, bank-clambering and hedge-peering, and since in default of these there was practically nothing to be seen other than the familiar blue-clad bulk of Luckraft himself, most people responded reasonably promptly to the demand that they keep moving.

Meanwhile, in Burraford, Routh's head was making the first of its three posthumous appearances.

A Routh-type female, so greedy for money and so lost to self-respect that she was prepared to work even for Mrs Leeper-Foxe, had agreed to cook the breakfasts at the Old Rectory, and was firm that on this particular morning there had been nothing amiss in the dining-room when she had put the food on the table. Two minutes later there was. Intent on bacon, sausages, kidneys, tomato and egg, Mrs Leeper-Foxe in her mauve housecoat at first failed to notice the last respects that were being paid her from the armchair in the corner by the open window. She had, indeed, actually sat down and served herself, and was lifting the first loaded forkful to her mouth, before she became aware of being stared at by a football-shaped object with no iris or pupil to its eyes, and with a nasty dent on one side. And even then, her reaction was not immediate. Her hand continued to move upwards, her mouth opened, and in went the food. She even started to chew.

Then realisation dawned.

The food exploded all over the table, making way for a screaming fit like a steam engine with its whistle stuck. In a few seconds more there were two steam engines, the Routh-type breakfast cook soaring high in hysterical descant, Mrs Leeper-Foxe becoming intermittent from lack of breath, as if an engineer had climbed up on top of her and was wrestling with her valve. Their combined uproar rushed headlong from the house and up the lane past The Stanbury Arms—where Jack Jones was so taken aback by it that he half got out of bed— and eventually came to rest against a buffer of alarmed people who had emerged from the various cottages along its route. Some sort of coherence being at last established, two men were despatched to the Old Rectory to investigate, neither of them, as it happened, having so far heard the news of the discovery in Bawdeys Meadow. They were consequently gratified, but not surprised, to find that Mrs Leeper-Foxe and the breakfast cook had apparently succumbed to a joint morbid hallucination: what the armchair contained was not Routh's severed head, or anybody else's, but a life-size eighteenth-century bust in white marble.

This object eventually turned out to be the property of Broderick Thouless, the composer. Through a tortuous sequence of bastardies Thouless was descended, or imagined he was, from William Augustus, Duke of Cumberland, the victor of Culloden; and it was Cumberland the bust purported to represent. It stood normally on a mahogany pedestal in a corner of honour in Thouless's parlour, but since he was currently engrossed all day and every day in working on a film called *Unalive*, he did not, as it happened, enter this room for a full forty-eight hours previous to discovering his loss and telephoning an indignant complaint to Glazebridge police station, which he did practically simultaneously with the bust's reappearing in the Old Rectory. In the commotions consequent on Routh's murder it took the police some time to make the necessary connection, and it was not, therefore, until evening that Thouless was visited by Detective-Inspector Widger, who by then was working under Chief Detective-Inspector Ling from County Headquarters.

"Now, sir, as I understand the matter, you keep a window open in here night *and* day. I mean, day *and* night."

"Yes, that's right. For air."

"Unwise of you, sir, if I may say so."

"Permits of burglarious entry all the way round the clock," said Detective-Constable Rankine, whom Widger had unwillingly brought with him. "Though not, of course, properly speaking burglarious unless after dark."

"Poor fellow's never boned up on the 1968 Theft Act," said Thouless unexpectedly.

"Quite so." Solidarity or no solidarity, Widger was not wholly without *Schadenfreude* at seeing his informative colleague discomfited for once. "Rankine, you've put your foot in it there. How you ever passed your examination for the C.I.D.—"

"The 1968 Theft Act, sir, had for its chief intention the—"

"Later, Rankine, later. Just now, for the moment, if you think you've quite finished, I'd like to ask Mr Thouless something else. What you're saying, then, sir, is that the bust could have been stolen at any time during the last two days."

"Yes, yes, of course. I keep telling you so. When can I have it back?"

"Not yet awhile, sir," said Widger. "There are tests to be made—fingerprints and so forth. Reminding me that we'll have to take your fingerprints, for elimination purposes. Your cleaner's, too."

"Mrs Dunwoody's? She's been away ill for days now. Cleaners," said Thouless testily, "have very little natural resistance to infection, I find."

While his fingerprints were being taken, he explained about Hagberd, who sometimes did gardening jobs for him. He had drawn Hagberd's attention to the bust, he said, as a matter of family pride, approximately a fortnight ago, taking the opportunity to give an account of Culloden and its aftermath, and Hagberd had seemed greatly impressed with Cumberland's nickname. "Butcher," he had kept muttering, "Butcher, Butcher," until Thouless, alarmed, had shooed him back to his hedging. In view of this it seemed at least possible— Thouless now told Widger—that it was Hagberd who had been responsible for the theft of this intrinsically not very valuable lump of marble.

And with this Widger was able to agree, for since morning it had become a moral certainty that Hagberd was guilty, if not of Routh's actual murder, at any rate of disassembling him and lugging his severed head round the neighbourhood; chief factor in this decision was the discovery of a knife, a saw and a hatchet—all of them bloodstained, all of them bearing Hagberd's fingerprints and no one else's—buried in a heap of Glo-Coal in an out-house at Hagberd's cottage. The man himself remained for a long time elusive. In Constable Luckraft's opinion, eventually proved correct, he hadn't gone into hiding or fled, but simply happened to be away on his own somewhere, working at something; and it wasn't until ten in the evening that he was at last located and taken into custody. In the meantime he had made further arrangements about Routh's head, and these had manifested themselves to an evening angler, a local unemployable called Don Goodey, who was futilely attempting to poach trout from a reach of the Burr where nothing was known to have been taken since the year of Alamein. Dozing over his wet fly, Goodey was roused by—as he said afterwards—"a Presence", and on opening his eyes found himself confronted by a raft—in fact, a packing-case lid—which was nudging the bank by his feet; on this was Routh's gory head, secured upright by long nails driven in aslant, and staring at Goodey's toe-caps "as if in entreaty". Too unnerved by this dreadful apparition to respond to its voice-less plea, Goodey had uttered a loud cry of terror, kicked the raft away from him into the current, dropped his rod and fled from the spot in search of suitable assistance. This, however, hadn't been close at hand, so that by the time the investigating party returned to the scene of the occurrence, the raft had vanished downstream towards the confluence of the Burr and the Glaze.

Attempts were made to recover it, but in vain. It was glimpsed just once more, in twilight, as it bobbed along in mid-stream past the Creamery in Glazebridge, but was identified only later by hindsight. After that it presumably either sank or else went on down river to Glazemouth and was carried out to sea. In any case it vanished completely, never to be seen again.

❀ ❀ ❀

The sequence of events, then, was as follows.

Sunday or Monday: Cumberland bust stolen from Thouless's parlour.

Monday, 7.30 p.m.: Routh murdered.

Monday night/Tuesday morning: Corpse dismembered and moved, and head taken away. (According to the medical evidence, the dismembering had been done between six and ten hours after death.)

Tuesday, 6.30 a.m.: Corpse discovered by Prance.

Tuesday, 10.00 a.m.: Head in Mrs Leeper-Foxe's dining-room.

Tuesday, 10.10 a.m.: Bust in Mrs Leeper-Foxe's dining-room.

Tuesday, 8.20 p.m.: Head entreats Goodey.

Tuesday, 10.00 p.m.: Hagberd arrested.

Tuesday, 10.15 p.m.: Head water-borne through Glazebridge.

Apart from these undeniable facts, however—these, and the discovery of Hagberd's tools in the Glo-Coal—the harvest of evidence was meagre. Hagberd had managed to wander round the district all day without being observed more than twice, and then in quite normal, innocuous contexts; he had no alibi either for the murder or for the Leeper-Foxe *débâcle*— but come to that, nor had quite a number of other people; his fingerprints were on the bust, but then, so were Thouless's and those of his housekeeper, Mrs Dunwoody. Even so, no one—in view of Hagberd's known preoccupations and antipathies— had any real doubt that the posthumous attentions Routh had received were the work of his mazed ex-employee, and he was therefore charged with conspiring to conceal a body: grotesque, as the Major remarked, when you considered the trouble he had gone to to display it to the widest possible audience.

As to the murder charge, that came later, after Hagberd had exhausted everyone by saying over and over again that he might have killed Routh, and then again he mightn't; he would have to wait and see, he added enigmatically. He said the same thing about the dismembering, driving even his own solicitor (supplied by Clarence Tully) to the limit of his patience by his constant repetitions. But these equivocal postures failed to save him. True, no one—not even the Director of Public Prosecutions—was wholly convinced that the felling of Routh had been Hagberd's doing; the murderer's behaviour, as attested by Anna May, militated against this supposition, as also did the fact that the wrench taken from Constable Luckraft's motorcycle proved to have been carefully wiped clean of prints: if that, then why not the implements hidden in the out-house? On the score of motive, however, the case against Hagberd was strong, and since it was evident that unfitness to plead would obviate anyone's having to arrive at a final verdict, the charge was proceeded with, and after the usual psychiatrists' reports, a judge sitting in chambers consigned Hagberd to an indefinite period in Rampton. His peculiar behaviour with regard to the corpse would have necessitated something of the sort anyway, so that even those who thought him innocent of murder had no need to feel that they must repine.

CHAPTER FIVE

In an English Garden

This is a riotous assembly of fashionable people, of both sexes, at a private house, consisting of some hundreds, not unaptly stiled a drum, from the noise and emptiness of the entertainment.

Tobias Smollett: *Advice, a Satire.*

"**WELL, WELL,**" said Fen.

He folded up the last of *The Western Morning Newses*, shuffled the pile together and put it back on the floor. Beside him on the chesterfield the cat Stripey had rolled over on to his back and was sleeping with his paws in the air, at intervals offering up faint moans of pleasure or dismay: possibly he was empathising, in dreams, the mixed emotions of the females he dutifully trod. Late-rose-scented, a gentle breeze stirred the Dickinsons' living-room curtains. All around stood post-war British fiction, unstably heaped, cross-lit by autumn sunshine.

"Mortimer, Penelope," Fen said.

"Different again," he told the cat, "different again is Penelope Mortimer, whose achievement is marred, is heightened, has been to, in part derives from." He stroked the cat's stomach, stopping the moans and inducing instead a jerky, metallic purring, like small cog-wheels unsatisfactorily meshed.

"In part derives from an acute apprehension of," Fen muttered.

A flood of light had not, he found, been thrown on the Routh-Hagberd affair by his consideration of it. Floods of light were evidently going to have to wait until such time (if ever) as more facts emerged. Was it worth going out into the highways and byways, and inviting more facts in? Fen felt reluctant to do this, not so much because he believed Hagberd guilty of murder—that, he thought, was a decidedly doubtful attribution—as because the case still seemed to him bizarre rather than challenging, its fishiness psychological, not evidential. Besides, the police, themselves none too sure that it had been Hagberd who had coshed Routh, would certainly have considered alternatives and ferreted for clues to support them. Putting out a random sweep in the hope of netting undefined further information would therefore almost certainly be supererogatory as well as wearisome.

The telephone rang and Fen answered it. "Yur," a voice said, "us wants a cow done." Fen gave the voice the number of the Artificial Insemination Centre, which closely resembled the Dickinsons' number, rang off, glanced at his watch, and saw that he must leave now if he was to arrive at the Fête in time for the opening. He got up, giving Stripey a farewell pat. Stripey started awake and at once began angrily licking his stomach where Fen's hand had touched it.

"An acute apprehension of everyday reality," Fen said, crouching his way out of the cottage. Whom had the sentence been going to be about? Never mind, it would do for almost anyone.

He passed Youings's pig farm and Thouless's bungalow, both seemingly deserted, and arrived at the junction of his lane with the lane which led from the Glazebridge direction through Aller to Burraford; this brought the Pisser's noise into earshot again. Suddenly a figure appeared round the bend, moving rapidly towards him. It was a great bandy-legged ape, wearing an ankle-length woman's black bombazine dress and carrying a cricket bag. It was the Rector.

"Is there going to be fancy dress?" Fen asked, stopping him.

"No, there isn't. This is for the fortune-telling," said the Rector. "I'm an old gypsy woman and I tell fortunes in a tent. Saves me having to walk about all the time, chatting people up."

"I thought that the Church had set its face against divination."

"You've been seeing too much of the Major," the Rector said, amiably enough. "Do you know what he does? He posts me ecumenical pamphlets under plain cover. Thinks I don't know who's sending them. Still, a very good chap, the Major, in his limited military way. And he has a point."

"Has he? What sort of point?"

"Says anti-popery puts me in some very dubious company, like that dreadful fellow in Northern Ireland, and Cooper."

"Who on earth is Cooper?"

"Anthony Ashley Cooper. My family agreed with his ideas on religion, but they always said the man himself stank."

"You're referring," said Fen with restraint, "to the reign of Charles II?"

"Am I? Yes, I suppose I am. Queen was a Portuguese girl—Popish, of course—and the Duke of York was whiffy with incense from morning till night. Good seaman, though. Anyway, as I say, my family thought this man Cooper was a horrible little cad."

"The same opinion seems to have been held by Dryden."

"Dryden was a horrible little cad too," said the Rector, "and I'll tell you another thing: if we go on standing here like a couple of wax images we shall never get to the Fête at all." They set off along the lane. "No, bless you, I don't *divine* anything," said the Rector, reverting to the fortune-telling. "I just pass on gossip. Harmless gossip, of course," he specified. "Nice dress, isn't it? It belonged to my grandmother." He hitched the skirt up to his knees and broke stride to do a couple of inchoate can-can kicks.

Fen saw that what he had first mistaken for a fichu was in fact the Rector's clerical collar. "How do you manage the bosom?" he asked.

"Rugger socks, rolled."

"Do they stay up?"

"They usedn't to," the Rector admitted. "But then I bought myself a forty-two bra, C cups, so they're all right now. The straps are painful, though, cut into your shoulders like knives. Can't think how women stand them. However, nowadays they keep their busts up with wax injections, or so I'm told. I don't put the hat and veil on till I actually start."

"Is that what's in the cricket bag?"

"That and other things," said the Rector. He seemed on the point of expanding on this, but at the last moment desisted. "The Major's gone on ahead to change," he said instead. "He likes to be a bit dressy on these occasions."

They were coming up towards a bend in the lane, where a large scrawled sign said BEWARE MUCK CATTLE CHILDREN. From beyond the bend they heard the sound of an approaching motor-cycle.

"Mind out," said the Rector.

The motor-cycle came into view only a few yards in front of them. It was being ridden at quite a moderate speed by a straw-haired skinny youth in a brown imitation-leather jacket and tight blue jeans. When he caught sight of the Rector, panic seized him. He swerved, skidded, lost control of his machine, and with a yelp of terror flung himself clear, landing heavily on his bottom near the verge. The motor-cycle went on for a bit and then fell over on to its side. Its engine sputtered out on a series of explosions like a Great Dane mastering a sneezing fit.

The youth gave a pitiful cry.

Fen and the Rector went back to examine him. He lay there supine, sniffling and rubbing his left arm, but not, apparently, very badly hurt. He broke into lamentations.

"You're all right," Fen told him.

At this, the youth ceased his lamenting abruptly. He stared up at Fen in horror. "You'm 'im!" he unexpectedly shrieked. "You'm 'im! La-di-da voice. You'm 'im! Oh, save me!"

"Who am I?" said Fen—sounding, he thought, like some Pirandello character grappling with doubts about his own identity. "What are you talking about?"

"You'm 'im," the youth moaned. "Blackmail, that's what 'twere. There you was, in the dark of the night, a-threatening to show this yur letter to the perlice, so be you wasn't give money. You'm 'im, you'm 'im."

"Must have hit his head," said the Rector.

"Mavis Trent," said the youth. "You was a-threatening 'm about Mavis Trent." Fen stopped, thinking it might be a good idea to get the youth at least partially upright. "'Old 'im off!" the youth bellowed at the Rector. "'Old 'im off, 'e's going to throttle me!"

"Nonsense, Scorer, of course he's not going to throttle you," said the Rector repressively. "People don't go around throttling people in broad daylight, with a clergyman present. And what's all this about Mavis Trent? No, don't answer for the moment. First, let's see if there's anything the matter with you. Move your limbs. Go on, move them. No, not just your left foot, *all* of them." Grey with apprehension, the youth obeyed. "Nothing much wrong there," said the Rector briskly. "Pelvis still in one piece? Spine? Ribs? Fingers? Any softness in the skull? Cough." The youth hawked feebly. "Any blood in your mouth? Tender tummy? Teeth loose?"

Fen went and heaved the motor-cycle in to the side of the lane. He propped it against one of the high stone retaining walls which here hemmed the lane in. Returning, he found the youth still lying supine, as if laid out waiting for his coffin to be brought, while the Rector diagnosed bruises and a possible, but not really very probable, cracked coccyx.

Satisfied that these ministrations were adequate for the moment, "Now, what's all this about Mavis Trent?" the Rector went on. "Explain yourself."

"No," said the youth uncompromisingly. "Shan't." With precaution he propped himself up on one elbow, meanwhile making a palsied attempt to brush some of his plentiful hair away from his eyes. "And it weren't 'im, either," he added, indicating Fen. "I sees that now. 'E'm tall enough but 'e'm not fat enough." But then all at once his eyes bulged in renewed alarm. "Listen!" he shouted agitatedly. "Listen!"

They listened. The noise, coming up fast from beyond the bend in the lane, was confused but distinctive.

"Tes Tully!" the youth wailed. "Tes Farmer Tully an' 'is cows! Move me! Move me!" The noise grew, bell-ringing, hooting, dogs barking, a car engine, a thunder of hooves. "*Move* me!" the youth shrieked, wriggling convulsively. "Oh, save me!" Fen and the Rector grabbed him at either end and heaved him on to the grass of the verge just as the cavalcade came into view.

At the head of it rode Clarence Tully's third cowman, whose duty it was to precede cow migrations on a bicycle; he was a jittery man whose nervous economy had been permanently affected, he believed, by having to toil up slopes in front of a herd of animals with more stamina, and a better turn of speed for hill work, than himself. Then came the cows, fourteen-hundredweight yearling South Devons. Last came Clarence Tully himself, bulging Falstaffianly behind the wheel of his Land-Rover, surrounded by excited, yapping sheep dogs, and with two of his many enormous sons standing up, as they all for some reason always did, in the back.

Clarence Tully waved. The sons waved. They waved using the whole of the arm, like castaways trying to attract the attention of a ship hull-down on the horizon. The third cowman pedalled frantically. The cows—each of which would have lost several pounds in weight by the time the new pasture was reached—mooed angrily as they lumbered along at an ungainly trot. Clarence Tully hilloed. His sons yipped. The third cowman rang his bell for the entrance to Fen's lane. The dogs fell into a paroxysm of barking. Still waving at full stretch, "All right, then?" Clarence Tully bawled, as the Land-Rover passed the group on the verge. "All *right*?" The youth whimpered, shielding his eyes from the dust. The Rector signalled reassurance. Fen watched the cows' smooth skins, glossy brown, sliding back and forth over their pumping haunches.

The procession receded, reached the further bend, was gone. The youth whimpered again; he seemed an exceptionally faint-hearted lad. The Rector took him under the arms and dragged him to his feet.

"Mavis Trent we'll hear about later," the Rector said, "and no two ways about it. Meanwhile you can come along with us to the Fête and have a word with the doctor about your bum."

In all its two hundred and thirty years, Aller House—designed by Hawksmoor, destined for ornamentation by William Kent which never eventuated—had never been properly occupied even for a single night. A series of dooms had attended it: ever since the first Sir George Stanbury had run decisively out of money in the course of building it, its owners had regularly gone mad or bankrupt or to the colonies, and it had continued to stand empty even during the Hitler war, when accommodation was at a premium. Now Clarence Tully had it—but not to live in; he had bought it for the arable which was its only recommendation other than the antiquarian and the aesthetic, had converted part of what had been going to be kitchens into a ground-floor flatlet, and had leased this at a nominal rent to the Major, on the thin pretext that the place needed a caretaker, if only to keep an eye on the occasional parties of sightseers from Museum Societies and other such bodies. The Major, who had only his pension—and that less than it should have been, thanks to a bureaucratic muddle at the time of the granting of Indian independence—had accepted this arrangement without false pride, as indeed almost everyone in the neighbourhood accepted almost all Clarence Tully's numerous dispositions for their comfort: he was a man whose unaffected goodwill made churlishness virtually impossible.

Either Hawksmoor had been in an uncharacteristically austere mood when planning Aller House, or else he had surreptitiously delegated his tiresome provincial task to some apprentice uninterested in the baroque. The place was really quite plain, its central mass rising in three well-proportioned storeys to a hipped roof with a balustraded surround, its two equal two-storey wings (flat-roofed) elegant, but apart from their balustrades, unadorned; its only serious concession to decorativeness lay in the pair of large circular bas-reliefs, depicting tangles of robust, helmeted Roman matrons, which were situated equidistant on either side of the pillared main door. Though very little had ever been done in the way of upkeep, Clarence Tully having confined himself to replacing two or three broken windows, weathering had been uniform, and the general effect was by no means dilapidated. Moreover, the gardens at the front had been kept under some sort of control, even though now reduced to trees, grass and shrubs exclusively. Their main feature was the huge lawn, bisected by the stony, unsurfaced driveway, where rankness had been kept at bay partly by sheep and partly by the occasional attentions of a man with a rotary mower: Clarence Tully was tidy-minded, and even on this white-elephant segment of his property had no intention of letting nature get the upper hand.

On the Aller House lawn, twice yearly, the Burraford Church Fêtes were held.

The youth Scorer, fearing for his rump, was wheeling his motor-cycle, not riding it; his original destination abandoned without even a pretence of argument, he trailed along the lane, sweating lavishly, behind Fen and the Rector. Presently they came to where the action was. And it was a surprising amount of action, Fen thought, for a place as small as Burraford:

despite its size, the Aller House lawn was crowded, as also was the adjacent field where cars could be parked.

"People come to our Fêtes from miles around," the Rector said complacently. "And it isn't all women, either; the men come because they can get pickled in the beer tent and enter their tykes for the dog show and gawp at the legs competition, though I'm bound to say, the standard of girls' legs hereabouts isn't exactly dazzling: more like two pairs of bolsters, most of them. The fairground stuff helps, too, makes a change from stalls selling doilies and jam and daffodil bulbs and musty old copies of Blackmore and Annie S. Swan. There's a sort of community of retired fairground people living in horrible little bungalows at Glascombe, and whenever we have a Fête I make them dig their gear out and bring it along here. The theory is that they're thrilled to get back into harness again. They pocket half the proceeds, of course, when I'm not looking, but they fill in the gaps and they're a draw, of sorts. There's one who has a dead mermaid on show, but the moths have been at her and she's beginning to look a bit odd. He ought to store her in polythene, I keep telling him, but for all the notice he takes I might as well be talking to a heap of boulders."

Trembling with exhaustion, the youth Scorer staggered into the car-park with his machine, while Fen and the Rector strode on along the rutted track towards the lawn. Ahead of them, a massive uniformed policeman in a white crash helmet was moving along unexpectedly slowly, swaying a little and from time to time waggling his head cautiously from side to side.

"What on earth's the matter with Luckraft?" the Rector demanded. "Looks as if he's half cut...Been at the bottle, Luckraft?" he enquired as they came abreast. Startled, Luckraft stumbled on a stone, recovered himself, said, "Oh, it's you, Rector," feebly, and attempted a smile. In point of fact he looked not so much drunk as ill. They passed him and were in turn passed by another cleric, small and wiry, running. The Rector bellowed a greeting at him. "That's Father Hattrick," he said. "A Roman, mind you, but a sound chap nevertheless. And nowadays he's allowed to wear trousers, liberalisation and all that tosh. Under another name, he's a sort of male C. V. Wedgwood," the Rector perplexingly added. "Always runs, says it's better exercise than walking. Comes for Mrs de Freitas's gooseberry jam."

They debouched on to the lawn where a double dais stood portentously apart. On its rear section, four grubby-looking girls with guitars, drums and a microphone were pottering about, trying to get themselves organised; lettering on the bass drum identified them as THE WHIRLYBIRDS. The front section, at a slightly lower level and with another microphone, was for the present unoccupied. Though a fair number of people were wandering about among the tents and stalls, reconnoitring, even more were assembled expectantly in front of the dais, and their numbers were increasing momently. The Rector detached himself from Fen and set about shaking hands. Father Hattrick stationed himself strategically. The youth Scorer arrived, peering about him in search of the doctor. P.C. Luckraft appropriated, and with evident relief slumped down on, a folding wooden chair which someone had left propped against a near-by marquee. From the car-park, engine noise signalled the return of Clarence Tully in his Land-Rover, his herding mission accomplished, his two huge sons still standing up stick-straight behind him. The crowd buzzed, the sun shone, in the distance the Pisser swapped continuity for irregular spasms, a light breeze rustled in the shrubs and the stands of trees which the first Sir George Stanbury had planted at the lawn's margins. Diametrically opposite from the dais, over by the west wing, the Misses Bale single-mindedly mounted guard on the Botticelli, and for the tenth time little Miss Endacott rearranged the incongruent jumble of items on the Rectory stall. Should she, she wondered, call out, "Come and buy! Come and buy!" The mere thought of it made her legs shake so much that she had to sit down.

The Rector consulted his wrist-watch, muttered a short prayer, hoisted his skirts, took a run at the front part of the dais and jumped up on to it; his impact shook the structure with such violence that an inattentive Whirlybird lost her balance, fell against the pedal cymbal and knocked it over the edge. More laboriously or with more circumspection, several other men and women followed the Rector, among them the Mayor of Glazebridge—since Burraford was in Glazebridge's extensive Rural District—complete with chain of office.

"We don't want hours and hours of talk, now," the Rector told his companions. It emerged in a roar from loudspeakers tuned to maximum amplification; an old man said, "Hear, hear!" and a child, panicking at the sudden din, broke into uncontrollable ululations of terror and dismay. "People don't come here," the Rector said, "to listen to hours and hours of talk." "Hear, hear!" the old man said again. "So let's get cracking," the Rector said.

The opener of the Fête was a short, slim, affable, loquacious Negro, educated at Winchester and New College, who lived twenty miles away, writing lucrative science fiction under the name of Dermot McCartney. (He had begun his writing career with delicate studies of coloured men teetering between two cultures, but these, though gratifying to the *Observer* and the *New Statesman*, had in addition to selling poorly proved to be too much like hard work, since their author had no recollection at all of what Negro culture was like and was obliged to look it all up in books.) "Count-down!" he shrilled into the microphone. "All systems 'Go'! Ten, nine, eight, seven, six, five, four, three, two, one, BLAST-OFF! *VROOM!* I declare this Fête open!" At 'Vroom', Father Hattrick, cheating, turned and ran, homing on the Jams Stall with his basket flapping against his thigh. Behind him, the Whirlybirds struck up with *Make the Scene, Do Your Thing.* The women made rapidly for the produce and garden stalls, and a sizeable proportion of the men made for the beer tent. The platform party descended, Dermot McCartney brandishing a well-filled wallet to signal awareness of the next stage in his responsibilities. J. G. Padmore, who had been standing at the front of the crowd appraising Dermot McCartney in an expert manner, headed for Fen. The Rector marched bandily away towards his fortune-telling tent. The fairground people, all of them well past their prime, could dimly be heard, through the Whirlybirds' amplified yowlings, crying their wares in cracked, senile voices.

"Any luck?" Padmore asked eagerly.

"Luck?" Fen was transiently bewildered; then he remembered. "Oh, you mean Youings. Yes, I did talk to him, briefly. And he's quite certain Hagberd wasn't at the Arms at 7.30 that evening."

"There, I knew it."

"So it's his word against Gobbo's."

"And not much doubt about which to choose," said Padmore contentedly, his burden of apprehension slipping from him.

"Did you see Gobbo again?"

"No. When I got back to the pub, he'd gone. So then I had to change the wheel on that bloody car...All's well that ends well, then."

"One supposes so."

"What does one suppose, my dear chap?" This was the Major, who had limped across the coarse turf to join them. He was dapper in well-creased checks and a mulberry tie.

"Gobbo," Padmore explained: "he was talking nonsense. Damn it, I *knew* he was talking nonsense."

"H'm," the Major said neutrally.

"How's the background and local colour going?" Fen asked.

"Not much so far," Padmore admitted. "Still, I only arrived yesterday. It's early days yet."

"Well, I suppose we'd better get moving and spend some money," said the Major.

"I want to see the mermaid," said Padmore. "I've never seen a mermaid. It's a dugong, I expect, a halicore. Still, come to think of it, I've never seen a halicore, either."

Since neither Fen nor the Major particularly wanted to look at the mermaid (the Major had in any case, dutifully looked at it several times already at previous Fêtes), they let Padmore drift away on his own.

"We circulate," said the Major.

They circulated: a Books Stall, a Linen Stall, a Cakes Stall, pennies to be rolled down slotted wooden slopes on to a numbered board. Fen bought Lord Garnet Wolseley's *Narrative of the War with China in 1860*, two tea towels imprinted in red with the Houses of Parliament, a dozen drop-scones; the Major bought an Ouida, some rather yellowed cotton handkerchiefs with the initials A.K.G., a seed cake; neither of them had any success, even temporarily, with the pennies. At the Lucky Dip the Major got a small whistle, which he thought might possibly amuse his dogs, and Fen got an apple. Next they came to where Broderick Thouless, the composer, at three balls for twenty-five pence, was persistently bowling for a pig; from what they saw of his performance it seemed very unlikely that he was going to win it.

"Where *is* the pig, anyway?" Thouless said, straightening up, red in the face from his exertions. "My *back*...Surely the pig ought to be *here*?"

But then suddenly it was. A young one, cleanly and wholesome, it arrived wriggling and snorting in the arms of big blond Youings, from whose farm it had presumably come. Apologising to the woman in charge for his lateness, Youings deposited the pig in its pen, where it examined its surroundings with an air of refreshed surprise.

"Now, you behave yourself, Bathsheba," Youings told it.

His Amazonian wife Ortrud sauntered up. She wore an expensive but ill-fitting beige linen suit, and her pale hair gleamed glossy in the sunshine. The Major raised his green trilby hat, but she simply stared at him. "*Komm' mit,*" she commanded her husband. Youings smiled flaccidly at Fen and shuffled away after her.

"I presume," said Fen, "that whoever wins the pig will have it slaughtered. Pity."

"No, that's all right," said the Major. "Youings always manages to buy it back. People don't want the bother of it, don't you know. New Nivea, smooth moisture," he sang, "right into your skin. Ergh."

"'Ergh'?"

"It's a sort of noise they make at the end, I can't think why."

"*I'm* going to win the pig," said Thouless, fishing in his pocket for money. "Three more balls, please." They left him still vainly trying to get a ball into one of the little doorways in the wooden trap.

A Treasure Hunt, the Jams Stall, a miniature rifle range, the platform for the legs competition, due at 4.30; this last had a wooden screen designed to occult the competitors from the groin upwards. Near it, the youth Scorer was talking tremulously to a middle-aged man—presumably the doctor—who was making soothing noises; Scorer kept turning his back on the middle-aged man and pointing to his bottom. The Garden Stall, a coconut shy, a queue of children waiting for donkey rides ("Serry your ranks, there," said the Major amiably as they edged past). The Bottle Stall, where they found the Rector, still in drag, swigging Coca-Cola.

"Business slow?" Fen asked.

"On the contrary, I've got a queue," said the Rector, wiping his mouth with the back of his hand. "I have to come out every now and again, though, to keep an eye on things." Fen noted with interest that he was carrying his cricket bag with him.

Their progress had by now brought them close to the west wing of the house, where the Botticelli tent was pegged down; for a tent housing nothing but a picture, it was unexpectedly large. At one side of the entrance flap, cash box on a little table in front of her, sat a stout elderly woman, presumably one of the Misses Bale. Opposite her, on a camp stool, sat P.C. Luckraft;

he had taken off his crash helmet, revealing a bandage round his head, and was cradling the helmet on his knees. Less explicably, another stout elderly woman, presumably the second Miss Bale, could be glimpsed sitting on another camp stool at the back of the tent.

Fen said, "What's *she* doing there?"

"All part of the security measures, my dear fellow," said the Major. "Very hot on security, the Misses Bale are. The one at the back, Tatty, is there so that no one can push the Botticelli out under the canvas without being seen."

"But they can't really think it's valuable."

"They do, you know."

"And is that why Luckraft's there?"

"Yes, he sometimes helps to mount guard, if he happens to be off duty. Makes them feel extra-safe. Good man, Luckraft, very patient. Wonder what he's done to his head?"

Fen began eating his apple. "Are you," he said, "going to have a go at the coconuts?"

"No, I'm not. I can hit them all right, don't you know, but I can never make them fall off. The fact of the matter is, they're wedged, or glued or something. Let's go and look at the Botticelli, get it over and done with."

"You can't look at the Botticelli now, because I'm going to," said the Rector.

"All right," said the Major amenably, "you can go first."

They strolled on, and in a few paces arrived in front of the Botticelli tent.

The Major stared.

In a choking voice, "My word," he said. "That's new!"

One sign—a sheet of cardboard on an easel—said THE BOTTICELLI. Another, pinned to the tent, said NO SMOKING. Another said ALL CONTAINERS BASKETS ETC TO BE LEFT OUTSIDE. Yet another said FIFTY P.

But it was the fifth sign that had provoked the Major's reaction. It consisted of two outsize cardboard discs pinned together concentrically with a brass clip; in the outer disc a window had been cut, revealing the word ENGAGED painted on the inner.

"My word!" said the Major again.

Father Hattrick came out of the tent, murmured something appreciative to Miss Bale, nodded to Luckraft, picked up his jam-crammed basket from under Miss Bale's table and trotted across to the Rector.

"Now?" he said.

The Rector said, "Give me five minutes, Father, will you?"

"Yes, surely. I'll stay somewhere around here, and then you'll be able to find me." He ran off down the fairway, braking to a halt at the Garden Stall.

Miss Bale got to her feet. Momentarily rooted to the spot, Fen, the Major and the Rector watched in fascination as she went across to the new sign and rotated the inner disc, replacing the word ENGAGED with VACANT.

The Major said, "My word!" for the third time. Then abruptly he dropped all his purchases on to the turf and doubled up in a fit of helpless laughter. "B.V.M. assumpting in the jakes," he spluttered.

"Lavater-y humour," said Fen.

The Major made an effort and got himself under control again. He stooped and gathered up his whistle, book, cake, handkerchiefs, narcissus bulbs and blackcurrant jelly. The Rector went across to Miss Bale, who was returning to her seat.

"Afternoon, Titty," he said. "Me next." Handing Miss Bale five tenpenny pieces, he made for the tent flap.

"Oh, but Rector," squeaked Miss Bale.

"Yes, Titty, what is it?"

"Your cricket bag. You must leave it out here."

"Nonsense, Titty, of course I'm not going to leave it out here. You don't think *I'm* going to steal the Botticelli, do you? Anyway, I couldn't, it's too big. Even if I cut it out of its frame and rolled it up and doubled it over, it still wouldn't go in my cricket bag."

"Oh, but Rector."

"Go and sit down, Titty, and stop being such an old hen," said the Rector, disappearing inside the tent.

"That'll be all right, Miss Bale," said Luckraft, his solid official face radiating reassurance.

"Well, I don't know, I'm sure," said Miss Bale disconsolately.

The Major said, "I'm going indoors to dump this stuff and fetch old Fred. Can't bring Sal, unfortunately, have to keep her shut up during these maffickings, otherwise she runs about biting everyone. See you later." He hobbled off, threading his way among stalls, marquees and sideshows in the direction of the house's east wing, where his flatlet was. Fen went and joined Father Hattrick at the coconut shy.

After a strenuous five minutes, during which neither of them succeeded in dislodging a coconut, they saw the Rector emerge from the Botticelli tent. He looked about him, caught sight of Father Hattrick, waved and beckoned affirmatively, and vanished round the corner of the Fruit Stall. Father Hattrick waved back, threw his last ball at random, grabbed his basket, said goodbye to Fen and ran.

The stall-keeper, impressed by Fen's obstinacy if not by his skill, picked up a spare coconut and made him a present of it.

Fen went to the Garden Stall and bought himself a large brown paper carrier from the pile on sale there; into this he stuffed the unwieldy acervation of objects he had acquired. Then he decided to go and look at the Botticelli. Miss Bale took his money and his carrier bag and graciously motioned him in, closing the flap behind him.

The tent was bisected widthways, he found, by an enormous piece of scuffed velvet stretching from side to side, and from the roof to the ground. At its centre, hanging by chains from the roof-strut, was the Botticelli, illuminated by electricity from several judiciously-chosen angles; and the Botticelli, Fen saw at once, was an almost supernaturally talentless picture—a gargantuan female form, angel-conveyed, with flowing robes, a halo, a vapid smirk and downwards-pointing bare feet. The style was two-dimensional, the composition monotonously symmetrical; the colours were mostly pastel blues, pinks and yellows; the halo was so pale that it looked as if it had developed a fault and was on the point of flickering out altogether. Fen went close up to the thing to see if there was a signature, but found none; the elaborate gilt frame, however, pointed fairly conclusively to some wealthy megalomaniac amateur, besotted with the pre-Raphaelites, round about 1870.

The only other object in this half of the tent was a spartan wooden chair without arms, set square in front of the picture.

Fen sat down on it, fixed his eyes on the Virgin's stubby toes and meditated—since this, after all, was what he was supposed to be doing—on religion.

❀ ❀ ❀

On leaving the tent ten minutes later, he was surprised to find the man from Sweb hovering outside—small, tubby and neat in his grey suit, grey overcoat and meticulously centred little grey hat; seemingly he was waiting to go in. "Hello," said Fen.

"Ah," said the man from Sweb, weakly.

"So you came after all."

"Yes, here I am."

"Enjoying it?"

"Oh, yes."

"Been to the fortune-teller?"

"No. No, not yet."

"You must be sure and do that," said Fen.

"Oh, I will, I will." The man from Sweb lowered his voice. "What exactly *is* the Botticelli?" he mumbled.

"A picture."

"A picture? Is that all? What sort of a picture?"

"Religious."

"Oh dear, and I've paid already."

Fen left him and sought out the Rectory Stall, where for the moment there were no other customers.

"Come and buy," said little Miss Endacott, blushing painfully.

"Certainly I'll come and buy, Miss Endacott. I'll have that purple lamp-shade."

"Oh yes, do, it's so pretty, isn't it? Only it's fifty pence, I'm afraid."

"Never mind, I'll still have it. And have you got some music of Broderick Thouless's, or has it gone?"

"Oh no, it's still here," said Miss Endacott. "Such a worry, it's been."

"Oh? Why?"

"Well, you see, I feel sure it must be very *valuable*. But then, when I asked the Rector how much I ought to charge for it, he said, 'Six pence'. I think he must have been joking, don't you?"

"Yes, I do. It's worth much more than that."

"Yes, but *how* much more? I don't know what to say to you, truly I don't," said Miss Endacott faintly. "Would...would a *pound* be too much, do you think?"

"No, it wouldn't. It'd be too little." Fen had been thumbing through Thouless's crumpled fistful of banknotes, which he had kept separate in his left-hand trousers pocket, and had discovered that there were fourteen of them. Thouless was well-off, but had he really intended Fen to spend the lot? Some sort of compromise seemed desirable. "Seven pounds, Miss Endacott," he said. "I'll give you seven pounds for it."

"There, I *knew* it was valuable." Glowing, Miss Endacott handed over a bundle of manuscript orchestral full scores, done in pencil. Opening one of the double sheets at random, "2 1/3 secs.," Fen read, in red ink, in the space between the percussion and the first violins, "Monster starts eating child," and then, several bars further on, "5 2/3 secs. Monster finishes eating child." He gave Miss Endacott the money.

At the hoop-la he found Padmore. The Whirlybirds, having run themselves into the ground, were taking a break, so that it was possible to hear Padmore singing "Ta-ra-ra Boumedienne" quietly to himself. He appeared to be trying to win a tin of Chivers Garden Peas.

Buying himself some hoops, Fen said, "So you think Youings's evidence settles the matter, do you?"

Padmore displayed alarm. "Yes, of course I do. I mean, from what you said, I gathered Youings was quite *definite* about Hagberd not having been at the pub, talking to Gobbo, at the time when Routh was being murdered. He was quite definite about it, wasn't he?"

"Yes, he was."

"Well, then."

"He might have been lying," Fen said mildly.

"Oh, *Lord!*" Padmore threw a hoop, distractedly, and knocked over a doll. "Why ever should you think that?"

"It's a possibility."

"Certainly it is, but *why* should he *lie?* He can't have done the murder, because when it was happening the Rector saw him four miles away at the pub...You're trying to make me re-write," Padmore said accusingly.

"I thought you were going to have to re-write anyway, so as to make Routh and Hagberd start out at one from the page."

"That's not re-writing, it's just a matter of sticking in atmospheric bits here and there. Do you know Clarence Tully?"

"Slightly. Why?"

"He's one man I ought to talk to. He employed Hagberd after Hagberd left Routh. I didn't see him when I was down here before. Is he here?"

"I saw him arrive, but I don't know if..." Fen glanced around him. "Yes, there he is." He pointed. "That huge man in the leggings and the green jacket."

"Ah," said Padmore, making the identification. "Good." Concentrating, he poised his final hoop. "If I win the peas, Youings isn't mistaken and he isn't lying," he said childishly. He threw. The hoop settled neatly over the wooden block on which the peas stood. "Look at that, then," said Padmore, triumphant.

Thouless joined them. He bought hoops, settled his bifocals on his nose, and prepared to throw.

"Wait a minute, Thouless," Fen said. "Here are your scores."

"Heavens, *I* don't want them."

"I dare say, but neither do I."

"Though on second thoughts, perhaps I do want them. When I finally run out of inspiration, which I'm bound to do sooner or later, I can crib bits from them for other films."

"Fen, you wouldn't like these peas, would you?" said Padmore winningly. "They're no conceivable use to me."

"No, thanks," said Fen. "I've got quite enough to carry already." Padmore sighed and departed, presumably in search of Clarence Tully. "Well, come on, take your scores," Fen said to Thouless.

"Look, why don't you come and have a drink with me some time, and bring them with you then?"

"No."

"Oh, all right," said Thouless resignedly. He accepted the scores and dumped them on the ground at his feet.

"I paid seven pounds for them," said Fen. "Here's the other seven pounds you gave me."

"Only seven pounds?" said Thouless, aggrieved. "I should have thought they'd have priced them a bit higher than *that*."

"As a matter of fact, I priced them myself."

"Well then, I should have thought *you* would have priced them a bit higher than that."

"Then you'd have had to pay more for them."

"Yes, that's true." Thouless threw a hoop, hitting the stall-holder lightly on the belly. "Now I come to think of it, seven pounds is quite enough. Exorbitant, in fact. You're sure you wouldn't like to keep the scores with you, for the time being?"

"Quite sure."

"I say, what a monstrosity of a lamp-shade you've got," said Thouless. "Where on earth do people find these things?"

CHAPTER SIX

Fate, Time, Occasion, Chance, and Change

Off with his head—so much for Buckingham.

Colley Cibber: *Shakespeare's Richard III, improved.*

THOUGH NOT LARGE, the fortune-telling tent was
relatively ornate; its use of arc-lines in the roof and the flap,
and its elaborate spiked finial, made it vaguely reminiscent of
paynimry at the time of the Crusades. It was labelled MADAME
SOSOSTRIS, FAMOUS CLAIRVOYANTE. A second placard, more
laconic, said FREE. Fen turned this over so that it read BUSY!
KEEP OUT!! THIS MEANS YOU!!!

He went inside.

Inside was murky, lit by an ancient hurricane lantern
perched on top of a step-ladder in the right-hand rear corner.
Its shielding must have been defective, for it was flickering a
good deal, casting alarming shadows on the canvas walls. On
a rickety oval table with cigarette burns and beer-glass rings
there were playing-cards, a skull, a crystal ball, a stuffed
lizard falling to pieces and a packet of ten Guards. Behind
the table sat the Rector; to his bombazine dress he had added
a wig and a peculiar hat with an impenetrable veil. In front

of the table was a chair for clients. In the corner opposite the hurricane lantern, a tarnished rococo thurible, apparently of silver, was emitting equal proportions of incense and thick black smoke.

Fen tripped on a corner of the Rector's cricket bag, which gave out a muffled clinking sound.

"Careful, damn it!" said the Rector. Then suddenly his voice went falsetto. "I mean, careful, damn it," he soprano-ed.

"Good heavens," Fen muttered.

"Be seated, stranger," said the Rector, still falsetto. "By Sebek, Tagd, Ler and Sokk-mimi," he hooted, "by Bile, Zerpanitu, Mu-ul-lil, Ubargisi, Ubilulu, say, stranger, what brings you to this place."

"I come to seek help," Fen hooted back.

"By Astarte, Gasan-abzu…Listen, if you're not going to be serious, there's no point in my going on with this," said the Rector waspishly, reverting to his normal tones.

"Are all those names real?"

"Certainly they're real: when I was at the Sorbonne, I did Comparative Religion. You don't mind if I drop the voice?"

"Glad of it."

"It hurts my throat."

"I should imagine so," said Fen. "And would you mind unveiling as well?"

"Anything to oblige," said the Rector, obliging. "Wretched things, veils. Stuffy. And when you yawn they get drawn into your mouth, by suction. Well now, what would you like to know?"

"The future."

"Very well." The Rector extended a huge brown hand. "Cross my palm with paper." Fen gave him a fifty-pence piece. "That's not much," said the Rector.

"I pay by results."

"Do you indeed. Well, now…" The Rector laid out some cards, perfunctorily, and made a pretence of peering first at them and then at the crystal ball. "I see you writing a book," he said.

"Right."

"I see you making a strange dish, of hog's brains, neat's flesh, herbs and spices."

"Right again."

"I see you making a long journey to a hot country," the Rector droned oracularly. "Beware an unexpected labour. Beware an ancient man."

"Sounds more like Padmore," said Fen. "Who do you think killed Routh?"

"Some benefactor."

"Hagberd?"

"Here, have a Guards." The Rector pushed the packet across the table to Fen. They both lit cigarettes. "Hagberd? No. I mean, *probably* not."

"Who, then?"

"*I* don't know."

"And who's Mavis Trent?"

"Ah, Mavis Trent." With deliberation, the Rector began building a card-house. "Mavis Trent is dead."

Fen waited.

"Died six months ago," said the Rector.

Fen still waited.

"Fell," said the Rector. "Or possibly was pushed." There was a silence while he erected the card-house's second storey.

"*More* crime?" Fen said presently.

"Could be." His cigarette projecting centrally from his mandrill face, the Rector, working rapidly, began on the card-house's third storey. The thurible fumed, the lantern-flame wavered, the crystal ball gleamed fitfully. "Could be," the Rector said again. "I understand that in the end the police plumped for accident—which was the verdict at the inquest. They had their doubts, though."

"What was that boy talking about? Any idea?"

"Scorer? Yes, I shall have to grill Scorer, when this lot's over," said the Rector. "He's easily terrorised, fortunately. Wonder if he found Doc Mason?"

"Yes, I think he did."

"Nothing the matter with him, actually...No, as to what he was on about, I haven't a clue." Tiring of the card-house, the Rector brought his hand down on it and squashed it flat. "Blackmail, indeed...He obviously wasn't romancing, though."

"No."

"It was something that had actually happened to him."

"Yes...Tell me, why do you call yourself Madame Sosostris, Famous Clairvoyante?"

"It was the Major. He suggested it."

"I see."

"I used to be Gypsy Rose Lee, but then I decided it was time for a change. Why?" said the Rector suspiciously. "What's wrong with Madame Sosostris, Famous Clairvoyante?"

"Nothing wrong with it. It's from a poem, that's all."

"A *poem*!" The Rector registered acutest disgust. "*Poem*! Just the other day," he confided, "the Major made me read some *poem* or other, about someone going into a church and donating an Irish sixpence. As if there weren't enough foreign coins in the offertory-boxes already. Let me just get my hands round that poet's neck," he said, brooding, "and I'll Irish-sixpence him."

"The unacknowledged legislators of the world," Fen said.

"Unacknowledged legislators grinding out unacknowl-edged legislation," said the Rector. "Do you want to know some more about your future?"

"No, I don't. I want to know about Mavis Trent."

"No reason why you shouldn't. But you'll have to cross my palm with paper again."

"I could get it from the newspaper files for nothing."

"Come on, come on, you're not a miser, are you?" With some reluctance Fen handed over another fifty-pence. "You mustn't take up too much of my time, though," the Rector warned. "Go and see how many there are in the queue, will you?"

Obediently, Fen got up, went to the tent flap and looked out. "There's no one," he reported, returning.

"My parishioners are a parcel of old muckworms," said the Rector resentfully.

"Well now, Mavis Trent," he said. "A widow. Fortyish, but looked younger. Very blonde hair—dyed—and one of those attractive mischievous faces, not really pretty, let alone beautiful, but somehow very appealing; it cheered you up just to look at her. Nice figure, and dressed well—plain well-cut clothes, nothing gaudy. Her husband died quite young of leukaemia, but luckily he was one of those people with a mania for insurance, and Mavis came into so much money that she didn't have to take a job, though as a matter of fact she did *do* quite a few jobs—casual or part-time—partly because she enjoyed the social side and partly because she wasn't the sort to sit about the house all day with folded hands. She did a lot of unpaid work too, cooking meals for pensioners and helping with kids and so forth."

"Sounds a paragon," Fen commented.

"She was a thoroughly nice woman, Mavis," said the Rector. "Everyone liked her. And most people went *on* liking her, even after her husband died."

"What did she get up to, then?"

"Men," said the Rector. "She suddenly started chasing after men. There'd been nothing like that while her husband was alive, or not as far as anyone knew, but then a few months after his death, whoosh, the balloon went up with a vengeance."

"All changed, changed utterly," Fen suggested. "A terrible cutie is born."

"That's more poetry, I take it. Mavis was a nympho, I suppose, but calling her that gives a wrong impression. She never seemed to flirt or ogle or any of that stuff. But then, she didn't have to, or anyway, not obviously: she was just naturally cheerfully sexy, with a sort of built-in spontaneous come-hither which gave you the idea, very powerfully, that making love to her would be all fun and no complications. It was, too—or so I gather. Damn it, I was quite taken with the girl myself. Not that I'd have married her, of course (*she* didn't seem interested in making a second marriage, come to that), and of course, me being a cleric and not approving of all this promiscuity anyway, there was no question of an *affaire* (besides, you can't stay properly fit if you keep fornicating all the time). Even so, I still got the impression that she wouldn't have minded nabbing me, on a temporary basis," said the Rector, with evident gratification. "So you can see, she wasn't exactly what you'd call choosy.

"And that was the chief trouble, really. Of course, there were rows about husbands, but not as many as you'd have expected, and not as bad as you'd have expected, either. Where Mavis was concerned, the injured wives somehow seemed to get half paralysed; they'd kick up a shindig, naturally, but it was always their husbands they were furious with, not, for some mysterious reason, Mavis; she was so bright and open about everything that it seemed to positively hypnotise people. Another thing was that with Mavis, absolutely nobody lasted more than a week or two; and *another* thing was that Mavis's men never seemed to *mind* getting the brush-off: they simply accepted it the way you accept the fact that when you've just had a meal, you don't want to eat any more."

The Rector rubbed his nose, ruminatively. "Mavis *looked* sexy, all right," he added. "But I've sometimes wondered if perhaps the poor girl wasn't very good in bed. That'd account for her men not bothering too much when she dropped them, and it'd also account for her gallivanting from one man to another to another to another."

Fen said, "Trying to find one who could rouse her, you mean."

"That's it. On the surface she seemed perfectly normal and...and fulfilled—easy and happy and comfortable in spite of being so active. Nothing neurotic, in fact. But that could have been misleading.

"Anyway, that's all academic now. What I started to say was that it wasn't the occasional hoo-ha over other women's husbands that made some people uneasy about Mavis, so much as the fact that she was so hopelessly undiscriminating. Some of her men were all right, but there were others who were really dreadful types, louts you wouldn't have imagined Mavis would have wanted to be seen dead with. And as I say, there were hordes of them; it was as if Mavis was trying to qualify for *The Guinness Book of Records*; and not just local men, either—men for miles around, even as far away as Plymouth and Exeter and London.

"The reason I know about all this is that Mavis wasn't in the least secretive about her goings-on. In particular, there was a friend called Ella Hamilton—gone to live in Walsall now; tiresome creature, actually, but Mavis seemed to like her. Anyway, Mavis used to tell Ella pretty well everything, not always naming names, but not keeping much else back. The two of them were as thick as thieves—but then Mavis made a pass at Ella's boy-friend, and Ella took umbrage, and among other things came to me and poured out a bucketful of murky gossip about Mavis—I tried to stop the silly chit, but she was half hysterical and I couldn't. The general idea was that I should *do* something about Mavis, preach her a sermon, I suppose, and show her the error of her ways."

"Which you didn't," Fen said.

"Which I didn't. Wouldn't have done the slightest good. No one takes any notice of the clergy nowadays, except for Humanists waiting to welcome South-Bank bishops into the fold...I say," said the Rector, "do you find it a bit close in here?"

"Not close, exactly. Smoggy."

"It's the thurible," said the Rector. "It's stepped up its output. I'd better do something about it, or we'll both suffocate." He produced a large earthenware teapot from under his chair, crossed to the thurible and emptied the teapot's contents into it. There was a hissing noise; the smoke first increased, then diminished, then vanished altogether.

"Interesting thing, that thurible," said the Rector, disposing of the teapot and sitting down again. "Belonged to that ass Dashwood. A relation of mine bought it when the Monks of Medmenham packed it in. I imagine they used it for their

Black Masses and so forth, burning goat's dung in it, or some such twaddle...Incidentally, I'll take my hat and wig off, if you don't mind, they're making me too hot. Where was I?"

"Ella Hamilton."

"Oh yes. Well, Ella doesn't come into it any more—parted brass rags with Mavis after the kafuffle over the boy-friend. Result: after the quarrel, for a month or two before she died, or was killed, nobody quite knew what our Mavis was up to. Ella had used to chatter a lot about Mavis, you see, and with that source of information cut off by the quarrel, the local tattlers found they no longer had anything much to get their teeth into; Mavis herself was quite open about things, as I told you, but on the other hand she wasn't deliberately indiscreet, so no one had any idea what man or men she was going with in the last few weeks of her life. There were the usual rumours, of course, but all very vague, very contradictory. The police questioned literally dozens of people when they were preparing for the inquest, but all they got for their trouble was wind and vapour. For all they could find out, Mavis might have given up men altogether.

"Well now, it was about the middle of March that it happened—can't remember the exact date, but it doesn't matter. You know Hole Bridge?"

Fen did. It was by way of Hole Bridge that the road from Burraford and Aller to Glazebridge crossed the Burr. Built in 1572 in grey granite from the moor, it had a single-lane carriageway lined on either side with V-shaped bays in which pedestrians could take refuge when wheeled traffic came along. The Burr was wide here: wide, shallow and fast-moving, with a jumble of big rocks beneath the surface.

"Yes, I know it," Fen said.

"Well, so it was there she was found," said the Rector, "by an old loon called Meiklejohn, a retired accountant, lives in Hole in the pink cottage with the bus-stop outside the gate. He was out for an early-morning walk. First thing he saw was Mavis's little white Sprite, parked in the old railway siding. He didn't take any notice of that, but then he went on, on to the bridge, and looked over the edge, and there she was, poor soul, stretched out on her back on a slab of rock directly under the V nearest the bank on the Glazebridge side, like a tumbled old bolt of dark cloth with the water bubbling over it. Meiklejohn's a coward or a half-wit or both—didn't try to make his way down to Mavis and see if there was anything he could do for her, just tottered off in a funk and phoned the police. However, there was nothing he *could* have done for her, as it turned out. She'd been dead for hours.

"A neighbour had heard the Sprite drive away from Mavis's house round about eleven the previous evening, so it was a reasonable guess that she'd had an assignation at the bridge; that was why the police were so anxious to find out who her current boy-friend was. But after she got to the bridge, what happened *then*? Was it an accident? You know how low the parapet is, scarcely comes up to one's crotch; if you were standing with your back to it, and lost your balance for some reason, you could topple over as easy as winking; and it's a long fall, and the water's too shallow over that rock slab to break your fall, you'd hit the rock full tilt.

"The most innocent possibility, then, was that Mavis arrived at the bridge ahead of the boy-friend and somehow tumbled over. Then along comes the boy-friend, fails to see her lying there under the bridge—there was a full moon that night, but on the other hand, there was also a lot of cloud—eventually decides she's stood him up, and tools off without the least idea that anything's seriously wrong."

"Wouldn't he have seen Mavis Trent's parked car?" Fen asked.

"Not if he'd come from the Glazebridge direction, and had just stayed on the bridge, without following the road on towards Hole and Aller and Burraford. The railway siding isn't visible from the bridge. Meiklejohn saw the car because he was approaching the bridge from the other direction, from Hole."

"I see."

"So that's one thing that *might* have happened," said the Rector. "Mavis wasn't at all the sort of person to get careless or giddy and fall off a bridge, but it just *might* have happened. However, there were four things—clues, if you like—which pointed to the possibility of violence.

"First off, after she fell, or was pushed, Mavis didn't die immediately, according to the medicos. She probably stayed alive for half an hour or more. She could have drowned—there's a good two feet of water over the slab she fell on—or she could have cracked her skull and gone out that way; but what she actually did die of, according to the post mortem, was internal bleeding, and that took a bit of time. Her right arm was all right, and they thought she must have used that to hoist herself up and keep her head clear of the water. She couldn't have done much else to help herself, poor soul—too badly smashed up; she suffered from osteoporosis, it turned out, soft bones, and there were a hell of a lot of fractures, too many to have allowed her to drag herself to the bank. *But*, she could have called out; weakly, perhaps, on account of her injuries, but loud enough to be heard by anyone on the bridge."

"Are there any houses close to the bridge?" Fen asked. "I can't off-hand remember."

"No, nothing very near—and of course, the river makes a good deal of noise. As far as houses are concerned, the poor thing could have yelled her head off, and still no one would have heard. Anyone on the bridge could have heard, though, which rather disposes of the idea of an innocent boy-friend hanging about there waiting, with no idea that there'd been an accident.

"The second thing was that the police found traces—freshly snapped twigs and so forth—suggesting that someone had pushed down through the bushes from the bridge to the water's edge, on the side where Mavis was lying. Also, they found a flattened patch in the grass on the bank, as if someone had squatted or sat there in the shadow of the bridge. They thought someone might have done just that, waiting for Mavis to die—perhaps talking to her, even."

"Good Lord," said Fen, appalled.

"Yes, very nasty. However, the traces weren't very definite, and in any case they could have been nothing to do with Mavis's death at all—could have been made the previous day. It was dry weather, like now, so there was nothing so decisive as a footprint; and there were no cigarette ends or shreds of cloth or what not.

"Thirdly, Mavis's handbag," the Rector went on. "The current isn't strong near the banks, so they found the bag in the water only a few feet away from her. So far, so good—but there was one odd thing. Did you know that fingerprints can survive under water?"

"Yes, I did."

"Well, so there ought in reason to have been a few prints on the bag. But there were none. The handle was a sort of fancy coloured cord—glorified string, really—and that wouldn't have taken prints anyway; but there ought to have been a few prints on the bag itself, because that was smooth pigskin."

"She could have given the thing a rub over before leaving home, to smarten it up," Fen suggested, "and then never touched it except for the handle."

"Oh, quite. On the other hand, she could have dropped it just before she toppled over, and then someone could have picked it up, and opened it and rummaged in it, and closed it again, and wiped it off, and finally chucked it into the water after her."

"Yes...She didn't have gloves with her, then."

"None were found. And no one could think of any reason why a murderer should have taken them from her, and taken them away from the scene."

"Yes," Fen said again. He was thinking that if Mavis Trent in fact had been murdered, the evidence of the handbag was particularly interesting, not so much because the murderer had examined it, or because he had then remembered to eliminate his fingerprints, but for another reason, a fairly obvious one, all things considered. It was at this moment that he had his first vague inkling of what eventually proved to be the truth. "Yes, I see," he said. "Equivocal, though: if Mavis Trent was a smartly dressed woman, as I think you said, she certainly could have polished the bag before setting out."

"It's *all* equivocal, unfortunately," said the Rector. "Grounds for suspicion, yes, but never anything conclusive."

"You said there were four clues. What was the fourth?"

"A handkerchief. Found clutched tightly in Mavis's hand. Don't know what the technical term for dead people clutching things is, but I dare say you do."

"Cadaveric spasm."

"I'll take your word for it. Anyway, there was this handkerchief, balled up in Mavis's hand. And it was a man's handkerchief, not Mavis's at all."

Fen said, "Even if it was a man's handkerchief, can you be sure it wasn't hers? Women do sometimes own men's handkerchiefs."

"I'm quite sure it wasn't hers."

"Was her own handkerchief in her handbag or her pocket?"

"No," the Rector admitted. "She didn't seem to have one."

"Well, then."

"What I imagine happened was that the murderer, if any, knew that his handkerchief had gone into the river in Mavis's hand, and took *her* handkerchief out of the handbag, and carried it away with him, to make it seem as if *his* handkerchief was *hers*."

"It's all wildly hypothetical," Fen pointed out.

"Yes, I know it is. All I'm trying to say is that Mavis was too well turned out to go out on a date carrying a ropy old cheap cotton man's handkerchief with her. She wouldn't have dreamed of it. And if that's so, then the handkerchief was handed to her, for some reason, by whatever man she was meeting."

"Not necessarily," said Fen. "Women sometimes borrow handkerchiefs from men, and afterwards get them laundered and give them back. Mavis Trent may have done just that—

brought the handkerchief along with a view to returning it; and she may have fallen into the river, accidentally, before the owner came along."

"Well, but in that case, where was her own handkerchief? Besides, this handkerchief in Mavis's hand was all crumpled, all balled up, not neatly folded as it would have been if it had just been laundered."

Fen sighed. "Yes, that's a point," he agreed. "Not exactly hanging evidence, but certainly it doesn't quite fit in with the accident theory, particularly taken in conjunction with the other three indications you mentioned. The police tried to trace the handkerchief, I take it?"

"They did, but no soap. Couldn't even find the manu-facturer, let alone the retailer; as I told you, it was a cheap, common thing. Widger, for the police, said at the inquest that either it was foreign or else the manufacturer had gone out of business, perhaps years ago."

"No initials? No laundry-mark?"

"No, neither. All the experts could say was that it had been washed a fair number of times. They didn't find any significant stains on it, either, blood or oil or anything like that."

"Most unhelpful. Even so, I'm surprised that the inquest jury decided it was accident. I should have thought that an open verdict was what was called for."

The Rector said, "So should I, but the Coroner thought differently. *His* idea was that there was never any man involved at all: Mavis simply decided to take a drive and a moonlit stroll over the bridge and along the river-bank; then at some stage she stood in the V with her back to the parapet, gazing up at the moon or something, and lost her balance and went head-long. He implied, even if he didn't actually say, that at the time of her squabble with Ella Hamilton, Mavis had a change of heart and decided to lay off men for a bit; that was confirmed, he thought, by the fact that the gossip about her had suddenly lost substance. Also, he pointed out that it had been pretty cold for a fortnight or more, and that in that sort of weather people didn't normally make arrangements for canoodling *al fresco*, moon or no moon. As to the handkerchief, he said that almost certainly that had been Mavis's. As to the handbag, he said Mavis herself must have wiped it. As to the traces in the bushes and on the bank, he said there was no evidence at all to connect them with the tragedy. And as to Mavis's being able to call for help, he said that if no one was within earshot, at any time, that just didn't come into it. He was very persuasive, I'm bound to say."

"And the jury went along with him."

"A majority of them did, yes. They weren't unanimous, though. And I gathered afterwards that the ones who'd voted against accident were the ones who'd known Mavis quite well. Knowing her, they simply didn't believe either that she'd given up men, or that she'd fallen off Hole Bridge unaided, or that she'd have gone out, even on her own, with a cheap man's handkerchief on her."

"And how did the police react to the inquest verdict?"

"I talked to Widger after it was over, and he said he was surprised: he'd expected an open verdict, perhaps even a murder verdict. However, the file would stay open, he said— and presumably it has stayed open, though if anything more's been discovered, I haven't heard of it."

Fen considered for a moment, and then said, "Was she pregnant?"

"No, she wasn't."

"And another point: could it have been Routh she arranged to meet at the bridge?"

"Psychologically, I'm afraid, yes." Uncharacteristically subdued after his long recital, the Rector was playing five-finger exercises on the top of the crystal ball. "As I think I mentioned, Mavis took up with some really appalling types. But Routh wasn't a womaniser, you know. In fact, he made a point of sneering at women, and you felt it was genuine, not just a pose. No, if anything, I'd say Routh was hostile to women. As you're probably aware, he was a pervert, a sadist, poor wretched unspeakable man. All his lust went into that ghastly business of tormenting animals.

"But in any case," the Rector added, "we now have every reason to believe that it wasn't Routh who killed Mavis, just as we have every reason to believe that Mavis didn't have an accident, that she was murdered."

"Scorer."

"Precisely: Scorer, babbling about someone threatening someone with going to the police about Mavis Trent."

"Doesn't Scorer realise the importance of whatever it was he overheard? Doesn't he realise that he ought to tell the police?"

"I'm quite sure he realises," said the Rector, without hesitation. "But he's a *Scorer*, you see—that's to say, one of a shower of feeble, dishonest, catchpenny aments; in spite of plenty of competition, the Scorers manage to be quite the most undesirable family hereabouts. No Scorer would go to the police voluntarily, about anything. A Scorer would just sit on whatever it was he'd found out, trying to think up some way of turning it to his own advantage."

"Rather risky in this case, I'd imagine."

"Extremely risky. I shall have to drag Scorer into Glazebridge to see Widger as soon as possible—this evening, preferably. I hope I'm going to be able to lay hands on him," said the Rector. "After blurting all that stuff out to us, he may take it into his silly head to slope off and hide himself. I ought to have handed him over to Luckraft, really, but what with one thing and another, it—"

Abruptly he broke off.

"What the hell is that?" he said.

From outside the tent, somewhere fairly close by, had come a sequence of sounds cutting across the expected turbulence of the Fête which had hitherto provided the unheeded background to their conversation: first the clang of a large bell, then a noise like a ship's mast coming down, then a chorus of feminine screams, then an agitated male voice shouting indistinguishable instructions, then a crescendo of voices raised in perturbation, then the thud of rapidly trotting feet. The Whirlybirds, who had been hacking their way into the hull of *Yellow Submarine*, faltered, tried to recover themselves, failed to do so and finally stopped altogether; their speaking voices, not much different from their singing voices except in volume, could be heard inside the fortune-telling tent twittering frenetically but obscurely through the amplifiers.

Indignantly, the Rector started to his feet.

"What the *hell*," he boomed, "is happening out there *now*?"

Padmore was one of those who saw it happen.

His interview with Clarence Tully had left something to be desired, the something consisting quite possibly of shortcomings in his interpellatory technique: prising facts from malign or unwilling black Press Relations Officers was one kettle of fish, substantiating Routh and Hagberd from the recollections of a Devon farmer quite another. Anyway, whatever the reason, nothing new or striking about either man had emerged. Like everyone else except Mrs Leeper-Foxe, Tully had found Routh repugnant and had avoided him. As to Hagberd, he, it appeared, had been always too busy working to have time to cultivate more than a nodding acquaintance with his employer.

"Proper old Stakhanovite, that one," said Tully. His father, fetching up with the British expeditionary force at Murmansk in July of 1918, had developed a good deal of interest in Russian affairs during his eighteen months of waiting to come under fire, and some of this had leavened the agrarian preoccupations of the family at large.

"I don't *see* Hagberd, that's the trouble," Padmore complained. "Or rather, I think I see him all right, but somehow I can't seem to get him down on paper."

"There, then," said Clarence Tully, whether in commiseration or polite surprise it was impossible to tell.

Padmore parted from him and plunged once more into the fun of the fair. Presently he found himself side by side with the Fête's Negro opener, Dermot McCartney, at the rifle range. They both banged away ineffectually for some time and then fell to discussing Africa, with particular reference to the Republic of Upper Volta. It was from the Republic of Upper Volta that Dermot McCartney had been brought to England at the age of three, and it was in the Republic of Upper Volta, in Ougadougou, that Padmore had once spent six painful weeks gathering material for his paper. During this period he had been pestered and pursued, he told Dermot McCartney, by a quadroon peanut planter who believed himself to be de Gaulle's illegitimate son. Moreover, he had had difficulty, when his stint was over, in leaving. Since he was *persona non grata* in Ghana at the time, the river was closed to him, and he was forced to charter a ruinous two-seater aeroplane in which he was flown, hair-raisingly, into Dahomey, arriving at Cotonou just in time for the latest of the country's biennial *coups d'état*. When the telegraph office re-opened, he had sent the *Gazette* a strictly factual cable about the recent days' events, and had been at once expelled.

"My people are mostly dolts, I'm afraid," said Dermot McCartney, consoling him. "Dolts or barbarians or both. They believe things which are either nonsensical or else manifestly untrue, such as that they are collectively capable of managing their own affairs, and that black is beautiful, and that jazz is an art form."

"Are you one of the Mossi?"

"Yes, I am, I'm sorry to have to say. A particularly rebarbative tribe, the Mossi, even for Africans."

"Well, I don't know about that," said Padmore, "but it certainly seems a very simple matter to get on the wrong side of them, one way or another."

Broderick Thouless strolled up, clutching his *Mincer People* scores in one hand, and in the other, various purchases bundled up in a Paisley shawl. He was accompanied by the Major, who now had the whippet Fred with him, on a lead.

"I want to try the Try-Your-Strength machine," Thouless said.

"Aren't you on the small side for that, my dear fellow?" said the Major, with less than his usual tact. "With these things, don't you know, it's brute size that counts."

"I may be small," said Thouless, affronted, "but I'm muscular...Mind you, they rig these contraptions somehow," he added, "so that the customer can scarcely ever win. So if I'm not successful, that'll be the reason for it. If it's rigged, I shan't succeed."

"Pleonasm," said the Major.

"I myself am certainly too small," said Dermot McCartney.

"So am I," said the Major.

"I'm *big* enough," said Padmore, "but the trouble is, I'm flabby. African food consists almost entirely of carbohydrates, so it's not surprising, really."

Exchanging further sorrows about their individual physiques, and about their individual states of health generally, the four of them wandered away from the rifle range and across the rough gravel driveway into the lawn's eastern half, where they wound their way in procession among crowded stalls and marquees, passed the fortune-telling tent—in which the Rector was at that moment concluding his account of the death of Mavis Trent—and so in due course came to a halt at the Try-Your-Strength machine near-by.

However, Padmore, Dermot McCartney and the Major were not, they saw, destined to watch Thouless excel himself immediately. (Or, as it turned out, ever.) The machine had just been pre-empted by Ortrud Youings.

It was a massive machine, traditional in design. With a long-handled mallet, you hit a metal plate set in the base-box, thus activating an arrangement of springs, cogs and levers which propelled a lead weight up a graduated slot in the tall central column; if you were lucky, the weight hit the bell at the top and you received a prize—a kewpie doll or a metal teapot or twenty Players or a psychedelic balloon, to judge from the adjacent display.

The machine was supervised, and indeed owned, by a fat barker called Arthur, well advanced in years, who stood beside it swaying benignly from side to side, the neck of a depleted whisky bottle projecting from a pocket of his raincoat.

"Come and watch the little lady!" he bawled hoarsely, ignoring the fact that Ortrud Youings was as tall, if not as obese, as he was himself. "Walk up! Walk up! Come on along and watch the little lady ring the bell!"

Ortrud Youings had taken off her jacket and given it to her husband, who was standing close to her with a love-sick smirk on his otherwise not unintelligent face; the onlookers saw the muscles ripple in her smooth white arms as she hefted the mallet. Grasping it firmly in both hands, she swung it slowly back over her right shoulder, then forward again, with lightning speed and colossal force, down on to the metal plate.

The entire machine seemed to totter at the impact. The plate crashed down on to the base box, the cogs groaned and the lead weight shot up the slot like a bullet, hitting the bell with a clang which momentarily drowned even the Whirlybirds. But there was more. Though solidly built from mahogany, round about the turn of the century, the machine had since then been sapped by decades of hard use and weathering, and a transverse crack had gradually developed in its column just beneath the vertex of the bell. Strained to crisis point by Ortrud Youings's tremendous blow, this crack now rapidly widened, and with a splintering of wood, to a hullabaloo of shrieks, gasps and shouted warnings, the top of the column sagged and broke away altogether. Bell and all, it plummeted earthward, catching its owner Arthur a glancing blow on the side of the head and collapsing him on to the turf, where he lay stunned, bleeding profusely from a wound in his scalp above his right ear.

The instantly ensuing commotion featured a single, rather ghastly, incongruity: wholly ignoring the unfortunate Arthur's fate—for which, though unintentionally, she had after all been responsible—Ortrud Youings dropped the mallet, clasped her hands above her head, brandished them back and forth like a victorious prize-fighter, and shouting *"Juchhe! Juchhe!,"* made for the prizes display, where she appropriated a teapot and proceeded to brandish that. His devotion temporarily quenched by her appalling behaviour, Youings seized his wife without gentleness and lugged her out of the way of the numerous people who were meanwhile milling round the recumbent Arthur, intent on administering help.

"Doc Mason!" a man shouted. "Someone find Doc Mason!"

"'E'm gone," someone else bellowed. "Saw en drive off, not ten minutes since."

"Well then, fetch First Aid Box!"

Two youths, twin brothers called Hulland, volunteered to do this. Side by side, they left the scene at a measured trot. In the interim, Dermot McCartney—partly because he seemed calmer and more confident than anyone else, and partly, no doubt, as an illogical result of people's frequent exposure to coloured doctors in hospitals—had been accepted as chief ministering angel. Down on one knee, he raised the injured man's head an inch or two, probing gently with his fingers at the place where the wound was. Arthur stirred; he moaned; he made an attempt to sit up; he wasn't, at any rate, dead.

"He'll do," Dermot McCartney told the circle of concerned onlookers, cheerfully.

"Even so, we'd probably better get the doctor," said the Major. "If he's gone straight home, he ought to be there by now. Thouless, my dear fellow, would you ring him up from my flat? You'll be quicker than I shall. The door's open, and the number's on the pad beside the telephone. Mind and not let Sal out, or we shall have more casualties." Thouless nodded importantly and strode off towards the house. As he passed the fortune-telling tent, the Rector emerged from it carrying his cricket bag, with Fen at his heels.

The Hulland twins had by now arrived at their destination, the Botticelli tent; *en route*, on the trot, they had thrown out brief explanations to the groups of people who were drifting, curious, towards the source of the disturbance. The sign on the Botticelli tent said VACANT. Titty Bale was still at the receipt of custom, and Luckraft with his crash helmet on was still sitting on guard opposite her.

"First Aid Box," said one Hulland twin, panting.

"Been an accident," said the other.

"Chap hit on the head," said the first.

"Bleeding all over the grass," said the second.

"Oh *dear*, oh dear," said Titty Bale, frowning. Neither she nor her sister Tatty (who was presumably still faithfully on watch at the back of the tent) had ever really approved of the custom that had grown up over the years, of storing bits and pieces in the Botticelli tent, behind the black velvet against which the Assumption was suspended. "Well, fortunately there's no one Meditating just at present. Even so, I shall have to speak to the dear Rector about it. It's quite ridiculous to keep the First Aid Box *here*, and I shall tell him so…No, no, you two stay out here. I'll fetch it." She got up and went into the tent, leaving the Hullands explaining matters to Luckraft.

Time passed—a matter of two minutes only, but to the Hullands this seemed (as indeed it was) needlessly long. Then Titty Bale reappeared through the tent flap. She had no First Aid Box with her. Moreover, she was moving slowly, and looked pale.

As they stared questioningly at her, "Luckraft," she said, speaking with some difficulty, "there's a man in there."

"A man, Miss Bale?"

"Yes. He's dead."

"Dead?"

"Yes, dead. And Luckraft, it's happened *again*," Titty Bale said faintly. She went back to her chair and slumped down into it. "Hagberd has been put away, but it's happened *again*."

They continued to stare at her, wordlessly.

"The man is not only dead," said Titty Bale, articulating with all possible care. "He has also been...been mutilated. That's to say, he's—that is to say, someone has cut off his head."

Collapsed in her wood-and-canvas garden chair, she added, "Incidentally, he is completely naked. In searching for the First Aid Box, I lifted a sheet of tarpaulin, or some such material—and there he was, bare as the minute he was born."

Alarmed, Luckraft surged to his feet. "That must have been very distressing for you, Miss Titania," he said.

"The nakedness? Pah!" Luckraft's concern for her spinsterly sensibilities re-aroused some of Miss Bale's mettle. "Rubbish, Luckraft, rubbish! Let me tell you, I've seen a great many naked men in my time."

"Oh, have you, Miss Titania?" said Luckraft feebly.

"Yes, I have. I dare say I've seen more naked men than you've had hot dinners."

Luckraft shifted his weight from his left foot to his right. "Gracious," was all he could find by way of response.

"There is nothing—*nothing*, Luckraft—that I don't know about naked men."

"No, I'm sure not, Miss Titania. All I was—"

"Nursing, Luckraft, nursing. Nearly twenty years of it I had, when I was younger. And you don't do a stretch like that without getting to know everything there is to know about naked men, do you now, Luckraft?"

"Well, no, Miss Titania, I suppose not." Luckraft squared his shoulders. "Now, if you'll just let me—"

"Yes, but be careful, Luckraft." Titty's brief outbreak of animation was now apparently exhausted; she began to fidget nervously with her untidy grey hair. "There is evil in there."

"Just so, Miss Titania. And it's my business to—"

"No, no, Luckraft, you misunderstand me. The murder is evil, true. The mutilation is evil, certainly. But what is worse is that they happened in the presence—or virtually the presence—of the Botticelli."

"And you think that that's—"

"I regard it as the worst evil of all. It is profanation, Luckraft—PROFANATION. It is the Unforgivable Sin."

"I'll bear that in mind, of course, Miss Titania. And now—"

"In fact," said Titty, "I think it may even be necessary to ask the dear Bishop to re-consecrate the picture."

Luckraft rolled his eyes. He was perhaps recalling that the Right Reverend had shown little stomach for his chrismal task when he had first performed it (the Rector had made an attempt—unusually, for him, an abortive one—to discourage and then evade the Bale sisters' ultramontanist requirements altogether), and was unlikely to be pleased at being summoned to do the whole job all over again. He had even, in reference to the Misses Bale, muttered something about Aholah and Aholibah, a tantrum which had struck Luckraft, when at last he succeeded in locating these two minxes in the Old Testament, as erring on the side of exaggeration.

From these not particularly timely reflections he awoke to the realisation that Titty Bale had given over her brooding on Satanas, and was now eyeing him expectantly.

"Well, don't just stand there like a dumpling, Luckraft," she said. "Go inside and get on with your detecting, or whatever it is you do."

The assembled crowd vibrated on a note in which Luckraft was now certain he could sense an element of censoriousness. *Why doesn't he do something, then? Ignorant Dogberry! Useless bumpkin! Calls himself a copper and doesn't even know where to start!*

Jerkily, like some mechanical toy too cack-handedly activated, Luckraft flung himself at the tent flap and disappeared inside.

It was two hours later—past six o'clock—when Fen at last got back home to the Dickinsons' cottage.

Police activity, though competent as far as it went, had had a provisional air, as of an organisation marking time tidily enough, but with no very clear notion as to the direction in which it would be most profitable to move. Following a brief personal inspection, Luckraft had left the Hulland twins in charge of the corpse, had sought out the Major and had asked permission to use the telephone in the Major's flat, in whose doorway he had met Thouless emerging, flushed with triumph at having made contact with Dr Mason, and summoned him back. Luckraft had then, keeping the Major's cocker bitch Sal at bay with well-judged kicks, rung up the police station in Glazebridge, given an account of the new enormity now brought to light in the Botticelli tent, and asked for instructions.

These directed him to sentry duty at the gate, where he took up his stand, fending off questions and preventing people from leaving; the latter precaution struck everyone, Luckraft himself included, as pointless, since by simply ducking through a twin-strand wire fence you could leave the lawn, and beyond that the Aller House grounds as a whole, practically anywhere. In general, however, the Fête's clientèle was showing more inclination to linger than to quit. Thanks to Titty Bale—who by now, to judge from her utterances, had come to regard what had happened as in some obscure fashion aimed at discrediting the Botticelli—news of the fresh murder, Burraford's second in two months, was spreading through the crowd like flame on a blowy day through an expanse of dry bracken, and almost everybody was anxious to stay and find out more. The lack of solid information, a Barmecides' banquet to curious appetites, was tantalising. No one could be certain who the corpse was, or how it had come by its end, or by whose malice; Titty Bale notwithstanding, no one could be certain, even, if it was a man or a woman; and with Luckraft baffling all inquisition by the simple process of slowly and silently shaking his head, it was clearly necessary to remain on the scene until something substantial emerged. Meanwhile, and much to the Rector's annoyance, the stalls and sideshows found themselves virtually deserted, and even the beer tent had emptied. As to Arthur, his mishap with the Try-Your-Strength machine was overshadowed wholly; attended by no more than a rag-end of his former numerous sympathisers, he continued, though now largely disregarded, to lie on the turf where he had fallen, exuding unrequited pathos, breathing plangently and holding a handkerchief to his head to staunch the bleeding.

His injury was not—said Dr Mason, re-appearing presently in response to Thouless's telephone call—anything to worry about, so long as he went home as soon as possible and rested, and kept off the bottle for a bit; reassured by this intelligence, Arthur staggered to his feet and tottered over to a chair, where he sat blinking and grunting in residual confusion while he was swabbed and patched up. His act of mercy completed, Dr Mason closed his bag, exchanged a few words with Luckraft, and then strolled phlegmatically across the lawn to the Botticelli tent, to await the arrival of the police reinforcements from Glazebridge.

These came on the scene ten minutes later; they consisted of Detective-Inspector Widger, two constables from the uniformed branch and Detective-Constable Rankine, who had beguiled the journey with a spoken catalogue of various hypotheses which he considered might apply to the situation confronting them.

"Seventhly," he was saying as the police car jolted up to the gateway, "the crime was committed by Hagberd, who had escaped from Rampton. But to this theory we can see objections. They are three-fold. In the first place, Hagberd has probably *not* escaped from Rampton, or we should have heard."

The car stopped. Widger got out of it and went to consult briefly with Luckraft. Delighted at being able to find Rankine something at once tedious and futile to do, he stationed him and one of the constables at the gate, with instructions to take people's names and addresses as they left, detaining only those who were blood-boltered or in overt possession of offensive weapons. He then, with Luckraft and the remaining constable, made his way across the lawn to join Dr Mason in the Botticelli tent.

Dismissed from their vigil, the Hulland twins lingered in the front part of the tent where the picture was, and were thus able to overhear part of Dr Mason's preliminary report. The corpse had been dead for some time, Dr Mason said, twelve hours at least, probably even more; the head (which like Routh's had been removed from the scene) had been cut off quite soon after death; the severed left arm, however, (and this, too, was apparently missing) had been cut off much more recently, perhaps within the last hour or two, and the abortive hackings of the right arm, and of the right leg, were equally recent. Excited by this information the Hullands broke into ejaculations of gratification and surprise, as a result of which they were detected and driven away to join the crowd milling around outside. Their news—which they rapidly relayed, spreading fresh *frissons* far and wide—turned out, however, to be practically the last piece of solid information the afternoon was to produce. In due course Dr Mason left, phlegmatic as ever but amiably impervious to questioning; and the Major's telephone was again commandeered, this time by Widger, who, it was rumoured, had decided to apply for help to County Headquarters. But there was little else, and after an hour or so the customers, bored with waiting, began to drift away. Some hung on grimly, whiling away the time in the beer and tea tents, transactions were few, and the craving to display or look at dogs and female legs had so far abated that in the end both competitions had to be cancelled.

"Pusillanimous lot," said the Rector, still a bizarre figure of menace, though an unavailing one, in his grandmother's black bombazine dress. He brandished his cricket bag, evoking a small cry of dismay from Father Hattrick, who, along with Dermot McCartney, was currently acting as sounding-board for his indignation. "*Pounds*, we're losing, *pounds*."

Father Hattrick said, "Does anyone yet know who the unfortunate man is?"

"Apparently not," said the Rector. "The Hullands didn't see anything about him they could recognise, and nor did Titty

Bale. Nor did Luckraft, come to that—I managed to get that much out of him. I dare say it isn't a local man at all: there've been plenty of strangers here this afternoon."

Fen strolled up, with Padmore. "We're going," he said.

"Feeble," said the Rector. "You haven't by any chance seen Scorer anywhere around, have you?"

"No, I haven't."

"I expect he's gone to ground, then," said the Rector gloomily. "*More* trouble. And where's my bank manager? He ought to have been here long ago."

"There doesn't seem much point in *my* hanging around, anyway," said Padmore. "I had a word with Widger, and the police aren't going to issue any statement until after their people have arrived from County. Anyone want a lift anywhere?"

"I wouldn't mind one," said Fen, "with all this stuff to carry."

"All right, then. Let's go."

"Decapitation," said Dermot McCartney. "The Itsekeri, of Nigeria, were at one time notable decapitators. Nowadays, however, they merely strangle people."

"Decapitation," said Father Hattrick. "A barbarous business, certainly...'I go from a corruptible to an incorruptible Crown'," he murmured, "'where no disturbance can be, no disturbance in the world'."

"You and your King Charles's head," said the Rector.

Back at the Dickinsons' cottage, lapped in peace after the brouhaha of the Fête, Fen contemplated without pleasure the next task which awaited him; though not normally liable to intuitive forebodings, he was certainly oppressed by them now.

He might as well, however, he thought, wait until Padmore had finished telephoning.

Fen was in the living-room. Padmore was in the big kitchen with his tin of peas on the telephone table in front of him, eating an Abernethy biscuit, sipping pink gin and dictating an account of the afternoon's events to a *Gazette* telephone reporter in London; through the open doorway his voice could be heard droning away, transforming the idiosyncratic Hulland twins into vapid stereotypes of popular journalism, each with an age in figures, an occupation in words and a talent for conversing in illiterate paragraphs of one short sentence apiece: a misprint to every sixth line, and a quarter of the quotation marks either misplaced or lacking altogether...Fen felt that he was becoming testy. He stared out of the living-room window at the lawn, where the tortoise Ellis was moving slowly round and round in a series of ever diminishing circles; near Ellis, the cat Stripey lay sprawled on his side, occasionally lashing out with his paw at some passing winged insect; beyond this precious pair were a hedge, the stony drive, an old barn used as a garage, a stand of mixed trees, a field, a glimpse of Thouless's bungalow, a glimpse of the Pisser and its adjacent criss-crossing echelons of other pylons, a glimpse of Aller House. In an upward-sloping meadow to the left, Friesians were grazing; urgent for insola-tion, they were drifting slowly upwards, eating as they went, following the gold light of the westering sun up to the slope's crest while the band of shadow below them steadily widened.

A fly making its way laboriously up one of the small panes lost its foot-hold and fell on its back on the windowsill, dead.

Fen played a few notes quietly, at random, on the Dickinsons' upright piano. He picked up a volume of Angus Wilson, gazed fixedly for some moments at its sturdy brown covers, and put it down again.

"Spark, Muriel," he said. An idea began to fizz feebly at the bottom of his mind, like stale effervescing aspirin dropped into a glass of water. "The use of ellipsis in Mrs Spark's earlier work," he intoned, "imposes patterns on her narrative which in addition to their intrinsic shapeliness sometimes make the reader—some-times make the reader—sometimes make the reader wonder if his wits are failing." No, that would scarcely do.

Padmore's. dictating drone modulated to easier, more conversational tones as he made his farewells. The telephone bell tinkled faerily as he rang off. Sighing, Fen collected his own pink gin from the pie-crust table, packed Muriel Spark off home with a promise to attend to her in the morning, and went through to the kitchen.

"Well, that's that," said Padmore. "But oh dear, isn't it all exasperating, isn't it all absolutely wretched? Because now it looks as if Hagberd didn't murder Routh after all."

"Oh, I don't know, you know," said Fen. "It's too soon to jump to a conclusion like that."

Padmore brightened a little. "You mean it might be an imitative crime? Yes, that's possible. Ah well, let's hope so, let's devoutly hope so...Incidentally, I reversed the charge on that call, but nowadays, even when you reverse the charge, you have to pay ten pence, so here's ten pence."

"Oh, thank you," said Fen vaguely. "What I'm wondering, actually, is whether you may not have to ring your paper again, almost immediately."

"Oh, why? Is there something else you've thought of?"

And Fen sighed again. "There may be," he said, putting his glass on the mantel-shelf above the Rayburn. "Yes there quite possibly may be. Just wait a moment, will you?"

Ducking into the scullery, he lifted his pig's-head sack off the top of the refrigerator, untied the coarse string which held it at the neck, and extracted from it a heavy spheroidal object wrapped in a good deal of *Daily Mail*.

"No snout," he said resignedly.

"What?" Padmore called from the kitchen.

"I said, no snout."

With more sighs, Fen unwrapped the newspapers, to discover that his intuition had been justified. The hair had mostly been torn out, the eyes were gone, and the other features were battered beyond recognition. But what he had—what, it seemed, he had toted round the neighbourhood for half the morning—was unquestionably a human head, not a pig's.

CHAPTER SEVEN

Omnium-Gatherum

Matters of fact, which as Mr Budgell somewhere observes, are very stubborn things.

Matthew Tindal: *Will of Matthew Tindal.*

"SO WE HAVE three possibilities."

"Surely only two."

"I ought to have said, four." With every sign of complacency, Detective-Superintendent Ling, from County, took his pipe out of his mouth, up-ended it, and set about thumping it noisily on a large electric-blue tin ash-tray, embossed in low relief about its perimeter with the name of an inexpensive proprietary cheroot. A minute amount of burned tobacco fell out, followed by a much greater quantity of unburned; Ling applied himself in silence to separating the two with his fingers. Looking on censoriously, Detective-Inspector Widger, himself a non-smoker, reflected not for the first time on the incivility of men with pipes, who commonly expect all social and business intercourse to be suspended while they tinker with their bits of hollowed briar. *Sexual* intercourse too? Widger somewhat wildly wondered. He must remember to ask Ling's wife Katherine about that, or rather, he mustn't.

"However, it's early days for theorising," said Ling, as though it had been Widger, and not himself, who had been guilty of dialectical foolhardiness. "Facts first, theories after. *In*duction, not *de*duction." He had read of this distinction years before in a Pelican book, and never tired of repeating it.

Widger's rancour grew. "The head, Eddie," he expostulated. "Now that you've had a look at it, oughtn't it to be sent off straight away to Sir John?"

"Ah yes, the head," said Ling weightily. "That's—it—it's a—" But at this point, regardless of Widger's gelid stare, he petered out: his winnowing operation completed, he had begun thumbing the unburned tobacco back into his pipe-bowl, thereby once again temporarily incapacitating himself for further speech. And now Widger frankly glowered. He glowered first at Ling; then, when that palled, as it very quickly did, he glowered at the Harris's Bacon sack, with its gruesome contents, which Ling had just deposited in the corner of the small office opposite the door; finally, he glowered out of the window, at the ring-road in which the police station was situated, and at the more distant prospect of Glazebridge itself, its spires and houses hazy in the autumnal Sunday-afternoon sunshine.

"A mess," said Ling. He had finished filling his pipe, but had not yet begun to address himself to the lighting of it. "Let's hope that Sir John can—that Sir John—that he—" He keeled over sideways in the desk chair, groping for matches in the jacket pocket thus exposed for use. "Let's hope that Sir John can do something to make it identifiable," he managed to conclude.

"Did you gather anything from it?" Widger asked. Ling's examination of the head had had to be deferred, owing to the lateness of his arrival, until after lunch; had, in fact, only just been completed.

"Can't say I did, much." Ling gave his Swan Vesta box an experimental shake, to discover if there was anything in it. "As to the sack, there must be tens of thousands of them knocking about. As to the string, it's just coarse, common stuff. As to the paper, that's two copies of the *Daily Mail*, Friday and Saturday the week before last, with 'Cobbledick' pencilled on both the front pages. Who's Cobbledick?"

"A market gardener. Lives a mile or two outside Burraford."

Ling stared vacantly first at the match-box in his right hand, and then at the pipe in his left, as if attempting to set up, in his mind, some rational association between them. He said, "That pile of old papers, in among all the rest of that junk in the...the Botticelli tent: what were they *for*?"

"Cobbledick brought them along because he thought they might come in useful for wrapping up stuff on the Garden and Vegetable Stalls."

"I see. Well then, why weren't they used?"

"I don't know. I imagine the stall-holders brought paper of their own."

"Did you have a chance to find out *when* Cobbledick brought his lot along?"

"Yes, I did. It was Friday afternoon."

Ling sighed. "So they just happened to be there, and they just happened to come in handy. Not very revealing."

"You're assuming the murder was committed during Friday night?"

"Well, it looks like it, doesn't it? And the head cut off immediately afterwards, and then...bashed about in that horrible way." Ling struck a match and held it poised above the blotter—this time giving priority to utterance—until it burned itself down to his fingers and had to be shaken out. "It's a pity the body was moved before I could see it," he remarked.

With difficulty quelling a fresh upsurge of umbrage, "C.C's instructions, Eddie," Widger said. "I didn't have any choice."

"Oh, I'm not blaming you, old squire. As you say, no choice."

"I probably ought to have taken the head to Sir John, too, as soon as it was found. In fact, I was just on the point of leaving here with it when your phone call caught me."

"It's been difficult for you, I realise that," said Ling placatorily. "I just felt I ought to take a look, that was all. As to this report of yours"—tapping the folder on the desk in front of him—"it's first-rate." He lit a second match. "I don't think I've ever—ever—" This time he had applied the match to his pipe's bowl, and was drawing smoke into his mouth with a popping noise, like small bladders successively punctured.

"I had to hurry it rather," said Widger. As a matter of fact it had taken him hours. "It's a bit sketchy."

"Oh, pop-pop," Ling said. "Ah, pop-pop-pop-pop-pop."

"But the essentials are there."

"...pop-pop-pop-POP." Ling withdrew the pipe, smirked at it and put it down in the ash-tray, where it fumed briefly and then went out. Articulacy restored, "You managed to cover a tremendous lot of the ground," he said. "Though of course, I have to go over it again."

"Yes, yes, of course."

"Something new might come out of it."

"Yes."

"And as I understand the matter, there were one or two people you didn't manage to catch up with. This boy Scorer, for instance. If what he let out to the Rector and, um, Fen means anything, his evidence may be crucial. You've got him safe now, I take it."

"Yes, quite safe. He's downstairs now with the others—and they're keeping a sharp eye on him; he won't have a chance to scarper again."

"What exactly happened to him?"

Widger explained. The youth Scorer, he said, was timorous, to put it mildly; to him, even the mildest perplexities of life took on the appearance of deadly ambushes designed to maim or even to extinguish. His impulsive babblings to Fen and the Rector, on the subject of Mavis Trent, had consequently preyed on his mind; either he feared some form of retribution, or else—which was also possible—he hoped by secrecy to gain himself some paltry advantage of a monetary sort; or both. In any case, having at the Fête brought his bruised bottom to Dr Mason's attention, and been reassured (in so far, that was, as it was ever possible to reassure him about anything), he had sloped off home, collected a rug, some corned beef and some Coca-Cola, and proceeded to establish himself for the night in the ringing-chamber of Burraford church. By these actions he apparently expected to be able to avoid further interrogation; a relatively brief unavailability, he seemed to have imagined, against all likelihood, would cause the Rector to forget his rash bellowings as he lay in the lane after falling off his motor-cycle. He was not, evidently, at all a good contingency planner. His family—all of whom were given to prolonged nocturnal expeditions in pursuit, or even just on the off-chance, of one illegality or another—would, it was true, evince no surprise, let alone anxiety, at his absence; that part of it was all right. Scorer had omitted from his considerations, however, the fact that the following day was Sunday—and as a result of this, the ringers arriving to ring for Matins had found him, at half-past ten that morning, heavily asleep on the chamber's dusty floor. They had delivered him promptly to the Rector, who had locked him in the vestry for the duration of the service and subsequently driven him in, panic-stricken, to the Glazebridge police station, where he had been kept pending Ling's arrival and the preliminary interviewing of all conceivable witnesses organised for that afternoon by Widger's two underlings (Detective-Constable Rankine and Detective-Sergeant Crumb, the latter a slothful middle-aged man good for nothing but paper-work) with the assistance of the uniform branch.

"This Scorer sounds half-witted to me," said Ling.

"Half-witted *and* dishonest."

"A difficult witness." Ling picked up his pipe and drew on it, grimacing in amazement when no combustion occurred. He reached again for the matches. "Well, well, we shall have to throw a bit of a scare into him."

"There'll be no difficulty about that."

"Another thing: I forget if you've got anyone with shorthand."

"There's Rankine."

"No," said Ling hastily. He remembered Rankine distinctly from the Routh-Hagberd investigation. "No, I think we'll just—"

"When he's taking things down he doesn't talk," said Widger. "Or at any rate, he doesn't talk so *much*."

"For the moment, I'll just jot down a few notes. Rankine can take proper statements, um, later. Where are we now?" Extending his crooked left arm at the maximum possible distance from his eyes, in the attitude of one hoping to ward off a blow, Ling peered at his wrist-watch. "Twenty-five past two," he said. "We ought to be able to get going in a minute." He applied flame to his tobacco and started pop-popping again. Widger, still testy from lack of sleep, reverted to looking out of the small office's one window.

It was a French window, giving on to an exiguous concrete balcony with a dangerously low wrought-iron railing. Beneath it lay the car-park, with the station's main door a little to the right. Widger's eye quartered the scene systematically, beginning with the ring-road's opposite pavement, where several girls of about eleven, coiffed and dressed like ageing tarts, were larking with a group of boys of the same age; they appeared to be, and in these enlightened days very probably were, making grabs at the boys' genitals. Frowning, Widger transferred his gaze to the nearer pavement, where the car-park's entrance was located, and where inquisitive Glazebridge townspeople were drifting up, coagulating to gape, and being shooed on by a constable. Finally, the car-park itself—and this, thanks partly to the numerous witnesses waiting down below and partly to a small army of pressmen, was fairly stuffed with waiting vehicles. At its centre stood a television van; linked to this was a camera with its generator buzzing; in front of the camera, a young man with womanish hair and a common accent was talking with unnatural rapidity into a hand-held microphone connected to the van by cables; a greatly loved character, no doubt, in innumerable homes.

The constable beckoned a car in from the ring-road: a gleaming white Saab from which, when it had succeeded in finding a space for itself, emerged the bulky, florid-faced form of P.C. Luckraft, in plain clothes. Widger frowned again. Luckraft, however, was presumably technically off duty, in so far as in present circumstances any of them could be said to be that; as to the car, Luckraft's wife had a bit of money of her own, Widger now vaguely remembered, and was not ungenerous with it...Now the constable was stopping, and after inquiry waving on in, a black Mercedes driven by a black man: Dermot McCartney, the science-fiction writer who had opened the previous day's Fête. He too, as one of the visitors to the Botticelli tent, might just conceivably have something pertinent to tell them...

Widger's eyes stung. His face, he found, was being subjected to a cloud of stale smoke. The pop-popping had ceased. "The head, Eddie," Widger said for the second time, as he turned away from the spectacle outside.

Nodding like a man of decision, so that his pipe waggled up and down between his teeth, Ling put out his hand to the telephone.

As he did so, it rang.

"Sir John Honeybourne? Yes, of course, put him on at once...Sir John? Superintendent Ling here."

"..............................."

"Really, sir? Sorry about that. It—"

"..............................."

"Yes, sir. I quite understand. Now, about the unfortunate man's head. It's been recovered, as I expect you know, and we have it here, and we can send it to you at once in a—"

"..."

"We can't, sir? But why not?"

".............."

"I see. But—"

" . . . . . . "

"Oh."

" . . . . . . "

"At seven this evening. Certainly, sir, if you say so. But will it be all right? I mean, ought we perhaps to, um, refrigerate it or something?"

" . . . . "

"Very good, sir. I'll be with you at seven. In the meantime, anything about the cause of death?"

" . "

"Nothing at all?"

" . . . . . . "

"Probably not poison."

" . . . . "

"Unless it's one of the volatile poisons like chloroform," said Ling, hypnotised into repetition. "You'll need to look at the brain before you can be sure about that…And identity, sir. Any special marks?"

" . "

"Nothing?"

" . . . "

"One small wart."

" . . . . "

"Below the left clavicle. No operation scars, no fractures?"

" . "

"The head's pretty badly damaged, sir, but do you think you might be able to, ah, reconstitute it to some extent, so as to give us some sort of a likeness?"

" . "

"Oh, good. Anything about age, height, things like that?"

" . . . . . ., ..., ..., ... "

Ling made jottings on a scratch-pad. "A well-nourished man," he mumbled, "slightly obese, age about forty, height about six foot two…Sir?"

" . ? "

"How about his hands—hand, I mean?"

".........., ..."

Covering the mouthpiece with his hand, "A manual worker in the past," he hissed informatively at Widger, "but not recently. Not for the last few years." Resuming contact with Sir John, "Well, that's very helpful, sir," he announced heartily.

"..."

"Till seven, then."

"."

"Goodbye."

Ling rang off, lay back in the desk chair as if exhausted, and said to Widger, "As a matter of fact, it isn't helpful at all. No cause of death, no pointers to identification, nothing. Ah well, perhaps when he sees the head, that'll give us something."

"What was it he *said* about the head?"

"Said if we didn't sit on it, or play football with it, it wouldn't come to any harm between now and seven. He's a bit eccentric, I suppose."

"I dare say he is," said Widger. "Seems to me, you're bound to get a bit eccentric, if you've spent your entire adult life cutting up corpses."

"What's he like?"

"He's like a corpse himself."

"Somehow you don't expect that," said Ling, "not with such a warm, cosy name."

"Why can't we take the head to him till seven?"

"Because he's going to bed."

"To *bed*?"

"Yes. Apparently he was up all night working on the, um, trunk. So it's fair enough, really," said Ling largemindedly. He put on a pair of spectacles, partially horn-rimmed as if the money had run out half-way, and again consulted his wrist-watch. "So now we can—"

A noisy knock on the door interrupted him. Sergeant Connabeer, the Duty Officer from down below, came in. He was brandishing a typewritten list of names with pencil ticks against them.

"They're all in now, sir," he said. "That Negro was the last."

Ling said, "Good lad," clipping the "a" and mooing on the "oo." It was one of his peculiarities that although he had spent his entire life in the south-west, he occasionally lapsed into a sort of generalised north-country accent, possibly from too much watching of *Softly, Softly*, or possibly in imitation of J. B. Priestley, whose works he was known to admire and whom, indeed, he to some extent physically resembled. "Everything under control, then?" he asked in less fanciful phonemes.

"Pretty well, sir—though it's a bit of a crush, of course, and I've had to send out for more chairs...The reporters are a nuisance. We could do without them."

"Get rid of 'em, then."

"They're talking to the witnesses."

"So boot 'em out—politely, of course. They've got no divine right to be on the premises. Tell 'em I shan't have anything for them till evening."

"They say they've got deadlines."

"I can't help their deadlines," Ling said. "For the moment, there just isn't any further information. I haven't," he said untruthfully, "got any further information myself."

Connabeer reflected on the situation, and found a ray of light. "Actually, Mr Ticehurst's here now," he said. "So they've homed on him. Oh yes, and he says could you possibly see him for just five minutes, before you get started."

And Ling sighed. "I suppose so," he said. "Yes, I suppose so. Send him up straight away."

Ticehurst—who had retired two years previously from the uniform branch with the rank of Chief Inspector—was nowadays the County Force's P.R.O. Relishing the job, he also excelled at it. Policemen whose activities he glozed and expounded for the media liked him because he had been one of them, and understood their problems. The media liked him because he had a flair for investing even the most banal of misdemeanours, even the most turgid of enquiries, with an arresting aura of sensationalism and even glamour. And down here, something of that sort was needful. The vast majority of crimes are committed by striking-class youths and young men living in conurbations—and in conurbations, unless you excepted self-important Plymouth, the county was almost completely lacking. Its malfeasances, therefore, were largely trivial; to make good copy, they required the intervention of a lurid mind; and this, to the immense gratification of reporters, Ticehurst was temperamentally well able to supply. Without ever going beyond the plain facts of the case, he could transform even so regular an occurrence as a farmer's hanging himself in a barn into something inapprehensibly monstrous; could convey the impression that a man who had neglected to buy his employees' National Insurance stamps constituted a gross danger to all peaceful citizens everywhere; could somehow manage to suggest, when hoodlums broke a shop window, that one more such episode was likely to topple six thousand years of civilisation ineluctably; could, moreover—and it was this more than anything which made him so popular with the County Force—mysteriously bring about a sea-change in the image of even the most bumbling police officers going about their duties, so that they emerged as prodigies of intelligence, zeal and kindness. Ticehurst would gesture vigorously; his small eyes would gleam with excitement, his cheeks would redden, a light sweat would break out on his brow. And his listeners—who till then had been wondering how on earth to inject a bit of interest into anything so obviously tawdry and negligible—would scribble away in their notebooks with a will. True, the hectic pieces which resulted almost invariably had to be much toned down by drab and heartless sub-editors; but for the time being their recipients were grateful.

Bald, obese and beaming, Ticehurst waddled into Widger's office with a copy of the *Sunday Gazette* tucked under one arm. Thanks to Padmore, the *Gazette* had had a scoop. Whereas the other Sundays had become aware of the body in the Botticelli tent too late to do anything at all about it, the *Gazette* had been in time to remake most of its front page. On this, Padmore's story had appeared, much altered. It had been embellished with seven literals, a fuzzily reproduced photograph of Fen (taken, seemingly, at the age of about fifteen), and a tribute to its originator in the form of the by-line 'J. E. Podmote'. Men had gone home late from the *Gazette* office, persuaded of having done a wonderful job.

"Eddie," Ticehurst said. "Widger. Well, seems you've got another lovely crime here," he said. "Another really *lovely* crime." With precaution, he lowered his bulk on to one of the office's inadequate chairs.

"Where have you been?"

"Holiday, dear boy, holiday." Waving the *Gazette* in the air like a fan, Ticehurst wriggled about in an approximation of flamenco dancing. "Sunny Spain, and a bit too sunny, even at this time of year, for yours truly. Don't like heat. Glad to be back. Come to that, Eddie, where have *you* been? I gather you didn't pop up here till this morning."

"London." Ling's pipe was dead again, and he was now slowly turning it between his hands, like a chicken on a spit; at each rotation, ash fell out on to the desk. "Helping the Met. Helping them over the Harding case."

"Oh, yes, that. Is there enough evidence to pull him in?"

"The D.P.P. says not. So everyone's trying again."

"So that held you up."

"Yes, it did," said Ling. "The Chief wanted me on this one, because it looked as if there might be a tie-up with Routh and Hagberd, so he didn't mind waiting till I got back this morning. Charles here was perfectly competent to deal with the preliminaries."

To his dismay, Widger found that tiredness was making

him simper. He set his mouth in a dour line, thereby somehow propelling droplets of saliva down his wind-pipe and bringing on a choking fit. Through his spasms he was aware of Ticehurst's fleeting surprise at this kaleidoscopic reaction to Ling's testimony.

"Yes, well, of course, naturally," Ticehurst said when Widger's noise had subsided a bit. "What time did you get here?"

"11:55. Charles met me at the station, and we went straight to the, um, fairground place. There's a mobile H.Q. still there, but it isn't doing much good any longer. The labs have got everything that seems relevant—the tarpaulin which was covering the body, and the hacksaw and so forth...Me, I've scarcely seen anything so far, apart from the head." And here Ling nodded towards the sack in the corner.

Ticehurst's in any case protuberant blue eyes bulged still further. "My God," he said, "that's not it, is it?"

"It certainly is. Want to take a look?"

"No, thanks, I don't. Don't think me impertinent, but why hasn't Easton got it?" Easton was the County Pathologist.

"He hasn't got it," said Ling, "because I wanted to look at it. The Chief phoned me in London yesterday evening, and I phoned Charles and asked him to keep the head here till I arrived. And anyway, it isn't Easton. Easton's on leave."

"Oh," said Ticehurst. "Well, but he's got assistants, hasn't he?"

"It's not them, either. It's Honeybourne."

"Honeybourne? Well, that's nice and distinguished, of course, and of course, I knew he was living down here, but I thought he'd retired."

"So he has, technically—though I believe he still does some sort of research. But he's a personal friend of the Chief's, you see, so with Easton away, the Chief asked him to take this on."

"Sounds most irregular to me," said Ticehurst. "However, the press boys'll love it. Honeybourne, the greatest pathologist since Spilsbury. Can I tell 'em?"

"I'd rather you didn't, not just yet. I don't want him pestered till I've had a chance to talk to him properly myself."

"You're the boss." Ticehurst heaved himself to his feet. "And I mustn't hold you up any longer. But you'll do a press conference, of course."

"Yes, I should think I'd better. Not until after I've talked to the witnesses, though."

"How long will that take you?"

"I can't really tell," said Ling. "Till six, perhaps."

"Can I lay it on for six, then?"

"Yes, all right. I'm due to see Honeybourne at seven, so I shall have to break off anyway, whether I've finished or not."

"Six it is, then," said Ticehurst from the doorway. "See you then."

Ling muttered something which sounded to Widger suspiciously like, "Gradely."

"And good luck." Ticehurst waddled out.

"And so now," said Ling, "we get started."

❀ ❀ ❀

"What I want to do," he added, "is take the whole business in chronological order. Which means starting with Mavis Trent. Anything new there, since the inquest?"

Widger shook his head. "Not a thing. She fell, or was pushed, over Hole Bridge. The Coroner thought she fell. I thought she was pushed. But I've got to admit that my evidence isn't strong. A man's cheap handkerchief clutched in her hand, some traces on the river bank, the improbability that she would have gone out at that time of night unless it was to meet someone—I agree, it doesn't add up to much."

"But now there's Scorer."

"Yes. Now there's Scorer."

"Scorer who apparently heard someone threatening to go to the police about Mavis Trent."

"Yes."

"*When* did he hear this?"

"The Rector got that out of him. It was Friday night."

"Somewhere about the time of the murder, in fact. The third murder."

"Well, yes, that's what we're assuming for the moment."

"Is it possible that Scorer actually witnessed the murder?"

"Quite possible, I should think."

"It's extraordinary," Ling mumbled. "Quite extraordinary. Is Scorer a half-wit, or something?"

"Not exactly. He's just secretive. And, of course, panicky."

Ling produced a small triune metal implement from his pocket and began poking about in the bowl of his pipe with it. "I'll panic him all right," he said. "Withholding crucial evidence— good God, whatever next? Yes, I'll certainly panic *him*."

"He could, I suppose," Widger said, "be protecting someone. Or, since it was night-time, he may not have been able to *see* who it was...Do we have him up now?"

"Routh and Hagberd really come first. But as far as I know, there's nothing new there either, any more than there is about Mavis Trent. We're still pretty sure, aren't we, that it was Hagberd who chopped Routh up? And was responsible for all that foolery with the head, and with the bust of whoever it was?"

"Yes, I think we can be pretty sure about that."

"Are we sure that he was Routh's murderer?"

Widger hesitated, then said, "The local feeling is that he probably wasn't."

"Yes, I know," said Ling gloomily. "But we simply had to arrest him, and after that it was pretty much out of our hands."

"Agreed."

"Not very satisfactory...Wait a minute, though, there *is* something new." Ling riffled through the pages of Widger's report. "There's this note you've got at the end here. About Gosprey."

"Yes, Gobbo. Everyone calls him Gobbo."

"Gosprey, it says here."

"I don't suppose it's connected in any way with this present case," said Widger. "But Fen volunteered it, so I—"

"Fen, Fen."

"The Professor who's rented the Dickinson' cottage at Aller."

"Oh yes, I remember…Well, so this Gosprey says he was talking to Hagberd, outside The Stanbury Arms, at the time when Routh was being hit on the head in Bawdeys Meadow, two miles away. Is Gosprey here now?"

"Gobbo. No, he's not. He's a very old man—and, as I said, it's nothing directly to do with this new business, so I didn't have him brought in."

"Old, you say. Vague?"

"Well, yes, I suppose so, to some extent."

"He might be getting his times and dates muddled?"

"Yes, I suppose he might. And in any case, there's Youings to say he's wrong."

"Youings, Youings."

"The pig farmer with the German wife."

"Yes, I remember now. Youings would be more reliable than Gob—Gosprey?"

"Probably. My guess would be that Gos—Gobbo is confused about which day it was."

"That's a relief, anyway," said Ling. "Be hard for us if it turned out that Hagberd had an alibi. You think we can afford to ignore Gosprey, then, at any rate for the moment?"

"Yes, I do. I think that for the moment we've got quite enough to cope with as it is. I just added that note to the report for completeness' sake."

In the car-park below, car doors slammed, and car engines started, as media reporters, balked until the press conference at six o'clock, set off to discover what recreation, if any, the small market town of Glazebridge could offer on a Sunday afternoon.

Widger said, "Scorer now, then?"

"Scorer now."

Dishevelled after his night in the ringing chamber, the youth Scorer opened the proceedings by demanding the presence of his attorney—a word which Widger presumed he had got from Perry Mason rather than from, say, Trollope. On being informed by Ling that since he wasn't, so far, being accused of anything, no attorney was necessary, he first reiterated his demand and then suddenly fell down on the floor.

"My God, he's having a fit," said Ling.

"No, he's not," said Widger. "It's his legs. They're too shaky to hold him."

One on each side, they clutched Scorer under the oxters, levering him up on to the chair recently vacated by Ticehurst. Here he sat, shuddering intermittently and peering at them through his tangle of grubby locks like one of the smaller dogs with hair-impeded vision: a Cairn, a Sealyham, a Skye. Ling went back to his chair behind the desk, Widger continuing to prefer to stand.

"Now, there's nothing to be afraid of," said Ling. "You just tell us the truth—the whole truth, mind!—and you've got nothing to be afraid of at all."

"Not a thing," said Widger in antiphon. "So you just pull yourself together."

Scorer licked dry lips.

"First of all," said Ling, "let's have your name. Your full name, I mean. Your Christian name."

"It's Mr Scorer,' said Scorer tremulously.

"Your *Christian* name."

Scorer said that he was called Clyde, after a famous criminal.

"Your *real* Christian name."

With the greatest reluctance, Scorer admitted that his real Christian name was Cecil.

"Well now, Cecil, what's all this about Mavis Trent?"

"Us bain't," said Scorer almost inaudibly, "goin' to tell 'ee naught."

"Yes, you are. You're going to tell us everything."

"Never 'eard of en."

"Oh, rubbish. Of course you've heard of Mavis Trent. You were talking about her to Professor Fen and the Rector, when you fell off your motor-bike."

"I never."

"You most certainly did."

"No, I never."

"Now, you just listen to me, Scorer," said Widger. "You're in danger, do you realise that?"

At this Scorer succumbed to a fresh fit of trembling. "Danger?" he whispered.

"That's right, danger. You *know something.*"

"Oh, aye," said Ling. Holding his pipe by the bowl, he levelled the stem at Scorer like a pistol, even going so far as to squint along it, as if taking sights. "Tha knows summat, all right."

"Something about blackmail," Widger went on, "and I dare say, something about this murder as well."

'Bain't goin' to tell 'ee n—"

"Be quiet and listen. Knowing something puts you at risk."

"Bain't—"

"You're a menace to this blackmailer, this murderer. He may well try to put you out of the way."

"Put me—"

"Kill you."

Scorer stared at them wild-eyed. "Oh, my God," he breathed. "Kill—kill…" His voice rose to a shriek. "No! No!"

"Yes! Yes!"

"You got to pertect me!"

"*We* can't protect you, Cecil," said Ling.

"No, we can't," said Widger. "Protect yourself, Scorer!"

"Save me!"

"*But*, so long as you've told us everything you know, there'll be no point in killing you, and you'll be perfectly all right."

Visibly Scorer made an attempt to master his fears. Visibly he began to consider Widger's proposition—whose defect, that the murderer might not know that Scorer had passed his information on, Widger hoped was going to pass unnoticed. And it worked. Suddenly, it worked. All at once, Scorer stopped swaying about on the chair as if he were going to faint; he even managed to sit up relatively straight.

"I'll tell 'ee," he said. "I'll tell 'ee all. And then 'ee'll pertect me."

"That's right, we'll protect you."

Scorer inhaled deeply. "Well, then…" he said. "What 'appened was…"

On the Friday evening, the evening preceding the day of the Fête, Scorer had gone for a midnight walk. And he was at pains to justify this expedition. First he said that he had wanted to admire the beauties of Nature. Then he said that he was unable to sleep, and had hoped that the night air would make him somnolent. Finally he alleged, with undiminished improbability, that he was a collector of moths.

"Some o' they's pretty," he said, apparently in the hope that this display of aesthetic sensibility would lend cogency to his tale.

"Never you *mind* about moths, Cecil," said Ling. "We didn't bring you here to talk about moths."

"Some o' they's real pr—"

"I said, never *mind* about moths. Just tell us what you saw and what you heard."

This he was at last persuaded to do. Shorn of divagations and shivering fits, his narrative amounted to something like this:

He had set out from the family cottage in Burraford at about twelve, armed with a torch: there was no moon that night, and the starlight was too faint to pick out more than dark masses and blurred outlines. Apparently he had made his way directly to the grounds of Aller House (*pilfering*, thought Widger disgustedly: moths, indeed), and had there wandered about a bit (dousing his torch, in case the Major happened to be looking out of the window of his basement flat) among the half-finished stalls and marquees.

One of the erections which actually was completed was the Botticelli tent, all ready for the installation of its pious treasure in the morning; and it was as he sidled towards this that Scorer became aware that he hadn't the Aller House gardens entirely to himself. Peering round a corner of the rifle range, he saw—and to some extent heard—two indistinct figures in conversation just outside the flap of the Botticelli tent.

"Sex?" Ling demanded.

But here, as elsewhere, Scorer was unhelpful. Visibility had been almost nil, the figures mere shadows. What he could say was that one of the shadows had been unusually tall, so if it had been a woman, she must have been a giantess. Then there were voices: one of them consistently whispered, the other was normal (though "la-di-da"), but low-toned; Scorer had been unable to make out which of the figures was the whisperer, and had certainly been unable to distinguish anything of what was being whispered. From the other voice, however, he had managed to glean a word or two here and there—Mavis Trent, a letter, the police.

These tantalising intimations reduced Ling to a subacute frenzy, and he wasted a good deal of time in attempting to get Scorer to enlarge on them. But when the dust had settled, it was found that nothing further had emerged. "Very well, then," said Ling, disgruntled, "What happened next?"

And what happened next was certainly sensational enough. There had been a sudden blur of movement, and a loud *crack*, and the tall figure had collapsed on the ground in a crumpled heap.

"*Crack!*" Scorer shouted quaveringly, almost falling off his chair at the recollection. "An' down 'e went!"

"*Crack!* Do you mean it was a gunshot?"

"Naw. More like a sort of thud, like."

"Then why did you say—no, never mind. More like a sort of thud. And then?"

Then, apparently, the shorter figure had stood quite still for a few moments (looking around him, Widger presumed, to see if the assault had been witnessed). He had then stooped over the taller figure on the ground, and had seemed to be examining its head. Finally he had grasped it under the armpits and dragged it inside the Botticelli tent.

Scorer had providently remained where he was; wild horses wouldn't have dragged him any closer. There followed an interim during which nothing much appeared to be happening. Then dim torchlight—so dim as to be almost imperceptible through the canvas walls—was switched on in the tent's rear section, where all the odds and ends were dumped, and moved about as if its owner were searching for something. Whatever it was, it was soon found. The torchlight steadied; there came a brief hiatus, and then a sound of *sawing*.

At this point, Scorer had apparently fainted.

The first thing he noticed when he recovered his senses was that although the torch was still on inside the tent, the sawing had ceased; the second, that a light was shining in a window of the Major's basement flat. A door banged, letting loose a tumult of barking; the torch inside the Botticelli tent was extinguished. The barking approached at an even pace, suggesting that its perpetrator was on a leash.

"'Twere the Major," Scorer explained, "taking 'is bluidy spannel for walkies."

Both Major and dog were still, however, a fair way off when the man in the tent decided to make himself scarce. Scorer saw him push his way out into the open—but this time his outline was strange, bulky and distorted (he must have been carrying the head, Widger reflected, and probably the clothes as well). Scorer cowered. But the shadow, unaware of him, was concentrating on the Major, who had now switched on his own torch and was perceptibly heading in his direction. The barking increased in volume; the bulky shadow slipped away into the darkness. And Scorer did the same: he had no wish to be discovered lurking in the grounds by the Major. Creeping away, he was slightly heartened to hear a car start up and move off distantly in the lane; that, he thought, must be the shadow. But he was still suffering from violent palpitations when he got home again, leaving the Major, his cocker bitch Sal and whatever lay in the Botticelli tent alone in the Aller House policies under the wan starlight.

"My God, what a witness!" said Ling, when Scorer, still clamouring for police protection, had been conducted out of the office and downstairs again by a constable summoned by telephone for the purpose. "Charles, I suppose that all that was true?"

"Oh, I should think so, yes."

"I mean, he wasn't just saying it all to make a sensation?"

"No, no, Eddie. He'd be too afraid of the consequences."

"So he actually witnessed the murder. That is, unless the tall man was just knocked out outside the tent, and finished off inside."

"Well, it doesn't make much odds, does it?"

"It might make a difference to the *method* of murder."

"Didn't Sir John say anything about that?"

"No, he didn't."

"Well," said Widger, "my bet would be that the victim was killed outside the tent—probably coshed, like Routh."

"The same murderer?"

"One supposes so."

"Or it might be imitative."

"Possibly...One thing is," said Widger with more energy, "that we shall have to keep after Scorer, and try to get some more out of him."

"And do you think we'll succeed?"

"No."

Ling sighed. He returned his pipe to his right-hand jacket pocket. Then he fumbled in his left-hand jacket pocket and brought out *another* pipe. "Looks as if the Major's in the clear," he remarked. "That is, if Scorer's telling the truth."

Widger stared. "Good God, Eddie," he said, "you weren't suspecting the Major, were you?"

"At this stage, old squire, we've got to suspect everyone. Anyway, we'll see the Major now, straight away, and find out what he was up to."

"He was taking his dog for a walk."

"I was thinking that perhaps he might have heard the sawing."

"We'll ask him."

CHAPTER EIGHT

Interviews

Nay, who but infants question in such wise?

Dante Gabriel Rossetti: *Fragment.*

THE MAJOR APPROACHED the office singing. "The savour, the flavour," he sang, "of the great liddle cube. Oxo," he explained, entering. "I find the high notes in that one bit difficult—though I suppose that if one started a bit lower down...The savour, the flavour," he rumbled.

Ling frowned. "Major," he said, "I don't have to tell you what a serious matter this is."

"Paraleipsis," said the Major. "No, no, my dear fellow, of course you don't. Dreadful business, dreadful—though not of course as dreadful as if one knew who the poor fellow was. And I suppose one doesn't know that, not yet awhile," he added hopefully.

"Please sit down, Major. We have a few questions to ask you."

The Major settled alertly on the edge of the chair. "Ask away."

"We understand that you were out and about after midnight on Friday."

"Yes, well, not exactly."

"Whatever do you mean, Major?"

"Well, I was in bed, you see, trying to read *Adam Bede*. I don't know if you've ever tried to read *Adam Bede*?"

"Please keep to the point."

"I was just coming to it. Let me see, where was I? Yes, *Adam Bede*. I was snug in bed, trying to read *Adam Bede*. And then, d'you see, I remembered."

"Remembered what?"

"Remembered that I ought to have put Sal out. Sal has a sweet nature, but there's no doubt she barks rather a lot. She barks when there's someone about. Come to that, she barks when there's no one about, except me. Come to that, she barks in her sleep."

"And you put her out every night?"

"Good gracious, no, my dear fellow. What a cruel suggestion. No, it was the Fête, don't you know. People leave things overnight—silly of them, really—and last year there was some pilfering. So I said that this year I'd tie Sal up outside the Botticelli tent which is where most of the stuff gets dumped, and then if anyone came around snooping she'd bark and wake me up, and I'd go out and find out what was going on. It was a mild night, fortunately, and if it had come on to rain Sal could have gone into the tent, and of course I was going to put down food and water for her. Only then I went to bed and forgot. It was only when she started chewing at *Adam Bede* that I remembered."

"You didn't hear any unusual noises from the grounds, at that time?"

"Well, that's a queer thing, because as a matter of fact I did. There was a sort of muffled sawing sound...I say: could that have been when the poor fellow was having his head cut off?"

"We think it may have been."

"Pity I missed it," said the Major. "I mean, pity I missed the person who was doing it."

"If you ask me, Major," put in Widger, "you were lucky not to blunder in on it."

"Yes, well, perhaps I am a bit old to go tackling ghouls in the middle of the night," the Major admitted. "Is Hagberd safe?"

"Safe?"

"Yes. I mean, he hasn't escaped or anything."

"Hagberd's perfectly safe," said Ling. "That was one of the first things we checked on."

"I wouldn't have minded if it had been Hagberd, d'you see? Nice gentle man, except where Routh and Mrs Leeper-Foxe were concerned."

"Well, it wasn't."

"That's a good thing, then. I remember once saying to Hagberd, 'Hagberd,' I said—"

"Major, will you please get on with your story."

"Well, yes, certainly I will. That's what I'm here for, isn't it? I managed to get *Adam Bede* away from Sal, and then I slipped on a dressing-gown, and then I got out the Supavite Doggy-woggy, and then I hunted about a bit for my torch, and by that time the sawing had stopped."

"You put on the light in your front room."

"Yes, naturally, my dear fellow. I wasn't going to do all that in the pitch dark, was I now?"

"Go on."

"There isn't much more. I put Sal on the lead, and went out, and headed straight for the Botticelli tent. Sal barked a lot at first, which probably meant there was someone about, but when we got nearer she quieted down a bit, which probably meant they'd gone. Anyway, I tied Sal up at the entrance, and went in and took a look round, just in case, but there was nobody."

"You went into the back part of the tent?"

"Oh yes, definitely, because that's where everything's put. The Misses Bale don't like it a bit, but I say to them, 'Titty,' I say—or as it may be, 'Tatty'—their names are Titania and Tatiana—that awful mother of theirs—"

"And there was nobody there either?"

"Quite right, my dear fellow. Nobody."

"Did you happen to notice a large piece of canvas spread out on the ground in a corner?"

"Well, yes, now you come to mention it, I did. Don't tell me that's where the body was."

"We think so."

"Terrible thing, terrible. And you'd think that at any rate I'd have smelt the blood, wouldn't you? A very distinctive smell, blood has. I remember once—"

"And it didn't occur to you to look under the canvas, to see if there was a pilferer hiding there?"

"No, it didn't, I'm afraid. You see, by that time Sal had stopped barking altogether, and she wouldn't have done that if there'd been anyone about for miles around, under a piece of canvas or not. So I just flashed my torch around and went out again. Then I did a little tour of the grounds, and then I went back to bed and *Adam Bede* again, with bits chewed out of it. That soon sent me to sleep, I can tell you."

"And you weren't disturbed at all?"

"No, I wasn't. As a matter of fact, I slept rather late, but then several local chaps turned up to finish off the stalls and marquees and so forth, and of course Sal started barking, and that was what eventually woke me."

"About when?"

"About ten."

"One other thing, Major. Did you hear any unusual noises apart from the sawing?"

The Major looked doubtful. "Well, there was a car," he said. Widger and Ling exchanged significant glances. "That," the Major went on, "was when I'd just come out of the flat with Sal, and was heading for the Botticelli tent. A car started up and drove off, somewhere out in the lane. Might have been lovers, of course, but I very seldom hear traffic so late at night. Usually it's dead quiet."

Ling nodded. He rummaged in the folder containing Widger's report until he found the page he wanted. "Now, Major, you were one of the people who visited the...the Botticelli tent during the Fête."

"Absolutely right, officer, I was. Mind you, it's quite outrageous for Titty and Tatty to charge fifty pence for looking at that frightful daub, and I can't really afford it, but I hate to disappoint the old girls. They're not mad about anything else, don't you know, just about the Botticelli. They think someone's going to steal it from them, and it's only because of the Church, or perhaps I should say the Rector, that they let it out of the house at all."

"And what did you do when you were inside?"

"I sat down and had a nap."

"I see. You didn't go into the rear section at all?"

"Not unless I was walking in my sleep."

"And you didn't hear anything from there? More sawing for instance?"

"My dear fellow, someone could have let off a bazooka, and I shouldn't have heard it. It was that pop group, d'you see? They were wired up to loudspeakers all over the place, and there was one just outside. Luckily Titty and Tatty are a bit deaf—you should hear them saying the Nicene Creed, quite out of time with everyone else—or I'm sure they'd have protested."

"Don't they wear deaf-aids?"

"They have one deaf-aid, which they share between them, passing it back and forth...I'm afraid," said the Major, "that you're going to find it a slow business, talking to *them*. What most of us do is just address the one who's wearing the aid, and ignore the other one completely."

"I see," said Ling again. "Well, thank you, Major. You've been most helpful."

"Oh, have I, my dear fellow? I'm so glad." The Major reached for his stick and got briskly to his feet.

"We'd like you to stay downstairs for a while, in case anything else crops up. And then later on—tomorrow, perhaps, or the next day—we'll be asking you to sign a formal statement."

The Major saluted smartly and hobbled to the door, where he paused for a moment.

"There are a great many journalists on these premises," he said severely, and went.

"He confirms Scorer's story, in some of its details," said Widger. "The sawing, the car..." He petered out despondently: the conviction had for some time been growing in him that despite the abundance of evidence, this was going to prove an extremely difficult case.

Ling roused himself from what seemed to be a catatonic trance. "Oh aye," he said. "There's that." While the Major had been talking he had been stuffing his second pipe (desisting regularly when he had to ask a question), and he now applied a lighted match to it. It at once emitted a shower of sparks, like a factory chimney in the early stages of the Industrial Revolution, and one of these fell on to the folder containing Widger's report, where it started burning a small black hole. Without troubling to extinguish it, Ling brushed it off the desk on to the carpet. "Ay, the car," he muttered. "Choommy made his getaway in a car, by the sounds of it. We'll have to check on that."

Widger pulled a notebook from his pocket. He selected a blank page, and on it wrote the word *car*.

"Put all the men you've got on to it." *Men*, Widger wrote, reflecting as he did so that Graveney's people (Graveney was the Inspector in charge of Glazebridge's uniform branch) weren't going to stretch very far. Constables would have to be borrowed from the neighbouring manors, and even if that were done, Widger doubted if their chances of finding out anything about the car—of locating anyone who had actually *seen* it, for example—were much better than nil. What they really needed—and here Widger's gloom touched its nadir—was the Regional Crime Squad, or even Scotland Yard. But the

Chief wouldn't have that, except in a really desperate emergency, which so far this wasn't, or at any rate not quite. The Chief considered his own men capable of handling absolutely anything...Touching, of course, but alarming as well.

"So what we have to do now is postulate," Ling was saying in his normal voice, through a cloud of smoke. "We postulate that Scorer and the Major were telling the truth, as far as they knew it. Our man was killed just outside the...the Botticelli tent. Then he was dragged inside, and stripped, and had his head sawn off...So if he wasn't dead to start with," said Ling in a sudden access of cheerfulness, "he was dead then. But now, along comes the Major, with his dog. Our murderer panics. He picks up the clothes and the head. He takes to his heels. He leaves the grounds. He gets into his car. He drives off. He..." His euphoria fading, Ling paused, unable to think of any evidence for what this ghastly figure did next. "He drives off," he repeated feebly.

"And from then on," said Widger, "we lose track of him until the head turns up again."

"Being carted all over the neighbourhood by this Professor Fen...Wait a minute, though."

"Yes?"

"There are three things Chummy almost certainly did that night, after he left the grounds of Aller House."

"Yes?"

"For starters, he mutilated the head, so as to make it unrecognisable. He wasn't going to let it out of his hands, not till he'd done that."

Widger saw several holes in this argument. He decided, however, that this was not the moment to specify them, and nodded instead.

"Then he had to get rid of his victim's clothes, or hide them somehow. Chances are he buried them. You'll have to put men on to that, looking for freshly turned earth."

Widger rolled his eyes but said nothing. In his notebook he wrote *victim's clothes*.

"And finally, he'd have to do something about his own clothes. He's bound to have got blood on them."

"Yes."

"So there are three lines of enquiry for you," said Ling, with the complacency of a man who is going to be obliged to do none of the leg-work. "Four, if you include the car. No, five."

"Five?"

"There's tools. That mess"—and here Ling swivelled round in the desk chair to indicate the sack in the corner of the office—"that mess wasn't made without the help of tools. A hammer is what we want, with bits of blood and brains on it. Tell your men to look for a hammer."

Without making any further entry, Widger put his notebook back in his pocket. "I suppose," he said, "that you'll be wanting to see Fen next."

"The professor? No, not quite yet. This Mrs Clotworthy first. Get her up here, will you?"

Widger picked up the house telephone and dialled the Duty Sergeant's desk. He sneezed. Ling said, "Hello, old squire, getting a cold, are you?"

"No, it's the smoke from your pipe."

"Oh, sorry."

The Major had made his entry singing; Mrs Clotworthy made hers talking. She was a dumpy little woman of seventy-five, with steel-rimmed glasses and a bun; she swayed from side to side as she walked, and was wearing an ankle-length black dress in continuing memory of her late husband, the butcher. All in all, she looked like a Mrs Noah from a Victorian Noah's Ark. As far as Widger could gather, she was complaining about something.

"Oh my dear soul, 'ow you do get a body on the run!" said Mrs Clotworthy. "An' that dratted Freddy Smale couldn't 'ardly wait 'alf a minute till I got on 'is bus an' clapped me money in 'is little bowl avore 'e was off again like a blue-arsed vly! Lucky

they sideways seats is up in front so 'ee can zit down quick
I say, unless somebody's set a push-chair on 'em, 'cus there
id'n time to see if you'm facin' yore nor back afore you'm in
town an' gettin' down again. Tid'n like I was late neither, just
stopped—"

"Mrs Clotworthy."

"Just stopped to pull up a few bits of stroyle round the gate
like, comes up easy now it's dying off a bit not that it's ever easy
to get up the root so it don't come back again avore you've had
a chance to make a bonfire of the last lot as that whatsisname
downstairs'll find if 'e don't get after 'is garden soon. Ought to
a knowd 'e id'n a real gennulman 'cus any road—"

"Mrs Cl—"

"—any road if the gentry can't till their own ground they
do know to get some'un as *can* avore it all goes to ruin an'
seedin' over other folks' plots."

"Mrs—"

"Still, I s'pose it takes all sorts an' 'e makes 'is way out
of books like that other chap makes 'is out of noting for the
pictures so they do tell me though it seems a funny trade to me
not like the gramophone or the wireless though they don't call
'em that nowadays seems, so."

At this point, either Mrs Clotworthy's jeremiad reached its
natural term or else she simply ran out of breath. At any rate,
it at last became possible for Widger and Ling to induce her to
sit down and bend her mind to the matter in hand.

Yes, well, she'd been given this nice pig to cut up for her
birthday; and then she'd met this gentleman who'd taken the
Dickinsons' cottage, and he was an M.A. the way her husband
had always wanted to be, and when she'd heard that he didn't
get on with the shop brawn, she'd decided to give him the
head so that he could make his own. So she'd told him she'd
put it in her porch if she went out, and he could collect it from
there; and that was what she'd meant to do. When was this?
Why, yesterday, of course, yesterday as ever was. Yes, *Saturday*:
didn't they know when yesterday was?

Mrs Clotworthy's kindly intention had aborted, however, it transpired. What had happened was that quite early yesterday she had received a message that a gravid great-niece, living on the other side of Burraford, was in labour; and though this occurrence was by no means novel, Mrs Clotworthy was convinced, as she had been on numerous similar occasions previously, that family ties made it mandatory for her to be present—if not actually in the bedroom, at all events in the house—during the delivery. She had accordingly locked up her cottage and hastened off to her great-niece's. And there she had remained all day (the great-niece's pains being fairly prolonged) until Doctor Mason had arrived from the Church Fête just in time to relieve the great-niece of a burly son.

All this was clear enough—so clear, in fact, that Ling made the mistake of not questioning Mrs Clotworthy further. She evidently had more to say, but this, Ling patently feared, would be bound to have to do with the great-niece and the baby, neither of whom could be construed as figuring in any way in the death and decapitation of the man in the Botticelli tent. Accordingly, Mrs Clotworthy was conducted downstairs again, while Ling mopped his brow with a tobacco-coloured handkerchief such as snuff-takers use and Widger said:

"It must have been Chummy, then, who put the sack in Mrs Clotworthy's porch, presumably after she'd gone out."

"Looks like it."

"An imitative crime, then, up to a point."

"How do you mean?—Ah yes, I get it. Hagberd dumps Routh's head through the window of Mrs Leeper-Foxe's breakfast room at the Old Parsonage, to give her a fright—and Mrs Leeper-Foxe owns factory farms. Chummy dumps *his* victim's head on Mrs Clotworthy, who's a butcher's widow and so more or less in the same line of business." Ling frowned and relit his pipe. "It isn't *really* the same though. Why didn't Chummy use Mrs Leeper-Foxe again?"

"Because she isn't here. She says that after what happened she's never coming back. She's selling the house."

"I see. So Mrs Clotworthy was a sort of rough equivalent. I shouldn't have thought that a *butcher's* widow would have got much of a fright from the head, though, not after a lifetime of cutting up dead meat."

"Humans are different from animals," said Widger. "At any rate, they are as far as Mrs Clotworthy's concerned. I once had to take her to the morgue to identify a nephew who'd been drowned. He wasn't messy at all—looked very peaceful, really—but she'd no sooner set eyes on him than she fainted dead away."

"Well, but that was a relative."

"Yes, but she's a tough old girl. I shouldn't have been surprised if she'd cried a bit—but *fainting...!*"

"Ah well, it's a small matter. We'd better have a word with Fen now, I think."

But Fen's evidence was brief and unenlivening. He had not particularly wanted to make brawn, he said, but had felt unable to reject Mrs Clotworthy's well-meant gesture, and consequently had gone along to her cottage about 10.30 yesterday, the Saturday. He had knocked on the one door, but there had been no reply. So then he had looked round the little wooden porch. It was very clean and tidy, with some potted plants on a shelf, and an empty milk bottle, and, of course, the Harris's Bacon sack, firmly tied at the neck with coarse string: this he had naturally assumed to be the pig's head, so he had taken it away with him without further examination. He had then gone to The Stanbury Arms, where he had met the Major, who knew all the gossip and who had told him about Mrs Clotworthy's great-niece, thus accounting for her absence from home. He had talked to the Major, and to Padmore, and to Old Gobbo, and later, upstairs, to Jack Jones. Then he and Padmore and the Major had strolled along the lane to see the Rector, and after that he had gone home to the Dickinsons' cottage, where he had left his sack, still unopened, on top of the refrigerator. In the afternoon he had attended the Fête, and when everyone was at last allowed to leave, had taken Padmore home with him, to have a drink and telephone the gory news to his paper. Meanwhile, however, he had been thinking about the Routh-Hagberd case, and had decided that the sack, still on top of the refrigerator, had better be investigated. Opening it, he had found the mangled head of a man. He had telephoned the police, and they had come and collected the head, and Padmore, enraptured, had rung his paper a second time, and that was that.

Ling said, "And was there any time when the sack you picked up at Mrs Clotworthy's could have been switched for another?"

"Certainly there was. There was the whole time when I was at the Fête. I didn't lock up, and even if I had, the Dickinsons' cottage is very easy to get into."

Widger said, "You say that when you were at The Stanbury Arms you went upstairs to talk to Jack Jones. Did you take the sack with you then?"

"No, I didn't. I left it in the bar."

"So there could have been a switch then?"

"I doubt it," said Fen. "Isobel Jones was there, I think—and the bar was beginning to fill up. So it's possible, but not very likely. A second sack would certainly have been noticed."

"Seems as if you had the head in your possession all along, then."

A faint gleam of amusement appeared in Fen's eyes. "It would seem so," he said.

Ling squinted into the bowl of his pipe. Then he sucked at its stem. Then he sat forward in the desk chair, so abruptly that his stomach knocked the blotter, and Widger's report, on to the floor. Fen leaned forward and retrieved them for him.

"Ah, thanks," he said. "Now, Professor Fen, we have you down as one of the people who visited the...the Botticelli tent during the course of the Fête. Is that right?"

"Yes, quite right."

"What did you do when you were in there?"

"Do? I thought about religion."

Ling was clearly taken aback by this; he could scarcely have been more flabbergasted, Widger reflected, if Fen had announced that he had conversed with Harold Wilson or the ghost of Rasputin. "Oh, ah," he said feebly.

"That's what you're supposed to do, so I did it."

"Quite, quite," said Ling hurriedly. "And did you go into the back part at all—behind the picture?"

"No."

"Did you *hear* anything?"

"I heard the Whirlybirds."

Ling stared. "Helicopters?"

"No, no. The Whirlybirds are a female pop group which was performing. They had one of their loudspeakers rigged up immediately outside the Botticelli tent. Full amplification."

Concealing his disappointment reasonably well, Ling said, "Yes, I remember. A pity."

"It was during the Fête that the arm was cut off, was it?"

"Yes," said Ling briefly. "Well, Professor Fen, you've been very helpful."

"Oh, have I, have I? I shouldn't have thought so."

"We shall be needing a signed statement from you, of course."

"Of course."

"Tomorrow or the next day."

"Yes."

"And will you please stay on the premises for a little longer? We're still in the early stages of the investigation, and something more may crop up."

"I'll do that. And good luck," said Fen benignly, as he disappeared out of the door.

Ling yawned and stretched.

"Thank the Lord for one lucid witness," he said. "And now, I suppose, we shall have to talk to that dolt of a constable of yours."

"Rankine?"

"No, Luckraft."

"Luckraft's not mine, he's Graveney's."

"Don't fuss, Charles." And since Ling seemed capable of no exertion greater than that required to fill a fourth pipe which he had conjured up from somewhere, Widger rang the Duty Sergeant and asked him to send Luckraft up.

Luckraft looked uncomfortable, both professionally and physically; and although his red, meaty face was not adaptable to any great range of expression, he also looked decidedly apprehensive. It being his day off, he was crammed into a light-weight grey suit too small for him. His shoes shone; his tie blared. He had a large piece of Elastoplast stuck to the back of his head, and he was sweating slightly.

Ling, a kindly man at bottom, told him to sit down.

Luckraft said that he would rather stand.

Ling, having consulted Widger's report, told him to tell his story.

Luckraft cleared his throat and began. And what emerged was this:

The Stanbury Arms was situated in Holloway Lane, and a little way along from it, in the direction opposite to Glazebridge, a footpath led through to Chapel Lane, debouching between Luckraft's small but newish bungalow on the one side and Mrs Clotworthy's cottage on the other. Mrs Clotworthy's cottage was one of a pair, but its neighbour had for a long time been uninhabited—unsaleable, seemingly—and was verging on ruin, its garden completely overgrown, its windows smashed, its paintwork peeled away, and a number of slates missing from the roof. To this deplorable condition vandalism had contributed much, and Luckraft, who knew the owner, had promised to do what he could about any vandals, vagrants, junkies and other such social undesirables as might come to his notice.

Yesterday morning, then—Saturday—he had left his

bungalow at about 10.15 and set off on his motor-cycle to ride into Glazebridge. Passing the abandoned cottage, he had thought he saw, out of the corner of his eye, an indistinct figure ducking into cover round at the back; and since he had time in hand, he had decided to stop and investigate, leaving his motor-cycle against the hedge and forcing his way into the desolation of the garden by way of a small, lop-sided wicket gate. A tour of the garden and cottage—peering into empty dusty rooms through broken panes—had brought nothing to light, and Luckraft had terminated his efforts by making his way into a ramshackle garden shed, still crammed with all manner of decaying household and garden rubbish. Here he had decided to remain for a little, on the watch: the shed's window, though grimy, was intact, and gave a good view of the surroundings, in case someone was still dodging about. And it was here that disaster had struck. Luckraft had scarcely had time to wipe a portion of the window, and so provide himself with a peephole, before he accidentally trod on the tines of a propped-up rake. Its handle fell forward, hitting him on the forehead (he was not wearing cap or helmet) and causing him to lose his balance and fall back with a crash on to an enormous old rusty iron mangle, whose roller caught him on the occiput with such violence as to actually knock him unconscious.

Ling was frankly incredulous. "Good heavens, constable," he said. "I shouldn't have thought that was possible."

Luckraft's face grew redder than ever. "It happened, sir," he said stiffly.

"You mean you actually knocked yourself *out*?"

"Yes, sir. I was talking to Doc Mason about it afterwards, and he says there are weak spots in the skull where quite a light blow will—will—well, it'll do what it did to me."

"I see. And how long did this condition last?"

"I fell down on to the floor, sir."

"Yes, I've no doubt you did. But how long *for*?"

"I suppose it must have been about ten minutes, sir. When I came round there was a boy standing over me with a bunch of herbs."

"What was he doing—waving them under your nose to revive you?"

"No, sir. He was taking my pulse."

"Good heavens."

"It was Oliver Meakins, sir."

Ling looked at Widger. "Oliver Meakins?"

Widger explained. Oliver Meakins, he said, was a stooped, studious Burraford lad of eleven whose unlikely ambition it was to become a male nurse. He was currently going through a homoeopathic phase—without, however, relaxing his grip on idiopathy.

"He was picking herbs in the garden, sir, when I came along," said Luckraft. "He knew, of course, that he didn't ought to be there, so while I was looking around he managed to dodge me, or hide, or something. It must have been him I glimpsed from the lane."

Again addressing Widger, "Is this boy here?" Ling asked.

"No. I had a few brief words with him before you arrived this morning, but—"

"Did you ask him if he saw anyone lurking round Mrs Clotworthy's cottage? That sack must have been dumped in her porch some time."

"Yes, but surely much earlier."

"Depends. What time did Mrs Clotworthy go off to see this great-niece?"

"I found that out," said Widger defensively. "It was shortly after eight. Come to that, though, the sack could surely have been put there during the night."

"In that case, wouldn't she have noticed it when she left?"

"She might not have. She was excited and in a hurry."

Ling grunted. "I'll have to ask her—though I should have thought that if she had noticed it, she'd have mentioned the fact. I'll have to talk to the boy, too. Luckraft"—he turned back to the sweating constable, who during this interchange had been shifting uneasily from foot to foot—"Luckraft, I suppose it's too much to hope that *you* noticed, before you knocked yourself out, if there was any—Wait a minute, though, I'm getting this wrong. Mrs Clotworthy's porch would be round the other side of the cottage, on Chapel Lane."

"Well, no, sir," said Luckraft, "as a matter of fact, it isn't. For some reason I've never understood, it's at the back. You get to it from the footpath which leads from Chapel Lane to Holloway."

"So you could have seen it from the toolshed window."

"Only the roof of it, sir, because there's a fairly high hedge between the two gardens. Besides," said Luckraft with some dignity, "I didn't have much chance to see anything."

"No one about?"

"No, sir. Apart from Oliver Meakins, I didn't set eyes on a living soul."

"All right. Go on."

But Luckraft had little more to tell. Oliver Meakins had heard the crash from the toolshed, and, his professional instincts triumphing over the urge to get out of there, with his herbs, fast, had crept up to the rickety erection, peered in at the door and seen Luckraft sprawled on the grimy boards with his head in a small pool of blood; and he had still been in the process of testing for unconsciousness—which, he had learnedly reported to Widger, was at the time of his entry complete—when Luckraft had come round. Reluctantly concluding that his medical qualifications were as yet too embryonic to cope with the situation, and that Luckraft had better see a proper doctor, he had punily assisted the unfortunate constable back to his bungalow and the arms of his alarmed wife, who had got in touch with Dr Mason. The doctor had bound the injury up, pronouncing it not serious, but advising a few hours' rest; Mrs Luckraft had telephoned Inspector Graveney in Glazebridge, to say that her husband had had a slight accident, and wouldn't be in that morning; Oliver Meakins, a helpful boy despite his eccentricities, had effortfully salvaged Luckraft's motor-cycle and put it away in the garage next to the white Saab; and Luckraft, after a cup of tea, had fallen asleep on his bed.

"But you woke up again," said Ling, "in time to go to the Fête."

"Yes, sir. By then I was feeling much better. And it's such a big affair, Mr Graveney likes to have someone on duty there."

"As far as I can make out, you spent most of your stint sitting outside the entrance to the...the Botticelli tent."

"Well, yes, sir, I did. The Misses Bale are so afraid that picture's going to get stolen, they're glad of a bit of extra reassurance, like. And besides, sir," said Luckraft with candour, "it was somewhere to sit down. I was better, yes, but I was still getting an occasional giddy spell."

"Did you sit there having giddy spells the whole time, then—until the body was found?"

"Oh, no, sir. I did a couple of rounds, just to make sure everything was all right. I even had a go at the hoop-la."

"Did you, indeed." Ling took all of his four pipes, and arranged them symmetrically on the desk in front of him; he then selected one, and levelled its stem accusingly at Luckraft. "So you can't for a certainty name everyone who went into that tent, or came out of it."

"No, I can't, sir. I can name some of them, though. There was—"

"Yes, yes, you've told Inspector Widger all that already."

"Miss Titty Bale would know, though."

"*She's* told Inspector Widger all that already. However, there were two people—men—whom she couldn't identify."

"Yes, sir. That Fête's that popular, people come to it from miles around."

"One of these men went into the tent while you were there."

"Quite right, sir."

"Well, come on, man, what was he like?"

A long pause followed. Then Luckraft said, "Ordinary."

"'Ordinary'?" Ling was outraged. "You're a policeman, and all you can say about a man you saw at close quarters, in broad daylight, is that he was 'ordinary'?"

"To tell the truth"—Luckraft's face coloured slowly from below upwards, like a July lupin—"To tell the truth, sir, I wasn't paying him any attention."

"Were you asleep, Luckraft?"

"Certainly not, sir."

"Well, what *were* you doing?"

"Thinking, sir. I wasn't to know that there'd been a—that there was a body in the— You can't take note of everyone," said Luckraft, rallying slightly.

"It may interest you to know, Luckraft, that Miss Bale can't describe the stranger properly, either. Either of the strangers."

"Sorry about that, sir."

"You may well be sorry. So how are we to set about tracing them, eh, *constable*? Can you tell me that?"

"Sir, I'm sure I wasn't there when the other one—"

"We know you weren't. Miss Bale has told us. You're useless, constable, useless."

"Yes, sir."

Ling picked up a ball-point pen, wrote *useless* on the blotter, and said, "Well, we shall have to test your memory with something else, shan't we? Did you yourself go into the tent at any time?"

"Yes, sir, I did."

"Well?"

"There was no one waiting, so Miss Bale let me go in free."

"You grudged giving fifty pence to the Church funds."

"No, sir, not at all. It was meant to be a sort of—a sort of reward. I wanted to pay, but Miss Bale insisted."

"Very kind of her, I'm sure. And you stayed in there ten minutes?"

"Yes, sir."

"Did you investigate the back part of the tent?"

"No, sir. I just sat down."

"You just sat down. And thought, I suppose."

"Yes, sir. I thought about my head. It was still hurting a bit."

"You sat for ten minutes thinking about your head."

"Well, sir, I'd seen the picture before, other years…I had a drag," said Luckraft, apparently in the hope that this admission would soften the heart of a fellow-smoker.

It didn't. "You had a drag," said Ling. "So now, of course, Forensic will be wasting time examining your nasty little cigarette butt, which no doubt you ground out on the grass before emerging. Did you see anything? Did you hear anything? Did you hear sawing?"

"I didn't notice anything out of the way, sir," said Luckraft. "And as to hearing—well, those girls were kicking up such a din—"

"We know, we know," said Ling wearily. "All right, Luckraft, that's all for now. We may need to talk to you again tomorrow, so see to it that you're available. Now go away."

Luckraft moved towards the door. Ling closed his eyes and began filling one of his pipes blindfold. He was starting to say to Widger, "What it amounts to, then…" when he opened his eyes again and discovered that Luckraft hadn't in fact left, but was still hovering in the doorway.

"Luckraft, did you hear what I said?"

"Yes, sir."

"I said 'Go away.' So why are you still here?"

"Excuse me, sir, but it's my leave."

"Your *leave*, Luckraft, your *leave*?"

"Yes, sir. It's due to start on Sunday. The Missus and I, we've got a nice little package tour laid on to North Africa."

"Impossible, Luckraft, impossible. You'll be needed. Yes, even you will be needed. Quite apart from all the routine work that's waiting to be done on this case, you may have to give evidence at the inquest."

"And if I may ask, sir, when's that?"

"Earlier today I talked to the Coroner's Office on the phone, and we've fixed it provisionally for Tuesday. It'll almost certainly have to be adjourned, of course. We can't even be sure that we'll have identified the victim by then." Ling had for once managed to get his pipe alight while talking, and this had mollified him considerably, so that he was prepared to be mildly chatty even with Luckraft. "However, we're taking the head along to Sir John Honeybourne this evening, after the press conference, and he may be able to make it recognisable for us."

Emboldened by these confidences, Luckraft nodded towards the sack in the corner of the office, and said, "Is that it, sir?"

"Yes."

"Can I look at it?"

"No, you can't. Why?"

"I thought it might turn out to be someone I knew."

"In its present condition, Luckraft, its own mother wouldn't know it."

"I see, sir. But about my leave. It had to be cancelled last time, when Mr Routh was murdered, and I'm sure I don't know what the Missus is going to say when I tell her it's having to be cancelled again. Set her heart on it, she has."

Ling said, "You talk to Mr Graveney about it, laddie, and see what he has to say...Besides," he added, with an assurance which Widger felt to be entirely premature, "by Sunday, chances are the whole thing will have been cleared up. And then away you'll go. Wish I were coming with you."

"That'd be nice, sir," said Luckraft in a tone which failed to carry much conviction; and this time he actually did go, closing the door quietly behind him. They heard his heavy tread receding out of earshot along the corridor towards the stairs.

"There are gaps still," said Ling, "and of course, someone may be lying. Even so, so far it looks fairly plain sailing. Our victim meets Choommy in the Aller House grounds, and— Wait, though: they *both* had to get there. Did they both come in that car Scorer and the Major heard?"

"Looks like it," said Widger. "Unless one of them lived fairly near by, and walked it."

"H'm, yes. Well, that's one gap. Never mind that for the moment, though. Choommy threatens blackmail over Mavis Trent—something about a letter. Would the blackmail be about Mavis Trent's death, d'you think, or would it just be that Choommy had been sleeping with her, and didn't want his wife to know? She did sleep about a lot after her husband's death, I think you said."

"She certainly did. But I think it must have been about her death, because according to Scorer the blackmailer said something about the police, and you don't go to the police to tell them someone's been copulating or committing adultery or whatever."

"Right, then. Choommy doesn't like being blackmailed, so he knocks the blackmailer down—perhaps coshing him with something and killing him outright, or perhaps finishing him off after he's dragged him into the back part of the tent. He strips the body to prevent identification, and cuts off the head, and maybe he means to go on with his butchery then and there. But then the Major and his dog come along. Choommy covers up the body with that big piece of tarpaulin, wraps the head in old newspapers, bundles up the clothes and slips away to his car. Then when he gets to where he's going, he disposes of the clothes, bashes the head about, puts it in a sack, and dumps the sack in Mrs Clotworthy's porch to help make the crime look as if it was similar to the Routh-Hagberd affair. Then all he has left to do is clean himself up and deal with his own clothes, and get into bed for the rest of the night."

"I doubt," said Widger, "if he put the sack in Mrs Clotworthy's porch during the night. I'm sure she'd have noticed it when she went off to see her great-niece, no matter how flustered she was."

"Well, all right, then. Riskier during daylight, though. What if she'd seen him through a window?"

"He probably lurked in that overgrown garden next door until he saw her set off. Remember, it was all of two and a half hours after that before Fen came along and took delivery."

Ling nodded. "You may be right. And it's a small point, anyway. After that, it's a fair bet that Fen had the head until we collected it from him in the late afternoon."

"Agreed. So then?"

"We don't know. But if the medical evidence is correct, something or other made our murderer take the enormous risk of coming along, and cutting off the arm and making the incisions in the legs, actually during the Fête."

"Fingerprints," said Ling. "He wanted to prevent identification, but the Major came along before he could do anything about the dead man's fingerprints. Then the dog was left tied up to the tent until quite late in the morning, and by that time there were people about."

"Really, Eddie," said Widger, a shade coldly, "you don't have to chop off a whole arm just to get rid of the fingers."

"People in and out of the tent the whole morning, too, I dare say," said Ling, ignoring this. "It's a miracle someone didn't move that bit of canvas and find the body sooner. I wonder if…"

"Yes?"

"I wonder if Choommy could have hidden himself in the tent before it, so to speak, opened for business, and then—and then…" His voice trailed away.

He's getting tired, Widger thought. He's going mad. It's all this abortive smoking. Perhaps it's like *coitus interruptus*— they say that can affect your wits…

"A van brought the picture to the Aller House grounds," he said. "And the Misses Bale came with it. They'd brought sandwiches and thermoses, and as soon as they'd seen the picture hung, they took up their positions outside. And stayed there. It's all in my report."

"What time was this? When they arrived, I mean?"

"About 10.30."

"Oh…Well, yes, come to think of it, it would have been safer to do the job during the afternoon, actually at the Fête, than during the morning: ten minutes alone inside the tent, with Miss Bale to keep intruders away, and that pop group to cover up any noise. The only other thing is, Choommy *could* have come back in the night; I don't believe that dog would have woken the Major up—he'd been reading this book..."

"But Eddie, the medical evidence is that the arm was cut off no earlier than one o'clock, and probably a bit later."

"We'll have to check that with Sir John, and make sure of it."

"Yes, certainly. But I still think we'll find that the person who cut the arm off was someone Titty Bale *saw*."

"And that's what I think, too," said Ling, to Widger's blank amazement. "It's the only possible answer," he said, his *sang froid* all of a sudden completely restored. He opened the file, and began rummaging through it. "Now let's see, where's that list?"

In silence, Widger took the papers from him and found him the right page.

"'Evidence of Miss Titania Bale', yes...Would you say that she's reliable?"

"Apart from being convinced that that awful great picture's a Botticelli, yes, completely."

"And she didn't herself go into the tent at all, during the Fête."

"She says not—not until she found the body. All she did was call through the flap to people, when their ten minutes were up. You're not starting to suspect *her*, are you?"

"No, no, old squire. From all the signs, this is a man's job. And according to this list, it was all men who paid their fifty pences (except for Luckraft) and spent their ten minuteses alone in the tent: Father Hattrick, the Rector, Professor Fen, Broderick Thouless—who's he?"

"A composer."

"Luckraft, the Major, J. G. Padmore—who's he?"

"A journalist from the *Gazette*."

"—Youings the pig-farmer, Dermot McCartney—who's he?"

"The Negro who opened the Fête."

"Clarence Tully, and two strangers. Not exactly a crowd, but I suppose the Fête wasn't nearly over when Miss Bale found the body. Also—ten minutes each. Also—the money. Charles, you're going to have to put men on to tracing those two strangers."

For a moment Widger said nothing. He was visualising the entire neighbourhood over-run like an ant-heap by blue-clad constables toting spades and notebooks. *If* they could be got. Recovering his voice.

"I don't quite see how we're going to set about that, Eddie."

Ling gestured seigneurially with a hairy paw. "You'll think of something, old squire, you'll think of something. Start with the list of names and addresses Rankine took at the gate when the mob was leaving."

"But Eddie, Chummy may have left before the body was found. And in any case, there are dozens of other ways of getting out of those grounds, in addition to the gate."

"You'll think of something," Ling reiterated exasperatingly. "Let's see, now, where was I? Yes. We've questioned some of the men who went into the...the Botticelli tent. So now we'll question the others."

They questioned the others.

No one admitted to going into the back part of the tent. No one admitted to having seen or heard anything out of the way.

They had passed the time in various ways: Father Hattrick had read his breviary, straining his eyes over it because of the awkwardly placed lights; the Rector had wondered if Father Hattrick could be converted to honest Anglicanism, and if so, how this could be accomplished (a wife?); Fen had thought about religion, on what lines he had not stated; Thouless (who had rather liked the picture) had attempted to compose celestial relief music in his head, in vain competition with the Whirlybirds; Luckraft had thought about his injured head; the Major had fallen asleep; Padmore had wondered if there was any way, apart from resignation, of stopping the *Gazette* from sending him back to Africa when its crime staff got out of hospital; Youings had mentally listed the merits and drawbacks of Gloucester Old Spots; Dermot McCartney had counted his money and examined, with no great enthusiasm, the purchases he had made so far; Clarence Tully had smoked a pipe and brooded over his milk yield.

The two strangers—the two strangers—

Ling wrote a question mark on his blotter.

The only mildly interesting question which arose concerned the Rector's cricket bag.

Yes, the Rector said, despite Titty Bale's objections he had taken it into the Botticelli tent with him; he had wanted, he said darkly, to keep it by him. "And I hope," he went on, scowling at Ling, "that you're not going to say *I* amputated this wretched man's arm, and took it out of the tent in my bag. For one thing, I doubt if it would have gone in, even if you bent it at the elbow. No, I'm sure it wouldn't. Think of a cricket bat, man: think of a cricket bat." Ling tried to look as if he were thinking of a cricket bat. "And I'll tell you another thing," said the Rector. "It's close on half-past five, and I've got to get back and take Evensong. So if that's all—"

"We won't keep you more than a few minutes longer, sir," said Ling meekly. "If you'll just tell us what was in the bag—"

"Curiosity killed the cat, but I suppose I must," said the Rector. "You'll have heard of F. X. Christopher."

"I'm afraid I haven't, sir."

"Good heavens, what does the higher constabulary read nowadays? Thrillers, I suppose. F. X. Christopher, Superintendent, is an expert on Charles I and his times. He's written a lot of books about them—scholarly as well as popular, a bit like C. V. Wedgwood only not quite so good. And F. X. Christopher is really Father Hattrick."

"I beg your pardon, sir?"

"Not at all, Superintendent. Partial deafness must be quite a handicap in your profession. I was saying, F. X. Christopher is really Father Hattrick. I dare say the 'F.X.' stands for 'Francis Xavier'," the Rector added. "Popish."

"Oh ay, I get you now. Sort of an alias."

"A pen-name, Superintendent, a pen-name."

"Yes, sir. But now, if we could get back to your cricket bag—"

"I was just coming to that. Superintendent, I have a lot of old junk in my attics."

Ling laughed feebly. "Most people have, sir."

"Yes, but much of mine is valuable."

"Indeed, sir?"

"So, being childless, I've decided to get rid of most of it. Over the last few months I've had a number of experts down from London—Sotheby's and so forth—to take a look at it all; and very pleased they've been. Some of it I'm going to have auctioned, in aid of the Church funds. And some of it—the association items—will go to museums. Among the association items, Superintendent, are four which concern Charles I: a lock of his hair, a letter, the wine-glass he drank from just before his execution (you can still just faintly make out the wine stains), and a coarse cotton handkerchief stained with his blood. They were left to my people by the Herbert family, I can't think why."

"Ah!" On Ling, light was dawning at last. "And Father Hattrick—F. X. Christopher—"

"Exactly. He wanted to see them before I gave them away. So I said I'd bring them along to the Fête and he could look at them in the Major's flat."

"I see. But surely, sir, if you'll forgive my saying so, a cricket bag—for four little things like that—"

"Oh, there were other things too," said the Rector airily. "Intrinsically valuable stuff, what's more. The bag was full—no room for any human arms. That was why I'd arranged to meet my bank manager at the Fête as well as Father H. What with some of the characters you see about the place nowadays, you can't be too careful."

"Your bank manager."

"Yes. When Father H. had seen the relics, my bank manager was going to collect the bag from me and take it straight to his bank and lock it up safely, pro tem. Only the miserable man never turned up, so eventually I had to cart the whole boiling back home with me again. Oh, one more thing: if you're thinking I could have done some sort of a switch at some stage, you can put the idea out of your mind straight away. Because when I came out of the Botticelli tent, the good Father was waiting for me, and he *ran* across to the Major's flat—he always runs; seems to prefer it to walking—and I ran after him without stopping anywhere—there must be dozens of witnesses to that—and when we arrived the Major was waiting, and I opened the bag in front of both of them, and there was no human arm in it. And now I'm going back to Burraford."

In the small office the shadows were lengthening, and down below, the car-park was filling up again as the media men returned in good time for the press conference. Widger suddenly realised that they had had no tea. Where was Rankine, where was Crumb? Their room adjoined this one, so why hadn't one or the other of them brought tea? What would Eddie think? Did it matter what Eddie thought? If he'd wanted tea, he could presumably have asked for it. What Widger wanted was a drink and then bed, but he realised that the day still had a long way to go.

When the Bale sisters were ushered into the office, Widger, slightly light-headed, perceived for the first time that their names were the wrong way round: Tatty (who had mounted guard at the back of the Botticelli tent) was large-bosomed but quite smartly dressed; Titty (who had been at the receipt of custom) was flat-chested but untidy, her upper half wrapped in a variety of long, diaphanous scarves. Facially, however, they were very similar—greying women of sixty or thereabouts. And although both were a bit deaf, Widger knew that they had all their wits about them, particularly where the Botticelli was concerned.

It was Titty who was wearing the hearing-aid, so Ling, mindful of the Major's warning, addressed himself first to her, while she fiddled with volume control in order to get him satis-factorily tuned in. Her evidence, however, was disappointing. She was adamant that her list of people who had entered the tent was complete and correct; she was adamant that no one could have smuggled even a baby's arm out, no matter how cunningly concealed; apart from the Rector's cricket bag, she had neither seen nor heard anything out of the way; and finding the body when she was looking for a medicine chest had of course been a shock, but at her age one got used to such things. (How on earth, Widger wondered, had she managed to come by this particular form of induration? Was she finding naked headless bodies all the time?)

Ling now indicated a wish to speak to Tatty, and there ensued a longish pause while Titty unscrewed the speaker of the hearing-aid from her ear, disentangled its cord from her scarves, unhooked the black microphone from the front of her blouse, and passed the whole contraption to her sister, who spent an almost equal amount of time putting it on. But Tatty, when the whole thing was adjusted to her satisfaction, proved to have even less to say than Titty. She had enjoyed the soft music (it was Titty who during the Fête had had custody of the hearing-aid), and could positively assert that no one had entered or left the tent by crawling under the back or sides, which had in any case been firmly guyed. Beyond that, nothing.

In a last desperate bid for useful information, Ling got the aid transferred back to Titty. How was it, he asked, that Titty was so completely unable to describe the two strangers who had gone in to see the Botticelli? Titty replied that she had only really looked at them when they came out again, and then solely with a view to detecting tell-tale bulges. Both were middle-aged, she thought. Ling went on questioning her for a while about clothes, hair, height, accent and so forth, but absolutely without result. Neither of the men had stolen the Botticelli, and that was enough for Titty.

Eventually, on both ladies' expressing a wish to go to church, Ling gave up and sent them away, warning Titty that she would have to give evidence (about the finding of the body) at the inquest on Tuesday.

He mopped his brow as the door closed behind them. "The funny thing is," he said, "that I *believe* them."

Widger crossed the room and switched on a light. He looked at his watch. "Time we went down and talked to the reporters."

Ling nodded, but made no immediate move. "Nothing from Forensic," he muttered.

Widger visualised the constables who had been, and presumably still were, collecting up every scrap of debris from the grass in and around the Botticelli tent, and placing their finds in little envelopes with locations carefully marked on them: fibres, sawdust, cigarette ends, toffee papers. "We're giving Forensic a lot to do," he observed mildly. "And they did send an interim report on the hacksaw I found in the back of the tent. I asked them to give it priority."

"Yes, there's that," said Ling, consulting the file. "Wiped. No fingerprints, and only the minutest traces of blood. Group A, rhesus negative. We'll have to find out from Sir John if that corresponds with the dead man's. Who did you say the hacksaw belonged to?"

"Cobbledick."

"Cobbledick again. So he left it in the tent over Friday night, and then—let's see, did he use it on Saturday morning?"

"Yes. Just briefly. He was one of the earliest to arrive. He used the saw, and then put it back in the tent just before the picture arrived, at 10.30."

"Didn't notice anything unusual about it, I suppose."

"No."

"So Chummy must have wiped it twice, once after cutting the head off, and then again after cutting the arm off."

"Yes."

"Nothing from the C.R.O."

"Have a heart, Eddie. That tent was fairly smothered in prints."

"They could have let us know if they had a match for the prints on the arm that was left."

"They've done that. They rang me up about it just before you arrived this morning. Negative: the victim didn't have form."

"Ground too dry to take footprints," Ling mumbled, unconsoled. "And then, of course, there's the paint."

They both thought about the paint. It had occurred to someone—specifically, to an officious little man called Wisdom—that the wooden parts of the Botticelli tent needed smartening up a bit, and he had accordingly spent most of Friday repainting them, scattering a good deal of the paint about him in the process. Unfortunately, the hue he had selected was that of dried blood, so that Forensic now had the headache of examining numerous pieces of dug-up grass and deciding whether their coloration was due to paint, or blood or both.

"Plenty of gaps still," said Ling, "but also"—and here he cheered up a bit—"plenty of lines to follow up." He stirred himself, putting three of his pipes into pockets and the fourth, and most impressive, into his mouth. He picked up Widger's report and made for the door.

"But you know what I really want to know most of all, Charles?" he said, as they stood in the corridor while Widger locked up the office.

"No. What?"

"I want to know how the *hell* that bloody great arm could have been smuggled out of the tent without anyone seeing."

CHAPTER NINE

The Short Arms of Coincidence and the Law

Quoth Hudibras, Friend Ralph, thou hast
Outrun the constable at last.

Samuel Butler: *Hudibras.*

T HE PRESS CONFERENCE was not a success.

In part this was because the Glazebridge police station had no room large enough to contain it: reporters squeezed in elbow to elbow, and many of them were without seats. But given the sensational circumstances (which were worth a little discomfort), the paucity of space wouldn't have mattered so much had it not been for Ling. He had made one enormous mistake already, in allowing pressmen and witnesses to mingle unimpeded while he conducted interviews in Widger's office upstairs; now he compounded it by trying to pretend that this juxtaposition had never occurred. In practice, of course, the reporters—those of them who had had the sense to continue hanging round the station instead of going out—had all the while been having a field day; and although Sergeant Connabeer, with a single constable to aid him, had attempted to keep the situation under control, his efforts, such was the excitement, had proved nugatory. The witnesses had found themselves hemmed in by a cloud of cameras, notebooks and cassette recorders, centres of a vast curiosity, targets for a never-ending stream of questions. And few of them had taken umbrage at this, or preserved a reasonable discretion; most had been delighted, and had talked freely. Moreover, they seemed to have felt no obligation to adhere calvinistically to the bare bones of truth, more particularly when they had nothing of great interest to recount: embellishment, often of the wildest sort, had been the order of the day. Scorer, much to his initial surprise, had found himself treated as a hero, and had responded with the assertion that he had not only seen the murderer but had chased him throughout the night, failing to tackle him and bring him down only by a hair's breadth. The Major dilated on Sal's unusual competence as a watchdog. Luckraft, omitting all reference to rakes, mangles and the therapeutic ministrations of Oliver Meakins, described how he had seen someone lurking in the garden next to Mrs Clotworthy's cottage; he also painted a lurid picture of his emotions on first seeing the body. Mrs Clotworthy specified to an interested audience the best way to cut up a pig, and gave it as her opinion that that Professor Fen wanted watching. All these people, and others, held opinions, mostly fanciful, not merely about this latest murder, but about Routh's death and Mavis Trent's death as well, and about the various links binding them together. Padmore came in for a good deal of cajoling, but kept what little extra he knew to himself, for the benefit of the *Gazette*; though he was certain to have to rewrite his book on Routh and Hagberd, he was consoling himself for this by a determination to do so well over this new murder that his stony-hearted superiors in Fleet Street would decide that it would be a waste ever to send him to Africa again. Fen too had his group of pursuivants, who were not only fascinated by his day-long custody of the head, but who knew him as having been a successful amateur detective and were anxious for his views on the present case. He fended them off, however, by stating, more or less truthfully, that he knew no more about the business than had been in the

Gazette that morning. The Misses Bale were eloquent about the insult to their Botticelli, and Titty's reactions to discovering the Corpse—ELDERLY SPINSTER FINDS NUDE MALE BODY BEHIND PRICELESS MASTERPIECE—were widely canvassed. The Rector contented himself with saying that there were a lot of dubious characters about. Flash-bulbs popped continually, the wildest rumours flew from tongue to tongue, and Scorer became such a nuisance that Sergeant Connabeer detached him by force from his inquisitors and locked him up in a cell. The reporters rejoiced, the more simple-minded among them assuming that far from having simply witnessed the murder, Scorer had now been found to have committed it, and had been summarily arrested.

Ling made his second mistake when the witnesses had at last been cleared out of the station and the press conference properly convened. At its outset it seemed to go well enough. Not unreasonably, in view of the fact that the investigation was still at such an early stage, Ling had intended, in his opening statement, to offer little more than had been in the *Gazette* that morning, together with a few harmless additional titbits such as that the murderer had probably used a car, and that in the absence of the County Pathologist the autopsy was being conducted by the celebrated Sir John Honeybourne; he could also, he thought, safely say that the body had not been positively identified yet, but that several promising lines of enquiry were being pursued. But beyond these banalities he was not prepared to go (in particular, he did not intend to say anything about Scorer), and it therefore came as a shock to him when the reporters started to ask questions based on their own interviews with the witnesses. If the questions had been anywhere near rational, Ling would very likely have kept his head. But they were not: most of the witnesses had interpreted the crime in terms of the wildest melodrama, and their exaggerations had been swallowed by the reporters hook, line and sinker. And now all this rubbish was being regurgitated for the benefit of Ling, who was expected to confirm or deny it; and his attempts to reduce the questions to a more realistic level, and at the same time not answer them, made him increasingly unpopular. What he ought to have done was simply shake his head, and leave the reporters with the responsibility of putting into their stories whatever fatuities they chose. Instead, he tried to master the situation, floundering deeper and deeper in a quicksand of wordy incoherence. His great pipe went out, a light sheen of sweat sprang up on his forehead, and his inter-locutors became momently more restive.

Ticehurst was sitting on Ling's right, behind a small table on an improvised platform which creaked loudly whenever anyone moved. Widger, stiff with embarrassment and a deter-mined non-contributor to the proceedings, was on Ling's other side. As Ling blundered on, Ticehurst's normally jovial features became a mask of dismay, and eventually, unable to bear it any longer, he plucked surreptitiously at Ling's sleeve. Ling was in the middle of trying to deal with a group of reporters who wanted Scorer to be brought on to the scene, and it was some little time before he had attention to spare for his P.R.O.

"Just say 'No comment'!" Ticehurst hissed in his ear. "Just keep saying 'No comment'!"

"As to Scorer," Ling told the assembled company, "he's a—NO COMMENT." It was like a speeding motor-cyclist braking abruptly to a halt.

A groan went up, and the reporters glared at Ticehurst, wet blanket at this stimulating jamboree. They went on trying for a few minutes longer, but Ling had belatedly learned: whatever they asked him, he sturdily came back with "No comment". Widger and Ticehurst leaned back in their chairs, to an outbreak of stridulation from the platform, in heartfelt relief; in between saying "No comment", Ling even managed to get his pipe going again. Finally, heartened by the success of his stonewalling, he was bold enough to look at his watch, get to his feet, and say, "Nothing more for now, ladies and gentlemen, I'm afraid. Thank you for your attention." With which he creaked down off the platform, followed by Widger and Ticehurst, and elbowed his way through the clumps of grumbling reporters into the comparative quietude of the station's entrance hall.

To Widger he said, "That went off quite well, didn't it?"

Widger swallowed. "You think so?"

"Yes, I do. *Quite* well."

Ticehurst caught up with them. He was peering nervously over his shoulder at the vanguard of discontented reporters emerging from the conference room.

"Well, I'll be off now, Eddie, if you don't mind," he said, and without waiting for a reply, waddled at a surprising speed to the entrance and so out into the night. Widger thought that he could hear him actually running to his car.

"Excuse me, sir," said Sergeant Connabeer to Ling, "but what am I to do with Scorer?"

"Don't mention that name to me."

"Where is Scorer now?" Widger asked.

"I locked him up, sir."

"Good," said Ling.

"Wait until the reporters have all gone," said Widger, "and then let him out and send him home."

"In a police car, sir?"

"Certainly not. There's a Sunday evening bus into Burraford. He can catch that."

"Very good, sir."

"No comment," said Ling to a reporter who had approached him with a question about the identification of the body. "As soon as there's anything solid, we'll let you know."

"You've no idea who the victim is?"

"Not yet, but we soon shall have…Charles, it's time we were on our way. You'd better go up and fetch that…that thing from your office."

"Yes, all right," said Widger, and made for the stairs. Ascending, he heard an increasing babble of voices from the entrance hall, and Ling saying "No comment" several times. The reporters were clinging like limpets to the last.

As he unlocked the door of his office, Widger spared a thought for his two subordinates, who had failed to bring tea. Detective-Constable Rankine, now...But then Widger remembered. He had put Rankine in charge of the mobile H.Q. in the grounds of Aller House—not a very onerous task, since all the actual work was being done by photographers, and Forensic, and the fingerprints boys, and the group of Graveney's constables who were maundering about picking things up off the ground; and there, presumably, Rankine was still. As to Detective-Sergeant Crumb, come hell or high water he always went home early. He was, indeed, so lazy and inefficient that Widger had excluded him from the murder investigation altogether (it seemed, in any case, not to have aroused much interest in him) and had left him to type up reports on such petty crime as the Department had been engaged on before the body turned up at the Fête.

Widger opened the door which led from his office to Crumb's and Rankine's office, and looked inside. As he had expected, the room was empty, its windows latched and its door to the corridor locked. For the thousandth time, he pondered the possibility of making a serious effort to get Crumb transferred to some other sphere of inaction. But it was really too late now: his appeal would certainly be dismissed, on the grounds that Crumb was nearly at retiring age.

Widger sighed, dismissed his useless subordinate from his mind, and turned back into his own office, where he picked up the Harris's Bacon sack, hefted it, and on an impulse put it on the desk and opened it. He was to reflect, subsequently, that this impulse could have been a sub-cortical adumbration of the trouble yet to come; meanwhile, he rationalised it with the thought that since its discovery the head had been very cavalierly—very *carelessly*—treated, and that it was up to him to make every possible check.

But all was well. Hideous as ever, and still wrapped in Cobbledick's copies of the *Daily Mail*, the head was there all right. Widger closed the sack and left the office with it dangling heavily by the neck from his right hand. Outside in the deserted corridor, he conscientiously locked up again.

In the entrance hall, the babble of voices continued unabated. Why on earth didn't Eddie march out and hide himself somewhere, instead of standing there like a dead whiting put down to lure congers? And suddenly Widger swore. It had just occurred to him that owing to the parsimony with which it had been designed and constructed, the Glazebridge police station had no back stairs, or at any rate none that were accessible from where he was: he, and the sack, were going to have to run the gauntlet of the entrance hall. And if the reporters didn't realise what the sack was, and what it must contain, after reading that *bloody* man Padmore in the *Gazette* that morning, they must all be quarter-wits. Good God, the moment they set eyes on him, they'd be down on him like a pack of wolves!

Widger counted up to five, slowly, meanwhile saying to himself, "You are an Inspector of Police. You will use your authority, and if necessary force, to brush these people aside and make your getaway." "Getaway" somehow didn't seem the right word: it carried overtones of the criminal, or anyway the craven. But it would have to do. The thing now was to make a move.

And in the event it looked to start with as if he were going to be lucky. For one thing, the ranks of the reporters had thinned, some of them having left to telephone their stories to their papers; for another, those who remained were concentrating on Ling, who was standing like a stuffed image at the centre of their circle, still saying "No comment". Widger sidled down the stairway, shielding the sack with his body, and then, with difficulty resisting the temptation to go on tip-toe, made his way as rapidly and noiselessly as possible towards the entrance. He could put the sack in his car, he thought, and then come back for Eddie.

Unfortunately, however, one or two of the reporters were getting tired of Ling; their attention was wandering, and

Widger had barely covered half the course before they noticed him. "The sack!" one yodelled loudly, and another chimed in with "The head!" In a moment Widger was surrounded, and babel broke loose, degenerating almost at once into a scuffle. Widger, tight-lipped, pushed and elbowed and thumped and inwardly cursed. Ling, initially paralysed by incomprehension, suddenly realised what was happening and rushed to the aid of his colleague, with Connabeer and a constable at his heels. Fearful that the sack was about to be wrested from him, Widger hurled it at Ling, like a rugby player making a pass, and more by good luck than judgment, Ling succeeded in catching it. Pitching and heaving and shouting, the whole mêlée burst through the swing doors and out into the car-park.

Here the Press came to its senses. It had undoubtedly gone too far. Apprehensively, it withdrew. Marshalled by Connabeer, it submitted meekly to being led back inside and having its names and addresses written down. Connabeer told it severely that he couldn't say what action would be taken, if any, but that its best plan would be to remain where it was for ten minutes or so, and then go quietly away. A left-wing reporter whom Widger had winded slightly muttered something about "police brutality," but when told that it was a pity he hadn't broken his neck fell silent; and from then on there was no more trouble.

Freed from pursuit but still breathing heavily, Ling and Widger hastened round to the back of the station where the police cars were kept, among them Widger's prized grey Cortina. Widger unlocked the passenger door and Ling got in beside him, clutching the sack to his breast as if it contained the treasure of the Incas. The doors slammed, the engine purred into life, and they moved through the car-park into the ring-road, where they turned left.

Peace at last.

Since Ling was uncommunicative, Widger concentrated on driving; despite the intricacies of the case, there somehow seemed, for the moment, to be very little to say. Two miles out of Glazebridge, they turned left off the ring-road towards the south-west, more or less at right angles to the Burraford direction, and lost the traffic coming home from a day's outing on the moor. It was by now almost completely dark, and Widger switched the headlights on.

At about this point, it occurred to Ling that there was no need for him to keep the sack on his lap for the entire journey. He twisted round awkwardly and deposited his burden on the back seat, bumping Widger's head with it in the process. Then he settled back, lit one of his pipes with a relay of six matches, coughed painfully and croaked out the single ejaculation "Ah". Widger supposed that this was intended to express contentment.

They plunged deeper and deeper into a nexus of ever narrower and narrower lanes. Wild flowers glimmered in the hedgerows, and the trees—even the sycamores, the limes and the horse chestnuts—were still leafy: it was certainly a freak autumn. As they went on, other traffic diminished to vanishing point, and the houses—almost all of them farmhouses hereabouts—became increasingly widely spaced. A Dutch barn loomed up on their right, and was gone. A rabbit appeared in the lane ahead, and bobbed along frantically in front of them, mesmerised by the glare of the headlights (Widger patiently reduced speed, so as to avoid running it down) until after about a quarter of a mile it found a gateway, veered into it, and was lost from sight. It was a lonely, unpeopled part of the countryside—and also, if you were going somewhere specific, a confusing one: Widger was glad that when he had ferried the body to Sir John, twenty-four hours ago, he had sat in front with the ambulance driver and taken careful note of the route.

He had not, on that occasion, seen very much of the great man. The door had been opened to him by a big-boned, silent, blond servant of some sort, who had switched on the porch light, nodded significantly and then gone out to the ambulance to help its driver, and the constable Widger had brought with him, to get the polythene-wrapped remains into the house. Widger had waited, and presently Sir John had appeared, pushing, with one extended forefinger, a large, rubber-wheeled trolley. He was tall, thin, gaunt, bald and cadaverous, with huge, splayed, brownish front teeth which he revealed to Widger, in what was more a leer than a smile, as he bade him good evening. He had then stood aside and watched while Chummy's victim was manhandled on to his trolley; had asked for, and listened to in silence, a brief account of how and where and when the body had been discovered; had promised a report as soon as possible; had slapped the body in a friendly way on its stomach; had said goodnight; and had shut the door in Widger's face. Widger had at first been slightly taken aback by this inhospitable treatment; but then, remembering that he still had an immense amount to do before Ling's arrival in the morning, he had dismissed it from his mind, had returned to the ambulance and had requested the driver to take him and the constable back to Glazebridge police station.

In these circumstances, he had had little opportunity to look about him. He already knew, however, the eccentric way in which the famous morbid pathologist, for so many years a star witness at the Old Bailey, had elected to dispose of his retirement; knew it by grace of detailed information supplied by Sir John's nearest neighbour, an astute, amiable farmer named Boddy whom Widger liked very much, and with whom he occasionally, on Market Days, had a pint at The Seven Tuns. Briefly, Sir John was independently quite wealthy, so that on leaving London he had been able to do more or less what he pleased; and what for some arcane reason had pleased him was to buy an enormous abandoned limestone quarry in the remotest spot he could find, and to build on its floor a massive bespoke ranch-style cedarwood house. This comprised three parts: on the left was a three-car garage; connected to it, by a short covered arcade, was the central mass of the lavish, roomy living quarters; and connected to them, again by an arcade, was a separate block containing three laboratories and an office. Sir John was apparently not a gardener, Boddy said: he had solved the garden problem by surrounding the entire complex of buildings with a wide apron of concrete beyond which the original wild growth was allowed to flourish unchecked, except on rare occasions when men with sickles and billhooks came along to lop off its encroachments on the concrete. The concrete included an elaborate system of gutters and drains to dispose of the rain-water which came pouring down the three sides of the quarry. There were servants living in, Boddy said, but he didn't know how many, and thought they were probably foreign.

And what—Widger reflected, as he twisted the wheel of the Cortina to take the last turn which led to their destination— did this wealthy hermit do with his time? Ah, but Widger knew that. Sir John researched. In his laboratories, he conducted experiments—experiments, moreover, which all bore on his lifelong preoccupation with crime, and more particularly with murder. Widger had always regarded forensic medicine as one of the most interesting aspects of C.I.D. work, and he really did know a good deal more than the average detective about it. The last he had heard, Sir John was currently engaged in mapping on a time chart the degenerative changes in dried blood, with allowance for temperature and other extraneous influences. True, as far as Widger knew he had not yet published anything on the subject, but even so, he seemed the ideal man to deal with the forensic-pathological aspects of the Botticelli murder. Much better, really, than Easton, the County Pathologist: Easton was a good man, but he was kept too busy to do much more than apply the established routines.

And now, here they were.

Sir John had no driveway—simply a gateless finger of the concrete apron which pointed down to the lane. Widger turned into it and ran the car up close to the front door. The place looked deserted; no light showed—but perhaps there were thick curtains on the windows, and they had been carefully drawn.

With the cessation of movement, with the switching off of engine and headlights, Ling roused himself. Widger suspected that he had been asleep. He peered out into the surrounding blackness.

"My God," he said. "Where are we?"

"We've arrived."

"What's the name of this place?"

"It hasn't got a name. It's just a house in a quarry."

"But isn't there a village or anything?"

"No."

"My God," Ling said again. "Talk about the back of beyond...Listen, Charles."

"Yes?"

"I have a hunch that Sir John's evidence is going to be important. It may even be the clincher."

"Yes."

"And we know that Chummy's pretty unscrupulous. He might benefit from killing again."

"Eddie, surely you don't mean that Sir John—"

"Yes, I do, though. If I'd known that Sir John lived miles from anywhere, in a place like *this*, I'd have put a guard on him."

"Oh, but you're being ridiculous," said Widger. "No one would—"

But that was where he stopped, because that was when it happened.

From somewhere behind the house came a long, high-pitched, bubbling, hideous scream.

Ling moved swiftly. He had grabbed Widger's torch from the cubby-hole in the dashboard, and was half way out of the passenger door, before Widger had sufficiently recovered from the unexpectedness of that ghastly cry to be able to make a single move. And once out, Ling switched on the torch and ran, at a pace astonishing in a man of his bulk and years. He pounded over the concrete towards the garage—this being the quickest way to get round to the back—and Widger, at last recovering the use of his limbs, flung himself out of the car and followed. He made the best speed he could; but Ling had a good start, and when he and the torch disappeared round the garage end, Widger was left in almost total darkness, and was forced to slow down. When eventually he groped his way round, he found that Ling, too, had dropped to a walk. He was flashing the torch around him as he went—expecting, presumptively, that it would presently illuminate some ominous dark huddled mass, moribund or dead, lying on the concrete. But there was no such thing. Catching up, Widger saw that the apron lay blank and untenanted all the way along to the laboratories and beyond.

"The bushes," said Ling.

With the escarpment of the quarry looming high above them, they plunged manfully into the tangle of undergrowth: elders, maples, red-leaved spindleberries, hogweed, willowherb, cow parsley, knapweed, stinging nettles. and everywhere the creamy fluffy, feathery fruits of Old Man's Beard; blackthorn which tore shreds from their clothes and lacerated their hands. They got separated, and Widger, torchless, found himself reduced to a mere palpating. At intervals they called out to one another, barely intelligibly, so that Widger was reminded of Horatio and Bernardo and Marcellus trying to pin down the ghost of Hamlet's father on the battlements of Elsinore: "'Tis here!"; "'Tis here!"; "'Tis gone." His first panic abating, Widger, as he stumbled on, realised how useless all this wild thrashing about was. There could have been half a dozen corpses lying in this fecund mish-mash on the quarry floor, and it would still have taken them hours, the way they were going about it, to find even one of them. More or less simultaneously, the same idea seemed to occur to Ling.

"Arc-lamps!" he shouted. "We shall have to get arc-lamps!" But even as he made this recommendation, he lost his footing and pitched head first into a five-foot-high clump of thistles. The torch flew from his hand, and Widger heard the tinkle as it smashed on a stone. They were in darkness again.

Suddenly a door at the back of the house opened, emitting a brilliant oblong of light. Two figures stood framed in the doorway, one of them, Widger was relieved to see, undoubtedly Sir John Honeybourne. Next to him was a much younger, much shorter man, a goblin with a shock of wiry hair and thick pebble glasses. They gazed out into the night; and:

"May I ask," said Sir John equably, "what is going on here?"

Ling scrambled to his feet, and for a moment he and Widger stood there waist-high in the undergrowth like a brace of startled pheasant put up by a game-dog. Then they pulled themselves together and struggled back on to the concrete. They hurried up to the door.

"Sir John?" said Ling. "Thank God you're safe, sir."

"Safe? Safe?" said Sir John. "Of course I'm safe. Why shouldn't I be safe?"

"But didn't you hear that scream, sir?"

"Oh, the scream. Yes, certainly I heard it. One could hardly *not* hear it, could one? Blood-curdling. And you thought that that was I, did you, in the grip of some ruffian or other? Well, it wasn't. I expect," Sir John added, "that it was an owl."

"An owl, sir?" Ling said blankly. Although he was a townee, the suggestion of an owl stretched his credulity to the utmost.

"An owl, yes." Sir John was firm. "Or possibly some other creature *ferae naturae*. At night-times the countryside is full of strange noises, I've found. It doesn't do to worry about them."

"But, sir—"

"Let's see, now, you will be Superintendent Ling."

"Yes, sir. At your service. But—"

"And this other gentleman, whom I've already met, is Inspector Widger."

"Sir," said Widger. He was uncomfortably aware that both he and Ling must look as though they'd just been dragged through a hedge backwards.

"Sir, about this scream—"

"Dear me, Superintendent, you're very persistent, aren't you? But haven't we more important things to do than go chasing after an elusive scream? Tomorrow morning, when there's some light, you may if you wish send a whole squad of men here to turn the place upside down. If they discover a cadaver, it will have come conveniently to the right customer. But they won't. They'll get badly scratched—incidentally, you must let me put some antiseptic on your own scratches—but they won't find anything, except perhaps a cat mangled by a fox. Meanwhile—"

"You're safe, sir," said Ling obstinately, "and this gentleman with you is safe. But how about the rest of your household?"

"I'm a lonely man, Superintendent," said Sir John, exposing his unlovely teeth in a leer, "and there are only two more of us—a married couple who live in and minister to my simple needs. They're Swedes, of course," he added, as though Swedishness were somehow mandatory in domestic servants. "And I've only just this moment been talking to them, so it was neither of them who screamed. But now, we really must get down to business. Where is this head you were supposed to be bringing me? I've been looking forward to sawing the top off that—and let us hope, of course, that it's a fit for the body I have."

Ling gave up. To Widger he said: "Get the sack from the car, Charles, will you, please?"

Widger hastened off, made his way round the side of the garage by brushing his fingers against the cedarwood wall, came in sight of the Cortina's sidelights, reached the car, retrieved the sack from the back seat, turned the sidelights off to save the battery, and with considerable caution—since for the first part of the trip he now had no illumination at all—retraced his steps to the rear of the house. The back door still stood open, but Ling and Sir John and the unidentified goblin had by now got themselves inside, and were waiting for him in a small unfurnished lobby. He joined them.

"Aha!" said Sir John, eyeing the sack. "We'd better go to the laboratories, I think."

He led the way through the bewildering complex of rooms and into the arcade, talking all the time.

"I have been remiss," he said. "Remiss in not introducing you sooner to Mr Morehen here. Superintendent Ling, Inspector Widger, Mr Morehen. I call Mr Morehen my little water fowl."

Mr Morehen spoke for the first time. "Drop dead," he said.

"Mr Morehen," Sir John continued, unperturbed, "is my assistant. My trainee-assistant, I ought to have said. For some reason best known to himself, Mr Morehen wishes to become a morbid pathologist, though he has really no talent for it, none at all."

"Belt up," said Mr Morehen.

"Mr. Morehen, you see, is by temperament not a pathologist, morbid or otherwise. He is a quantitative analyst. Above all, he loves to *measure* things. Give Mr. Morehen anything—absolutely anything—and he will at once measure it for you. Take alcohol."

Since at this point they were passing a sideboard laden with bottles, Widger imagined for one wild moment that they were being offered a drink. But this was apparently not so.

"A good thing you've got me, if you ask me," said Mr Morehen.

"Take alcohol," said Sir John again. "We wish to test blood for its alcohol, so what do we do? We supply ourselves with a millilitre of blood and a millilitre of saturated potassium carbonate solution and we place them in one compartment of a diffusion vessel without allowing them to mix. Then we take a solution of potassium dichromate in sulphuric acid and place it in the *other* compartment. Seizing the sealed vessel, we proceed to mix the two solutions by tilting—and if alcohol is present, the dichromate will turn a charming green. What could be more satisfying? What could be more delightful? But for Mr Morehen, this isn't enough."

"I should think not," said Mr Morehen.

"Mr Morehen wants to know *how much* alcohol. While you are admiring the green, Superintendent, Mr. Morehen is indifferent. He is thinking

$$1.15 \times \frac{(y - z) \times 100}{W} = \text{mg of alcohol per 100 g of blood}"$$

"I never knew you knew," said Mr Morehen.

"Well, these things have to be done, unfortunately," said Sir John. "So in that sense, you could argue that Mr Morehen is really quite useful to have about the place: a sort of purblind human computer. Nor, luckily, does his usefulness end there. For Mr Morehen, Superintendent, is an International Socialist, whatever that may be, and believes in the dignity of manual labour. With him, even more luckily, the manual labour takes the form of disagreeable housework, and his efforts save the poor Hetmans all manner of unpleasant chores, as well as enabling me to economise on wages. I don't say that Mr Morehen isn't rather limited. But within his limits, he's quite a paragon."

"When the Revolution comes," said Mr Morehen, "you'll be one of the first for the lamp-post," and on this affable note they reached the end of the arcade, and Sir John led them into the largest of the three laboratories, where dazzling fluorescent strip lights were burning.

Widger looked about him with interest; but his knowledge of forensic medicine was almost entirely theoretical, and he could make little of what he saw. There were flasks, retorts, blenders, Bunsen burners, rubber hoses, jars with specimens in pickle, microscopes, a fluoroscope, test tubes, surgical instruments—scalpels, scissors, forceps—and an electrically-driven circular saw. At one end of the big room he recognised X-ray equipment—and the utility of that was obvious. So was the utility of the surgical instruments. But as to the rest, Widger could only stare and wonder.

At the centre of it all, on a sort of operating table with guttering and pipes, lay the sheeted figure of the murdered man.

Sir John went up to it and whipped the sheet away.

"Well, here he is," he said cheerfully. "A bit mottled by now, of course, but apart from his paunch, a fine figure of a man. I don't know if you'd like to see his organs? They're in that row of jars over there."

"No, thank you, sir," said Ling. He approached the body gingerly, made a pretence of studying it, choked slightly, backed off and slumped down heavily on a small stool.

Mr Morehen was closely examining the abdominal incision; he almost had his nose in it. "This stitching's a bit of a cock-up," he said.

"You did it yourself," Sir John said.

"I never said I didn't, did I? Ah well, it doesn't matter now." And with this, Mr Morehen appeared to lose interest in the proceedings; he began wandering about the laboratory, picking things up, sniffing at them and putting them down again, not always where he'd got them from.

Sir John went to a bench and swept a lot of chemical glassware to one side with a large hand, in order to clear a space. "Come along, Inspector," he said to Widger. "You can put it here." Widger went across with the sack, deposited it, and retreated again to join Ling. "Well now, gentlemen," said Sir John, "if you'll excuse me, I'll get on with this straight away. I dare say you can find your own way out, or if not, Mr Morehen will take you."

"But sir," Ling bleated.

"Yes, Inspector?"

"There are some questions I need to ask you. I know you gave me a few pointers on the telephone this afternoon, but—"

"Now, now, Superintendent," said Sir John, as if soothing a fractious child. "I'll give it you all in my written report. It'll be on your desk by tomorrow evening at the latest. So you see you've nothing to worry about, nothing at all. Meanwhile, I want to get at this head."

"I'm very sorry, sir," said Ling with unexpected decisiveness, "but there are a few things which just won't wait."

Sir John looked wistfully at the sack. Then he turned away from it with a sigh of long-suffering. "Very well, Superintendent," he said. "But please make it quick, because I want—"

"Quite, sir, quite. First off, how old was he?"

"About forty-five."

"In good shape?"

"Apart from being a little overweight, in very good shape. Muscular. And the condition of the internal organs is excellent."

"Any fractures?"

"None."

"What was his blood group?"

"A, rhesus negative."

"Same as we found on the grass."

"That's a good thing."

"Would he have bled a lot?"

"That depends partly on how he was killed."

"Well, sir, *how* was he killed?"

"Good heavens, man, *I* don't know. If you'd just let me take a look at the head..."

"We think he may have been coshed, sir. Some sort of a blunt instrument."

"You do, do you? Well, I'm afraid I'm not in a position to supply confirmation. Or the opposite. If you'd just let me—"

"If he was coshed, would he have bled a lot?"

"Probably. Scalp wounds usually do bleed a lot. There are exceptions, however. There was that farmer fellow, Routh, for example. I understand that he didn't bleed much."

"Would he have bled a lot when his head was cut off?"

"Since that was done so soon after death, almost certainly yes."

"And you're sure it was done soon after death?"

"Quite sure."

"When his arm was cut off, and the cuts made in his thighs, would he have bled a lot?"

"Probably not."

"And what *was* the time of death? We think," said Ling helpfully, "that it may have been about half past twelve on Friday night."

"Then what you think agrees with the medical evidence."

"When was the arm cut off?"

"Somewhere between two and four on the following afternoon."

It was Ling's turn to sigh. "And there's absolutely no doubt about that, sir?"

"None whatever. The degenerative changes in the blood can be accurately timed, Superintendent."

"What implement was used to cut off the head?"

"I should say a hacksaw."

"Ah!" said Ling. "We found a hacksaw."

"With blood on it?"

"Just traces. But enough."

"Good," said Sir John. "Superintendent, you're home and dry. And now I really think that I ought to—"

"Earlier on, sir, you mentioned alcohol. Had he been drinking?"

"No, he hadn't. And to judge from the state of the liver and the kidneys, he very seldom drank...The scrotum," Sir John threw in as a bonus, "was not collapsed."

"I beg your pardon, sir?"

"I mean, Superintendent, that he had not recently been making passionate love."

"Sounds like a dog's life to me," said Mr Morehen from a far corner. "No drink, no women. And then, look at the *food* he ate!"

"Ah yes, sir," said Ling. "I was just going to ask you about that. When did he have his last meal, and what was it?"

"He had it about three hours before death, Superintendent," said Sir John, "and it was fish and chips. I dare say," he added, "that Mr Morehen could give you the dimensions of the cod fillets, if you were to ask him."

Mr Morehen named items of the male pudenda.

"And now we come to the crux," said Ling. "We've absolutely got to identify the man, and so far, his head is the only hope. *But*, it's been horribly bashed about. I was wondering if there was any hope that you could, so to speak, reconstitute it, with wax or something, so that we could have a photograph to issue to the press."

Sir John considered. "It's just possible," he said cautiously. "It all depends on how bad the damage is. And of course, even if it is possible, it will take me quite a time."

"Of course, sir."

"So now you'd better let me take a look at it, hadn't you?"

"Yes, sir."

Widger sank on to a stool next to Ling's as Sir John, rubbing his hands, crossed to the bench where the sack lay. He was between them and the sack, so that they couldn't see what he was doing as he untied the string and lifted out the contents; but they heard the rustle of the newspapers as he unwrapped them.

There was a long pause.

Then Sir John said, in a curious voice: "I've been underestimating myself, Superintendent. The answer is: yes, I can reconstitute your head for you, quite easily. And then perhaps after that I can have it for my dinner."

Widger froze. "Have it for your..."

But for once, it was Ling who was quicker in the uptake. Six giant strides took him to Sir John's side, with Widger clattering along bemusedly behind.

On the bench—neatly cloven down the middle, eyes closed in the big sleep—lay the head of a small pig.

The drive back to Glazebridge was characterised for the most part by a deathly silence. It was only when they were approaching the police station along the ring-road that Ling at last spoke.

"We've been conned," he said.

"Yes."

"Chummy switched sacks on us."

"Yes."

"When?"

"Well, not before we left the station," said Widger. "Because when I fetched the sack down from my office, I looked."

"It must have been at Sir John's house, then."

"Yes."

"That scream wasn't a real scream. It was a decoy, to draw us away from the car."

"*I* thought it was a real scream," said Widger. "Come to that, so did you. Whoever produced it must be a marvellous actor."

"We oughtn't to have left the car unlocked."

Since there was nothing to be said to this, Widger said nothing.

"Chummy was there waiting for us," said Ling. "He must have had a car, parked out of sight somewhere up the lane, and—Did you hear a car drive off? Afterwards, I mean?"

"No, I didn't. I'd guess that he parked it a good way away. Did you hear one?"

"No. Anyway, he parked his car. Then he hid the substitute sack, with the pig's head, somewhere in the bushes at the front. Then he slipped round to the back, and when he heard us arriving, he produced his scream. Then when we were going round by the garage end, he went back to the front by the laboratory end. Then he switched sacks and crept away to his car. He had plenty of time for all that."

"*Why* did he do it?"

"I suppose he realised, a bit late in the day, that Sir John might be able to make the head recognisable again. And he wasn't going to risk that: better get the thing back and bury it somewhere. Landing us with the pig's head, though, was sheer malice. He was mocking us," Ling said bitterly. "Very sure of himself, is Chummy."

The car turned right off the ring-road into the police station's now deserted car-park. Ling said:

"I take it you realise I'm going to have to ring the Chief and tell him what's happened?"

"Yes."

"He only lives twenty miles away. He'll get straight into his Alfa and drive down here."

"Probably."

"And then—and then—for God's sake, Charles, what is he going to *say*?"

"YOU MEAN TO TELL ME THAT YOU HAD THIS UNFORTUNATE MAN'S HEAD *ACTUALLY IN YOUR POSSESSION*, AND THAT YOU THEN *LOST* IT?"

"It was stolen from us, sir."

"*STOLEN* FROM YOU. AND I SUPPOSE THAT AT THE SAME TIME, YOUR WATCHES WERE STOLEN OFF YOUR WRISTS."

"No, sir."

"SO NOW ALL YOU'RE LEFT WITH IS A PIG'S HEAD. A *PIG'S* HEAD."

"We'll get him, sir, you can be sure of that."

"I CAN, CAN I? SUPERINTENDENT, YOU RELIEVE MY MIND WONDERFULLY. ALL I CAN SAY FOR THE MOMENT IS THAT ALTHOUGH I'VE MET PLENTY OF NUMSKULL COPPERS IN MY TIME, THERE'S NEVER YET BEEN ANYTHING TO COMPARE WITH YOU TWO."

"If you'd just lower your voice a little, sir..."

"I WILL *NOT* LOWER MY—Yes, I will, though," said the Chief Constable reluctantly. "We don't want everybody in the station to know. And you two keep your mouths shut about what's happened, do you hear me? If it gets out, we shall be the laughing-stock of the whole of Devon."

"Sir, we—"

"And just one other thing before I go. I'm giving you a week—one week exactly—to get this mess cleared up to my satisfaction." The Chief Constable stormed to the door of Widger's small office. "After that, it's the Yard—and a fat lot of thanks *I* shall get, for calling them in so late. As for you two," he flung over his shoulder, "you'll be out of the Force and looking for jobs as bank guards. And now, GOOD NIGHT."

He went out, slamming the door furiously behind him. Widger and Ling continued to stand like waxworks until they heard his car roar out of the car-park, and dwindle, and fade away to nothingness. Then Ling moved.

"Come on," he said.

They drove to Mrs Clotworthy's cottage in Burraford's Chapel Lane. Why, yes, Mrs Clotworthy said, she had visited her great-niece a second time; that very morning, in fact, just to make sure that the mother and baby were going along well. And this time, yes, she'd managed to remember about Fen's pig's head. How she could have forgotten it the day before, the Saturday, she really couldn't think. In fact, she was sure she *hadn't* forgotten it: she recalled distinctly putting it out in the porch when Mrs Prendergast came with the news about Sandra. Still, when you gets old, you does go a bit queer in the head, as they, Ling and Widger, no doubt know from their own experience. You think you've done a thing, when actually you haven't; so that was what must have happened to her, yesterday. Today she was sure about, though. She'd been proper flammagasted, this morning, to find the sack there in the corner of her kitchen: couldn't call to mind ever having put it there in the first place. Anyways, she'd took it out to the porch right off, and "'There! I've put you there now, and there you stays till the Perfesser comes and fetches 'ee, see?' I says to it. Then I locks up, and off I goes to Sandra. 'Ad to leave her at dinner-time, because of you making me come into Glazebridge for questions, but I looks in 'ere on me way along, quick-like, and sure enough, sack was gone. 'Ah! Perfesser's got 'ee now, me 'andsome,' I says, and as you'd expect, I was thinking 'e'd say a bit of a thank 'ee when I saw 'im at p'lice station. But no, never a word! 'M.A. or no M.A., that's no real gennulman,' I says to myself. 'That's no'—What? What was that you were—Oh, beg pardon, I'm sure. The sack, yes. Well, that was one I bought months ago, it'd be, from a chap wi' a van driving around 'ere wi' a 'ole pile of 'em for sale, only three pee each. Lots of us 'ad one or more from 'im, they being so useful for so many things. Yes, all the same they were, an' all 'Arris's. Not after that chap for pinchin' of 'em are yer? 'E seemed all right, not that you can ever tell for sure, what with that stuck-up M.A. 'ardly able to give 'ee a civil 'good day', let alone thank 'ee for a lovely pig's 'ead yer 'ubby would 'a' charged three bob for if a penny. But that's life for yer. That's life all along. Folks doan 'ave not a particule o' gratitude in 'em these days, simly."

"That's life for you, all right," said Widger grimly as they got back into the car. "The whole ruddy district smothered in Harris's Bacon sacks. That's going to be a great help, that is."

From Mrs Clotworthy's they went to the Dickinsons' cottage, to see Fen. No, he told them, he was afraid that today he hadn't given the pig's head a thought. Mrs Clotworthy had said that she'd put it out for him today, having apparently forgotten about it yesterday, but in all the excitement and commotion it had slipped his memory: and certainly he'd been nowhere near Mrs Clotworthy's cottage, not today, not a second time. He'd been surprised to find her standoffish, during the gathering of witnesses at the police station, but had thought it wisest not to enquire what the matter was: she was perhaps nervous about the coming interrogation.

"Anyway, where is it?" Fen asked.

"Where's what, sir?"

"My pig's head."

Ling succumbed to a stammering fit. "I—I—It's—" he babbled. "Mrs Clotworthy put it out in her porch this morning, sir, but someone else must have taken it."

"Oh, did they, did they?" said Fen. "What a pity. I was looking forward to making that brawn. Will you have a drink before you go?"

This, however, they refused. As Widger negotiated the Cortina along the narrow lanes which led back to Glazebridge, he said feebly: "Well, at any rate it wasn't the Rector."

"Why not?"

"He would have been in Burraford church, taking Evensong. The Bale sisters said they were going to church, too."

"We'll check on all three of them. We'll put men on it," Ling said vacantly. "A week...Old squire, I think that's about all we can do for today. We'd better find a bite to eat, and then bed. Tomorrow," he said in a phantom recrudescence of his customary optimism, "we'll be fresh, and then we can really get on with it. It was a disaster, losing the head, but we'll get by without it. Let's see now, who knows about the head? Us two; the Chief—but he's much too proud to blab; and Sir John and that Morehen. Well, *they* won't blab either, because before we left I told them how important it was not to, and they agreed. At the end," he said rather pitifully, "I think they were really quite sorry for us...So although I don't imagine the business can be kept under wraps indefinitely, nothing ought to come out about it for a week at the very least."

But he had reckoned without Detective-Sergeant Crumb.

Crumb had spent the morning laboriously typing out a vandalism report, about a smashed shop window; this was because Rankine was in the room with him. But then Rankine had gone out somewhere, detecting, and Crumb had forthwith abandoned his activity, put his feet up on his desk, and immersed himself in a paperback Mickey Spillane. This, and the lunch hour, had occupied him pleasantly until three o'clock, his usual hour for going home.

Unfortunately, he forgot to take the Spillane with him, and when evening came, and he was settled comfortably in front of a broiling fire, he found himself without diversion. He might have watched television, but he was too mean to have a set, though he could well have afforded one; and he had long since ceased paying any attention to his wife's conversation. Nothing but Spillane would do. With a great deal of grumbling, Crumb heaved himself out of his chair and returned to the police station, arriving there just in advance of the Chief Constable.

It took him a little time to find his book, and he was just about to make off with it when he heard voices raised in Widger's office. Curious, he tip-toed across to the connecting door and glued his ear to it. And what he heard, he understood perfectly.

Crumb was delighted. He nourished a consuming hatred of all his superiors, and of Widger in particular, and it was wonderful to know that they had been so humiliatingly laid low. Waiting only until Widger's office finally emptied, he hurried home again and with much lip-smacking and thigh-slapping told his wife all about it. Then he settled back to his diet of sex and sadism, still chuckling occasionally, and his wife, who knew that there would be nothing more to be got out of him before bedtime, went out to have a cup of tea with a neighbour.

Mrs Crumb was an inveterate gossip, and it was too much to expect that she wouldn't pass on to the neighbour what she had heard. That neighbour told another neighbour, and that one, another. The news spread like flame through parched bracken.

By mid-week, practically everybody in Glazebridge and district knew that Widger and Ling had lost the head.

CHAPTER TEN

Wasp Chewing

A wild and dream-like trade of Blood and Guile
Too foolish for a Tear, too wicked for a Smile!

Samuel Taylor Coleridge: *Ode to Tranquillity.*

T HE INVESTIGATION languished.

Thanks to Ling's Sunday-afternoon arrangements, and to his press conference, Monday morning's papers presented a strange spectacle. The Botticelli murder was sensational enough, in all conscience, and all of the public sheets, even *The Times*, gave it extensive coverage. But they differed widely as to detail, and were often mutually contradictory. Reporters continued to hang about the district, causing the Major's antennae to quiver; Ling, however, avoided them as far as possible, and when a confrontation was inevitable, faithfully ground out "No comment". They tried to get at Sir John, but he never seemed to leave his house, or to be willing to talk on the telephone, and not one of them managed to make contact with him. Mr Morehen was once accidentally discovered at a mass Trotskyist rally in Glazebridge (five people), but seemed to have forgotten so completely about the Botticelli murder that his interviewer, who at first had had great hopes, was in the end obliged to write him off as an incurable mooncalf. That really left only Ticehurst, to whom Ling occasionally communicated scraps of useless, almost entirely negative intelligence; and from these, Ticehurst, looking far from his normal self, was obliged to construct such frail edifices of melodrama as he could. To him both Widger and Rankine (holding himself in with the greatest difficulty) referred all queries; while Crumb—resentful, morose and surly at the ever-increasing additions to his normally inconsiderable work-load—simply refused to say anything at all, consoling himself, so far as that was possible, with the knowledge that news of the loss of the head had got about, branding both Widger and Ling forever as incompetent cretins.

For the reporters, it was a barren time.

Nor, on the Tuesday, were they helped by the inquest, which ran for about ten minutes before the Coroner, at Ling's urgent request, adjourned it for three weeks. There was evidence of the finding of the body, from Titty Bale, from Luckraft and from Widger. But there was no evidence of identification, no mention of the cause of death, no medical detail; and the Coroner, sitting without a jury, refrained even from saying that he thought it was murder, even though so evidently it had been. He released the body, still armless and headless, for burial, and on the Thursday it was taken from Sir John's laboratory and put underground, hugger-mugger in the cheapest possible coffin, in Glazebridge churchyard. The Rector attended, to conduct the graveside service, the Press attended, a bored-looking constable attended, and so did a variety of sensation-seekers unconnected with the case. There were no mourners, however, so that the whole business was conducted briskly and with despatch. The one wreath, unticketed, was discovered much later to have been sent by Dermot McCartney, less in a spirit of grief than because he believed that the conventions of his adopted country must be observed at all costs.

Meanwhile, the police had been furiously busy—and with absolutely no significant results. Widger thought that there could never have been a case with so many possible leads and so little to show for them.

Reluctantly, the Chief Constable had agreed that extra men were needed, and these had been drafted in, so fulfilling Widger's nightmare vision of the district (Burraford and its surroundings especially) overrun as if by a plague of blowflies. The extra men conducted house to house interrogations; they sought to identify the two strangers who had passed time in the Botticelli tent during the Fête; they searched out-houses for recently used spades and for blood-stained hammers; they combed fields and woodlands and gardens and lane verges for freshly turned earth; they rummaged for blood-stained clothes; they questioned everyone who might have noticed a car, either at Aller House about midnight on the Friday, or in Sir John Honeybourne's lane between six and seven on the Sunday (they were not, however, given any reason for this latter question); they reported and reported and reported, triggering off numerous false alarms, all of which had to be checked and none of which proved to be the slightest use. Widger's small office became a crowded welter of loose papers, files, extra telephones and extra furniture; and in the room adjoining, Rankine and Crumb found themselves hemmed in similarly. Rankine bustled about importantly, insisting on reading even the most hollow, inconsequential and negative bulletins out aloud in their entirety. Crumb, the lethargic tenor of his ways grossly disrupted, was several times forced to remain at his desk until six or even seven. The placid routine of the Glazebridge C.I.D. had never before—not even for Mavis Trent, not even for Routh—been so horridly deranged.

And the week wore on, and nothing came of any of it: victim and murderer alike remained obstinately unidentified.

Missing Persons was no good; the C.R.O. was no good; Forensic was no good. True, Forensic did come up with the information that the sack from which Sir John had taken the pig's head had at some stage been employed for storing potatoes (Arran Pilot, Forensic rather thought), and that the string which tied it at the neck bore faint traces of a common brand of engine oil, and this intelligence led, on the Thursday, to those who grew their own potatoes, or had private garages, or both, being investigated all over again, again without significant results. Interviewed by Ling, the bacon factory stated that it had used the same sort and size of sack for as long as it could remember, and that there must be hundreds of them knocking about; interviewed by a Detective-Constable from the Met., the manufacturers of the sack stated that they had used the same materials for their sacks for as long as *they* could remember, and that it was impossible to assign a date to any particular one. Police frogmen plunged into the depths of the Burr and the Glaze, coming up again with assorted irrelevant debris, and there were even a couple of dogs with their handlers, though what these animals were expected to do, since they had been trained simply to knock people down or to bite them, passed Widger's comprehension. The witnesses were all questioned a second time, this time in more detail, but failed altogether to cast any fresh light on the problem. There were only two more days to go before the Chief Constable's ultimatum expired on the Sunday, and Widger and Ling were still no further forward than they had been at evening on the previous Sunday.

Not surprisingly, they became increasingly morose, their morale markedly lowered by the realisation—which had been bound to come in the end—that the news of the victim's head's being cheekily filched from them—had somehow leaked. Ling took this very badly indeed. He slunk about the station throwing furtive glances over his shoulder at the men of the uniform branch (who remained, in his presence, conscientiously wooden-faced), in deadly fear that he would catch someone jeering at him behind his back; after the Wednesday, he went out increasingly seldom, pre-empting Widger's desk chair for most of the day and endlessly re-reading reports; he even abated his smoking. And Widger, though not quite so disastrously affected, was none the less a thoroughly unhappy man. By the Friday, they were scarcely speaking to one another.

A dun fog of depression had settled on them, and nothing at all came along to dissipate it.

There seemed to be only one frail hope left.

Unlike the majority of policemen, Widger had no great objection to, or contempt for, amateur detectives, so long as they didn't meddle with evidence or get under the feet of the authorities. If they could solve crimes by just sitting in their armchairs thinking, the best of British luck to them. There had been some business about an Oxford toyshop, Widger remembered. Other things too, though the details escaped him for the moment...

Wan and exhausted from lack of sleep, Widger lunched that Friday at home with his wife. He kept silence, and, being a sensible woman, so did she. Lunch over, he kissed her, returned to the police station, and climbed the stairs to his office. Here, as expected, he found Ling established behind the desk. He was leafing listlessly through a bundle of colour photographs of the body in the Botticelli tent and of its surroundings. On Widger's entrance, he neither raised his head nor spoke. Widger regarded him sadly for a moment. Then, without himself speaking, he turned round and left the office quietly.

He went to where the police cars were parked, got into his Cortina, and drove out alone to Aller to talk to Gervase Fen.

Fen was not thinking about the murder.

Instead, he was smoking a cigarette and reading *The Times Literary Supplement*—nowadays vulgarly retitled T.L.S, without even a full stop after the "S"—one of three special issues given over to modern Albanian poetry. The warm, sunny weather continuing, he was doing this in a deck chair on the Dickinsons' side lawn. Ellis the tortoise had not been glimpsed for twenty-four hours or more, and conceivably was making a second attempt to hibernate; Stripey the cat had absented himself on one of his priapic itineraries. To the right of the deck chair, on the grass, lay Fowles, John, and Taylor, Elizabeth, temporarily discarded. To its left stood a transistor radio, which was emitting, and indeed had been emitting for some considerable time, a symphonic movement of vaguely romantic cast; from the movement's excessive length, vacuity and derivativeness, Fen judged it to be by Mahler. In the distance, and out of sight, the Pisser was making a new kind of noise, suggestive of a small cataract harbouring a swarm of hornets. And from close to Fen's ear came a tiny scrunching sound, the product of a late wasp which for reasons best known to itself was boring determinedly into the woodwork of the deck chair's side support.

What with all these things, and the modern Albanian poetry, the atmosphere was decidedly soporific.

Fen was not thinking about the murder because since Monday he had been working quite hard at his book. He had had to go to Glazebridge police station a second time, but his only visitors at home had been his daily, Mrs Bragg, and on one occasion the Major. Apart from the trip to Glazebridge, he had stayed put.

"Edna O'Brien," he muttered, "is the Cassandra of female eroticism." Certainly Edna O'Brien's women didn't seem to get much fun out of sex. If he were they, he would give it up altogether.

A car crept up the Dickinsons' stony drive towards him, and he roused himself to look at it. It was being driven by Detective-Inspector Widger, he saw, and he was on his own. More questions, presumably.

Widger caught sight of Fen over the low beech hedge. He stopped the car opposite the little gate which gave access to the lawn, climbed out, passed the gate, and headed for the deck chair. Fen extinguished Mahler's violins by means of a useful knob and got up to greet his visitor.

He offered a drink or tea or coffee. He offered the deck chair. Widger politely refused them all, easing himself down on to the grass with a little sigh of contentment.

"It's restful here," he said.

Not quite the usual official visit, Fen thought, relapsing into the deck chair, where the wasp was still scrunching away. Not at all an official visit, in fact, for now Widger fell silent, gazing out across the countryside; he was wondering if this was a sort of betrayal—and wondering, too, how he was going to open the conversation. He was very tired, and tiredness had congealed his normal modest self-assurance.

The ensuing pause lasted for so long that in the end Fen decided he had better help. He said non-committally, "I hope the case is going well."

"It isn't."

"I'm sorry."

"It's a devil of a business," said Widger with slightly more animation. Relaxing a little, he thrust out his legs and fixed his eyes on his toe-caps. "Slippery, you see—nothing at all you can get a grip on."

"Yes, I can imagine it's difficult. Have you identified the body?"

"No, we haven't."

"Oh," said Fen—and was glad that Widger, looking away from him in the general direction of Burraford, was unable to see the surprise on his face.

And with that, suddenly Widger's tongue was loosened. Driving over, he had planned this interview carefully: he would be casual, confident; above all, he would preserve a decent reticence. But now, all at once, his good resolutions were swept away. His embarrassment dropped from him, and he found himself talking; and talking; and talking. Sprawled on the grass, he told Fen every detail of the case—everything that he and Ling had seen and heard and done, balking only at the visit to Sir John Honeybourne and the switching of the sacks. Fen, however, noting his hesitation, at this point interrupted for the first and only time.

"Yes, I know you lost the head," he said mildly. "Very bad luck. Still, it could have happened to anyone—and I certainly don't see what else you could have done. The Major told me," he explained. "He didn't say where he got it from—but I have an idea that by now it's common knowledge, even if the details are a bit vague."

For a moment nervous again, Widger lapsed unconsciously into a childhood Devonism. "You must," he said, "be thinking we're a pair of girt dawbakes."

"I don't think that at all. Please go on."

And Widger, his conscience relieved of the burden of treachery, did go on. He went on, all told, for over two hours—and because his eyes were averted, missed the one or two occasions when Fen's brows lifted. At the end of his recital he was hoarse, and tireder than ever, but he felt purged; though he hadn't been behaving in the least like a responsible officer of the law, he didn't care a damn. If the Chief didn't sack him on Sunday, he was due to retire soon anyway. And as to Eddie, to hell with Eddie. The probability was that he would never get to hear about this visit, and even if he did, and turned nasty about it, let him do his worst.

Widger stretched luxuriously, and swivelled his head to grin at Fen.

"Well, that's it, sir," he said cheerfully if indistinctly. "Any comments?"

Fen said, "I think that now you *do* need that drink." He went into the cottage to fetch whisky, and when he returned, the two of them sat sipping for a space in companionable silence. Finally Fen said:

"You were right. It *is* slippery. For one thing, although it's a very far-out guess, I suspect that you have *two* murderers to look for."

"*Two*, sir?"

"Yes. One for Routh (and I don't mean Hagberd), and another for Mavis Trent and the man in the Botticelli tent."

"Any proof of that, sir?"

"No. As I say, it's a guess. And I don't at all know who killed Routh. But as regards the Botticelli murderer, I can make a rather closer guess."

"Again, sir—any proof?"

"Nothing that would really satisfy you, Inspector."

Widger swallowed his disappointment, telling himself that he had never really had any great expectations.

"On the other hand," said Fen, "our Botticelli murderer has been going to a good deal of trouble and risk to muddy the waters. He's been trying to prevent, or at any rate delay, the identification of his second victim."

"Agreed, sir." This was a conclusion Widger had come to himself.

"Which in turn means that identification would point to him alone."

"Yes, sir. I agree again. But we've tried everything. We've—"

"No, you haven't Inspector. It ought to be perfectly easy to identify that body."

Widger stared incredulously. "But, sir, how?"

"Just by making some telephone calls."

"I think, sir," said Widger, "that perhaps you'd better explain."

Fen explained. And Widger scrambled to his feet with as much celerity as if his host had picked up the radio and hurled it at him.

"But that means—"

"Yes."

"It means that the way the arm was smuggled out of the tent—"

"Yes."

In high agitation, Widger said, "I must get back to the station, sir. At once. I must—I must make a start on that tele-phoning you suggested." Recovering something of his official manner, he said, "Well, you've been most helpful, sir. Very helpful indeed. Thank you. And thank you for the whisky."

"You haven't finished it."

Widger picked up his glass, drained it at a gulp, and put it down again. He rushed back to his car, and Fen watched in some amusement as he turned it in the space in front of the cottage, and headed down the narrow driveway towards the lane. He was still in sight when a slight hitch occurred. For Fen had more visitors, on foot, stumbling excitedly up the driveway towards him. They were Thouless, Padmore and the Major, and they all looked as if they had been drinking. Confronted with Widger's Cortina, they temporarily lost their heads. The Major hobbled rapidly to one side, Padmore and Thouless to the other. It was evident that Widger was not going to be able to squeeze between them, so Thouless caught Padmore by the sleeve and dragged him to where the Major was, while at the same time the Major crossed to join *them*; the situation, though reversed, thus remained as difficult as ever. Padmore now decided to make a rapid traverse and align himself with the Major, but Thouless, while calling out to him irritably, seemed equally firmly determined to remain where he was. So it was still deadlock. Finally, all three of them made up their minds to move simultaneously, and collided in a clump at the centre of the driveway, where they stood irresolutely, blocking Widger's progress altogether.

Widger slowed down. He honked his horn. Eventually, he was compelled to come to a stop. He wound down the driver's window and thrust his face out, saying, "Will you get out of the way," and this broke the paralysis. Thouless, Padmore and the Major all huddled themselves into the same side at once, and Widger scraped past them, disappearing into the lane with an irate roar of his exhaust. With him gone, they hurried on up the driveway to where Fen was waiting for them on the lawn, and flung themselves down around him on the green.

"That was Widger," said the Major. "We ought to have told him."

"We phoned the police," said Padmore, "so there was no need."

"What's happening?" Fen asked. "What is all this about?"

Thouless snorted. "You may well ask. Heavens, what an afternoon! I drank too much gin, for one thing, and that never does me any good. It gives me a headache. In fact, I can feel the headache coming on now." He dredged in a pocket, producing from it a box of non-ethical, and indeed totally inefficacious, tranquillisers, such as could be bought without a prescription across the counter of any chemist's. "Here, have a CWYETEWD." He offered the box around, but there were no takers, so he ended by cramming a handful of the small white pills into his own mouth. And the Major, who seemed marginally soberer than the other two, said to Fen:

"We thought we really must come and tell you, my dear fellow. It's Ortrud Youings. She's bolted."

All three of them tried to tell the story simultaneously, so that a good deal of confusion and squabbling resulted. In its main outlines, however, it emerged clearly enough.

That afternoon, Padmore and the Major had dropped in on Thouless for a drink and a chat. They had originally had no intention of staying very long, but Thouless had been pleased at having an excuse for not going on composing bugaboo music in his hut in the garden, and the revels had prolonged themselves, as these things will. Then at shortly after four the front door bell had rung, violently and repeatedly, and Thouless—euphoric from gin and from the prospect of expanding the party—had gone to answer it, finding himself confronted on the doorstep with a large, bloodied, bruised, hairy young man, dressed in blue jeans and an imitation leather jerkin, and with great grubby bare feet. This vision was at first so agitated as to be barely articulate, mumbling, "Fuzz! Fuzz! Telephone! Ambulance! Help me!" and "Oh, my God!" But Thouless nevertheless conducted him into the living-room with its bust of Cumberland, there compelling him to lie down on a sofa while he supplied witch hazel for the bruises, iodine for the cuts and grazes, and brandy for the stomach. Recovering partially, and watched with acute interest by Thouless's other two guests, the young man presently managed to raise himself on one elbow and speak rather more lucidly.

"Fuzz," he said. "We must telephone for the fuzz. And for an ambulance. Oh, my God, if I'd ever realised what a ghastly bitch she was—"

"There, there," Thouless soothed him. "You're quite all right here. The danger's over."

"No, it's not," said the young man. "Not so long as that dreadful woman's on the loose. I can't think what possessed me. I can't think why I didn't see through her. Oh, my God."

"Have some more brandy," said Thouless, pouring. "Why don't you tell us quickly what's happened, and *then* we'll telephone."

The young man looked at Padmore and the Major. "Who *are* these people?" he said suspiciously.

"Visitors."

"And who are you?"

"My name's Thouless."

"You must know her, you live so near. Perhaps you're a friend of hers. Perhaps you're *all* friends of hers. Perhaps you're in league. Perhaps you're hiding her out here. Oh, my God."

"We're not hiding anyone out," said Thouless a shade impatiently. "Come on, man, come on. Tell us what's happened. Have you been knocked over by a car?"

"If only it was just that," the young man moaned. "If only I'd never set eyes on her. Oh, my God." He mastered himself with an effort, again made an inventory of the room, and apparently concluded, with reluctance, that he'd have to trust them. The whole story—not a very lengthy or complicated one—came pouring out.

He was a student from the University, he said, and had recently been having a bang with Ortrud Youings; his name, aptly enough, was John Thomas. He did not dilate on how and where he had first met Ortrud, but simply said that she had invited him to come and stay. Her husband, she told him, was away, so they could have a delightful, *höchst erfreulich*, time together; and since (his hearers gathered) Thomas had so far made no great mark with his studies, he had felt no compunction about putting the University behind him for a week or two, and accepting the invitation. Though Thomas had had no notion of this, to her meek and doting husband Ortrud had simply said, as on a number of previous occasions, that she was going to move a man into the house; and grief-stricken but obedient as ever, he had taken himself off to the flatlet over Clarence Tully's stables. Thomas had at first been slightly surprised to see a large, blond man drive up to the pig-farm every day in a battered black Volkswagen, and attend lovingly to the pigs. He had concluded, however, that this was an employee, and soon dismissed the matter from his mind.

At first, all had gone well. Ortrud was a good cook, and had had not the slightest objection to her lover's lounging in bed for most of the day, reading light fiction or slumbering. But her sexual demands were heavy, and Thomas, though young and strong, had found it more and more exhausting to keep pace with them: he had begun to pine, to imagine lethal ailments, to find it increasingly difficult to do the simplest thing without getting giddy spells. He had begun to think wistfully that the University syllabus was less demanding than he had previously imagined. On the other hand, he was much too afraid of Ortrud to make a unilateral break. He could only hope that she would quickly get tired of him, and make the break herself; and since he was becoming alarmingly subject to impotence, there did seem to be a very real hope that she would shortly do this.

It was at this stage, on the Friday afternoon, that Youings, who had come as usual to attend to the pigs, made the mistake of entering the house; he had needed a clean shirt, and had thought that he could abstract one from the bedroom without arousing notice. Creeping in at the front door, which gave on a combined entrance hall and parlour, he had discovered Ortrud and Thomas there entangled in an embrace, and for some reason this had proved too much even for his infatuation. He had embarked on a mild remonstrance, but had never had the chance to finish it. For Ortrud was enraged at seeing him. Thrusting Thomas from her arms, she had picked up a heavy poker from among the fire-irons and had hit her husband a colossal blow on the head with it, flooring him.

It had all happened too quickly for Thomas to do anything about it; he had witnessed the assault aghast; all he knew was that he must get away from this terrible woman as rapidly as possible. Moreover, he knew now that this big, blond man was not an employee, but was married to Ortrud. He, Thomas, had been ruthlessly deceived. He stood there paralysed by dread while Ortrud bent over the body on the floor, favoured it with a cursory inspection, and straightened up again, the poker still in her hand.

"*Tod*," said Ortrud sepulchrally. "He has gone to his fathers."

"Oh, my God," said John Thomas.

He himself looked at the sprawled figure, and although he had little experience of such things, it occurred to him, sanguinely, that this victim of Ortrud's impulsiveness, even if very seriously injured, might not actually be dead: for one thing, his head was still bleeding freely. Ortrud, however, had no such *arrière-pensées*: she must clear out of here, and fast. Pausing only a moment to arrive at her decision, she seized John Thomas in an iron grip, propelled him hapless into the small, stone-walled downstairs lavatory, threw down the poker beside him, and before he could collect himself, had locked him in and taken the key away.

His first reaction had been one of relief: here, he felt, was at least a temporary refuge. He heard Ortrud climb the stairs, heard her bumping about in the bedroom—packing, presumably; heard her come down again (and at this he cringed, deadly afraid that she was proposing to fetch him out); heard her leave the house (relief, relief!), clamber into the Volkswagen and start it up. Peering with precaution out of the lavatory's little window, he watched the car drive away. He even had the presence of mind to take its number, which he wrote down on a piece of lavatory paper with a stub of pencil he luckily happened to have on him.

Apart from the intermittent grunting and squealing of the pigs, the farm was mercifully quiet.

And now Thomas began to gather his wits together again. He must somehow get out, he must somehow escape. Moreover, there was the matter of the unfortunate husband who was still, in all likelihood, lying gory and unconscious on the floor of the entrance hall: patently he needed a doctor and an ambulance, and it was up to him, Thomas, to summon these aids as fast as possible. He tried the door, but it was solid and unyielding. He fished in his pockets for some implement to unscrew the lock, but they yielded nothing. It had to be the window, then. Balanced precariously on the lavatory seat, Thomas put his head out and called, "Help! Help! Oh, my God, help!" He did this for some time, as loudly as he could, but no one came.

Nothing for it, then, but to try to get *out* of the window.

Unhappily, the house was old, and the window consequently diminutive.

Thomas struggled and heaved and pushed, eventually managing to get his head and shoulders outside. But here he got stuck, his upper parts projecting like a gargoyle's from a church tower, his legs waving feebly inside. A further interval passed while he remained in this uncomfortable position. Then, summoning up the last of his resolution and valiantly disregarding the pain to which he was subjecting himself, he began to wriggle systematically. At first he thought that that was going to be no good, either. But his shoulders were wider than his waist or his buttocks, and presently he found that he was moving. As he re-doubled his efforts, he soon found, indeed, that since there was nothing for him to hold on to, he was moving altogether too quickly for safety. But by then it was too late to stop, and finally he emerged from the window like a cork from a bottle, and fell heavily on the paving below.

He was grazed and bruised and stunned. By good chance there were no bones broken, however, and after a minute or two he lurched to his feet, looking round him wildly for assistance. Through a rift in the trees, he caught sight of the roof of Thouless's bungalow. Making as much speed as his injuries allowed, he left the pig-farm and hastened down the lane towards it.

And here he was.

Rousing themselves hastily from the morbid fascination induced by this saga. Thouless, Padmore and the Major all went into action. The Major set out at once for the pig-farm, to see if there was anything he could do for poor Youings. Thouless, lingering only to snatch the piece of lavatory paper with the car number which was still clutched crumpled in Thomas's still tremulous hand, made for his telephone and rang Sergeant Connabeer at the desk in Glazebridge police station, giving him a succinct, accurate account of what had happened, and asking for an ambulance; this done, he adjured Thomas to remain resting on the sofa, and hurried after the Major. Padmore, having grabbed the telephone when Thouless was finished with it, dictated the story to the *Gazette* and then followed the other two. They found Youings barely conscious, and did what they could for him until the ambulance arrived and he was carried out to it. The Major remonstrated with the ambulance men: surely, he said, nothing ought to be done until the police arrived. But the ambulance men merely shook their heads. They knew a critical injury when they saw one, and this wouldn't wait. They drove Youings away to the Glazebridge Hospital, and the three rescuers were left kicking their heels, with nothing more that they could do.

Eventually, the police still not arriving, they had posted on up the lane to the Dickinsons' cottage, to put Fen in the picture.

"So that's it, my dear fellow," said the Major, who had gained control of the latter part of the narrative. "Terrible woman, terrible. I hope they catch her. And I do hope that poor silly Youings is going to recover."

"But what a story!" said Padmore. "On top of everything else, what a *story*! I'm sure the *Gazette* won't send me back to Africa now, after all I've done for them here. They're absolutely bound to assign me to Crime."

"My headache's worse," said Thouless.

The sun was low in the west. Abandoning its activity for the day, the wasp on the deck chair settled on the lobe of Fen's ear, stung him, and flew away. Leaving the others still sitting on the grass. Fen went into the cottage to see if the Dickinsons had any blue bag.

Meanwhile, in Glazebridge that afternoon, there had been a great brouhaha of which none of them heard until later, when Padmore got a statement out of a revivified Ticehurst, and after ringing the *Gazette* again, passed it on to the others.

At 2.15, Widger left the police station and drove to Aller to see Fen.

At 3.15, Ling, jaded and despondent, sneaked out, appropriated a police car, and sought out an unpopulated stretch of country where he went for a slow, melancholic walk in the woods, revolving in his mind the Chief Constable's ultimatum and all the other injustices of life.

At 4.30, Sergeant Connabeer at the desk received Thouless's telephone call.

At 4.35, having vainly searched the building for Widger or Ling, Connabeer hurriedly entered the room where Rankine and Crumb were working. After one look at Crumb, he summoned Rankine out into the corridor and gave him the gist of Thouless's message.

Rankine was highly gratified. Despite being outranked by Crumb, it was evidently he, Rankine, who for the time being was going to be in charge of this fresh development, and he was determined to make a success of it. Pausing only to ask Connabeer to send an ambulance to the pig-farm, and to put out a general alarm for Ortrud and the Volkswagen, he borrowed a constable, a Panda and a jemmy and drove off towards Aller at a great pace, beguiling the constable, as they went, with a homily on the principles of safe motoring. On the Burraford side of Hole Bridge, however, they received a check: the Panda came to a halt, and was found on investigation to have run out of petrol. Despatching the constable to fetch a spare can from wherever he could, Rankine sat fretting, constantly on the look-out for Ortrud, but thinking it unlikely, if she were trying to escape, that the rascally woman would have taken this particular route. There was no traffic. Once an ambulance from Glazebridge swept past, ignoring Rankine's signals and cries, and fifteen minutes later it came back again in the opposite direction, going faster than ever and still obstinately disregardful. Rankine paced up and down beside the Panda, gnawing at his nails and sometimes talking to himself.

After about twenty minutes the constable came back with petrol borrowed from a reluctant householder, and they got on the move again. The pig-farm was deserted, but the pool of blood on the entrance hall floor restored Rankine's spirits, and with great energy he went to work with the jemmy on the locked lavatory door, forcing it open eventually with a loud detonation and a shower of oak splinters. Inside, he found the poker, wrapped it carefully to preserve fingerprints, took a quick look round and then, notebook at the ready, conveyed the constable—who apart from fetching the petrol had contributed nothing yet, and was destined to remain thus unemployed throughout—down to Thouless's bungalow, intent on getting preliminary statements from Thouless himself and, more importantly, from John Thomas. But here he was brought to a stand, for the bungalow too was deserted. Revived by Thouless's brandy, and in any case thoroughly apprehensive at being left alone, John Thomas had decided to escape, and was already hitch-hiking his way back to the congenial familiarity of the University campus. It not occurring to Rankine to visit the Dickinsons' cottage and find out if Fen had anything to say, he wandered round the outside of the bungalow, baffled and perplexed and peering in at windows, tried the doors, which were all locked (the front door had locked itself automatically on John Thomas's departure), and at length, reluctantly concluding that he had better report to Widger, drove the Panda back to Glazebridge police station, arriving there just in time to witness, and even assist in, the arrest.

At 5.00, since Rankine had not come back, Detective-Sergeant Crumb judged that it was time for him to go home. Preparing himself with some disingenuous excuse for the interruption, he tapped on the door of Widger's office, and on receiving no reply, opened it and glanced in. The room was empty. Good. Crumb put on the overcoat which he wore even in the warmest weather, and went confidently downstairs.

Here, an impulse which he was shortly to regret led him to stop for a few minutes for a gossip with Sergeant Connabeer; and Connabeer, who had been longing for a confidant and was even willing that it should be Crumb, gave him all the details of Thouless's telephone call. Crumb paid relatively little attention to these, but inevitably some of them stuck, and he was as well primed as he was capable of being when he emerged from the station, crossed the car-park to the ring-road, and stood there on the pavement for a moment, waiting for the traffic to allow him to cross. Immediately to the right of the car-park's entrance, the Gas Board's hole in the road had deepened, he saw; the three men delving in it were now penned in by tarmac up to their shoulders. It was surrounded by small cones, feebly lit up at nights, but although only single-line traffic could pass it, it was not yet extensive enough for the Board to have put up temporary traffic lights.

As Crumb stood on the pavement close to this hole, he looked first down the road, towards Glazebridge town, and then up it, in the Burraford direction. And from the Burraford direction he saw approaching a battered black Volkswagen such as he dimly remembered Connabeer's having described to him a minute or two ago. It was being driven by a large young woman with blonde hair assembled in a bun at the back. No one knew, either then or afterwards, what was in Ortrud Youings's mind. The best guess was that, in her instant determination to escape after hitting her husband on the head with the poker, she had originally set out from the pig-farm in the direction opposite to Glazebridge, intending to get to a port or an airport, and so leave the country; but that then, in an access of low cunning, she had changed her plans and circled round through the lanes *into* Glazebridge, arguing that her pursuers would not expect her to do this and so would be thrown completely off the scent. Anyway, whatever the reason, here she was on the ring-road close to the police station; and here too was Crumb, watching her approach.

Crumb had long sight. He could make out the Volkswagen's number as it came nearer, and there was no doubt in his mind that it resembled, roughly, the number which Connabeer had mentioned to him, and to which he had paid such scant attention at the time. Suddenly madness seized him. Policemanly instincts which he had thought buried thirty years deep abruptly reasserted themselves. Single-handed, he would make an arrest—an *important* arrest. It would be a good mark on his undistinguished, indeed dubious, record. He might even, he thought maniacally, be awarded the Police Medal. He might even, he thought even more maniacally, get promotion and swell his impending pension. Yes, he, Crumb, would make an arrest. He would be the hero of the hour...

Besides, it was only a woman. Arresting a woman would be a piece of cake.

Crumb moved. He moved faster than he could ever recall moving before. He planted himself on the ring-road between the Gas Board's hole and the opposite pavement, directly in the path of the oncoming car, and held up an imperious hand.

The Gas Board men suspended their labours to regard this tableau with fugitive interest; they were not, however, given the opportunity to contemplate it for more than a few brief seconds, for the Volkswagen was only a short distance from Crumb, and still moving at an undiminished speed, when it was suddenly borne in on Crumb, on a wave of dread, that it wasn't going to stop. Instead, it was going to run him down.

He hurled himself on to the pavement with only inches to spare, and stood there gasping with indignation and relief. The Volkswagen drew level with him, passed him, and then with a strident squealing of brakes stopped. As Crumb started forward to apprehend its driver, it suddenly and rapidly reversed. Then it came forward again, mounting the pavement with a jolt and once more heading towards Crumb. The Gas Board men scrambled out of their hole and stood gazing in paralytic bemusement. Cars approaching from both directions scented imminent disaster, possibly a pile-up, and came to a halt. As to Crumb, he remained gazing at the Volkswagen in dazed incredulity for a moment, and then turned on his heel and ran. The woman was *mad*! She was out to *kill* him! Crumb had never experienced such horror in all the days of his career.

Crumb ran and the Volkswagen, its off-side wheels in the gutter and its near-side wheels on the pavement, inexorably followed. True, in this condition it couldn't go quite so fast as on the road, but it could still go quite fast enough to overtake Crumb, and that in no very long space of time. Crumb heard its engine roaring immediately behind him, and knew that short of a miracle he was lost. In a last frantic attempt to save himself, he turned, and as the front fender caught him agonisingly on the shins, flung himself on to the Volkswagen's sloping bonnet, where he lay spread-eagled, clutching the windscreen wipers to hold himself on.

Ortrud Youings was annoyed: this silly man had tried to stop her, and her attempts to dispose of him had so far failed. Moreover, he was obstructing her view. Moreover, the Volkswagen was a rotten little car; she needed something much bigger and faster, with better acceleration, and through her rear-view mirror she could see just the thing, immobile at the head of a queue of several other vehicles back along the road. With a bump which she hoped would dislodge Crumb, but which didn't, she drove back off the pavement. With a violent swerve which she again hoped would dislodge him, but which again didn't, she performed a U-turn, ending up facing the way she had come from. Meanwhile, Crumb, aspiring to throw himself clear before the car gained speed again, had contrived to raise himself acock on one elbow. Eyeball to eyeball with Ortrud through the windscreen, he was now blocking her vision entirely. Wavering and yawing wildly, the Volkswagen first lost momentum and then, with a noise like a bomb going off, dived head first into the Gas Board's hole.

The by now numerous witnesses of this occurrence confidently expected that the gas would blow up, or the Volkswagen's petrol tank catch fire, or both; they also had no doubt that the two people who had so dramatically disappeared from sight would be seriously injured, or even, perhaps, dead. But nothing of the kind. Crumb, thrown clear of the bonnet, was lying uncomfortably on a grille of rusty but unbreached gas pipes, contused and with his left leg broken, but still with sufficient strength left to search in his pockets for his police whistle, which he presently found and began to blow piercingly. The Volkswagen failed to ignite. And as for Ortrud, there was general astonishment when she clambered out of the hole, tousled and grubby but apparently scarcely scratched, and set off at a run towards the Rover 2000 which she had previously noted and coveted. Its driver was a man, and he was alone. Reaching him, Ortrud wrenched the driver's door open, and he gaped out at her anxiously.

"Is there anything I can do to help?" asked this gentlemanly person.

Ortrud punched him on the nose, fracturing it to the accompaniment of great gouts of blood, and while he was still reeling from the shock, dragged him out of his seat, adding a chop to the neck for good measure, so that he collapsed in the roadway. But here nemesis overtook her: before she could fling herself into the Rover and make her escape, the two brawnier Gas Board men, who had recognised Crumb as a policeman, ran up and seized her from behind, attempting to pinion her arms behind her in a double lock. One of them she sent staggering with a left hook to the jaw, but the other was more tenacious and hung on. Also, by this time Crumb's frenetic whistling from the depths of the hole had had its effect: Connabeer with two constables came running out of the police station, and simultaneously, Rankine and *his* constable arrived back from Aller, and leaped out of the Panda to lend a hand. The tenacious Gas Board man continued somehow to hang on until these reinforcements came up. His mate, recovered, joined him. In the midst of a milling cluster of seven men, even Ortrud had no chance. Kicking, scratching, punching and shrieking obscenities in German, she was hustled into the police station and thrown into a cell.

Ruffled but contented, Connabeer returned gratefully to the peace and safety of his desk in the entrance hall. He telephoned for an ambulance, warmly thanked the two Gas Board men, and sent three constables outside to attend to the man from the Rover, get the traffic flowing again, and see if Crumb could be extricated from the hole without worsening his injuries. He then settled down to write out a full report of the incident, and was still doing this, to an accompaniment of distant screams and objurgations from Ortrud Youings's cell, when Ling returned from his solitary walk.

With wordy interpolations from Rankine, Connabeer told Ling all that had happened.

"Crumb?" said Ling incredulously. "*Crumb* was responsible for the arrest of this woman?"

"Yes, sir. I can't think what got into him, I'm sure. But it's a fact."

"Well, well." Ling's melancholy had lifted markedly as he listened, and he was now almost his old confident self again. "Marvels will never cease…What on earth is that noise, Sergeant?"

"It's her, sir. Seems she doesn't take to being locked up."

"And where's Inspector Widger?"

"I don't know, sir. I don't think he's in the building."

"I see. Well, I'd better go and talk to the woman, I suppose. Rankine, you can come with me and take shorthand notes."

"If you don't mind my saying so, sir," said Connabeer, "I should take some other men with you as well as Rankine. She's a proper wild-cat, that one."

As it happened, Ling had never met Ortrud. "Pooh," he said loftily. "These people are all the same. Once they're arrested, all the stuffing goes out of them. Where's the key?"

Connabeer handed over the key to Ortrud's cell, and Ling stumped off towards it with Rankine at his heels. Connabeer then summoned a pair of constables and went in pursuit. Ling was not so intent on fitting the key into the lock that he failed to notice this addition to the party, but although he raised his eyebrows sarcastically, he said nothing.

The door of the cell opened, and he marched in.

"Now, Mrs Youings," they heard him say, "what's all this I've been told about AAAAAAAGH." For there was no time for him to complete the question: Ortrud had her fingers round the back of his neck and with her thumbs was exerting considerable pressure on his eyeballs.

Rapidly, though not without a strenuous struggle, they rescued him from being blinded permanently. Connabeer knocked Ortrud to the floor and dragged Ling back out of the door, himself hastily following. He slammed the door and locked it, and they all stood together for a moment in the corridor outside, breathing stertorously.

"She attacked me," Ling gasped. "She attacked me—*me*. She tried to gouge my eyes out. My God!" With great caution he slid open the judas window. "Now, you just listen to me, Mrs Youings," he said, but all he got in reply was a stream of German, a language with which he was unacquainted.

"We shall have to get an interpreter," he said, recovering slightly. "Sergeant, is there anyone in the station who speaks German?"

"I don't think so, sir."

"Try and find someone, then. But there's no hurry about it. It's obviously useless to try and question her when she's in this...mood." He squared his shoulders. "Meanwhile, I'd better see the husband. He's in the hospital, I think you said."

"Yes, sir. But I don't know how bad he is."

"Never mind, I'll go there anyway. Lay on a car and a driver, will you? Oh, and when Inspector Widger turns up, tell him what's happened and where I am."

"Very good, sir. Do you want him at the hospital too?"

"No, I don't think so. Just ask him to wait for me in his office here. This, Sergeant, may be the break we've been waiting for."

Arrived at the hospital, Ling found that Youings had had a very narrow escape. Ortrud had struck hard. But fortunately, her husband possessed a thick skull, and to some extent his cloth cap and his thatch of fair hair had protected him. He had been concussed, and there was an extensive, painful scalp wound, but he was no longer on the danger list. A middle-aged, grim-visaged, moustached nurse conducted Ling into the private room in which, at Connabeer's insistence, he had been accommodated, and there Ling found him lying in the high bed with his head swatched in a bandage, pale in the face, drowsy from drugs, but still quite coherent, quite capable of answering questions, and surprisingly firm despite the normal mildness of his character.

A constable who had been sitting in a corner with a notebook and pencil stood up as Ling entered and whispered, "He hasn't said anything so far, sir."

"Ten minutes only, mind," the dour nurse said. "He needs rest." She consulted the watch pinned to her bosom and stationed herself by the window. Ling crossed to the bed.

"Well, Youings, how goes it?" he said in a hushed voice.

Youings smiled wanly. "Oh, I'm all right," he said. "I'll live. Glad you've come, because there's things I got to tell you. About Ortrud. I loved that woman, Superintendent. Doted! Would've done anything for her—well, look at all the money I paid out. But 'tis all over now. She never did treat me right. And this business, 'tis the last straw. I go into me own house for to fetch a clean shirt, and what do I find? I find her kissing some awful College git wi' bare feet. Well, I've put up wi' things like that for a long time now, and I suppose I'd have gone on putting up wi' it. But picking up the poker and trying to kill me, that's different. Enough's enough, I reckon. I never want to think about her or see her, ever again. I don't care what happens to her, however bad: 'tis all right by me. From now on, I just want to live me own life, *on* me own."

The constable scribbled busily. The nurse said disapprovingly, "You're talking too much, Mr Youings." Ling said, "She tried to put my eyes out." He was still smarting under this humiliation.

"Did she, now?" Youings seemed neither surprised at the revelation nor specially interested in it. "Well, well, fancy that."

"Did she kill Routh?"

"Course she did. Who else? That's why I paid out all that money. Blackmail. Someone knew I doted on her, and took advantage."

The constable scribbled even more busily. "Blackmail!" Ling exclaimed. "Shhh!" said the nurse.

"'Twouldn't be that Hagberd who killed Routh," said Youings. "'E wer' mazed, but 'e weren't no killer. 'E just came on the body, accidental like, an' made up 'is mind to chop it up."

"I see," said Ling. "Tell me about the blackmail, then."

Youings yawned; his initial burst of garrulity was spent, and from now on Ling was obliged to ask him specific questions. The day after Routh's murder he had received an unsigned typewritten letter, he said, informing him that his wife had committed the crime, and that if he didn't pay up, the writer would go to the police. Every Tuesday he was to put fifty pounds in used notes in the hollow of a particular tree in Holt's Wood; he was not to linger there, or notify the authorities, or Ortrud would be arrested. Youings had a few investments; he had hurriedly realised these, and had done exactly what he was told. Ortrud was then still infinitely precious to him, and the thought of her in prison had pierced him to the heart. He had never even dreamed of disobeying.

"But proof, man," said Ling incredulously. "What proof did the letter-writer give that your wife was involved in the Routh murder?"

None, Youings said, causing Ling to sigh heavily: he hadn't had any actual proof. But he had taxed Ortrud with the accusation, and she had cheerfully admitted its truth, saying it was good riddance. Shocked, Youings had none the less been able to see the force of this: like everyone else except Mrs Leeper-Foxe, he had thought Routh a horrible man; and no doubt there were extenuating circumstances, though Ortrud had not deigned to give him any details. Anyway, at all costs she must be kept out of prison, so he had paid, and had continued to pay right up to this afternoon, when Ortrud had hit him with the poker and radically changed his mind for him.

Had he kept the blackmailing letter? No, he had burned it. Had he any idea at all who the blackmailer might be? No, none.

The nurse again looked at her watch, saying, "That's enough for now. Time's up. You can come back tomorrow." And Ling was content to go: there were still details to be filled in, but he had the main outline.

"And you can take him"—here the nurse indicated the constable—"away with you. We don't want a lot of bluebottles cluttering up the place." She propelled both men towards the door.

"Ask Farmer Tully to send someone to see to the pigs, will you?" were Youings's final words. "I'll soon be back."

Then quite suddenly he fell asleep.

Heading for the exit, Ling and the constable encountered Crumb being trollied back beneath a blanket from the operating theatre to the ward. He was much bandaged, and his broken leg was in a plaster cast. Still under the anaesthetic, he was snoring squeakily. They ignored him and went on out to the car.

On the drive back to the police station, Ling could barely contain his exhilaration. He burst into Widger's office, where he found Widger, at last returned from Aller, in the desk chair finishing off a telephone call.

"We've got her!" Ling said exultantly.

"We've got Ortrud Youings, certainly," said Widger. He stood up, so that his superior could have the desk chair.

Ling, however, waved the offer graciously aside. "You've heard what happened?" he said.

"Yes, Eddie, I've heard what happened this afternoon. Connabeer told me. He also told me you'd gone to the hospital to see Youings. How is he?"

"Oh, he's all right. But now, just you listen, Charles, to what *he* had to say." And Ling gave Widger the gist of the interview. "She *admitted* it," he gloated. "She admitted to her husband that she killed Routh."

"So we were wrong about Hagberd," said Widger. "Poor Hagberd."

"Never mind about Hagberd," said Ling. "Hagberd's insane. He's where he belongs anyway. The great thing is that we've got the woman."

"Yes, I can visualise Ortrud coshing Routh," said Widger thoughtfully. "She pinches the wrench from Luck-raft's motorcycle kit. She goes for a walk, carrying it. She meets Routh accidentally. He takes her into Bawdeys Meadow, pretending he wants to seduce her. But then when it gets to the point, he only jeers at her. She's furious. She loses her temper and hits him. Yes, it all fits."

"Of course it fits. She's a devil, she'd try anything. When I went to talk to her, she tried to blind me."

"But what about the other two murders—Mavis Trent and the man in the Botticelli tent?"

"She did those too."

"Why?"

"*Why*? Well, I suppose as regards Mavis Trent, she pushed her over Hole Bridge because she was jealous."

"You mean Mavis was having an affair with Youings?"

"Could be. She had affairs with lots of men."

"Um," said Widger. "And what about the other murder?"

"I dare say it was some boy friend she wanted to get rid of."

"But, Eddie, we haven't got a shred of proof. It's—"

"Don't you worry about that, old squire. We'll find the proof all right, now that we know where to look for it."

"But—but how did she get the severed arm out of the tent? Everyone agrees that she never went *into* it."

"An accomplice. Probably her husband."

"Well, then, how did he get the arm out?"

Ling seemed slightly miffed. "Don't just stand there raising objections, Charles. We'll find out, never you fear. The case is closed. Now it's only a matter of tidying up a few loose ends."

"Listen, Eddie—"

But Ling wasn't prepared to listen. "As for me," he said, "I'm going out to have a drink and celebrate. I feel I've earned it. Coming?"

"If you don't mind, I've still got a few things I want to clear up here."

"Suit yourself." Ling made for the door. "Oh, by the way, get in touch with Ticehurst, will you? Ask him to meet me in the bar of The Seven Tuns, and we'll work out a statement about the Youingses which he can pass on to the press."

"All right."

"And one other thing. Youings is worried about his pigs. Ask Tully if he can send someone to look after them till Youings gets out of hospital."

"All right."

"Be seeing you, then, Charles." And Ling went jauntily out, leaving Widger gazing after him sceptically.

Widger made satisfactory contact with Ticehurst and with Tully, and then, alone in the office, reverted patiently to his own chores.

But it was not until the following morning that his efforts bore their unexpected fruit.

CHAPTER ELEVEN

Galloping Major

Then came…the flyndermows and the wezel and ther came moo than xx whiche wolde not have comen yf the foxe had loste the feeld.

Anonymous, translated by William Caxton: *Reynard the Fox.*

SATURDAY MORNING CAME, a week after the Fête, and found Fen and the Major perched up in a large old apple tree, straining their eyes for signs of the Hunt. The apple tree had been the Major's suggestion, and Fen, though he rather doubted the wisdom of a man of the Major's age and disability clambering happily about in branches like a bird, had decided that it would be tactless and wounding to raise objections. The Major sat dangling his legs on a lower bough, and Fen was on the bough above him. Fen was smoking a cigarette, and the Major was eating a diminutive sour apple.

The apple tree was part of the hedge bordering the southern verge of the lane which led westward from Burraford past Aller and Hole Bridge to Glazebridge; technically, it belonged to Aller. Behind it and at the opposite side of the lane, on the far side of another hedge, were pasture fields, at present empty, belonging to Clarence Tully. To Fen's right could be seen the Rector's great ugly house, its Y WURRY board cloven, faded and dangling from a single nut and bolt, set in its disorderly gardens with their paddock at their back. Almost facing the house's front gate, a minor lane—tarmac-ed but barely wider than a footpath—led off northwards, and in this it was possible to make out the roof of a parked Mini; here, at the turn, a stone had been daubed with yellow paint to indicate part of the route of some imminent motor-cycle scramble. To Fen's left, and about a hundred yards away, the main lane which he was surveying from his eminence took a sharp turn leftwards and downhill, and by twisting round you could follow it for quite a distance before it took another turn and disappeared from sight; in the corner of the nearer turn, a wooden field gate stood partially open. If you walked eastward past the Rector's house, you came after about half a mile to the wynd which led to Thouless's bungalow and Youings's pig-farm and the Dickinsons' cottage; further on, to your right, lay Aller House and its grounds; next, and again to your right, came the large field in which the Pisser (at present mute) eccentrically conducted its high-tension scare-mongering; next came the Old Rectory, abandoned in panic by Mrs Leeper-Foxe, locked, shuttered and deserted; next, a couple of semi-detached cottages; next, The Stanbury Arms; next, the pathway to Chapel Lane, where Luckraft and Mrs Clotworthy lived; and finally, as protégé to these various outriders, the bulk of Burraford village itself.

The weather continued to hold, and the surroundings were altogether restful. In the time which had elapsed since Fen and the Major had lost the Hunt, and its followers on foot or in cars, they had seen nothing and no one except for a Central Electricity Generating Board lorry, three men aboard it, hastening in the direction of Burraford.

The meet had been at The Stanbury Arms—not a very good choice, since there was scarcely room for all the huntsmen, the Hunt followers, the hunt saboteurs, the cars, the horses, the horse-boxes, and the notoriously ill-disciplined bitch pack, all of whom were obliged to spread themselves a considerable distance in both directions along the lane. Even so, possibly owing to the sunshine, a general good humour prevailed. Isobel Jones, assisted by a blowsy girl from the village, did a busy trade in the overcrowded bar; Jack Jones looked down with keen approval from his bed at the upstairs window; and even the hunt saboteurs, some of whom had burdened themselves with scrawled, strangely-spelt objurgations on placards, seemed more or less at a loss, managing only a meagre jeer when the horses and hounds eventually moved off. The chief of the saboteurs, a small, dark-suited, bespectacled man whom Fen recognised as a dispensing chemist from Glazebridge, stood in the car-park in earnest but apparently amicable conversation with the Master, who was taking intermittent swigs from a gleaming silver hip flask; he seemed for the moment subdued, perhaps because he had recently put an advertisement in the local paper offering a £5 reward to anyone who could give information about the smuggling in of foxes, in crates, by British Rail, and their subsequent release in the wilds to provide targets for the blood-lust of the huntsmen. This had provided a good deal of sour amusement to farmers who kept hens, and who were accustomed to waking up in the morning to find whole rows of the birds lying about the yard with their heads bitten off; the district was already infested with foxes, and Mr Dodd (which was the dispensing chemist's name) had hurriedly withdrawn his advertisement after only one issue.

The Glazebridge and District Harriers were an inefficient lot, and although they often found, deaths among the Canidae they put to flight were few and far between. Nor were they a very distinguished Hunt: the men mostly turned up in ratcatcher (Fen had that morning noted one, with waist-length hair, who was wearing a hoicked-up caftan and prayer beads above his shining riding boots); the women, though lending a little colour to the proceedings by putting on pink, were preponderantly ill-favoured and dull; the horses, with only a few exceptions, looked as if their sires and dams had been mated by some primitive, flawed computer-dating system; and of the hounds, several were so fat and old and lenient, with rheumatism and sore pads, that they could scarcely be trusted not to abandon the chase after a mile or less. Still, what the Hunt lacked in usefulness it more than made up for in enthusiasm and optimism, emotions with which it was infected less by the Master, a neurotic figurehead who held his position chiefly by virtue of his money, than by the cheerfulness of Clarence Tully and his huge sons, all of them splendidly mounted, who moved chatting among the crowd like yeasty catalysts in an inert chemical mixture.

The Hunt eventually got under way, heading along the lane in the Glazebridge direction and pursued by pro and anti fanatics walking or in cars. The cars soon disappeared, and at various stages the pedestrians dropped out. Owing to the Major's arthritic hip, he and Fen made relatively slow progress, dropping further and further behind; and by the time they reached the apple tree, they had the lane to themselves. It was at this stage that the Major proposed that they cease walking and climb instead. And so here they were, reasonably comfortable in their point of vantage, and with a grandstand view of the cumulative havoc which was shortly to develop down below.

The Major finished his apple and threw the core into the field behind the tree. "Widger visited you yesterday afternoon, my dear fellow," he said. "Whatever did he want?"

"He was telling me about progress in the investigation of the Botticelli murder," said Fen from above. "Or rather, about the lack of it."

"They're not getting anywhere, then?"

"Apparently not."

"Silly fellows, letting the wretched man's head be stolen from them like that," said the Major severely. "No wonder they're stuck. Were you able to help them at all?"

"Not very much, I'm afraid."

"And do you think that harpy killed Routh?"

"Ortrud? Yes, probably. She seems to like hitting people on the head."

"Killing Routh is practically the only good thing you can say about her, don't you know. Question is, can they prove it?"

"If she keeps her mouth shut, I dare say they can't."

"Ortrud can no more keep her mouth shut than she can get along without sex."

"Anyway, they can charge her with trying to kill her husband. What with one thing and another, it'll be an insanity plea, I imagine. That's if they can keep her quiet, and stop her boasting about it all."

"In any case," said the Major, reaching for a second apple, "it seems as if Youings has seen through her at last. Whatever happens, he'll be able to get a divorce, won't he?"

"Certainly he will."

"So all's well that ends well. What about the other two —Mavis and the man in the Botticelli tent? Did Ortrud murder them as well as Routh?"

"I don't think so."

The Major was shocked. "You don't *think* so? Are you telling me that there's *still* a murderer on the loose?"

"Ortrud's half mad," said Fen. "She wouldn't go to a lot of trouble to cover up her tracks, as the Botticelli murderer has. Their mentalities are completely different."

"Well, my dear fellow, if you say so. But who *is* the Botticelli murderer?"

"*I* don't know."

"But you must know by now, my dear fellow," said the Major plaintively. "We're practically at the end of the book." All at once he straightened up on his bough. "I say, look, there's the Hunt coming this way. Or part of it. Drop-outs, I think. They've given up and are going home. Lost the hounds, perhaps, not that that's easy, with the lazy brutes averaging about five miles an hour on the straight. But they may have over-ridden them, however hard they reined in, and lost them that way."

Following his gaze towards the field gate up the lane at the bend, Fen saw that in the pasture beyond it three huntsmen were riding slowly over the sky-line. Circumspectly this party descended towards the gate, and passing through it gained the lane, where two of them waited while the third conscientiously dismounted to close the gate and latch it. He then got astride his horse again, and still at a funereal pace the three of them, riding abreast, came on towards the apple tree where Fen and the Major were watching them. And by this time it was possible to make them out properly: they were two men flanking a girl with Bible-black hair peeking out from under her cap, and with the strained, wan face of one to whom the preliminaries of Armageddon have just been announced by some notorious practical joker. She, and the man riding on her left, wore pink; their companion was the man in the caftan and prayer beads whom Fen had noted at the meet. The near-side rider sported a long, thick, wiry, square-cut black beard—what Urquhart, in his translation of Rabelais, describes as a "great buggerly beard"; he seemed taciturn and straight-laced; the caftan man, who kept leaning from his saddle to pat the girl's arm consolingly, and to murmur to her, was patently less rigid and more humane. Both, however, looked as if they were in the act of honourably rescuing the girl from peril, and neither of them noticed Fen and the Major, who in addition to being above eye-level, were in any case partially concealed by leaves.

"My word!" said the Major. "They all look a bit glum, don't they?"

The horses' hooves kicked up a little puffs of dust in the lane, like spurts of powder from an aerosol container. A vehicular noise was heard approaching, from somewhere along the lane beyond the Rector's house, and the huntsmen got themselves into single file to let whoever it was get past. Coming into sight at a good pace, and making a considerable racket about it, the noise revealed itself as an enormous estate wagon of indefinite make. It was ancient and damaged and painted all over in psychedelic swirls of hideous pastel colours. Sitting in the back of it, horn-rimmed-spectacled and dark-suited and revealed by his expression as being far from in comity with his much younger companions, was Mr Dodd the dispensing chemist, leader of the hunt saboteurs; next to him sprawled a girl with long, tangled hair; in front, and driving, was a completely bald youth (alopecia? Buddhism?) in a stained roll-neck sweater. Even above the engine's stuttering din, Fen and the Major were able to hear the girl's shriek of glee when she saw the three huntsmen, and to glimpse her leaning forward urgently to speak to the driver. He nodded; the estate wagon slowed, swerved in to the verge; and by a series of rapid manoeuvres managed to get itself sideways on across the lane just to the right of the apple tree. It was now blocking the way entirely, and the riders, after spreading out again, perforce came to a halt.

The bald youth switched off his engine and jumped out, facing the horses; he was revealed as wearing sneakers and old trousers as well as the roll-neck sweater, and appeared to be just as grim and laconic as the bearded huntsman. He was followed by Mr Dodd, who confronted the man in the caftan with a mien of intelligent reasonableness. Disentangling herself from a placard which said (in faded lettering) FREE THE SHREWSBURY PICKETS, the girl emerged last. She looked by far the most overtly bellicose of the party, in a T-shirt across whose bosom, and redolent with the charms of a long-lost Golden Age, were shakily stencilled the words I LOVE CHÉ ("Don't suppose she'd love him much if he turned up in his present condition," observed the Major. "Remember *The Monkey's Paw*?"); she wore also shapeless slacks apparently tailored from jute, and high-heeled black patent-leather shoes whose chrome buckles were studded with paste to simulate diamonds. In this ill-considered get-up she stood glaring for a moment at the demoralised girl on the horse, who lost the first round by incontinently bursting into tears. While she dried her eyes with a lacy handkerchief about the size of a chequer-board square, the man in the caftan again patted her on the arm, consolingly. Then he addressed himself to Mr Dodd.

"Would you mind," he said mildly, "getting that thing out of our way?"

"A little talk first," said Mr Dodd with equal civility. "All we're asking is to have a little talk with you. A *reasonable* talk."

"Fascist pigs," snarled the hunt saboteuse, brushing hair out of her eyes.

"We just want you to think a little about what you're doing," said Mr Dodd, "when you go out hunting innocent, helpless animals."

"Blood-lust."

"Consider how uneven the contest is," said Mr Dodd. "All those horses, all those dogs. And just one terrified little fox, running for its life."

"Go and live in South Africa," said the hunt saboteuse. "Those tyrants there will give you something better to hunt than foxes. They'll give you blacks. That's it, go and live in South Africa, you bourgeois scabs."

"And then, think how it all ends," said Mr Dodd, still endeavouring doughtily to keep to the point. "The fox is cornered. Trembling, he has no hope left. The hounds surround him. Then they pounce. Their great teeth tear gobbets from him. In his intense agony, his blood gushes like a fountain. He dies slowly. He is literally rent in pieces. And all around him, the huntsmen sit astride their horses, laughing."

"Sado-masochistic élitists."

"Miss Davenant"—here Mr Dodd addressed the hunt saboteuse in mild reproof—"I don't think your approach is getting us anywhere. Peaceful persuasion, that's the line to take. It—"

"Power-crazed murderers."

"Well, I scarcely—Peter, what are you doing?"

What Peter—the bald youth—was doing soon became obvious. He had reached into the estate wagon for a large glass jar full of colourless liquid, had unstoppered it, and was now splashing its contents freely on the surface of the lane. The odour of aniseed rose up and engulfed them all. Miss Mimms started crying again.

The second huntsman's teeth gleamed in the forests of his beard. He made his first and only contribution to the discussion. Glowering at the bald youth, he hissed "Scybalum!" twice—an arcane obscenity which, whatever its appropriateness, failed to have much effect, since only Fen understood what it meant.

Mr Dodd, who had his choleric side, said testily, "What on earth is the use of that, Peter? You're just wasting the stuff. The hounds are nowhere near."

The hunt saboteuse gave Mr Dodd a withering look. "You just go ahead, Peter," she shrilled. "You just *show* the pigs."

Peter followed up action with speech. "We did ought to have laid a false trail," he said, frowning at the bearded scybalum-merchant. "And we did ought to have unstopped the earths, and sprayed the dogs with Anti-Mate, and used firecrackers and thunderflashes and horns and whistles. That's what we did ought to have done." He transferred his displeasure to Mr Dodd. "And why haven't we, that's what I want to know? Why haven't we?"

Mr Dodd groped for the vanishing tatters of his leadership. "As regards this particular meet," he stammered feebly, "I made an arrangement with the Master that we shouldn't—that we shouldn't—In short, that we should confine ourselves to banners and to verbal protest. You see, the police—trespass—"

"Revisionist!" the hunt saboteuse said. "You're nothing but a dirty bourgeois revisionist. Trespass, hell! I tell you, these bloody aristo land-owners have got it coming to them anyway. And as to being scared of the fuzz, all I can say is—"

"You're a bourgeois yourself, come to that," said Mr Dodd stoutly.

"Still, you didn't ought to have done it," said the bald youth in more moderate tones. Thoughtfully, he poured more aniseed on to the ground.

During this interchange, the man in the caftan had wearily dismounted. He let go of his horse's reins—it was a sixteen-hands bay, apparently of a very equable disposition—and on being released it wandered to the grassy bank above which the hedge grew, coming to rest immediately beneath the branch on which the Major was sitting. Here it stood grazing as voraciously as its bridle allowed; and here it remained unperturbed throughout all the subsequent disturbances, until its fate finally caught up with it.

The man in the caftan approached Mr Dodd on foot, watched suspiciously by the hunt saboteuse and the bald youth. The bearded man imitated him in dismounting, to stand in the lane in silence glaring at the scene. Miss Mimms stayed up, quietly weeping, with no one now to pat her on the arm.

"Look, said the man in the caftan, "I don't in the least mind talking about the pros and cons of hunting, but this isn't the time for it, or the place. Miss Mimms has been thrown. She's hurt herself. We're taking her to see Dr Mason, and you're in the way. So will you please get *out* of the way?"

The hunt saboteuse laughed harshly and performed a little dance of triumph. Mr Dodd said, "Oh dear, I am sorry. Perhaps in the circumstances we'd better—"

"She don't look hurt bad to me," said the bald youth.

"Miss Mimms is suffering from extensive bruises and from shock."

"Serve her right," said the hunt saboteuse.

"Come, now," said the man in the caftan.

"Yes, I think in the circumstances perhaps we'd better—"

"She can still ride her horse, can't she?" said the hunt saboteuse. "If she wants to see a doctor, tell her to go jump a hedge."

Miss Mimms dissolved into a niagara of tears. "Shock can be very dangerous," said the man in the caftan sternly.

"Yes, I think perhaps—"

But what the issue of this conflict would have been, neither Fen nor anyone else would ever know, for at this point a new element was added to the situation. From down the lane beyond the Rector's house a locally familiar aggregation of sounds came within earshot, approaching rapidly: shouts, a bicycle bell, a drumming of hooves.

One of Clarence Tully's herds was on the move.

Fen, the Major, the huntsmen and the hunt saboteurs were alike struck dumb, peering into the east to catch a first sight of this fresh complication. And they had little time to wait. In the van of the procession, as usual, came Tully's third cowman on his bicycle, pedalling away frenziedly. Then the South Devons—luckily only about twenty of them, but all moving precipitately, at their utmost speed. Finally, to draw up the rear, trotted Clarence Tully's youngest son, a brawny eleven-year-old whose penetrating voice was on the change, and who carried a long hazel switch with which to lash out at the bony rumps of the hindermost cows if they showed signs of strag-gling or of losing momentum. This rowdy, intimidating muster came belting up the lane at full tilt, and it seemed impossible that it would be able to stop in time to avoid breaking against, and deluging, the obstacle of the hunt saboteurs' estate wagon, as an Atlantic roller drenches a shingle bank.

"My word!" said the Major.

Matters were not improved by the fact that the third cowman seemed to have lost his head: apart from ringing his bell, he seemed proposing to do nothing to avoid a collision. At almost the last possible moment, however, he recovered himself and took action. True, this consisted of nothing more constructive than veering into the bank, hitting it with his front wheel, falling off his saddle and inflicting on himself some painful, disabling injury of the ankle; but it was just sufficient to bring the cows to a halt. Once relieved of their hurry, the creatures immediately began to disperse in various directions in search of food. Some attempted to wander back in the direction from which they had come; a second group decided to explore the offshoot opposite the gate of the Rector's house, in which the Mini was parked; a third tackled the nearest verges and hedges; a fourth—three cows only, including the leader— remained standing more or less still, sniffing at the paint-work of the estate wagon. Tully's youngest son, whose name was Alan, ran hither and thither, cursing, making cow noises like "Coop, coop", and plying his switch in an effort to re-assemble the herd in a homogeneous mass in the lane, all facing the right way. Sometimes he shouted at the hunt saboteurs, "Get that bloody thing out of the way!" Sometimes he shouted at the third cowman, who was sitting on the bank moaning and nursing his ankle.

"Git yer arse up off o' there, Enoch, an' come an' help!"

"Can't," Enoch shouted back. "I think I gone an' broke me bloody leg!"

"Pity you 'asn't broke yer bloody neck," said Alan unfeelingly, fluctuating between treble and bass. Panting, he continued to chase the errant cows single-handed.

"I think, perhaps—" said Mr Dodd.

"Capitalist feudalists," said the hunt saboteuse.

The Major said, "I say, my dear fellow, do you think we ought to get down and help?"

"As far as I can see," said Fen, "the only way we could really help would be by knocking the two younger saboteurs unconscious and moving their car."

"Well, I wouldn't mind doing that."

"Good heavens, what's happening now?"

What was happening now, and what inhibited them from moving for the moment, was that the leader of the herd had come to the conclusion that the grass was greener on the other side. Eyes rolling, she proceeded doggedly to scramble across the bonnet of the estate wagon, its rusted metal buckling under her weight, and to descend somehow on the other side. The hunt saboteurs got expeditiously out of her way. So did the two huntsmen and Miss Mimms, all of whom had been contemplating these goings-on in pessimistic silence. Only the bay belonging to the man in the caftan remained unperturbed, still stationed beneath the Major's branch and apparently on the point of slumber.

Alan Tully was roused to a fresh access of rage.

"Can't 'ee bloody stop 'er, you useless lot?" he shrieked. "Enoch, get after 'er, can't 'ee?"

"It's me leg," said Enoch, not attempting to get up. Seemingly in an attempt to justify his existence, he grabbed at his fallen bicycle and began trying to straighten the handlebars. The leader of the cows, meanwhile, had set off briskly towards the field gate at the bend of the lane, had reached it, and was now doing her best to lift it off its hinges with her head. From their position on the other side of the estate wagon, such of the remaining cows as Alan had managed to herd together stood regarding her admiringly.

"Stop 'er! Git after her!" Alan bellowed despairingly. But no one answered him and no one moved. Both huntsmen and hunt saboteurs, indeed, seemed to feel that the time had come for them to re-open hostilities, and with the exception of the bearded man were all talking simultaneously when a menacing wave of assorted internal-combustion resonances reached their ears from the direction of Glazebridge. Fen and the Major heard them too, and Fen rotated on his bough to see a large number of machines strung out and roaring up the hill towards the bend.

The motor-cycle scramble had arrived.

There were Hondas and Suzukis and Yamahas and even a few Norton Commandos, ranging in capacity from 400 to 750 c.c. They were being ridden by youths and young men, who, unaware of what was awaiting them, were all going at a tremendous pace—so much so that when they rounded the bend, and the man in the caftan (by now perceptibly losing his cool) dashed forward to flag them down, their helmeted leaders were only just able to stop short of Miss Mimms's horse. With the exception of the cow at the field gate, who went on striving unabatingly at her furative task, the herd panicked, and the unfortunate Alan Tully was back to square one. Enoch continued to sit on the bank, grizzling and groaning and calling for medical aid and intermittently wrestling with his bicycle. The hunt saboteurs lined themselves defensively up against the side of their vehicle. The bay had apparently fallen asleep entirely. The bearded huntsman spat in the lane. The man in the caftan lifted its hem and wiped the sweat off his face with it. Miss Mimms again burst into tears. Fen and the Major stayed safely up in the apple tree, by this time so selfishly riveted by the scene as to be psychologically quite incapable of deserting their grand-stand view and climbing down to offer assistance.

Motor-cyclists went on pouring round the bend and stopping short until eventually the lane became crammed with them. Some remained astride with their engines idling; others switched off; yet others dismounted. All looked grim and resentful. To the stink of aniseed and horses and cows was now superadded the stink of petrol fumes. Back along the lane to Glazebridge, far away from the hurly-burly, a rearmost motor-cyclist had got off and was pressing himself and his machine hard into the hedge, though nothing at all was approaching him from either direction. Fen took this distant, terrorised figure to be Scorer.

The nearest motor-cyclist, who appeared to be fugleman for the rest, propped his Honda against the bank and after a quick assessment of the situation advanced minatorily on Mr Dodd. He was a muscular but rather stunted youth, scarcely taller than the chemist but a good deal more single-minded. He jerked his head towards the estate wagon and said, "That thing yours, Dad?"

"Yes," said Mr Dodd. "No. Well, in a way."

"Move it."

"I don't drive," said Mr Dodd. "You'll have to ask one of these other two."

"You ask them—*Dad*. It's you I'm talking to, not them. You're in charge here, aren't you?"

"Well, in a way. Up to a point, that is. In actual fact, we're a democratically elected—"

"Stow all that, Dad, and get weaving. I know what you lot are," said the motor-cyclist. "You're hunt saboteurs, that's what you are."

"And proud of it," said Mr Dodd, drawing himself up to his full height.

"Cissies, dykes, fags. Nosey parkers. Busybodies. Spoilsports."

"Polluters," said the hunt saboteuse. "*Lumpenproletariat.* Why don't you rise up against the exploiters and be men instead of serfs?"

"Kindly leave this to me, Miss Davenant," said Mr Dodd, who was losing his temper fast.

"I said, move it, Dad."

"And stop calling me 'Dad'."

"I'll call you what I bloody like, you crazy old crank." The motor-cyclist raised his eyes to heaven, as if imploring it to rescue him from this superannuated donkey. "Ninety if you're a day, and can't even drive a car yet. Don't you argue with *me*, Dad, or I'll knock your dentures down your throat. When I tell you to get that wreck out of the way, you don't argue, see, you just do it."

For Mr Dodd, this was the last straw. "Oh no, I don't," he said, bearing down on the motor-cyclist. "Don't you dare tell *me* what to do, you miserable young puppy. I'll teach you to tell *me* what to do." He clenched his fist and swung wildly at the motor-cyclist's face, but was still too far off for the blow to connect. Taking several steps nearer, he tried again, and this time, if the swipe had ever got under way, it might have rocked the motor-cyclist slightly. It did not, however, get under way; in fact, it had only just started when Mr Dodd, still moving forward, tripped over a tortoise and fell abruptly into the motor-cyclist's arms, clutching him round the back for support. It was possible to judge from the motor-cyclist's face when confronted with this assault that his aggro was strictly verbal, that he avoided physical fights and that he feared that even such a decrepit relic as Mr Dodd, once roused, had the capacity to do him an injury and cause him much unacceptable pain. Accordingly, he confined himself to putting his own arms round Mr Dodd, and for some moments, in a confined space, the pair of them gavotted unsteadily round in circles—in what would have looked like a fraternal embrace but for the feeble wrestling motions to which one or other of them occasionally resorted—watched with mild interest by everyone present. The motor-cyclists made no move to come to the aid of their leader, and the hunt saboteurs made no move to come to the aid of theirs. Mr Dodd's spectacles were shaken from his nose and at once trodden on by Miss Mimms's horse. Eventually both combatants lost their balance altogether, and fell down, still locked together, on to the dusty tarmac. Disentangling himself, the motor-cyclist got upright again; he stood glaring round and brushing himself off with the palms of his gloved hands. Mr Dodd remained on his knees, groping about him vainly for his spectacles, which presently the hunt saboteuse, striding forward contemptuously, picked up for him and thrust into his hand. He put them on, but on discovering that with their lenses cracked and their frames buckled he could see better without them, soon took them off again, heaved himself to his feet, and with arms extended in front of him like a somnambulist's, began making his way towards the estate wagon.

"I'm getting out of this," said Mr Dodd.

"Male chauvinist mouse," the hunt saboteuse hissed at him. It occurred to Fen that although she could only be about sixteen or seventeen, her package of progressive *idées reçues* was already a bit out of date, not to say rather blurrily cross-referenced. What would it be next, he wondered? Namibia? The perennial C.I.A.? Chile again? The Black Papers on Education?

"Oh, shut up," said Mr Dodd to the hunt saboteuse.

"1 suppose you think I'm just a sexual object," said the hunt saboteuse.

Mr Dodd was normally a polite man, but now the last vestiges of chivalry left him. "You're not even capable of being that, I'm afraid," he said; and got into the estate wagon and scrambled into the back, where he huddled down morosely, dissociating himself from all further part in the circumjacent turmoil. As to the hunt saboteuse, she was uncharacteristically for the moment bereft of speech.

The leader of the herd of Clarence Tully's South Devons had meanwhile succeeded in getting the field gate at the bend off its hinges, had pushed it open and was now browsing in solitary splendour in the field beyond.

Two cars came round the bend from Glazebridge. They braked hurriedly on seeing what confronted them, and began playing protracted, angry fanfarades on their horns. To cries of rage and despair from Alan Tully, the cows on the far side of the estate wagon, unnerved by this fresh source of noise, again scattered.

The second of the two cars was a Panda, containing a brace of uniformed constables. The first, a grey Cortina, had Widger driving, with Ling sitting at his side puffing miasmally at a pipe. In the back sat Detective-Constable Rankine, lovingly nursing a pair of handcuffs. Rankine's mouth was moving, so it was to be presumed that he was beguiling his superiors' journey with a commentary on the landscape, or the weather, or the Botticelli murder, or the blockage in the lane, or some other topic which had struck his fancy. Both cars were forced to a halt, and a constable leaped from the Panda to clear a way for them, efficiently herding, by virtue of his uniform, all of the horses, the huntsmen, the motor-cyclists, the motor-cycles, and even the bald youth and the hunt saboteuse, on to the southern side, the apple-tree side, of the lane, where they joined the man in the caftan's bay, which was still drowsing peaceably almost immediately beneath the Major. The constable then stood on guard while the police cortège nosed cautiously forward along the narrow route thus provided until once again checked, this time by the estate wagon.

"My God, it's the pigs," said the hunt saboteuse disgustedly. "That was all we needed. Well, come on, arrest us for something," she shouted at the Cortina.

"Ah, belt up, Elaine, can't you?" The bald youth might share the hunt saboteuse's views on the evils of venery, but it was far from certain that he shared them on any other issue, and in his taciturn way he had become almost as irritated with her as had Mr Dodd: only rapidly fraying generation ties were still binding the two of them together. "I'm going to move your junk dooly, that's what I'm going to do. I don't want no trouble with the fuzz."

"Coward. Conformist," the hunt saboteuse spat at him. She turned her attention again to Widger. "Come on, then, arrest us," she bellowed. "It oughtn't to be difficult for brutal fascist pigs like you to find some excuse for arresting and beating up innocent people."

Widger stuck his head out of the window of the Cortina. "Does this...this motor-car belong to you, Miss?" he asked.

"For the love of the Lamb, let's get going, Charles," said Ling fretfully. "We're in a hurry."

"Ms." The hunt saboteuse wobbled her breasts under the T-shirt to show that they were un-brassiered, a token of liberation which had little effect, since her torso was almost entirely concealed by long shanks of tangled, parti-coloured hair. "Ms, if you don't mind."

"I do mind," said Widger, who had no time for such inanities. He got out of the Cortina and advanced on the hunt saboteuse with an air of menace. "I said, *is this your car?*"

"Yes, it is, and I'm not going to move it. You can—"

"Do let's get *going*, Charles," Ling shouted. "Our man—"

"I really *will* arrest you, you know," said Widger. "For obstructing the police in the execution of their duties. Now if you'll kindly—"

"Scybalum!" hissed the bearded huntsman, while Miss Mimms wept, the motor-cyclists' leader judiciously picked his nose, and the man in the caftan contemplated the scene in despair. Enoch could still be heard grieving, and Alan Tully swearing monotonously as he tried to organise his cows. The Major reached for yet a third apple and Fen lit a fresh cigarette.

"The police seem to be putting on a show of strength," said the Major. "Do you think they've found out who the murderer is, and are on their way to arrest him?"

"Either that or detain him for questioning. They certainly seem to expect resistance."

"Let's hope it isn't one of us, then," said the Major. "Because we're well hidden and they haven't spotted us yet."

"Very well, if you refuse to move it," Widger was saying to the hunt saboteuse, "I shall have no alternative but to move it myself." He turned away from her and began clambering into the estate wagon, where for the first time he perceived Mr Dodd hunched in the back. "Mr Dodd!" he exclaimed. "What on earth are you doing here?"

"Oh, hello, Inspector," said Mr Dodd uneasily, having managed to identify Widger at the cost of some optical strain. "I—I've got myself into rather bad company. I'm afraid. These young people—I'm sure they mean well, but such language… And they just won't see that reason is the only weapon, calmness and reason." He shook his head sadly, doing his best to look an injured innocent. "We shall never get reform in any other way."

"Oh, so it's hunt sabotage, is it?" said Widger, enlightened. "Calmness and reason, eh? And just what's this aniseed I smell?"

"Aniseed," said Mr Dodd rather more stiffly, "has its place."

"I see. Well, you just stay where you are while I try to get this ruin of an automobile into the side of the road."

Widger edged himself into the driver's seat, switched on, started the engine with a roar, let the clutch in, put the gear lever into reverse, twisted the wheel, and let the clutch out again. The estate wagon twitched once, but otherwise made no move, and the engine died. Widger restarted it and tried again, with the same negative result. Nor did any of the forward gears make any difference: the vehicle remained immobile where it was.

"We really must get *on*," Ling bawled through his pipe.

Disembarking, Widger addressed himself to the bald youth, who happened to be nearest. "What's the matter with this thing?" he demanded irritably.

"You tell me, cock," said the bald youth. "She was okay when I was driving her. It's something you've done."

"Oh, rubbish...RANKINE!"

In his anxiety to be of help, Detective-Constable Rankine almost fell out of the back of the Cortina. He was still dangling the handcuffs from one fist. "Sir?" he said.

"You're supposed to know something about cars, aren't you?"

"I think I may assert without immodesty, sir," said Rankine, "that I have some practical experience of the internal combustion engine." He lifted a forefinger, presumably in order to engage Widger's closest attention. "Its basic principle is simple. Petroleum vapour under pressure is ignited by a—"

"Yes, thank you very much. Rankine, but we don't want a lecture on mechanics just at the immediate moment. The point is, can you do anything about this bloody estate wagon? I think the brakes must be jammed. Can you unjam them?"

"Certainly, sir."

"Well, don't just stand there, Rankine. Get on with it."

"Sir."

"*Quickly.*"

"Sir."

Ling could be heard groaning aloud. "I said, *quickly*, Rankine." Widger repeated.

"I shall have to borrow some of your tools, sir." "Borrow anything you like, but for God's sake, man, get weaving."

"Very good, sir," said Rankine, recovering from his uncharacteristic stupor and at once becoming a blur of purposeful activity. Flinging the handcuffs into the back of the Cortina, he rushed to its boot, opened it, and abstracted the tool-kit which the manufacturers had thoughtfully provided in case their workmanship should fall to bits the moment it got on the road. Armed with this, he ran to the estate wagon, flung himself on to his back on the ground, and wriggled underneath until only his shoes, socks and trouser-ends remained visible. He set to work, and from time to time his muffled voice could be heard giving a blow-by-blow account of his procedures ("I select a spanner of the correct size. I apply it to the nut. I take a half turn to the right.") while his large audience looked on sceptically.

"Charles, hadn't we better turn and go round some other way?" Ling said restively from his seat in the Cortina.

"It's a long distance, Eddie," said Widger. "And I think Rankine will be able to manage," he added without much confidence.

"If only he didn't *talk* so much."

"Yes, I know. But he just gets bewildered if you try to stop him."

A helicopter marked SWEB ground its way towards them, appearing suddenly from beyond a distant rise in the terrain, and although originally flying at a height of about five hundred feet, dipped to examine the snarl-up in the lane below; like all helicopters, it sounded like an inexpensive clockwork toy enormously amplified, and inevitably its uproar panicked the cows again. Serenely unconscious, like all his kind, of the obnoxiousness of his tawdry expertise to the vast majority of the public, the pilot waved through his Plexiglas. Then his machine lifted again, its damage done, and made off in the direction of the Pisser, where it could remittently be glimpsed buzzing round in circles, no doubt making some sort of inspection from above. Collecting his cows together for what seemed the umpteenth time, Alan Tully now sensibly gave up all attempt to get them to their proper destination, instead driving them up the lane opposite the Rector's house, where the Mini was parked. Here a second gate gave on to the field in which, for sometime now, the more enterprising leader of the herd had been peaceably stuffing her rumen, honeycomb, manyplies and abomasum with Farmer Droridge's grass, and here Alan Tully harried her companions to join her. They could go to their proper pasture later. Meanwhile, Alan knew that his father, returning from the hunt, wouldn't when he heard all the circumstances in the least blame him. And as to Farmer Droridge, to hell with the old fool.

Noted initially only by Fen (the Major was eyeing Miss Mimms, Mr Dodd in the estate wagon was nursing an aura of gloom, Alan and the cows were gone, Enoch the cowman was too preoccupied with his ankle to have any attention to spare for anything else, and the remainder of the participants were on the wrong side of the estate wagon, or, in Rankine's case, active underneath it)—noted only by Fen, a new phenomenon was at this point added to the situation. In the Rector's gateway there materialised a familiar pink blob; apart from shining black shoes, a white shirt and a conservative navy-blue tie, it was surmounted and underpinned entirely by palest grey; it was the man from Sweb. In his arms he was lugging an ornate metal coffer, and this, though not particularly large, evidently weighed a good deal. He looked back anxiously over his shoulder; he gaped in some dismay at the brouhaha up along the lane. Then, summoning up his determination, he scuttled across to where his Mini was parked, levered himself and the coffer into it, started the engine, reversed rapidly, and drove off towards Burraford. By this time the Major's interest was aroused, and he and Fen watched in some fascination as the Rector himself emerged, beamed up the lane and down it (where the Mini was just disappearing from sight), and abruptly gave tongue.

"STOP THIEF!" shouted the Rector. "STOP THI-EEEEEF!"

The Rector's voice, at the best of times stentorian, when fully exerted was of a colossal volume. Its effect—except upon Rankine, who continued to hold forth about cogs, crankshafts and joints—was to arrest instantly the squabbling which had again broken out on the Glazebridge side of the estate wagon, and to bring about a virtually complete silence during which policemen, huntsmen, motorcyclists and hunt saboteurs all craned their necks to peer over and around the obstructive estate wagon in an effort to discover what was going on now.

"*STOP THI-EEEEEF!*" the Rector continued to bellow— though it occurred to Fen that for a man who had just been robbed he looked unnaturally cheerful, from cracked shoes through bandy legs to apish face and noble brow more like a gorilla at large in an unguarded banana promptuary than the hapless victim of an unscrupulous crime against his possessions. "Stop thief!" he said once more, quite quietly this time. Then with a broad grin he turned and set off at a trot in the wake of the Mini; though how he could ever hope to catch up with it, Fen was unable to imagine.

"D'you know what this is?" said the Major. "It's the man from Sweb, and he's burgled the Rector." He began sidling along his branch to where it directly overhung the lane. "Can't have goings-on like that. The Rector and I may have our points of disagreement, from time to time, but even so—"

"Major, what are you…"

"Never trusted that fellow," said the Major. "Too slavish, don't you know, too slavish by half. Toadying, too. Squeaky. Now, let's see. I've watched John Wayne and so forth do this sort of thing on late-night films on the telly, so it must be possible, but can't say I've ever tried it myself. The trick, apparently, is to…"

Fen leaned forward and tried to grab the Major by the scruff of his neck, but he was too far away, by now immediately above the man in the caftan's slumbrous bay, and already edging himself off the branch, legs parted and preparing to jump.

"Major!" Fen ejaculated loudly and warningly. But the only effect of this was to draw everyone's attention to their presence in the tree; the Major it left unintimidated and unmoved.

Immediately above the bay's saddle, the Major launched himself into air.

His aim was excellent, but he had apparently forgotten all about his arthritic hip, and let out a vehement howl of anguish as he landed astride the pigskin.

The bay instantly recovered consciousness. Somnolent she might be; insensitive she was not. Indeed, anyone who knew her was aware of the fact that before she was ridden she had to be coaxed fairly slowly and cautiously from the fringes of sleep, since otherwise there was liable to be trouble. And there was trouble now. For a creature superficially so equable, the bay was very easily excited and upset. She was unused to being violently mounted while still deep in the arms of Morpheus; in particular, she was unused to being mounted by someone who had apparently dropped on to her without warning from the skies. To this phenomenon she reacted violently, kicking and plunging and rearing and whinnying as if a javelin had been thrust into her rump. Groping for reins and stirrups, the Major contrived to hang on somehow or other. Policemen (excepting always Rankine, who was in any case already largely protected by the chassis of the estate wagon), motor-cyclists, hunt saboteurs and huntsmen, even the lachrymose Miss Mimms, all took hasty refuge wherever they could. The bay cavorted wildly in what little space remained, the Major meanwhile managing by sheer horsemanship to gain control of her harness. Fen looked down from the apple tree in solemn wonderment. The man in the caftan emitted an uncouth cry of protest.

"My horse!" he yelped. "What are you doing with my horse? Xantippe! Xantippe!"—this being seemingly the bay's name. Her owner had for a long, time been neglecting his role as consoler of Miss Mimms, and had now, in his extremity, evidently forgotten about her entirely. "XANTIPPE!" he shrieked—though it was noticeable that he avoided any attempt to seize his volatile loved one's head. "Bring my horse back! Bring her *back*, I tell you! BACK!"

But it was doubtful if the Major could have succeeded in doing this, even if he had wanted to: Xantippe had glimpsed a route to freedom, and was already careering along it, towards the bend in the lane where the field gate stood ajar. However, the Major had her increasingly under discipline: by the time the rearguard of cringing motorcyclists were passed, she was doing more or less what he ordered. Arriving at the field gate, she skidded to a halt while the Major, loosening his right foot from the stirrup, kicked the rickety structure wide open. Then they were into the field. Then they were turning. Then, just as everyone was beginning to relax slightly, they came thundering back again, through the gateway, across the lane, and thence, in a prodigious leap, over the hedge into the field behind Fen. The Major screeched again as man and horse hit terra firma on the other side, then went on to gallop almost *ventre à terre* in the direction of the hedge which gave on to the paddock behind the Rector's garden.

His purpose was now clear. He was pursuing the man from Sweb through the fields which ran parallel to the lane.

Fen sighed. He didn't think that the Major on horseback was any more likely to catch up with the Mini than was the Rector on foot. He decided that the time had come to climb down and reveal himself to Widger and to Ling.

Ling too had meanwhile come to a decision—namely, that his superior rank made it now obligatory for him to take a hand in the extraordinary occurrences which he had so far witnessed—admittedly ducking out of sight at the Major's passing—only from the passenger seat of the Cortina. He lurched into the lane, where Miss Mimms and the man in the caftan were presently weeping in synchronisation, eyed with disgust by their companion in the beard. To Widger he said, "Charles, what the *hell* is going on here?"

"Don't ask me."

"Who was that man on the horse?"

"That was the Major."

"The Major. What was he—what was he—"

"I think he was trying to chase after the man in the Mini."

"I see. Well then, who's that other person up in the tree?"

"It looks like Professor Fen."

"Good God, is it really? What's *he* doing there?"

"*I* don't know, Eddie. He seems to be coming down now, so we can ask him."

"Everyone's mad."

"Yes."

"Deranged."

"Yes."

"And so, to conclude, a weeny squeeze of the oil-can," came Rankine's voice from the depths, "and the task is completed. Not that what I have been enabled to do is more than provisional. An inspection pit is required, welding equipment, at least two engineers. And there is more. For perfect safety, we undoubtedly need—"

"Never you mind about perfect safety, Rankine," Widger shouted from the stooped position he thought likeliest to reach his subordinate's ears, and to interrupt his flow. "Just do enough to get that thing into the side of the road, and let us pass."

"Yes," said Ling, scrutinising his wrist-watch from a serviceable distance. "Yes. We really must get *on*. I've said it before and I'll say it again—"

"And again and again and again." Fen had joined them, mopping fragments of mud, grit, and apple tree from his person. "Any chance of a lift, Inspector?"

"Yes, of course, sir. I mean, no, certainly not."

"Dear me," said Fen.

"Confidential police business, sir, I'm afraid," said Widger, distressed; he was remembering what he owed Fen—remembering, too (which increased his embarrassment) that he had not yet been able to bring himself to confide the fact of his indebtedness to Ling. With a hasty glance at this individual, who was glaring contumaciously at Mr Dodd in the back of the estate wagon, he muttered, "Come and tell you all about it, sir, as soon as it's tied up."

Ling had lowered his gaze, and was now contemplating Rankine's protruding feet, which were showing signs of motion. "I think he's finished now, thank God. I think he's coming out."

This projection seemed to be correct, for first Rankine's turn-ups came into view, then his flies, then his hands (the one scrabbling for a purchase on the lane's surface, the other clutching Widger's tool-bag), then his belly, then his tie, then his shoulders, and finally his face and dishevelled hair. He had spots of grease all over him, and to these, smudges of dust had adhered.

"My God, Rankine, you do look a sight," said Ling.

Unabashed, Rankine lurched to his feet, beaming. "All present and correct, sir," he told them. "I don't think you'll be having any more trouble there, not for the time being. You'll be anxious to know the method I used. My first step—"

"Get back in the car, Rankine," said Widger, exasperated, "or I'll put you on a charge."

"Yes, sir, but I thought you'd be bound to want to hear—"

"*Back in the car, I said.*"

"Oh, very good, sir, if that's orders," said Rankine pathetically. "All I was thinking—"

"BACK!"

"Your tools, sir," said Rankine. "First of all I shall have to—"

"No, you won't, Rankine. You can take them into the car with you."

"Sir."

"And for heaven's sake, try and clean yourself up a bit. You look as if you'd been crawling through a pig-bin."

"Sir."

"*Move*, Rankine, *move.*"

"Sir," said Rankine, wounded. He moved, thrusting himself into the back of the Cortina, where they saw him pick up the handcuffs and attempt to scrape some of the oil off himself with them. Ling swung round on the bald youth and the hunt saboteuse.

"Now," he said.

The bald youth, at least, needed no additional urging. He shinned without further argument into the estate wagon's driving seat and started the engine.

"Imperialist running-dogs," said the hunt saboteuse to Widger and Ling.

"You just shut yer cake-'ole and get in 'ere with me, Elaine," the bald youth told her, "or I'll fetch you a clip on the ear you won't forget in a 'urry."

"Capitalist lackeys."

The bald youth reached across the estate wagon, pounced on her wrist, and hauled her squealing into the seat beside him, where he slapped her hard on the cheek—so hard as to induce a temporary bemused silence—slammed the door and at once began manoeuvring the estate wagon in the direction of Burraford. Fen sat down on the bank beside the inconsolable man in the caftan; the huntsman with the great buggerly beard collected Miss Mimms's reins and remounted his own horse; Widger and Ling ran back to the Cortina; the motorcyclists raised a cheer and their leader, who had observed the comeuppance of the hunt saboteuse with approval and who had stridden forward (but without enough celerity) intent on shaking the bald youth warmly by the hand, a salute which would probably in any case not have been particularly well received, was forced to beat a retreat to his machine, striving to make it appear that this was what he had intended all along. With the departure of the estate wagon the injured Enoch was revealed, still preoccupied with his personal vexation to the exclusion of all else. A hideous amalgam of smells infected the air—horse-droppings, petrol fumes, cow-dung. The Major, astride Xantippe, had long since passed out of earshot, not even his ululations provoked by thumping down intermittently on dry turf with an arthritic hip being now audible.

It rapidly became apparent, by the time the estate wagon had passed Y WURRY, that Rankine's tinkerings had not merely unjammed the brakes: they had made them inoperable altogether. The lane sloped slightly here, and in order to bring his vehicle under control, the bald youth was forced first to change down as rapidly as possible, and then to bring himself to a stop by nosing—admittedly not at any lethal pace—into the bank. The police cars edged past him and swept away. The man in the caftan heaved himself on to the crupper behind the man with the beard, who with Miss Mimms in tow followed more restrainedly. The motorcycles sputtered into life and took the turn to the left, where the Mini had been parked and where Alan Tully had eventually disposed of his cows. After a rather long wait a put-putting was heard and Scorer, at last assured of his safety, came in sight at about twenty miles an hour, presently disappearing well to the rearward of his fellow-enthusiasts. The three occupants of the again-immobilised estate wagon had observably lapsed into a violent quarrel on some topic or other, the hunt saboteuse doing most of the talking. Fen went across to the now abandoned Enoch, Clarence Tully's third cowman.

"Are you all right?" he asked.

"Naw, I bain't. Broke me bloody leg, that's what I've done. And where's that boy, that's what I wants to know. 'E did ought to 'a' come back for me. But they're all the same nowadays—no 'eart."

"Oh, I don't suppose it's as bad as that," said Fen consolingly. He meant Enoch's leg, not the callousness of the young. "Have you tried standing on it?"

"Wouldn't dare."

"Well, you're never going to find out until you do dare," said Fen a shade impatiently.

"Yur, maister."

"H'm?"

"'Ave 'ee got a drop o' water with 'ee?"

Fen tried to imagine himself—or anyone else, for the matter of that—tramping the countryside with a small bottle or flask of unfortified water in his pocket, and failed. "No, I haven't, I'm afraid," he said.

"Me throat's fair parched. Tes the shock, see?"

"Yes, I can see that in some circumstances—"

"Tes the shock, that's the only reason I arst. The shock, an' then the pain. Turrible bad, the pain is."

"I'm very sorry to hear that."

"Ah. Turrible bad. Dries a man's throat up. So that's why I arst, see?"

Fen stared about him, but no gleam of water met his eye, and he remembered, now, that no stream or even rivulet ran near-by. Closest was the Burr, at least two miles off, and even if Fen had been prepared to walk that distance and back again, he still possessed nothing in which he could convey the desired fluid to Tully's unseated hind, who would in any case probably have been picked up by some passing vehicle by the time he got back. As to human habitations, there was only one in sight, the Rector's house, Y WURRY.

Worth a try, perhaps.

"Wait," said Fen.

But the doors of the Rector's house proved, when he got there, to be either locked or bolted, and no ground-floor window stood open. He went back, accordingly, to where Enoch reclined, alternately clutching his ankle, trying to straighten the distorted steering-gear of his bicycle, and moaning, and reported failure, with the result that Enoch yammered more loudly than ever. Eventually rallying his powers of speech:

"So be 'ee 'a'bb'n got water," he said, coming at last to the nub of the matter, "'ee've got summat a mite stronger, mebbe?"

At this, Fen's heart hardened a little. Ordinarily a clement man, he now found himself somewhat out of sympathy with Enoch's predicament, which he was inclined to feel was being much exaggerated by its victim. No, the person Fen was really anxious about was the Major, whose elderly, brittle bones, in his headlong career across fields and hedges, must certainly bring him to grief sooner or later, if they had not done so already. Fen understood the Major's motives, all right: his dislike of horses was genuine, and he couldn't possibly have imagined that he had any chance of catching up with the man from Sweb in his Mini. What had happened was that quite simply, a spirit of boyish mischief had entered into him at the sight of Xantippe browsing almost immediately below him, and he had been wholly incapable of resisting it; then, once mounted, he had decided that for appearance's sake he must do something putatively purposeful in order to justify his action, and so had set heels to flank and taken off in pretended pursuit with a gusto worthy of the cavalry charge at Lewes (whose leader, Fen now uneasily remembered, had nearly lost the day owing to too prolonged a pursuit).

Which didn't mean that the Major wasn't at this moment pinned with a broken leg beneath a capsized hulk of squirming equine flesh, his cries for help unheard; for Xantippe had clearly not at all relished being descended upon, not, as Zeus descended upon Danae, by a shower of delicate manageable guineas but by a single vast, bifurcated ingot; and there had been the devil in her eye.

Fen decided to give Enoch one last chance.

"You must try to stand," he said. "You must put your weight on it." And when Enoch's mouth opened to protest against the anguish this would entail, he added hastily: "Not *all* of your weight. *Some* of it. Otherwise we shall never be able to find out whether that ankle of yours is broken or not."

"There's them X-rays."

"So there is. Are. But we haven't got them *here*, don't you see?"

"Didn't 'ee ever know what tes to 'ave a parched throat, squire? Tes a'most worse'n the pain, and that be—"

"Turrible; Yes, quite…I'll tell you what," said Fen, brightly and also rather abruptly, as if some entirely new-fleshed theophany had just presented itself to him. "Yes, I'll tell you what we ought to do. We ought to get you to a doctor."

"Can't move."

"We'll get a doctor to come to you here, then. I'll go and find a telephone and arrange for it."

"Doan leave me!"

"But, Mr Powell, how on earth can I fetch a doctor if—"

"Everyone leaves me!"

Fen lost patience at last; he was visualising the Major, steadily breaking up under Xantippe's hairy form like coal under the blows of a sledge-hammer; by now he might even be unable to call for help, whereas this—this preposterous chawbacon—

"Me too," he said, and pursued, diminishingly, by Enoch's heart-rending pleas, set off rapidly along the lane in the direction of Burraford, well to the rearward of the rest of the cortège. Passing the estate wagon, whose occupants seemed still locked in contumely, he considered briefly, and not for the first time, asking Mr Dodd to exercise his pharmaceutical skills on the ailing cowman. But once again he rejected the idea: Mr Dodd was patently at the moment in no frame of mind to relinquish his vituperations, even if the patient needing his attentions were in the final throes of a bout with the King of Terrors.

Fen left them behind, their offside wing still puncturing the bank, and lost them from earshot as he rounded the first bend of the lane.

He broke into a trot.

CHAPTER TWELVE

Bliss Was It in That Dawn to Be Alive

There is…a current of strong, leaking electricity.

Anthony Carson: *A Train to Tarragona.*

THE SCENE NOW changes dramatically to a point about three-quarters further along the lane towards Burraford, where Jack Jones is reclining against his pillows recuperating from the excitements of the meet, Isobel Jones is hammering a spigot into a kilderkin of one of the few potable ales left in the country and Mrs Clotworthy is making a steak-and-kidney pudding with a thick suet crust—to a point, in fact, at which the Pisser, its high-tension current like a loaded automatic rifle in the hands of some senile bedlamite, stands in rusty, antique ambush behind the hedge, terrorising with its noises not merely the passing natives but even strangers who know nothing of its habits but who sense instinctively that all is not well with the thing. For the moment, however, the Pisser is mute, and, with the exception of a single cable, literally unstrung; all is placidity and peace; the uproar from the Glazebridge quarter is inaudible here, and even if it were not, would evoke little remark, for the countryside is full of unaccountable phenomena, acoustic and otherwise, and to puzzle over each and every one of these would necessarily preoccupy the mind to the exclusion of all else. And certainly, none of the four persons present has attention to spare for anything but the anxieties and problems of his immediate vicinity; one of them, indeed, appears to be paying no attention whatever even to these.

The two engineers from the Central Electricity Generating Board are hard at work. Caps crammed down unhealthily to the very tops of their ears, they are labouring to make sense of the Pisser and its doings, and if possible to cure, or at least to modify, its present bogleman repute. Between the Pisser and the hedge they have erected, and somehow fixed firmly in the ground, a very much smaller pylon—as if the Pisser's noises had been a product of labour pains, and it had at last managed to pup—and an exact equivalent of this object stands on the *other* side of the lane (twins, then, one of them thrown further than the other in the process of parturition). Slung between these miniatures, and so crossing the lane, is a sort of mesh cradle constructed of heavy, many-plied wire. In this there repose the massive cables which (all but one) have been disconnected from the Pisser's terminals, and whose ends now lie coiled at random, large basking blindworms, on the grass near the Pisser's splayed, Lynn Chadwick feet.

On the Burraford side of all this obstruction is parked the C.E.G.B. lorry glimpsed earlier by Fen and the Major. It can be seen to be elaborately equipped, even to a radio-telephone.

But things are not going well, and the radio-telephone is unable to help. So, at least, diagnoses Don Goodey, third of the quartet. Goodey, it will be remembered, is the angler who, on the bank of the Burr, suffered the traumatic experience of being nudged on the toes, while dozing, by farmer Routh's severed head, or to be more accurate, by the impro-vised raft to which that horrific *memento mori* was nailed. He has, however, by now had plenty of time in which to recover from his dismal arousal—plenty of time, too, for his dining out on ever more and more gaudy accounts of his experience to have at length palled. Accordingly he has reverted to his normal chief recreation, which, angling apart, is watching other people at work. And in this, clearly, it is the two workmen who are the star turns: the fourth person present, though admittedly in some sense working—working, moreover, with hardly a moment's pause for reflection or rest—lacks, for Goodey, the pleasing charisma of intense muscular effort; moreover, the nature of his association with the workmen, though patently such an association does exist, is hard to define. He is a tall man in leggings; his dress and general demeanour suggest that he is socially a cut above the other two; he holds a large mill-board, its spring clip fairly bursting with paper. Much of the paper has been written on, and is hanging over the edge of the board, but a considerable wad remains virgin, and on this, Leggings is busy writing with a silver ballpoint pen. He is some sort of supervisor, then, some sort of foreman, and his occupation is to keep a record of the work being done on the Pisser, the assiduity or other-wise of its doers, the triumphs they may achieve from time to time, and so on and so forth. Yes; but here Goodey's interest turns to perplexity. Surely Leggings is writing *far too much* for these simple explanations to be adequate? Glittering in the autumn sunlight, his Biro is travelling from left to right of the page with the rapidity of a shuttle operating a loom. It reaches the end of a line; in a flash it whisks back, a notch lower, to the beginning of the next line—and with undimin-ished rapidity the whole process is repeated. Now Leggings has come to the end of his page; he flips it over the edge of the mill-board and instantly commences work on another. Scarcely an official report, then, even though such things are apt to be wordy to a degree. Goodey, though unemploy-able through idleness, is by no means uneducated. Possibly, he conjectures, Leggings is whiling away his time with the C.E.G.B. with the composition of a large panoramic novel, something of the order of *Little Dorrit*, say, or *War and Peace*.

He is not, in any case, very exhilarating to study for long, and Goodey's gaze reverts to the two workmen.

These are now both on the Pisser's side of the lane, struggling in unison, and still vainly, with some sort of winding mechanism attached by a hawser from the mini-pylon to the nearer end of the wire cradle. The cradle jolts and jerks under their combined assault, but remains obstinately blocking the throughway. Goodey feels very sorry for this pair. On such a hot morning, it must be aggravating to strive so hard and meet with such poor success. Goodey decides—mistakenly, as it turns out, but he is one of those people who are chronically error-prone—that perhaps a little encouragement from an outsider will be consoling, and may even weight the scales in the workmen's favour.

"Having a bit of trouble?" he calls.

Unheeding, Leggings scribbles on. But the two workmen are far from being unheeding. For a moment, they seem as if turned to bronze. Then, with one accord abandoning the mini-pylon and its winch, they make for the gate against which Goodey has been leaning. Something in their demeanour disquiets Goodey, who retreats a few steps into the lane. The workmen come out through the gate, and so forward to confront their Job's Comforter. The older man leads, but the other is close behind him. The older man looks at Goodey and then speaks.

"You bugger off," he says, confidingly.

Goodey is six foot tall, but his interlocutor tops him by at least three inches. Moreover, he is brawny, brown and very muscular from long hours of work in the open air. No thought but the conciliatory crosses Goodey's mind. "No offence meant," he mumbles.

"But some taken," says the workman. He stares at Goodey fixedly for a further few seconds, as though engraving his features in some personal Rogues' Gallery prominently on display somewhere behind his central sulcus. Then he turns to his companion, nods briefly, and leads the way back to their scene of joint arduousness at the mini-pylon, carefully closing the gate behind them.

Leggings stops writing for long enough to raise his eyes briefly to the heavens, presumably in search of inspiration. He finds it, and the ball-point at once goes into action again.

Goodey wonders whether he had better take himself off altogether, and look for diversion elsewhere. But there are elements in this present situation which are irresistible: Goodey absolutely *must*, he feels, wait and see how it is eventually resolved. Cautiously—indeed, almost on tiptoe—he re-approaches the gate.

Leggings pauses for long enough to take out a handkerchief and wipe his eyes: he has perhaps just embarked on an extended and pathetic death-bed scene.

Rattling like a rabid mongrel with dozens of empty tin cans tied to its tail, a helicopter comes into sight over Worthington's Steep, apparently steering by the line of pylons to which the Pisser belongs. Reaching the Pisser itself, it begins deafeningly to circle, conceivably—thinks Goodey, transferring his attention from workmen to chopper—with a view to taking aerial photographs.

But helicopters are not really very absorbing, the way frustrated workmen are.

The wire cradle across the lane squeaks and gibbers like the sheeted dead, at the same time shivering like those Romans unfortunate enough to be abroad and observe them.

The older workman keeps shouting, "One, *two*, THREE! One, *two*, AGAIN!", and at each climax a groan goes up, accompanied by the sound of sinews cracking.

The cradle remains earth-bound.

Having propped the infant Grand Duchess up against her frilly damask pillows (bed-side toys by courtesy of Fabergé), Leggings resumes writing. The infant Grand Duchess smiles bravely and lisps a request for a glass of *eau de vie*. No, better make that lemonade or passion-fruit juice.

The cradle seems to be lifting now. No, it isn't. Yes, it is. No, it isn't.

It has fallen back on to the lane again. Sexual, scatological and religious oaths are uttered in quick succession by the two workmen.

Even above these, and the rumpus of the helicopter, sharp-eared Goodey picks up a new sound. So now, he reflects, there really *will* be trouble.

Up along the lane from the direction of Glazebridge, a cloud of dust has appeared, moving rapidly.

Presently this resolves itself into a grey Mini, driven by a small, pink-faced person in a grey trilby hat.

It is the man from Sweb.

By temperament, the man from Sweb was an evader, not an escaper. He had been put away three times—the first time for half a stretch, the second time for one and a bit, the third for a pontoon; but since he was a stair dancer, a walk-in thief, judges had been inclined to be lenient until the last occasion, when his offence had been said by prosecuting counsel to have been aggravated by his having broken a window to "effect an entrance" (the man from Sweb had denied this, squeaking out from the box some long, rambling fantasy about people who didn't keep their houses in proper repair; but unluckily the judge hadn't believed any of this). Still, on the whole he had had it off all right, thanks to working alone, to making careful reccys, to a considerable knowledge of works of art and to lying low in between jobs; and his previous arrests had all been peaceable, unexpected affairs, the work probably of some anonymous snout, and had left him with no time in which to get seriously nervous. But this business was different: now the hounds were on his scent with a vengeance, and he was running for cover instead of being relatively amicably, as it were, unveiled; now he had to get to his bolt-hole in a hurry, against expert competition—and his bolt-hole was a long way away. No wonder he was scared, and driving somewhat erratically as a consequence. Instead of watching the road ahead, he kept peering into his driving mirror, and even twisting round to look back through the rear mirror. The rozzers were after him, not a doubt about that...

He looked for all the world, Goodey thought wonderingly as the little car raced nearer and nearer, like a fugitive from justice.

Emerging from Y WURRY with his, or rather the Rector's, ponderous iron coffer, and intending to slip away with it as quietly as possible, the man from Sweb had been dismayed to hear voices raised in wrath, together with motor engines and various animal noises, only a short distance away; and an unobtrusive survey of the situation, through a small hole in the outermost of one of the Rector's many hedges, had increased his alarm almost to a point at which he had considered returning the coffer to the Rector's attic, and its obviously matching key to the hall table on which it had carelessly been left; he could then, if discovered on the premises, easily have fabricated some innocent reason for his presence there. But now—police! And in force! True, for the moment they seemed much preoccupied by the mellay still gathering impetus in the lane. True, if he had been thinking clearly the man from Sweb could easily have unlocked the coffer, seen if there was anything of value inside it, and if not, have thrown it away and made off. But his emotions at the prospect—the *possible* prospect—of yet another dose of porridge were such that he was as incapable of thinking clearly as he would have been of throwing a grenade at Princess Anne. No blagger he. On the contrary, he was, for an experienced criminal, a markedly timorous man, and the forefront of his mind was wholly preoccupied with the notion that the anonymous snout had struck again, and that Old Bill consequently knew not only that he was here, but also that he had chosen this particular afternoon, when the Rector had publicly announced that he would be away at a Diocesan Synod, to turn that clergyman's drum over and make off with the best and most disposable of the many *objets d'art et de virtu* its top floor were said to contain. Had he known that Old Bill, in the shape of the Rector, was gleefully watching his every move from the inside of the house, he would probably have fainted from fear. As it was, he simply panicked and decided to take a chance, rushing out of the gate, and into the Mini, and away, before the police had any opportunity to disentangle themselves, or even to become seriously aware he was present. He did, however, as he drove off, hear the Rector's cry of "Stop thief!", and knew with a heart-sick prosternation that he was discovered. The only thing to do now seemed to be to drive as fast as possible and hope that some wildly improbable contingency would rescue him at the last.

Accordingly, he was so busy looking at the road behind that he was almost on top of the Pisser's cradle, stretched across his route, before a chorus of warning cries, including even that of Leggings, awoke him to his peril. Stamping on the foot-brake, he skidded violently and somehow managed to bring the Mini to a halt, nearly sending himself head first through the windscreen, mere millimetres short of the obstruction. With the dust settling round him, but with the lane towards Glazebridge still void of pursuit, he scrambled out and stared pitifully at the two workmen, who in turn stared blankly back at him. Leggings had returned to his writing, trying to decide whether the infant Grand Duchess was exhibiting a deathly pallor or a hectic flush.

Goodey, who was closest, spoke.

"Well, you nearly copped it that time, chum," he said, friendily.

The man from Sweb's mild and diffident manner was genuine, not a pose: he knew that if he were a professional actor, he would be permanently "resting". "Shall you be long?" he asked. "I don't want to be a nuisance, but—"

"At this rate, looks as if we're going to be all day," said Goodey cheerily, associating himself gratuitously with the electricity men. "I'd back up and go round by Hole Bridge, if I was you."

"But I've *got* to get through. I've *got* to!"

"Well, if you was to hang on for a bit, I dare say—"

"No, no! You don't *understand*!"

Goodey, who had a fine conceit of himself, was unprepared to admit this. He said: "You've got to get through. Right? But you can't get through till that cradle's shifted. Right? So you'll have to ask"—here Goodey looked doubtfully at Leggings, who had again momentarily paused in his writing, perhaps meditating the literary advisability, or otherwise, of petechiae—"you'll have to ask those two chaps there how they're getting along. Right?"

The man from Sweb cleared his throat. "Shall you be long?" he called. But his tone as well as being squeaky was humble and muted, and the two workmen, though conscious of being addressed, failed to catch his drift. "What?" they bellowed. "What was that you said?"

More loudly, "I said, shall you be long?" the man from Sweb repeated. "I—I'm in rather a hurry, you see."

The two workmen looked at one another, and evidently decided that this was not a foeman worthy of their steel. "We'll be as long as a donkey's," the older one said—at which witticism he and his colleague clutched one another in a joint paroxysm of mirth. "Tell you what, matey, you want to get through, you just come in here and lend us a hand." Leggings frowned fractionally at them, but the Muse was too strong for him, and he resumed composition without speaking. "They don't *understand*," squeaked the man from Sweb desperately. "*No one* understands."

"Yes, yes, they do," Goodey soothed him. "I understand. Your problem, as I see it—"

But the man from Sweb was no longer attending to him. Instead, he was staring back in horror along the lane, where a second, smaller cloud of dust had appeared. This solidified shortly into a bandy-legged ape wearing clerical black, moving towards them at quite a considerable pace.

"It's him!" shrieked the man from Sweb. "It's him! They're after me! They'll catch me!"

Though beginning to wonder if he was dealing with a lunatic, Goodey made another attempt at consolation. "Now, that's only the Rector," he said. "I don't know why he's running like that—shouting something too, by the sound of it—but unless you've been visiting him, and have left something important behind...Come to think of it, I heard he was at some conference or other this afternoon, but I suppose—"

He got no further, for at this point the man from Sweb gave vent to a cry like a live mouse being torn asunder by contesting tabbies. For now two further clouds of dust had appeared, approaching rapidly in file and emitting engine noises. These passed the Rector at speed, and were quickly seen to be a Cortina followed by a police Panda car. The man from Sweb threw up his hands in dismay—a gesture Goodey had hitherto imagined to be confined to the stage, and even there to have died the death about the time of the production of *The Second Mrs Tanqueray*—and looked round him wildly. Then he lunged back into the Mini, emerged from it clutching a large heavy iron chest, and with this upborne in his arms thrust through the gate, setting off at a tottering run towards the patch of scrubby woodland which signalled the nearest available shelter. Goodey had been right the first time: the man was a fugitive from justice. Should he, Goodey, therefore now give chase? He was still inwardly debating this problem when it was solved for him by the Cortina and the Panda screeching to a sudden stop immediately behind the man from Sweb's abandoned Mini.

Widger and Ling were as a matter of fact still unaware of the man from Sweb and of his nefarious activities back at Y WURRY: they had bigger fish to fry. All they knew was that there was yet *another* impediment to their real momentous mission; and by thrusting their heads out of the car windows they were able to glimpse the heavy wire cradle, strung across the lane, which had brought the Mini to its present chrysalid, sloughed condition.

"That car yours?" Widger bellowed at Leggings.

His pen momentarily halted, Leggings shook his head.

"Well, is it yours, then?" Widger demanded of Goodey.

Goodey said that No, it wasn't.

"Is it theirs?" said Widger, indicating the two workmen but addressing himself to Leggings.

Leggings frowned at this renewed interruption and again shook his head.

Widger got out of the Cortina.

"Whose is it, then?" he enquired angrily of the world at large.

"It's his," said Goodey.

"His? Whose?"

"His." And Goodey pointed to the man from Sweb, who by now was several hundred yards away and in some slight danger from the helicopter; this had been circling lower and lower over the Pisser and was now evidently intending to touch down near by. Its ratchet clatterings were making conversation increasingly difficult on the ground.

"Who is he?" Widger shouted. "What's he running away for?"

Goodey shrugged. "Don't ask *me*," he shouted back. "I think he may be trying to escape from the police."

"Why should he be doing that?"

"What?"

"*I said, why should he be doing that?*"

The Rector joined them. For a man of his years, his long run had left him remarkably unpuffed. "After him, Widger!" he said, his normal tones amply the equal in decibel power to everyone else's special efforts. "After him, I say! Tally-ho! Thar she blows! Yoicks! Never say you let him get away from you now!"

"There, there, sir."

"What?"

"*I said There, there.*"

"Could have told you from the first he wasn't from Sweb," said the Rector. "Not nasty enough, for one thing. You know why he came to see me, Widger? He was casing my joint."

"You mean to tell me, sir, that he was a—is a—"

"I was ready for him, though," said the Rector. "First time he came to see me, I said to myself, *he's* not from Sweb. So I rang them up, and sure enough, he wasn't. Good disguise, mind. Nowadays we're all such a parcel of tegs that we'll believe anyone who says he's anything to do with any part of the Government or the County Council or any of that drivel. There were ninety and nine who safely lay," said the Rector, "in the shelter of the fold. Only I was the hundredth, you see." He paused, possibly because the context of his quotation struck him, coming from a Christian cleric, as not wholly apposite. "Anyway, he didn't take *me* in, not for a single second. Here's a bad egg, I said to myself. And sure enough, he was. Mistake *he* made, though, was in casing my joint too soon. Because during the last week, I've sold practically everything valuable off, and it's all been taken away, by Spink's and people. So then, when I gave it out that I wasn't going to be home this afternoon—"

"Wait, sir, wait," bawled Widger. "Are you trying to tell me that that man"—he gestured towards the by now fairly distant little grey figure still stumbling in laborious haste across the tussocky grass towards the woods—"that that man is a *burglar*?"

"Course he's a burglar. Got criminality written all over him, like some outsize *graffito*. It says, 'I am a criminal,' that's what it says."

The near-side door of the Cortina opened to emit a thick nimbus of tobacco smoke through which, as the breeze wafted it away, the irate figure of the officer in charge of the investigation presently became discernible. "What in hell is going on *now*?" it wanted to know, as it circled the car to join Widger, Goodey and the Rector in the shadow of the Pisser.

"It's the Rector, Eddie. As far as I can make out, he think's he's been burgled."

"What?"

"*I said, As far as I can make out, the Rector thinks he's been burgled.*"

"Inspector, arrest that man," said the Rector.

"Superintendent, sir. I smoke a pipe."

"Superintendent, arrest that man."

"I—I—" said Ling, in what was apparently a nautical affirmative.

"He stole a Victorian jewel-safe from me."

"Oh, in that case, sir—"

"Get him back here and make him…make him"—here the Rector's normal vibrant tones acquired a marked and significant tremor—"make him open the safe in your presence."

"Very good, sir, I'll…" Ling called to the two constables in the Panda. "Crosse! Tavener!" he called. "Go after that man"—pointing—"and bring him back." The two constables leapt from their car and trotted off into the Pisser's field in the wake of the man from Sweb, who turned and saw them coming but who, burdened as he was, could do nothing to put on speed other than abandon his spoils. Still scraping vaguely at himself with the handcuffs, Rankine left the Cortina and joined the continually enlarging group by the gate.

"Not that I didn't *mean* him to, mind," said the Rector.

Ling felt that the primary purpose of their mission was becoming diluted by trivia. To the workmen he shouted, "Eh, coom on lads, git tha' bluidy thing out o' t'way, can't 'ee?"

"We're police," Widger bawled over the ever-increasing stridor of the descending helicopter.

"You're police, you better stick us in the cells," bawled back the workman who had terrorized Goodey, wiping sweat off his brow with a hairy forearm. "Be a sight cooler there than it is here, I reckon…Here, Bert," he added, addressing his colleague, "get on over the other side and see if that roller's got stuck again, will you?"

Pushing his way unceremoniously through the assembly at the gate, Bert crossed the lane, somehow forced his way through a hole in the hedge and disappeared from view. The cradle began to twitch and shudder again.

Rankine had produced a notebook. "Shall I take some details, sir?" he asked Widger.

"No."

Now two horses became members of the static troupe. The first carried Miss Mimms, not at the immediate moment weeping, but with all the look of a storm-cloud sucking up moisture in readiness for a fresh deluge. The second carried the bearded huntsman, ready no doubt with his single expletive, and on its crupper the man in the caftan, peering anxiously about him in all directions for a sight of his missing mare. This was the situation when with the exception of Leggings ("Please, please, Uncle Stanislas, make me well again") everyone had his or her mouth open in preparation for speech.

And this was when, virtually simultaneously, three separate climaxes occurred.

In the first place, the Pisser exploded, as everybody but the experts had always said it one day would. First giving brief warning with a hiss like a thousand pitsful of Fu Manchu's death-dealing snakes, its one remaining connected terminal first discharged a corona of brilliant blue and orange sparks and then produced a dentonation so ear-splitting and colossal as to make people even as far distant as Hole Bridge leap to the conclusion that nuclear warfare had become a reality at last. Of those gathered together to witness this *dénouement* (apart from the horses, which plunged and whinnied as if suddenly assaulted on all sides by Gargantuan gadflies), for many seconds only one was able to move: swearing terribly and still clutching his mill-board, Leggings raced up to the cradle, somehow manoeuvred himself underneath it, grabbed up the radio-telephone on board the C.E.G.B. lorry and began gabbling frantic warnings. The Pisser's single cable had left at least a small part of the neighbourhood able to use electrical appliances; now all lunch-time ovens cooled, electric irons ceased to make proper creases, spin driers ground to a halt and television assumed a stupefying blankness for many miles around. One music-lover, his stereo tape-deck only a second away from the enormous climax of *Also Sprach Zarathustra*, genuinely supposed, for a few frantic seconds, that Jahweh,

on account of his sins, had determined to strike him instan-
taneously deaf, with the result that, instead of a thunderous
chord, dead abrupt silence met his ears.

The second explosion came hard on the heels of the first,
and although not nearly so loud, was shocking enough in all
conscience. Looking around and seeing Crosse and Tavener
closing in on him, the man from Sweb had done what he ought
to have done long before: he had paused, dumped the Rector's
box on the grass, fished its key from his pocket, unlocked it and
opened its lid: unencumbered, he might—just *might*—succeed
in reaching the woods, and taking cover there, before the fuzz
caught up with him. If he had had any sense, he wouldn't even
have worried about the box's contents—but the acquisitive
instinct in thieves is naturally very strong, and the man from
Sweb was psychologically incapable of not taking just a quick
look, the more so as the helicopter was just touching down and
so temporarily concealing him from the two pursuing uniforms.
He opened the box, and suffered a humiliation which almost
made him decide to spend the remainder of his life in some
blameless occupation, such as politics or hawking encyclopae-
dias from door to door.

The helicopter's rotors were slowing to a standstill as the
Pisser began its hissing noise. From the pilot's cabin jumped
the pilot. He wrenched open the passenger door and let down
a short flight of steps, down which, barely credibly in those
surroundings, there started to descend two men in bowler
hats, each with brief-case and neatly furled umbrella, both in
pin-striped black trousers and black coats. These, presumably,
were an arm of the C.E.G.B.'s top brass, come to give their
personal attention to the technical problem confronting their
subordinates.

The first of them, however, had not yet reached *terra
firma* when the Pisser let fly; and the second bang, following
so rapidly afterwards, broke their nerve completely. Shouting
something at the pilot ("Take off! Take off!" it might have
been), they turned and rushed back up into the shelter of their

aircraft. Of sterner stuff, the pilot shrugged, whipped the little flight of steps back into its concealment, slammed the door, clambered back into his cockpit, and obeyed. The machine lifted higher and higher. Then it veered away and clickety-clacked rapidly southward over the top of Worthington's Steep, where it vanished, being, indeed, never seen in those parts again.

The second bang, meanwhile, had been the product of the man from Sweb's opening the Rector's box, and was shattering enough in itself. But there was more. Accompanying the bang, a thick black cloud jetted from the box's interior, totally smothering the man from Sweb's frontal aspect from the tip of his hat to half way down his trousers, so that it appeared as if the make-up artist from *The Black and White Minstrel Show* had gone berserk or was protesting against racism, or (since the two things are not dissimilar) both. Nor was even this quite all—though for the time being only the man from Sweb and the pursuant Law were suitably placed to appreciate the Rector's delicate final touch. And the pursuant Law, coming up to where the man from Sweb, all notions of escape banished from his mind by his dreadful condition, stood acquiescently awaiting it, could be seen from the gate not merely to hesitate, but even to recoil slightly. But then Duty, stern daughter of the Voice of God, took over again. The pursuant Law, possibly mindful of the Force's unofficial motto (*"YOU JUST COME ALONG O' ME, ME BUCK-O"*), trod forward again. Crosse took the man from Sweb by the arm, and set off with him towards the gate; Tavener gingerly picked up the box, following on with that.

They arrived, and at their approach it soon became evident what this third element in the booby-trap had been. It had been hydrogen sulphide.

The man from Sweb smelled like a cargo of broken addled eggs.

A faint whimpering came from the edge of the group. This was the Rector, trying to suppress his laughter.

The man from Sweb, who when desperately hard pressed could show an irascible side, glared. "Call yourself a man of God," he squeaked. "Call yourself a man of God, and look what you—look what you—look what you've—" Words failed him.

"The Hulland twins made that for me," said the Rector. "Very clever with their hands, the Hulland twins. Don't know how they managed to make the hydrogen sulphide into a spray, though. I always thought it was just a gas."

"It's a gas, all right," said Crosse, who was prone to Americanisms. "Phew! I never smelled anything like it."

"He pongs, he pongs, he's black and he pongs," the Rector intoned, to the first part of the chant generally used for the Psalm *Justus es, Domine*. "And the soot, too. Lovely. It was all damp and caked when I gave it to the Hulland twins from the chimneys of my house. They must have dried it out very carefully and then sieved it over and over again. But it's the pong that's the best. Haw-haw," chortled the Rector, bending forwards in his mirth and clutching with both hands at his stomach as if it contained a great rent from which, if unstemmed, his puddings would come bursting out. "Ah, haw-haw-haw-haw-*haw*!"

"What's happening?" This was Fen, who had at last caught up with them all. "What's happening, and where's the Major?"

"The Major," said Widger, pointing, "is *there*."

For this was the third of the three things whose simultaneity, and whose immediate consequences, make them so difficult to describe, intelligibly, in any sort of chronological order.

While the Pisser was preparing to detonate, and the man from Sweb was fumbling in his pocket for the key to the Victorian jewel-safe, there was heard, though amid all the other agitations not attended to, the ker-a-lop, ker-a-lop, in the next field towards Glazebridge, of a galloping horse. This approached with great rapidity, ceasing to be sound and becoming vision at precisely the instant when Xantippe, the Major still up, jumped the hedge into the Pisser's field. Unfortunately it was also the instant when the double squib went off.

Now, it is not physically possible for any horse totally unconnected with the ground to stop dead in mid-air; yet this was what, to Goodey's dazed and deafened senses, Xantippe appeared fractionally to do. Then, like a cinema projector resuming normal working after a frame has jammed, all was movement again. Xantippe came on over. She touched down. And now she really did stop dead, all four hooves thrust forward while her head and body hinged backwards from her fore-arms, stifle joints and quarters.

So abrupt and violent an arrest of impetus can, for the rider, have only one result.

The Major flew over Xantippe's head.

He had had his first fall.

He was not dead, however, or even, it seemed, seriously incapacitated. First he moved; then he lifted his head; then he got somewhat groggily to his feet, and, leaving his mount in an unhorsemanlike manner to its own devices, began hobbling towards the group at the gate. Fen went to meet him.

"Major, are you all right?"

"Yes, perfectly, my dear fellow, perfectly. And didn't you *see*?"

"Yes, I arrived just in time to see. But the thing is—"

"I had a *fall*, my dear fellow, I had a *fall*. I had my first *fall*...Mind you—nasty treacherous brute, that. She refused three times, and each time I had to take her back and put her at the fence all over again. Still, we got here eventually."

On catching sight of his horse, the man in the caftan had uttered a single shriek of "XANTIPPE!", had practically fallen off from behind Beaver, and had rushed to the rescue of his kidnapped love, Miss Mimms, though a horsy girl herself, gazing after him in considerable resentment at being so absolutely forgotten in favour of an animal of so little apparent breeding. She threw a pleading look back over her shoulder at Beaver, who said "Scybalum!", apparently on general principles rather than for any particular cause. Passing Fen and the Major, the man in the caftan paused for long enough to hiss "Horse-thief!" at the Major, and then raced on to administer consolation to his maltreated darling, who, though sweating fairly freely, seemed not much the worse for her adventure. She had already recovered from her terror, and was browsing, and would quite soon—it was possible to surmise —be falling asleep again. The man in the caftan patted her nose and gave her sugar and wiped her with the hem of his garment. He mouthed comforting phrases at her, but these were unfathomable to those who heard them, since they were couched in some unidentifiable language—stable-boys' argot, perhaps, or even, in view of the horse's name, demotic Greek.

"What happened to the man from Sweb?" the Major asked Fen.

"They caught him. He's here now."

"Super," said the Major, who had been watching too many David Frost programmes recently. "Can't have characters like that ballsing up the Rector's property. Ah, and there he is."

"Who?"

"The Rector. In at the death, as usual. It's the human deaths I mean," the Major explained kindly. "The Rector isn't a hunting man."

"You're sure you haven't broken any bones?"

"No, no, my dear chap, nothing awkward like that. Just bruises. Witch-hazel, now have I got any witch-hazel at the flat? Yes, I believe I have. I tried to use it on Sal once, only she bit me. Postman kicked her, the wretched brute."

"Well then, what about your head? Are you concussed?"

"Certainly not. Do I *sound* concussed...? Though come to think of it"—they were now nearing the gate—"there does seem to be something a bit odd about my sense of smell. For example—"

"Oh, that's all right," said Fen. "That's just the man from Sweb."

"Is it really? I don't remember his smelling like that before. But perhaps it's one of these men's toiletries they're always advertising."

"It's sulphuretted hydrogen," said Fen. "Seriously, Major, I'd be easier in my mind if you let Dr Mason take a quick look at you."

"It's very kind of you, my dear fellow, but really, there's not the least need. A few hours' rest, and I'll be as right as rain again. Come to think of it, I do believe the fall's done my arthritis good: it doesn't seem nearly as painful as usual."

On arrival, they found Widger at odds with the Rector. "No, of course I'm not going to charge him with anything." the Rector was saying. "I set him a booby-trap and he fell into it, that's all."

"He surreptitiously entered your premises, sir."

"Yes, I know. Dozens of people do, because apart from anything else, I never keep it locked, except for the attic rooms. And even the attic rooms have been left unlocked these last few days, since Spink and Sotheby and Christie took all the valuable stuff away...You should have heard them ohh-ing and ah-ing, for all the world like Billy Bunter offered a huge plate of chocolate éclairs. Yes, dozens of people come in and wander about the house, calling 'Rector! Rector!' when all the time I'm hiding in the cloaks cupboard. I'll admit, they have souls to be saved like anyone else, but the trouble is, I've saved most of them already, and it only makes them pester me all the worse."

"Well, I don't care," said Widger in one of his rare spasms of irritability. "If you won't bring a charge against him, I *shall*. I'm not having any stair dancers wandering around loose in *my* manor...Rankine!"

"Sir?"

"Arrest that man."

"Sir."

With some reluctance Rankine approached the man from Sweb. "I am a police officer," he said, "and I arrest you...I arrest you...I arr—What's his name, sir?"

Widget glowered at the man from Sweb. "What's your name?" he said.

"It's Humphrey de Brisay," squeaked the man from Sweb.

Ling snorted his disgust. "Oh, rubbish," he said.

"No, hang on a minute, Eddie," said Widger. "I think that actually *may* be his name." To the man from Sweb, "I've heard of you," he said. "You've just come out of the nick for breaking and entering and stealing a Koekkoek and a Bosboom from a house in Wiltshire. You've got a record as long as my arm."

"I never broke. I never entered," squeaked de Brisay indignantly. "Half of the people with valuables go out for the day leaving their front doors and their ground-floor windows open, so there's no need to break. All that happened in Wiltshire was that I noticed one of their billiard-room windows had a bit of a crack in it, and I gave it a little tap, just to see if it was firm, and the whole lot fell in." He subsided into gloom. "Only the judge wouldn't believe me," he concluded bathetically.

"I don't believe you, either," said Widget. "Come on, come on, Rankine. Get on with it."

"Sir…I am a police officer, and I arrest you, Humphrey de Brisay, in that you did—did—What *did* he do, sir?"

"Broke and entered, of course."

"There's no such thing," said de Brisay.

Rankine lifted a forefinger. "We have now to consider," he began.

"We have now to consider, Rankine," said Widger, "whether you remain in the Force or whether I recommend that you—"

"Yes, sir," said Rankine hurriedly. "I am a police officer," he said. Ling groaned.

"IamapoliceofficerandIarrestyouHumphreydeBrisayinthat youdidsteal—did steal—exactly what did he steal, sir?"

"It's my Grandmother's jewel-safe," said the Rector. "Spink and Co. wanted it, but I kept it for sentimental reasons. It's not very valuable I understand, but these London dealers— Sotheby and so forth—would call their mothers 'Ma'am', and bow at them and bob at them, their aged souls to damn."

"He keeps a lady in a cage most cruelly all day," said de Brisay.

"There," said the Rector triumphantly. "there's good in all of us, if only you know where to look for it."

"What are you two talking about?" said Widger, his choler growing momently. "RANKINE!"

"—in that you did steal the Rector's grandmother's jewel-safe of the value of—of the—"

"About a hundred," said the Rector.

"ofthevalueofaboutahundredbelongingtotheRectorcontr-arytoSectionsoneandsevenTheftAct1968."

"Bravo," squeaked de Brisay. "So now let's have it all again, from the beginning."

"I am a p—"

"Rankine, get back into the car at once. And take de Brisay with you." Suddenly Widger frowned. "No, wait a minute. Now I come to think of it…"

"Exactly," muttered Ling.

"Is it really going to need five of us, Eddie? If not, Crosse or Tavener could take de Brisay to the factory in the Mini, while the rest of us—"

But Ling shook his head. "It *could* need five," he said, still more or less *sotto voce*. "And we'd look pretty silly if we started economising on man power in a thing like *this*." Then he brightened slightly. "Tell you what, though. The Rector could take him back to Y WURRY in the Mini and lock him up there until we had a man free to fetch him."

"I'm not locking anyone up," said the Rector, who had overheard the last part of this. "I'll take him home with me, yes. And I'll get the pong off him. And I'll clean him up. And I'll find some fresh clothes for him. And I'll give him some lunch—*Tournedos Barbara* today, so he ought to enjoy that… And in return," he said to de Brisay, "you can help me with my sermons for tomorrow. All these endless Sundays after Trinity, it gets very difficult to think of anything to say that has any bearing on anything."

"I've already told you," squeaked de Brisay, "that I'm not religious."

"We'll soon cure that," said the Rector. "The Repentant Thief, now. Of course, it's not exactly the right time of year for him, but you could help me over him, even so. We could even stick you up in the pulpit, and you could Bear Witness."

"But I'm *not* repentant."

"H'm. You could read aloud to me over lunch, then. John Dickson Carr, *The Crooked Hinge*. Good stuff. And then after you've paid your debt to society, perhaps you'd like to be my valet."

De Brisay was bereft of speech. "Your *valet*, Rector?" said the Major, almost equally bemused. "What on earth do you want a valet for?"

"Well, I always look a bit of a mess, you know," said the Rector cheerfully, "because my housekeeper isn't any good with clothes. So of course, although I don't want to peacock around the place like a Papist, I do feel that I ought at least to be a bit *neat*, due to my ordination and so forth. So I thought you might come in useful there," he said to de Brisay, "once we get rid of that frightful pong of yours. Ha! Caught you neatly there, didn't I? Oh, haw-haw," said the Rector. "Ah, haw-*haw*-HAW-*HAW*. That's right, you settle in quietly and be my valet. Sunday evenings off, and two whole weeks' holiday a year. Five pounds."

"You get better conditions than that in stir," squeaked de Brisay. "So the answer is, No, I bloody well *won't* come and be your valet."

At this point, they were rejoined by Leggings, who had presumably terminated his telephone call. He was clearly in a foul temper; and for some reason which no one was ever able to fathom, either then or later, he instantly fastened on de Brisay as the author of all his misfortunes. Striding up to the little man, he raised his mill-board—which despite appearances turned out not to be a mill-board at all, but a stout plank of wood—and brought it down with colossal force on the top of his chosen victim's head, crushing down his soot-bedecked trilby so that de Brisay, blinded, off balance and partially stunned, reeled into the arms of Detective-Inspector Widger. Almost overpowered by the smell, Widger withdrew hurriedly from this unwelcome embrace, while de Brisay, after careering round several times in circles, eventually succeeded in recovering both his balance and his power of vision, and so managed to bring himself to a stop.

"Now, now, sir," said Widger weakly, to Leggings, "you'd no call to be doing that, you know. No call at all." But Leggings was of too stern a mettle to be affected by such feeble objurgations; without making any reply, or even paying any noticeable attention, he returned to his original post and began writing again.

"Well, I'll be getting back to my flat, I think," said the Major. "An hour or two lying down watching the telly'll work wonders, you'll see. Can you tell the butter from Stork Margarine?" he sang. "Course you can't, course you can't, course—you—can't. I can, as a matter of fact, quite easily, but it's a pretty little tune, charming. See you later, then, at the pub. Toodle-oo meanwhile." And with this he hobbled up the lane in the direction of Aller House, which was just visible beyond the hedges and the trees.

It was the beginning of the break-up of the party. "Rector," said Ling, "I know we can trust you to keep an eye on de Brisay for us. We'll send a car for him as soon as we possibly can. In the meantime"—he turned to Widger—"I've been wondering if a horse could jump that wire cradle thing and take a message on ahead for us. We've got the horses, we've got—we've got—we've—"

Astonishment, as he looked round him, stunned him into silence; and Widger, following his gaze, was equally flabbergasted. For during the preceding alarms and excursions, the horses, together with Beaver and Miss Mimms, had disappeared as completely as if the ground had opened and swallowed them all up; they were quite simply nowhere in sight. It was Widger who first saw the reason for this apparently supernatural happening.

"Look!" he shouted. "LOOK!"

The two workmen had met with success at last. Just how long previously they had met with it was to provide matter for acrimonious dispute between Widger and Ling in the bar of The Seven Tuns that evening. The important thing, for the moment, was that at some undefined juncture their sweaty toil had been crowned with triumph. The cradle was no longer obstructing the throughway; instead, it was suspended high in the air between its mini-pylons, with ample space for a ten-foot-high lorry to pass beneath.

Ling was galvanized into activity. "Quick!" he bellowed. "Quick! Crosse, Tavener, back into the Panda. Rankine—"

A new but filth-encrusted Volvo, coming from Burraford way, screeched to a halt alongside them. In its back seats were Beaver and Miss Mimms, the latter of whom was resting her head sideways against the former's chest, so that it looked (her cap was now off) like some monstrous hirsute pectoral growth which had burst through the veil of his beard and was exuding liquid (she was sobbing again). At intervals Beaver would hit her quite hard with the flat of his hand, supposedly as a therapy for hysteria. But her tears merely increased, making an embarrassing segment of Beaver's riding breeches dark and sopping wet.

Alone in the front, driving, was Dr Mason, who put his head out of the window to address Widger and Ling. "Anything I can do?" he asked cheerily. "I picked these two up when I was on my way to a call in Glazebridge—it's only Mrs Teacher's prickly heat again, so I'm in no hurry—and they said the girl had had a fall, and I said she'd better come in to Glazebridge for X-rays, so they left their horses at The Stanbury Arms, and here we are. They said something about an accident up the lane." He eyed de Brisay, who certainly made a woeful spectacle, and then sniffed. "You the accident? You look as if you could be. If so, you must have fallen into a Kipp's apparatus and then tried to climb a chimney. No?" Dr Mason eyed Rankine. "Come to that, you look a bit the worse for wear, too."

"I am a p—"

"Get in the car, Rankine, and try not to say anything for at least half a minute. No, Doc, we're all okay," said Widger. "And now, if you'll excuse us, we're in rather a hurry. So..."

"There's a cowman," Fen volunteered, "who fell off his bike and thinks he's broken his ankle. That's up beyond Y WURRY."

"Get in and come and help me find him," said Dr Mason. "just between you and me and the gatepost," he muttered, "that pair in the back, between them, are about as much use as a sick headache, and not nearly so easily cured."

"All right," said Fen. He felt glad to be relieved of his moral obligation to the afflicted Enoch—though the chances were that some passing vehicle had already picked him up and carted him off to somewhere where remedial measures could be applied. The police cars roared off towards Burraford. Dr Mason roared off towards Glazebridge. Looking back, Fen could see de Brisay and the Rector climbing into the Mini, the Rector ostentatiously holding his nose...

Peace descended on Pisser land.

The man in the caftan was leading Xantippe—at a snail's pace, in view of her presumed infirmities and exhaustion—towards the woods. They grew smaller. And smaller. And presently were gone. Disarmed, the Pisser stood mute, just another constructivist monster left out too long in the rain. Or was it practicable to rustproof metallic structures, as one did cars?

The two workmen neither knew nor cared. Another stage of their labours completed, they were taking a break for lunch, sitting with dangling legs on the lowered tailboard of the C.E.G.B. lorry while they consumed sandwiches and beer. The sandwiches had crisp fresh lettuce in them, so that the two men scrunched as they ate. The beer they swallowed straight from the bottles, so that they slurped as they drank.

The infant Grand Duchess smiled bravely through her tears.

Enoch was still there, and at the approach of the Volvo roused himself sufficiently from his self-pitying torpor to make feverish checking gestures with his hands. The car stopped beside him and the doctor jumped out.

"Ha! What have we here?" he said with that settled eupepsia which at one time or another had numbed the sensibilities of most of the inhabitants of the district. "What seems to be the trouble, now?"

"It's me ankle, Doctor."

"Yes? And what about your ankle?"

"'Er'm broke."

"Dear, dear. Which one is it?"

Silently, Enoch indicated a point on the narrow grass verge precisely half way between his outstretched feet. Guessing, the doctor seized hold of his right foot and twisted it violently. The howl of anguish which went up from Enoch indicated that he had guessed right.

"Yes, well, it's a bit swollen," said the doctor. "Probably only a sprain, though. Can you wiggle your toes?"

"Doan know."

"Well, don't just *sit* there. Find out."

Gouts of sweat stood out on Enoch's forehead as he made the experiment. Presently, with some reluctance, he said, "Ar."

"It's a sprain then, for sure," said the doctor. "Still, better be safe than sorry. I'm taking this young lady into Glazebridge for X-rays, so you can come and be done too."

"Can't move."

"Then you'd better make preparations for spending the night here. Fen, come and give me a hand, will you?"

With Enoch's arms fastened vice-like round their necks on each side, they managed to get him, hopping on one foot, to the car, and to cram him somehow inside. "You coming with us, Fen?" the doctor asked.

But Fen shook his head. "I've had quite enough excitement this morning already," he said. "I'll walk back home and have a quiet afternoon, I think."

"Me bike!" shouted Enoch from inside the car. "What about me bike?"

Fen sighed. "I'll look after your bike for you," he said, and waved them on their way.

With its handlebars all twisted, Enoch's bike proved intractable, and Fen, after being forced virtually to heft it for a short distance, decided that he was tired of philanthropy and carried the machine into the Rector's garden, where he hid it behind a hedge, skulking there himself until de Brisay and the Rector had arrived in the Mini and gone inside. Then he made his escape. The psychedelic estate wagon, he noted in passing, was empty now. (It remained in position, slowly falling to bits, for months and months afterwards, while the police vainly tried to ascertain its ownership, and eventually had to be towed away to be pulped. The bald youth and the hunt saboteuse, Mr Dodd's intimates later learned, had suddenly got tired of quarrelling—had, indeed, all at once shown every sign of nursing the warmest affection for each other—and "We're going to copulate," the hunt saboteuse announced, rather as if referring to a visit to some festival such as Glyndebourne or Bayreuth, "and we're going to do it behind a hedge, the way all decent animals do." With this much preliminary, they had gone off together to find a suitable gate; though whether their congress was successful or not was never known, since no one in Devon ever set eyes on them again. As to Mr Dodd, he had reeled unsteadily along the lanes leading to Glazebridge and home and a spare pair of glasses, being mercifully picked up near Hole Bridge by a customer who took him the rest of the way. Thereafter, his interest in hunt sabotage became increasingly theoretical, eventually petering out altogether despite the impassioned reproaches of his whilom fellow-crusaders.)

So Fen passed the marooned estate wagon and continued on his way, soon reaching the turning which led up to the Dickinsons' cottage. In the hut in the garden of Thouless's bungalow, dreadful dissonances suggested that he had been compelled to abandon his relief music in favour of yet another monster, and at Youings's pig farm a man sent by Clarence Tully was attending to the requirements of Youings's pigs.

"Boo," he said, turning at Fen's approach. "Boo, ah boo-boo."

"Boo?" Fen answered amenably, and was at once subjected to a perfect storm of boo-ing, an opera-singer's nightmare. When this had subsided a little:

"Boo," Fen said, "Oh, ah, boo-boo."

The idiot was plainly delighted at this incisive, thoughtful response. "Boo," he said, waving his hand in friendly dismissal, and reverted to feeding the pigs. "Boo."

"Boo," Fen agreed, and passed on up the lane. Trudging up the rocky defile which did service as the Dickinsons' drive, and which looked as if it marked, unaltered, the passage of some small but implacable glacier of the quaternary, Fen reflected that village idiots were something of a rarity these days, whereas in previous times the mating of two members of a particularly stupid family (MUM [*on her death-bed, to her eldest daughter* GWLADYS]: And you, Glad my girl, you just see to it, after I'm gone, that yer Da's kept comfy-like. Know what I mean? GWLADYS [*with enthusiasm*]: Oh yes, Mum! MUM: That's all right, then. These nasty things are best kept in the family, that's what I always say. [*Dies; after a seemly interval for weeping,* GWLADYS *hies her blithely to incestuous sheets.*])—whereas in previous times the mating of two members of a particularly stupid family could virtually be relied on to engender an ament of one sort or another. Now the breed had largely died out, possibly because in 1908 incest was made illegal, possibly because of the efforts of such as the Rector, possibly because—

At this stage of his meditations, Fen woke to the awareness that there was a tortoise-shaped lacuna in his garden. Good. The pansies were mostly wilting or dead, Ellis was fussy about what else he ate, and it was time for him to be having another go at hibernation in any case. (Fen vaguely recalled glimpsing a tortoise somewhere quite recently, but where?) Meanwhile, Stripey was waiting with a haunted look—he had been over-doing the sex again—outside the front door for someone to come and let him in. Fen did this, and they rushed side by side to the scullery, Fen only remembering to duck his head in the nick of time. Here, with Stripey performing figure eights between and around his ankles, Fen opened Kattomeat, chopped it up in a dish and dumped it on the mat, subsequently, in addition, supplying fresh milk and water, with a sense of the vanity of human endeavour which arose from the fact that Stripey seemed partial to neither fluid: at all events, Fen had never witnessed his sampling them. Turning now to his own requirements, Fen took a terrine of *foie gras* from the refrigerator, along with a half-bottle of Roederer Kristal Brut; supplemented this nourishment with a glass, a plate, a spoon, a knife and some water biscuits; and was about to carry the whole lot into the living-room when his attention was caught by an unfamiliar white blur on the mantelpiece above the Rayburn. Disburdening himself temporarily, he went to investigate, finding a message for him scribbled on a sheet torn from a Shopping-List pad. It was from his cleaner, and it ran:

I singed for this as it seamed alright,

BRAGG.

(Mrs Bragg for some reason always referred to herself in this synoptic fashion—and indeed to her whole family of whatever age or, sex, even including the baby ["Bragg cut another tooth during the night"]. She apparently feared that any further fissidity in the naming of the clan, other than what was required to differentiate it from the rest of the world, would result in estrangements among its various members, or even in total cataclysmic disintegration; as a consequence, no one in her household could ever be sure whom she was addressing at any given time.)

Her note was propped against a letter marked in one place "Special Delivery", and in another, "Recorded Delivery". The scrawled address on the letter was in the handwriting of Henry, the St Christopher's College porter at Oxford with whom Fen, unfortunately, as Dean, was in a constant state of muted enmity. Leaving for his sabbatical, Fen had given Henry instructions that nothing whatever was to be forwarded to him, at his Devon address, unless it seemed of the first importance—and Henry, conscious of the limits which the lowliness of his position *vis-à-vis* dons imposed on his disobedience, had so far forwarded nothing. This, however, he had dared to forward, so what could it be? Fen tore open Henry's envelope to find another envelope inside it, addressed to him at the College in a cursive, clerkly hand. Also, it was registered; its flap was secured, in addition to the usual gum, with a large, impressive red seal. Below this, in print, ran the legend, "If undelivered, return at once to the Senior Official Receiver, Thomas More Building, Royal Courts of Justice, Strand, W.C.2." It read like an instruction from an obstetrician to a lady whose gestation has gone long beyond its proper term, and who has been given oxytocin to hurry matters up.

Anyway, it explained Henry: Henry had fancied that Fen's absence had given his creditors the chance to file a suit in bankruptcy against him, and had been anxious that he should know about this, and be reduced to a fit of the tremors, at the earliest possible moment—for, as la Rochefoucauld remarked, there is always something pleasing to us in the misfortunes of others, especially when the others are Professors and you are merely a porter. Fen snorted, thrust the envelope unopened into his jacket pocket, reassembled his meal and carried it into the living-room, where—suppressing his usual qualms about obese poultry with induced hepatitis—he unsealed the terrine, opened the Roederer and settled down on the chesterfield to eat and drink. In order to keep in touch with civilisation while he did this, he grabbed the topmost book from the nearest pile and began to read it. It was called *Hackenfeller's Ape*, and was the work of Brophy, Brigid.

Stripey, meanwhile, unsated by Kattomeat, had slunk into the room, jumped up on to the coffee table, and was attacking the *foie gras*. Fen noticed this pilfering too late to put a stop to it. He fetched a second terrine from the scullery, ran the knife round that, took off the top, and had scarcely settled back again into the chesterfield before he observed that with terrine one still not half consumed, Stripey had moved on to terrine two, and was making heavy inroads on that. Grateful that the creature was in both senses a pussyfoot, Fen drank some champagne and returned to his reading.

Hackenfeller. It sounded like a Groucho alias—Otis B. Hackenfeller, Licensed Chiropractor. Not more than twenty pages, however, were needed to convince Fen that in this particular script, S. J. Perelman had had no hand.

Abruptly tiring of literature, Fen remembered the registered letter, took it from his pocket and wrenched it open, a large proportion of the splintered red wax going into the Roederer. Jobson and Ellis (who had commissioned the book on modern British novelists) were unhappily, he learned, going into voluntary liquidation, owing to being unable to meet their debts; all contracts with authors were consequently suspended until matters had been clarified; further information would be forthcoming in due course; pending this, the writer was Fen's very obedient servant, Squiggle.

Fen pondered this; and the more he pondered it, the more he liked it. Some of the reading had been enjoyable, of course—*The Doctor is Sick, I Want It Now*, "the Balkan trilogy", Elizabeth Bowen, *The Ballad and the Source*. But much more had not—and a great deal that was pending wasn't going to be, either.

"Wasn't going to be"? What did he mean, "Wasn't going to be"? "Wouldn't have been," because he wouldn't now be doing any of it.

With a sigh in which repining played little part, Fen abandoned Brophy, Brigid, and reached for Gibbon's *Autobiography* instead.

CHAPTER THIRTEEN

The Chesterton Effect

And then comes answer like an Absey book.

William Shakespeare: *King John.*

"**S**O THE MAN FROM SWEB** wasn't the murderer after all," said the Major. "Pity. I rather fancied him."

"You'd fancy an earthworm to win the National," said the Rector.

"Extraordinary you should say that, because I once actually knew a horse called Earthworm. He was called Earthworm because he kept trying to burrow, I've no idea why. Heaven only knows what goes on in those ghastly great pop-eyed heads of theirs."

The Rector drank soup. "Not wanting to be my valet," he said. "Preferring to go to prison. Can you imagine such a thing?"

"Well, yes, my dear chap, since you come to mention it, I can."

"I seem to be losing my thaumaturgical touch, too," said the Rector, uncomforted. "Talked to him about Christianity all through the *Tournedos Barbara*, and at the end of it all, do you know what he said?"

"One could make several guesses," said the Major reservedly.

"Said he had a nice little nest-egg tucked away, and would I sell him my cook. I said my cook wasn't to be bought and sold like some Nubian slave, but afterwards I caught the two of them muttering together in a corner, and he was saying something about people who play horrible practical jokes on innocent bystanders, and she'd taken one of his hands and was patting it. *Patting it*! I didn't think much of *that*, I can tell you. Gave them both the sharp end of my tongue, in a way they won't forget in a hurry."

"They haven't," said Fen. "I was passing your house earlier this evening, and your cook was getting into a taxi, along with a lot of luggage."

"*Appropinquet deprecatio*," said the Rector, rolling his eyes to the ceiling and momentarily forgetting the popish effluvium which hung about the Latin language like butterflies round a buddleia. "Ah well, I suppose it's scrambled eggs and chips from now on. They're the only things I can do," he said to Fen. "However, when I do do them, I do them well. As my grandmother always used to, say, 'You can't cook scrambled eggs too slow, and you can't cook chins too quickly.' It's true, too."

The Major faintly groaned. On the one or two occasions when this sort of thing had happened before, he had been expected, he remembered, to enthuse over stirred-together yolks and whites of virtually uncooked egg, dotted with splinters of adamant butter and served on a substratum of charcoal sticks. He made a mental resolve that until the Rector got himself a new housekeeper, he, the Major, was going to find himself subject to painful aftermaths of his Fall whenever issued with an invitation to eat at Y WURRY. To change the subject he now said:

"De Brisay won't get much of a sentence, though, will he, so long as you don't testify against him?"

"Well, I shan't do that," said the Rector, spooning up more soup. "I most certainly shan't do *that*. Wretched misguided fellow's more than repaid his debt to society, as far as I'm concerned. Lovely soot, stink like a polecat, half deafened, and then that fellow in leggings comes along and conks him on the nut with his mill-board. Haw-*haw*," said the Rector, his Christian charity momentarily in abeyance. "No testifying from me. No bringing charges, I mean."

"But the police are going to bring charges," Fen pointed out.

"Let 'em."

"Which means you're bound to be sub-poena'd."

"Oh Lor', does it?"

"Of course it does. So what are you going to say?"

The Rector thought about this; then: "I shall tell Hizonner," he announced eventually, "that I deliberately lured the man into my house. And it'll be quite true. I did."

"And that you then deliberately lured him into surreptitiously making off with your grandmother's jewel-safe?"

"H'm. Yes, I see what you mean. That's going to be a bit more difficult."

"I never saw any good that came of telling truth. Dryden."

"That wet."

"Yes, fancy anyone thinking that *Paradise Lost* would make a good light opera," said the Major. "I'm surprised Milton let him in the house. Now, let's see, where was I?"

"It was I who was speaking," said the Rector, peeved. "Though evidently not to much effect...Fen, if you were in my position, what would *you* do?"

"I'd tell them the whole thing from beginning to end, just as it happened. It really is quite funny, you know. The judge'll be so sorry for poor de Brisay that he'll get off very lightly, you'll see." (And this, in the event, was what happened.)

The fine spell had broken at last: it was not only blowy and rainy, the gusts flinging the raindrops against the old window-panes of the Dickinsons' cottage like handfuls of tiny pebbles; it was cold as well, and Fen's two guests were grateful when he moved the kitchen table close to the Rayburn. A farewell party, this was to have been, but two of the invited had proved unable to come. Thouless was all agog, since for once he had been commissioned to compose the score for a film not involving more work for the makeup people, the special effects men and the art director than for anyone else. True, he told Fen, a very similar type of music seemed to be expected of him, but he was hoping to insinuate a late-Romantic chord or two here and there. Anyway, he was very sorry, but he was committed to go to Pinewood to see the film a second time, and so couldn't, much as he would have liked to, share in the jollifications Fen had presumably planned.

"What's the film called?" Fen had asked, mildly interested.

"*Warts.*"

"I see. And what's it about?"

"Almost entirely, it's about several couples having a bang in bed in Paris. They keep switching around, but I'm not sure of the reason. Anyway, some of the things they get up to—! You'd scarcely think they were anatomically possible. I mean, there are some angles the human skeletal and muscular structures are quite simply incapable of, so I suppose a lot of it must be trick photography. The great thing is, though, from my point of view, that it's not about monsters, it's about sex. There are bits I can use up, too, one long section in particular, for where the hero and heroine seem to be standing on their heads, mother-naked, with their toes intertwined. I don't know," Thouless said doubtfully, "that I should very much want to try that myself."

"Anyway, the point is, you've already got the music for it."

"For that particular scene, yes, I have. Quite a big bit which they cut out of *The Blob*. I shall scarcely have to alter it at all."

"And what was it for originally?"

"It was for beaked dekapods being slowly incinerated by a death-ray in a space-ship. Much the same sort of thing, really. Well, cheerio. Been nice knowing you. Have a good time."

Padmore's leave-taking had been considerably less ebullient. "I can't think what I've done wrong," he kept saying to Fen, who had gone to Glazebridge station that morning to see him off. "I just can't think what I've done wrong. They said I was doing such a good job down here, and—"

"Yes, of course you did a good job, but the telegram explained that, didn't it? The Crime Staff is fit to go to work again."

"Yes." Padmore stared for the umpteenth time at the message on the piece of paper which had been delivered to him with his breakfast: "Come back to London soonest prepare leave for Libya soonest terrorists blowing up all the oilwells there." "I don't like bombs," said Padmore. "I don't *want* to be bombed."

"Never mind," Fen consoled him. "I expect you'll have been expelled by Gadafi long before anyone has a chance to bomb you. Besides, just think. It might have been Uganda."

"Oh God."

"Or Angola."

"Oh God, God…Gervase, you know what I'm going to do?"

"No. What?"

"I'm going to buy myself a little cottage here in Devon and just write books about murders."

"There aren't *many* murders down here, you know. These last few months have been quite exceptional."

"Oh, I don't mean just Devon murders. Murders everywhere, and particularly the old ones, which have never been properly solved. There was an extraordinary business in Victorian times in Balham, for instance—"

"I'm afraid you'll find that about six thousand books have been written about the Bravo Case already."

"Well, *something*." Padmore fixed his eyes on one of the innumerable B.R. symbols dotted about the station—simplified representations, they seemed, of a particularly nasty derailment. "There must be *something*. Your own cases, now—"

"Crispin writes those up," said Fen, "in his own grotesque way.* And there's not much money in it, John. In writing about any murders, I mean."

*I include this fragment of dialogue only at Fen's personal insistence.—E.C

"I don't need much," said Padmore lachrymosely. "A roof over my head, a warm fire in winter, beans on toast, clothes, whiskey, wine, a car, a stereogram, records, books, just a few decent sticks of furniture—that'd have to be Georgian, I certainly couldn't afford Queen Anne—a daily, a gardener, a—a—"

"A crooked Tax Accountant," Fen suggested.

A whistle blew and the train began to move. Padmore grasped Fen's hand through the open window, and bade fair to drag him at increasing speed right along the platform and off the end of it unless he literally wrenched himself free. The newspaperman—whose vocation, Fen judged, though misguided, was unlikely ever to be replaced by anything else—continued despite this forcible parting to wave from the window until the train rounded a curve and his atebrine-yellowed face was lost from sight.

So now, in the cosy warmth of the Dickinsons' cottage's kitchen, it was just Fen, and the Rector, and the Major. Stripey, judging the weather too inclement for venery, was asleep in the adjoining room.

"Good soup, this," said the Rector. "I'll have some more," he added, never backward in making his requirements known.

"That's the way," said Fen, ladling the fluid on to the Rector's plate from a saucepan on the stove.

"And what's for afters?"

"Cold roast partridge, salad, mashed potatoes. Peaches in brandy and Brie."

"Sounds all right."

"Mostly from Fortnum's, I'm afraid. But the soup," said Fen, "I made myself."

"Delish."

"You, Major?" Fen asked. "Basis is shin of beef."

"Excellent, my dear fellow, excellent."

"It ought to be excellent, because I've been boiling it up every day for more than a week now."

"So I can imagine," said the Major, paling slightly. "Yes, really quite excellent. Very...very *strong*."

"The wine's good, too." The Rector picked up one of the two bottles and stared incredulously at the label. "La Tache, 1953?" he exclaimed. "I didn't know there was any left in the world. However did you get hold of it?"

"There are still a few dozen in the College cellars."

"Bibulous dons," said the Rector, holding his glass to the light. "Lovely orangey colour. I'll have some more of that, too."

"Join me in a Sweet Martini," the Major chanted, to the tune of *Frère Jacques*. "It has taste! It has taste!"

"You've had quite enough to drink already, Major," said the Rector severely. "And besides, it's very ill-bred to sing at table."

"It's gotta be Tide—Noo Tide!"

"Kindly be *quiet*. Fen, did Ortrud Youings kill Routh?"

"Oh, I should think so, yes. In fact, she boasted of it when they arrested her. But then she changed her mind, when they got a lawyer in to look after her. And after that, she wouldn't speak anything but German—she's one of those women who can never stop talking, but she had the sense to wrap it up until they could get an interpreter, and that took quite a long time. After that, it was German for days on end, and Not Guilty all along the line. Of course, they'll have her for bashing her husband, but as to Routh—well, there's some independent evidence against her, from X, but that may not be quite enough. What obviously happened was that she went out for a walk on the evening before the Bust girl found the body, met Routh, and tried to seduce him, as she did anything in trousers. And Routh, I think, must have simply jeered at her (he wasn't a one for the women anyway, let alone a tigress like that), so that she got enraged and knocked him on the head."

"Was she the woman Hagberd was referring to when he said he was 'crook with a sheila'?"

"I imagine so, don't you? She'd have tried her little games on him, all right. But Hagberd was—is—a bit of a puritan. He'd have been shocked to the core at the idea of having an *affaire* with the wife of another man—especially if the other man were someone he liked, such as Youings. So Hagberd turned our Ortrud down, and she was fresh from that humiliation when miserable little Routh had the nerve to turn her down, too. It was too much, and she simply brained him—and went on her way singing, I've no doubt, as happily as a lark. And then Hagberd chanced on the body, and although he wouldn't himself have *killed* Routh (almost everyone in the neighbourhood agreed about that), he was quite dotty enough to do the dismembering and play all the foolish tricks with the head."

"Will the Court find Ortrud guilty but insane, or whatever the phrase is nowadays?"

"I expect so. And then after she's been put away for a few years, some lunatic Parole Board will decide that she's now fit to be a member of society again, in which case"—Fen shrugged—"the whole thing will probably happen all over again, somewhere else."

"Which brings us," said the Rector, "to X."

"Ah yes, X." Fen nodded. "Psychologically, I think, the most interesting murderer I've ever had the pleasure of meeting. Great cunning combined with crass stupidity. Great unscrupulousness and great sense of duty. Great bravado—with a humorous touch to it, even—and ridiculous timidity. Great good luck, and great bad..."

The Rector drank wine. "Luckraft," he said. "Police Constable Andrew Aloysius Luckraft. Seen him about the place for donkey's years, and until the papers printed them, for the life of me I couldn't have told you either of his Christian names."

"Brothers," said Fen, rather as if addressing a trade union of two. "Andrew Luckraft had a brother, George. They didn't greatly resemble one another either in looks or in temperament. As regards temperament, although it was Andrew who committed the fratricide, George was in character by far the more criminal of the two. If he hadn't decided to blackmail

Andrew for every penny Andrew could produce, he wouldn't have been killed—and probably, when the money ran out, Andrew would have gone to the authorities and told them the whole dismal story, including the virtually certain murder of Routh by Ortrud Youings. As it was, he got the wherewithal to pay his exigent brother from a *second* blackmail. Youings, as we know, doted on Ortrud—though he's got over that now, thank heavens; and Youings had a bit of money in addition to owning the pig farm. So when Andrew found out that it was Ortrud, almost incontrovertibly, who had broken Routh's pate for him, he knew where to turn in order to meet his brother's demands. Youings would believe him, all right, when told what Ortrud had done—for all his uxoriousness, he had no illusions at all about his wife's occasional shocking malignancy and violence—and Youings would pay. In his turn, Andrew would pay George out of the proceeds. And that was really the only link between the two cases. It's unique, though, as far as I'm aware—A blackmailing B for the cash to silence C, who in a sort of circlet is blackmailing A."

"Yes, I see that much, my dear fellow, and as far as it goes it's very clearly put, if you'll forgive my mentioning it. But there must have been a lot of factors which haven't appeared in the papers, as far as I know. F'rinstance, I don't understand how—"

"And you never will," said the Rector testily, "if you don't keep your mouth shut and let Fen get on with it in his own way. As to the papers, the police, since it concerns one of their own number, aren't giving out a scrap more information than they absolutely have to. What I don't understand is how Fen comes to know so much more about the business than anyone else. What *I* can't see—"

"And never will," said the Major, "if you don't belt up for a minute or two, while our host puts us in the picture—"

"Stop it, you two," Fen reproved them mildly. "I know what I know simply because a few days ago I read Andrew Luckraft's confession."

"So he *did* confess!"

"To killing his brother, yes. Not to killing Mavis Trent. He says it's true he was having an *affaire* with her, but he doesn't know anything at all about her death."

"Wise of him," said the Major dryly. "He might confess to killing his brother, and the jury might be a little bit sympathetic, particularly since the brother was a blackmailer and in general, as far as I can gather, pretty much of a bad hat. But Mavis Trent a jury certainly *wouldn't* forgive him for...I say, what a lot of nymphos there are in this case. Now if only Mavis and Ortrud could have got together and organised a sort of joint lesbonympho, probably none of this would have happened. Just goes to show what a powerful force sex still is."

"'Still'?" said the Rector. "I can't think what you mean by 'still'. Anyway, Major, you brood far too much over sex. It'll ruin your health, just see if it doesn't."

"My dear fellow, I hardly ever think about it at all. Not voluntarily." The Major sounded quite put out at this presbyteral slur on the purity of his imaginings. "Much too old. The only time I think about it is when I wish I lived in a country where somebody or other wasn't bedevilling you with sex, in one form or another, every five minutes. It's like being infested with gnats. Do you think they'd take kindly to me in Éire?"

"No."

"There was a girl on the telly doing the washing up in just high heels and panty-hose. Whatever would you think if I were to do that?"

"I shouldn't be surprised in the least. Fen, how did you *come* to read this confession of Luckraft's?"

"Widger showed it me."

"Oh, he did, did he? Why?"

"He seemed to feel," said Fen evasively, "that he owed me some sort of a favour."

"And did he?"

"Nothing to speak of."

"You didn't mention it yesterday or the day before."

"No. I was asked not to. But now that Luckraft's safely surrounded by lawyers, they feel they can release most of what he said. It'll be in all the papers tomorrow, so there's no reason why you two shouldn't know about it now. Sir Robert Mark has been informed. So has the Queen. Though what *they're* expected to do about it, except waggle their heads," said Fen with some candour, "I really can't imagine."

"I've watched the Queen closely," said the Rector, who as a matter of fact couldn't remember ever setting eyes on her, "and she never waggles her head."

"Well, anyway, it's all public knowledge by now," said Fen. "So if there are any questions—"

An instant and simultaneous babble erupted from the Rector and the Major. Fen waited for it to minify, and then fastened on the last (indeed, first) enquiry that was more or less wholly intelligible.

"Begin at the beginning? Well, there's good precedent for that—as well as for stopping when you reach the end. The beginning, of course, is Mavis Trent and her men. It was inevitable that sooner or later she would set her cap at Andrew Luckraft, and sure enough, she did. And he fell. His wife isn't a marvellously agreeable person, I understand, and probably the only reason he stuck with her so long was that she had this bit of money of her own, and wasn't too ungenerous with it; so he needed sympathy as well as sex, and Mavis Trent was good at supplying these in a single attractively wrapped package. But the wife, though open-handed enough, had from the point of view of Luckraft's *affaire* one serious disadvantage: she was a maniacally jealous woman; one hint of the Mavis Trent business and Luckraft would have whizzed through the Divorce Court like a naked man running the gauntlet through two rows of sadists with spiked whips, and been back in no time to living on a humble copper's pay. Not so impossible to do that, you may say; but like most criminals, Luckraft failed to see that you can hardly ever, on this turning globe, rob Peter without paying Paul; and he knew that Mavis, though she had money too, was altogether too fond of variety in her men to be likely to want to keep him indefinitely in the rather better-than-average style to which he'd become accustomed.

"So—it all had to be a dead secret. And a dead secret it actually was until one fateful day when Luckraft agreed to meet Mavis in a pub in Plymouth, and take her out to dinner.

"Because, you see, there just happened to be someone else in that particular pub on that particular evening: Andrew's brother George.

"Their lives had taken different courses, and they'd never even attempted to keep in touch. Andrew, always the more law-abiding of the two, had become a policeman; George had gone into the Merchant Navy, and despite a few dubious incidents *en route*, had eventually got his Mate's ticket. He never ranged far afield, I gather—none of that xenophile curiosity to see the world—but stuck to the British ports and the closed Continental ones; so there was nothing intrinsically surprising about his turning up in Plymouth.

"It took half an hour's surreptitious staring for the brothers to recognise one another; and when they finally did, their meeting wasn't exactly a joyous one. But booze works marvels, and one of the marvels it worked this time was to make a gift to Mavis of a brand-new and, she thought, infinitely superior man—infinitely superior to Andrew, I mean. Andrew was stolid and socially unenlivening; George could draw the long bow, in an endless stream of amusing nautical anecdotes which always, as well as being mildly scabrous, made himself out the duffer until the final touch of self-aggrandisement which represented him as being by a hair's breadth the victor in the end.

"Mavis was enchanted by all this. When Andrew went off to the Gents, she responded eagerly to George's suggestion that they should meet again. He would probably be in Plymouth for several weeks, he said; so if she didn't mind being seen about the place with a poor old crock of a shellback like him—

"Mavis didn't mind: it was as if Andrew had never existed. She arranged her first date with George there and then…"

"And never lived to keep it."

Fen sighed. "And here, I'm afraid, is where it all becomes very vague and conjectural. We do know, though—because Luckraft has told us so—that Mavis wrote George a long letter at his Plymouth address, in which she expressed her undying affection for him and poked fun at his brother, whom, she mentioned in passing, she was due to meet late the following evening at Hole Bridge. She was going to give Andrew a bit of a fright, she said, just because he was such an old stick-in-the-mud. But then she'd tell him it was all only a joke—and she'd tell him, too, that it was George she wanted now, someone who'd seen a bit of life, and not someone whose highlight of the year was keeping an eye on things at a perfectly well-behaved and completely boring old Church Fête."

"Yes, I suppose we are a bit boring," said the Rector meditatively. "But what are we expected to do? Hire the cast of Raymond's Revuebar?"

"Goodness gracious, my dear fellow," said the Major, "I never realised you knew about such things."

"Oh, I know about them, all right," said the Rector darkly. "Beast is beast and pest is pest, and ever the twain shall meet. The Bishop of Southwark was telling me all about the Raymond's Revuebar girls only the other day. But then somehow we got on to Bangla Desh (where I've been, by the way, and he probably hasn't), so I never got round to asking him how we could brighten our Church Fêtes up, short of breaking all the Ten Commandments simultaneously to a fanfare of slide-trombones." Plumbing the depths of gloom, "I dare say he's never come across the Ten Commandments, anyway, not to remember them," the Rector said. "And, you know, it's all very well and fine" ("hendiadys", the Major muttered) "but what is one to *do*? What is one ACTUALLY TO DO?"

"Talk less, for one thing," said the Major. "Fen here has scarcely got started, and here are you babbling about the Bishop of Southwark. You just leave the Bishop of Southwark alone."

"I wish he'd leave God alone," said the Rector. "God has managed for centuries without the Bishop of Southwark, so why—now—"

"THE LETTER!" the Maior shouted. "I want to hear more about THE LETTER!"

This contrived to silence even the Rector. Pouring them all some more La Tache, by way of vinous irenicon, Fen obligingly resumed his tale.

"George got this letter from Mavis, then," he said, "and to start with it simply amused him: his brother as a settled adulterer—and with an obvious flighty wanton like Mavis —struck him as one of the funniest things he'd ever come across. But his amusement altered—not to regret, but to sharp self-interest—when he read in *The Western Morning News* of the "sad fatality" at Hole Bridge. Details were at this stage scanty: but the date was right, and the time of night was right, and above all, the place couldn't have been righter. On Mavis he wasted no emotional capital: plenty of girls around, and most of them as easy to lay as one brick on top of another. Nor did he worry, to speak of, about whether the thing had been accident, suicide or murder. In fact, if it *had* been murder, then bully for dull Andrew: who would have thought the old man had so much blood—or at any rate, spunk—in him?

"No, the question was, what was in it for George? And what was the best way to play his cards? (He had at that stage not the faintest fear that what bridge players call a Yarborough, a hand with no honours cards in it, was what was eventually, in the shadow of Aller House, to be dealt to him by the "quiet" one of the family.)

"Yes, what was in it for George? Circumstances hadn't been kind to him recently (I'll explain that presently), and his first temptation was to milk Andrew for every penny he was worth, and then do a flit. But he soon saw the folly of that:

Andrew wouldn't be able to raise very much of a sum, all at once, and meanwhile there were debts (many of them due to an opinion which he was inclined to share with the Major, of the unreliability of horses) pressing on him urgently. He was in this frame of mind when a conversation in a bar with a man who owned a large electrical store decided him on his future course.

"'No, you don't make any profit to speak of just by selling things,' the man had said. 'You make it by persuading the mugs how lovely it would be if they could have some rubbishy gadget straight away, and then pay for it bit by bit. After that, it's only a matter of dickering with some finance company over who gets what proportion of the profits, and you can go straight out and order your first Rolls. The cash customers—well, half of 'em don't even ask for a discount; the rest you tell it's a one-off order, so they can only have five per cent. When you've done that a few times, you own a Merc as well. Or better still, become a finance company yourself.'

"George had listened, and he had learned: Andrew, or little by little. Because he had no doubt that the letter, if given to the police, would sink Andrew, good and proper."

"*Another* hendiadys. I say, we are having a—"

"Silence, Major! Silence, I say!"

"With that letter to guide them, Andrew's colleagues would start investigating his private life; and from that it was only a step to Mavis's death at Hole Bridge. Besides, Andrew's wife would go up in smoke; no hope of help or support from *that* quarter. All in all, Andrew had better pay—or else.

"Well, he paid. The first demand was for £100, and he managed that out of his own small savings. The same with the second. But with the third, he had to start asking his wife for money. He got it, on one specious excuse or another. But the demands continued to come in, regularly once a week, and Wifey soon became suspicious. The situation was desperate, until—"

"Until Ortrud Youings snuffed Routh," the Major interposed.

"Exactly. It was Prance who discovered Routh's dismembered corpse; but then Andrew Luckraft was left alone on the scene for quite some time. He wandered about Bawdeys Meadow looking for clues. And he found a clue, all right. He found the weapon."

"But, my dear fellow, I always understood that it was a wrench from his own—"

"No, of course it wasn't. It was Ortrud Youings's cosh, simply chucked away—that woman really is quite mad—somewhere among the trees."

The Rector stirred. "Her *cosh*?" he said. "Do you mean that thing she used to go about with, with the—"

"Yes. I gather almost anyone in the neighbourhood would have recognised it. During the Hitler war, her father was a concentration camp guard, you know—Auschwitz—and at the Nuremberg trials he was condemned to death for torture and for murder among the wretched inmates. Not before he'd engendered Ortrud, though. She was born subsequent to his execution, but his effects came to her through her mother, and among them this loathsome object which ought by rights to have been burned, if only because of the swastika decorating, in plaited leather, the handle. Anyway, she has it—had it—and used to carry it about with her most of the time. She was savagely resentful of her father's death, and the cosh became a sort of horrible cult-object to her, a sort of memorial to him. I'm surprised that she threw it away after killing Routh with it, but perhaps she had enough remnants of common sense left to imagine that she'd hidden it successfully, and could more safely come back to collect it after all the turmoil had died down. In any event, she didn't hide it very effectively, because Luckraft discovered it inside ten minutes, with Routh's hair and blood and brains still sticking to it.

"And there he saw his opportunity.

"His brother was still pressing him, and pressing him hard. He was frantic for money to keep Mavis Trent's letter out of the hands of the police.

"And here now was virtually incontrovertible evidence that Ortrud had murdered Routh.

"And here was a husband who doted on her.

"And the husband had money.

"There was never the smallest difficulty about it, Andrew says in his confession. For all his infatuation, Youings knew his Ortrud, and he paid up without complaining, without proof, on nothing but an anonymous letter-writer's say-so (it enclosed a gory Polaroid colour photograph of the truncheon; but Youings had already noted its absence, and when Routh was killed, had wondered). He had no thought of going to the police. He simply left the money, each week, where he had been told to leave it, and went away again. Next week, when he returned, it was gone, and he obediently left more. This couldn't have gone on for ever, of course: Youings's resources were by no means unlimited.

"But then George Luckraft precipitated matters.

"A hundred pounds a week doesn't buy all that much, these days. He could scarcely be said to be living in luxury. Moreover, he was the type of man who craves not just luxury, but unlimited idleness as well. Moreover—again—even if he had wanted work, he would in his present condition find it none too easy to get. He visualised quiet comfort, good food, decent clothes, a Jag at the very least, a blonde or two to go with the Jag, and plenty of doubles, morning and evening, at the local, where he would be one of the most welcome and popular customers they'd ever had. Most of this his brother Andrew could manage—*if* he went to live, to settle down permanently, in his brother's house. Some of it he might have to wait for, but he'd get it in the end...

"And so: that was the situation when Andrew drove in the Saab to Plymouth to plead with George—only to find that George, bag and baggage, was waiting to move in on him in the bungalow at Burraford.

"In Plymouth they ate and they drank together, that Friday evening just before the Church Fête. And to Andrew, one thing became abundantly clear: that though his wife would no doubt put up with an in-law for a week or two, the notion of his staying on indefinitely, as a subsidised lodger, would have no appeal to her whatever. One of the two had to go, wife or brother; and since with his wife dead he would still have George on his back, literally an old man of the sea, the one who went would have to be George. In any case, Andrew was heart-sick over the whole business, and not just for his own sake: he pitied Youings, and he liked Youings, and every time he milked Youings of more cash, he felt himself utterly contemptible.

"Yes, George would most certainly have to go."

In the momentary pause which followed this, the Major's diffident voice was heard. "Forgive me if I back-track just for a moment, my dear fellow," he said. "I'm being stupid, I know. But Luckraft 'came on what appeared to be—and indeed was—the weapon with which the murder was done.' Well, what he came on, you say, was this truncheon of Ortrud's, this cosh. But what he gave Widger and Co. was a wrench, a wrench from his—his own—" The Major gave way to what he would certainly have recognised as aposiopesis. "Oh," he said blankly. "Oh, yes, I see. I *am* being stupid."

"Glad to know you realise the fact," said the Rector rather acerbly. "It's all this drink you've been taking, you're not used to having so much. Obviously, what Luckraft did was (a) find the cosh, (b) recognise its blackmail potentialities, (c) hide it in his tool-kit, taking out a heavy wrench to make room for it, (d) smear the wrench with Routh's blood (he couldn't manage brains or hair, because Hagberd had made off with the head, and was using it to scare the wits out of that snobby hell-hag Leeper-Foxe, by dumping it through her breakfast-room window, and then, when she and the other woman rushed out to raise the alarm, taking it away again and substituting the bust of Butcher Cumberland which he'd snitched from Thouless's bungalow, probably with the idea of doing a war-dance round it and then pulverising it somehow, though what he actually did, one doesn't know, because one hears nothing more about it till it nudged Goodey on the foot) where had I got to?"

"'Lastly'," the Major suggested, "I counted three 'lastlys' in your sermon at Matins last Sunday, Rector, not to mention an 'in conclusion', 'finally' and a 'to sum up'. There were intervals of about five minutes in between. As Pepys tells us—"

"Never you mind Pepys," said the Rector darkly. "Yes, (d) continued: no brains or hair for Luckraft to smear on the wrench, but plenty of blood. So Luckraft uses that, then (e) he wipes the wrench clean of fingerprints, and puts it exactly where he found the cosh, and (f) displays it to Widger and the others when *they* turn up...Very clever of him, really," said the Rector in grudging admiration. "I mean, using his *own* wrench, and pretending it might have been stolen from him at any time, anywhere, in the previous few weeks. Diverted suspicion from him completely—because if he *had* killed Routh with the wrench, Widger would imagine that he would clean it up afterwards and put it back in his tool-bag, not display it publicly."

"Conditional clause syntactically a bit groggy there," said the Major. "Or to be more accurate, the main clause following. 'Would have cleaned', not 'would clean'."

"If there's anything in this world I hate," said the Rector, "it's a purist. And now, perhaps, if Dr Dryasdust can keep a still tongue in his head for just a few more minutes, we can get on. Fen?"

Fen absently nibbled at his Brie, which had just the right degree of runniness. "We left George and Andrew in Plymouth." he said. "And in that unhappy little discussion, George was—or at any rate seemed to be—the victor: Andrew agreed to drive him home to Burraford, and put him up in the bungalow there, at least for a few days, until, as he said, 'something more sensible could be worked out'. They ate fish and chips, and off they went. I don't think that at the time Andrew planned to kill George immediately; but then Fate, in the unexpected form of Andrew's conscientious police training, took a hand. Passing Aller House on their way into the village, Andrew suddenly remembered that he had promised to take a look round the site of the Fête once or twice during the night, to see if there were any pilferers on the prowl, as there had been occasionally in previous years. He told George this. George simply laughed, not dreaming that Andrew was actually going to *do* what he'd promised. However, Andrew *did* mean it: it's one of the strange contradictions in his character that although he was already in intention a murderer, and a fratricide at that, he still took it as morally essential that he should perform this trivial duty. He stopped the car; George, who never trusted anyone an inch—and in this case, how right he was!—said that although he considered the whole thing a lot of rubbish, he would come too; and while they were getting out of the car, Andrew, who trusted George no more than George trusted him, managed to smuggle his police truncheon on to his person without George's noticing.

"Outside the Botticelli tent, their quarrel flared up again, George speaking in whispers and Andrew ("lah-di-dah voice") in more normal tones. And from the youth Scorer we've heard, *ad nauseam*, what happened then. Andrew lost his temper, killed his brother with the truncheon, and dragged him into the Botticelli tent. There were essential things he had to do in the attempt to cover his tracks, and in the rear part of the Botticelli tent he would probably find the tools he needed…

"He did: a strange hacksaw, a heavy axe and a sharp knife had all been left there overnight. You see, the moment the corpse was identified as a Luckraft, Andrew would be lost: whatever the other evidence, he would be under observation continuously until he confessed, or was arrested, or killed himself; his chances of escape would be practically nil. But delay the identification of the corpse, and there was still hope. Remember, eight days from the inevitable discovery of the remains he was due for leave, when he had arranged to go on a package holiday to North Africa with his wife. And in Africa, it oughtn't to be too difficult to disappear. There's a constant demand for mercenaries in Africa, and so long as they're tough and can shoot, no one asks many questions about where they've come from, and why. Well, our Andrew was tough all right—

and Widger tells me that he was also considered a very good marksman. Wifey would languish in Tangier or somewhere until rescued by the British Consulate, and Hubby, meanwhile, would be growing a harvest of facial hair and working out plausible answers to any queries there might be about his experience and background and papers. From that time on, reliable old P.C. Luckraft of Burraford would be eliminated, for ever, from the face of the earth."

"Interpol?" the Major queried.

"Oh, no doubt in the end a telex would be sent to them at that hideous cuboid they inhabit at St Cloud. But Interpol's writ doesn't run—or at any rate, doesn't function—the whole world over, by any manner of means. Besides, the message would arrive too late: Andrew would already be deep in the Dark Continent by the time some bored Arab official received the telex and took action."

"So Andrew cut off his brother's head," said the Major.

"Yes."

"That's all very well, but surely he'd have been physically capable of dragging or carrying the complete body back to the Saab, and taking it away to some remote spot and burying it."

"Certainly. And that was what he originally intended to do—except that he was going to bury the head in one place and the rest in another, as a sort of double indemnity. Oh yes, and the clothes: George might conceivably have been identified by them, so they were to be parcelled up into lots and buried in yet more places. Quite a busy night, our Merry Andrew was proposing for himself—all the more so when you consider that his *own* blood-spattered clothes had to be got rid of too, and all traces of blood washed from his hands and fingernails and so forth. Luckily, his wife was quite used to his being in and out of the house at all hours of the day and night (he'd persuaded her that this was an unavoidable part of his police duties). At all events, he'd got as far as stripping the corpse, and cutting off the head, when there was an interruption."

"An interruption, my dear fellow?"

"Yes. You."

"Oh Lor'."

"You and your, um, conversible cocker bitch, Sal."

"'Conversible'!" The Major for a few moments was ecstatic. "The very word I've always wanted for Sal. 'Conversible', yes. Not a yapper, as unkind dog-haters are always saying, just con—"

"We take your point, Major," said the Rector. "And on the day Sal dies there'll no doubt be weeping and wailing and gnashing of teeth, all of it audible, for a change. Anyway, *I* think you had a very lucky escape."

"An escape, Rector? Escape from what?"

"From Luckraft, of course, you numskull. Here was a murderer standing over his victim, and here were you, within an ace of finding him. If Luckraft hadn't had scruples, we should have been walking along slowly behind you a week ago, wearing black and carrying our hats in our hands, and there'd also have been a freshly dug little grave in the Doggies' Cemetery."

"Phew!" the Major produced a gaudy silk handkerchief and swabbed his forehead with it. "Damme, I never once thought of it that way. Thank God Luckraft *did* have scruples."

"Yes, he's an odd bundle of inconsequences," said Fen. "Killing you, as a means of saving his own skin, is something which would simply never have occurred to him. Anyway, he heard you and Sal coming towards the Botticelli tent, and abruptly changed his plan. Pausing only to make preliminary slashes in the corpse's thighs, and to drag a big piece of tarpaulin over it in case you took it into your head to look inside and flash your torch around (he was still very much playing for time, remember), he grabbed up the clothes and the head and made himself scarce, with Scorer following as soon as it seemed safe to do so. So—when you got there, the cupboard was bare. Did you look inside the Botticelli tent, by the way?"

"Yes, I did, but it was just a quick glance around, don't you know. If anyone had actually been there, Sal'd have been yelling her h—I mean, she would have told me."

"Quite. So although Luckraft still had a pretty busy night, it wasn't as hectic as it could have been. Apart from anything else, although it took him a long time to smash the head up, he decided to keep it."

"His change of plan," said the Rector, "being to make the authorities believe either that they'd made a mistake, and the killer and mutilator of Routh wasn't Hagberd at all, but someone still at large; or else that this was an imitative crime. Hence using Mrs Clotworthy as a sort of rough substitute for the Leeper-Foxe. George's mangled head in its bacon sack was deposited in Mrs Clotworthy's porch surreptitiously next morning; at the same time, the pig's head—which Mrs Clotworthy *had* remembered to put out—was taken away; and Luckraft (supposed by his wife to have gone off on duty) kept watch from the tool-shed of the abandoned cottage next door. He knew Mrs Clotworthy's terror of human remains. He knew that when she saw the head, she'd simply drop it and run shrieking for help. And when she did that, he'd nip around, retrieve the head, and leave something equivalent to the bust of Cumberland in its place. What, I wonder?"

"It was a bust of Gladstone, as a matter of fact," said Fen. "It had lain underneath a pile of rubbish in Luckraft's garage for years now, and as Widger found out, *Mrs* Luckraft not only didn't know it was there, she'd never even set eyes on it or heard of it. Luckraft himself was very ashamed of it, because he'd paid through the nose for it at a junk shop in Exeter, only to find, when he took it to a genuine antique dealer for valuation, that it was worth about five shillings. He'd brought it home, but he'd never mentioned the shaming business to anyone, and only remembered about it when he was casting about in his mind for something to use in imitation of Thouless's bit of marble."

"Just a couple of questions, my dear fellow, if you don't mind," said the Major. And the Rector sighed histrionically. "First," said the Major, "did you ever suspect that it was him?"

"Not really, no," said Fen. "This wasn't a case in which there was too little evidence; it was a case in which there was far too much. The only thing was that when I heard the details of the death of Mavis Trent, it did just occur to me that if she'd been murdered, the killer might be a policeman."

"Why was that?"

"The fingerprints had been wiped off her bag before it was thrown into the Burr after her. Now, most people think that water, and especially running water, will eliminate prints; and sometimes it will. But then again, sometimes it won't—and that's the sort of detail that would be likely to be known to a policeman rather than to anyone in any other profession, except perhaps detective-story writing."

"Did Luckraft murder Mavis, do you think?"

Fen shrugged. "Let's say that I think it wasn't an accident. She *could* have been wiping her bag, using a man's cheap handkerchief, immediately before she tumbled and fell; all one can say is that it makes a rather queer sequence of accidents...As to the fun she was going to have with Andrew before dismissing him, which she mentions in the letter to George, I'm afraid it was that same old silly thing; I'm pregnant by you, darling, and what are you going to do about it? Then, after a bit of teasing, no, of course I'm not really, I was just having you on. But I'm afraid she was never allowed to get to the stage of issuing her *démenti*. One shove, and over she goes, dropping her bag on the way. The murderer picks it up, wipes it, and throws it after her. Then he waits until he's sure she's really dead. Then he goes home."

Despite the warmth of the Rayburn, the Major shivered a little. "Ghastly," he said. "Poor, poor silly child...What does Luckraft himself have to say about it all, in his confession?"

"Doesn't deny the *affaire*. Doesn't deny the letter. Doesn't deny the assignation. Doesn't deny that he went to Hole Bridge that night. But Mavis, he says, never turned up. So he waited half an hour or so, then left. *È finito*."

"Well, so *do* you think he did it?"

"Oh yes, obviously he did. For one thing, eliminate the letter and the blackmail over it, and there's no strong ascertainable reason left for Andrew's murdering his brother. Incidentally, regardless of the fact that it's what used to be called a capital charge, he's going to insist on pleading Guilty, and nothing the lawyers say will budge him. He'll just make a short statement saving that George was sponging on him, and that he suddenly lost his temper and killed impulsively. So there won't be any testimony that isn't purely formal—nothing about Mavis, nothing about the letter, nothing about anything. He'll simply go to prison and be kept there a good long time. And the Press will be furious, but there'll be nothing whatever they can do about it."

"Reporters," said the Major. "Never could stand the fellers. Padmore quite a decent sort, but the rest of them..."

"Mrs Clotworthy." At their current rate of progress, Fen was beginning to feel, his dissertation would last all night. "Mrs Clotworthy in her cottage, Luckraft in the old tool-shed (where he'd carefully hidden the bust of Gladstone, in readiness for its metamorphic function), the boy Oliver Meakins on the look-out for healing herbs, me passing The Stanbury Arms on my way to the footpath which leads from Holloway Lane to Chapel Lane.

"And then it all dissolves into farce. A puffing female messenger hammers on Mrs Clotworthy's door, which is at once opened to her. She delivers her tidings: Sandra is about to become a mother again. Enthralled, Mrs Clotworthy locks up and dashes away. So Luckraft's bit of misdirection has for the moment failed. Not quite certain of what to do next, he moves forwards, treads on the rake, whose handle clouts him on the brow, loses his balance and falls backwards, hitting his head so hard on the old mangle as to render him unconscious for ten minutes or so. Meanwhile, enter me. I see the sack with George Luckraft's head in it, assume it to be the promised pig's head, and pick it up and take it away without thinking to examine it more closely. It is either my constant companion, or sitting on top of my refrigerator, till early evening, when at last, following the discovery of a headless corpse in the Botticelli tent, it occurs to me to take a proper look at it—and if there was ever a detective in fiction more ridiculously circumstanced, I have yet to hear of him.

"So the head gets back not to Luckraft—who for hours hasn't the remotest idea what can have happened to it—but to the police.

"Widger and Ling interview Luckraft, as they interview everyone who entered the Botticelli tent during the time when the medical evidence says that the corpse's arm was cut off. And during that interview, Widger has told me, they inadvertently let a couple of cats out of the bag. In the first place, Luckraft learns that Sir John Honeybourne has said that the head, no matter how badly damaged, can be 'reconstituted', and a reasonably accurate simulacrum of it produced. In the second place, he learns that Widger and Ling are themselves going to take the head to Sir John as soon as their press conference at six o'clock is over.

"So Luckraft is once again in deadly peril—in peril that the head will be identified before he has a chance to get away to Africa. (He daren't, of course, try to get away before he has the excuse of the leave due to him: the hounds would be in full cry almost before he was across the Channel.) And that chance he simply must have. All leave will probably, in the circumstances, be suspended. But Luckraft has had his leave cancelled once. If he takes it now, in spite of its being cancelled again, his action will be put down, for a few days anyway, to simple bloody-mindedness. And by the time anyone gets to know anything different, he will have disappeared: no summons to Interpol will do the smallest good, if he can only have a little breathing-space in which to vanish.

"The thing for him to do, then, is to muddy the waters. The police are no fools, but even sages are confusable up to a point. And Luckraft's next step in this direction almost makes me feel an affection for him, ghoul though he undoubtedly was. Lingering with the other witnesses until the press conference began and they were free to leave, he happened to find in a pocket of the civilian suit he was wearing a relic of a small nephew's birthday party which he had attended some weeks previously. There had been crackers—good crackers, crackers as they used to be before the manufacturers decided they could get away with fillings of the cheapest possible rubbish. Luckraft had won a Dying Pig; and there, in his pocket, it had remained ever since its charms, at the party, had given place to rival attractions.

"You know the thing I mean, of course: it's a sort of small balloon which you blow up with a view to letting the air out and producing, by means of an ingenious device in the neck, one of the most hideous and realistic bubbling screams you ever heard.

"And Luckraft thought that he could use this. He *had* to get that head back before Sir John Honeybourne could work on it. So, he would set a trap. He would so horribly distract Widger and Ling, before they had a chance to make contact with Sir John, that with any luck at all they would plunge into the fray leaving Widger's car unlocked, with the head in it for the taking.

"And so it happened: the dreadful shriek from the back garden, Widger and Ling rushing round one side of Sir John's house, Luckraft slipping round the other—and the substitution of sacks.

"That substitution was, of course, strictly a bravura touch. Luckraft had the sack with Tabitha's head in it, which he had taken that morning from Mrs Clotworthy's porch (more misdirection!). Before driving to Sir John's isolated house, and concealing his car up the lane, he went home and retrieved Tabitha. Then, concealing himself in the twilight, in the wilderness at the front, he waited for Widger and Ling to come. They came. Luckraft crept round to the back and operated his Dying Pig. Then, while his superiors vainly beat the bushes in their search for the cause of the scream, it was back to the front, exchange Tabitha for George, gumshoe back to his car and drive quietly away.

"And this time, he was taking no more risks with George's head. He weighted it with stones and sank it in the Glaze—where the frogmen, I understand, at last found it yesterday morning. No, Luckraft was taking no more risks with George's head—or with anything else. He was wise there, I think; what with one thing and another, Widger and Ling were completely bemused already, and by the Friday afternoon, nearly a week after the murder, they still hadn't the ghost of an idea who the victim was, let alone who had murdered him. But then Widger suddenly realised something very simple that he ought to have realised long before."

"He was visiting you that Friday afternoon," said the Major dreamily. "There wouldn't be any connection, I suppose?"

"Certainly not. No connection whatever. He needed a rest, so we just talked about life in general."

"H'm," said the Major.

"Yes, Widger had this idea, and he made a lot of telephone calls, and one of them was successful. Hence the police cavalcade—somewhat obstructed, you'll remember, by a variety of factors—which we saw heading from Glazebridge into Burraford on Saturday morning. They were on their way to pick up Luckraft, and if not actually arrest him, at any rate take him back for some pretty strict and prolonged questioning. Well, they got there just in time: Luckraft and his wife were packed and on the point of leaving. And the questioning proved not to be necessary—any more than the small army they had with them proved necessary to overcome Luckraft's resistance. He came quietly. In Glazebridge, after all the due warnings had been given, he offered his confession, regarding which the only doubtful thing was his refusal to admit that he had killed Mavis Trent. I think he did it, but I also think that he was deeply ashamed of having done it. Ah well, I suppose now we shall never know. Not for sure."

"Ah," said the Major. "No wonder Widger and Ling didn't want to take de Brisay with them, and have him watch them arrest one of their own people."

Fen yawned and stretched. "And that, gentlemen, I think, is that. I don't know if anyone would care for a hand of bézique, or a—"

"Oh, no, you don't," said the Major. "You don't get away without answering the one really fascinating question."

"And that is?"

"How was almost all of a big man's arm smuggled out of the Botticelli tent? The Bale sisters were watching everyone like hawks, and I'll take my dying oath their evidence is reliable. The only thing the arm could possibly have been in was the Rector's cricket bag—which it wasn't, as Father Hattrick and I can both tell you."

"Ta ever so," said the Rector.

"So how was it spirited away? *How*?"

Fen seemed amused. "By the Chesterton Effect," he said.

"The *what*?"

"There are two Chesterton effects, actually, which are used in the Father Brown stories. The first you've just exemplified. It consists in asking the wrong question."

"In what way was my question wrong?"

"You should have asked, *Why* was the dead man's arm spirited away?'"

"Well, because it identified him in some fashion, that's obvious."

"Y-yes. Fair enough."

"If you ask me," the Rector interposed, "the whole puzzle arises simply because the medicos foozled their job. The arm wasn't cut off during the Fête at all, but at some much earlier time."

"No, the medical evidence was all right," said Fen. "And that brings us to the second and more important Chesterton effect: even when you've picked the right question, the answer to it is a paradox. So: 'Why was the dead man's arm cut off?' Answer: 'Because he hadn't got an arm'."

For a second or two the Major simply gaped. Then, with a moan, he collapsed in his chair like a pricked bladder. "Amputation," he mumbled.

"Exactly. And a fairly recent one, too, or the evidence of it would have spread upwards into the shoulder, and could hardly have been missed. But a recent amputation—George had got his arm crushed in a winch, by the way, and had to have it taken off, almost in its entirety, at Freedom Fields— would be much easier to disguise. There would be clip marks in the skin, and suture material in the wound; the main blood vessels would still fairly evidently have been recently tied. But there would still not be much shaping of the stump—it'd still be rounded rather than pointed; the main nerves would still be cut straight across; the sawn edge of bone would still be obviously fresh. To make it seem as if the *whole arm* had just recently been hacked off, you'd only have to remove a segment about half the length of your index finger. And the Bale sisters certainly wouldn't be on the watch for as small a bulge as that would make; if they noticed it at all, they'd simply assume that Luckraft had overstuffed one of his pockets.

"There was Widger's problem; and once he'd thought of the simple and only answer to it, all he had to do was ring hospitals and ask them what arm amputations had taken place recently, and what the name of the patient was. It took him a bit of time to get round to Freedom Fields and the (unusual) name Luckraft. But he did it in the end."

There was a long silence when Fen finished speaking. The wind had dropped but the rain had increased, and there were already bubblings and gurglings in the gutter which ran along the front of the cottage. With its two picked partridge carcases, the table had a slightly mortuary air; but the wine was completely gone, and no trace remained, either, of the bran-died peaches and cheese. Two thin slices of peeled cucumber clung to the sides of the salad bowl, in whose bottom a baby radish sat steeped in a little pool of French dressing. From the stove came the pleasant sound and scent of coffee percolating.

At last the Rector spoke. "Hagberd," he said.

"Is not at all a happy man," said Fen. "Or so Widger tells me. They don't quite know what to do about him."

"Why isn't he happy?"

Fen explained. For fear of an outbreak of books and articles by Ludovic Kennedy and Paul Foot, the authorities had hastened, when the news from Devon came through, to shift Hagberd from Rampton to some less penal, more analeptic, institution. But like so many well-meaning human endeavours, this change had failed to meet with its deserved success. Briefly, Hagberd loathed his new ambient and wanted to go back to Rampton again, where the warders were proper warders, and you could issue a bonzer hop out and mix it till you were dragged off. But lobbing in here had been quite different. Here, the warders weren't warders, they were long-haired, pebble-lensed cissies dolled up in white coats who gave you a chit to see the doc if you offered to punch them on the snout, and all the doc did was ask you if you hated your Mam. Also, here he wasn't allowed to do any work—not what you'd call *work*. Also, here they objected to him keeping a fowl-run. The whole place stank, and if this was going to be the alternative, he'd far rather they strung him up like any decent horse-thief.

"Yes, well, one sees his point of view," said the Rector, interested. "Still, I dare say they'll let him out altogether quite soon!' (They did; he went back to work for Clarence Tully and when getting on in years married an Aller girl who bore him a child regularly every ten months for nine years. He doted on this brood, and though still passionate about cruelty to animals, showed no further disposition to chop people up into pieces.)

"And you're leaving us tomorrow," the Major said to Fen. "Sad."

"The Dickinsons come back from Canada the day afterwards, and I've got to give Mrs Bragg the chance to clean up after me. Don't you get on with the Dickinsons?"

"Oh yes, quite well, but he's not a pubber, and nor is the

Rector, come to that, because people feel they oughtn't to drink much when he's there, and he stays away out of—out of"—here the Major dubiously studied the Rector's simian countenance—"well, out of delicacy, I suppose you'd have to say. Still, there are always books, and the dogs, and the telly, and showing visitors round Aller House, so I'll find plenty to keep me busy."

"Military Cross, Albert Medal, D.S.O., Conspicuous Gallantry," Fen murmured.

The Major flushed slightly. "Oh, I was very young and silly in those days," he said. "Besides, we were still on horses, and whenever you tried to turn tail and run, the half-witted creatures plunged on regardless, and one had to fight so as to get away. Besides, it's all ancient history now. Just hearing the Rector announce a hymn gives me a cauld grue nowadays...Oh, and by the way, did you know? The Rector's going over to Rome."

Fen stared. "I beg your pardon?"

"Woppie wrote and invited me," said the Rector complacently, as if this accounted for everything. "So I felt I had to accept. Woppie's my *amicus Curiae*."

"Excuse me, my dear fellow, but I don't think you're using that phrase quite correctly. It means 'a friend at court'."

"Not when it has a capital 'C', it doesn't," said the Rector contentiously. "When it has a capital 'C', it means a friend at some nasty popish court or other. Still, Woppie's on it, so it can't be all bad, I suppose."

"If you'd kindly explain," said Fen, "who Woppie is—"

"Woppie's a boy I was at school with," said the Rector. "He's a Cardinal now, of course, but he used to be great fun. His real name was Vittorio Nono, but he was called Woppie because he was a Wop, see? I can never understand," said the Rector, divagating, "why people object to being called Wops and Frogs and Huns and so on, when that's what they are. F'r instance, when I was in the States, people used to call me an effing Limey sky-pilot to my face, but I never objected. Why should I? 'No, I'm just a humble navigator,' I'd say. 'It's Jesus who's the pilot, and the engines are powered by the Holy Ghost, and the fuselage —the fuselage—'"

"Yes, what's the fuselage?" the Major wanted to know.

"It doesn't do to press these analogies too far," said the Rector rather coldly. "And in any case, by the time I reached that point, my audience had always somehow managed to disappear. Anyway, Woppie didn't mind being called Woppie in the least; he just laughed. Fine little chap—and the best three-quarter the school had had for generations. He could still teach Jarrett a trick or two, I'll bet."

"Woppie's going to show the Rector round the Vatican," said the Major. "And he's even arranged for him to have an audience of the Pope."

"No, he hasn't," the Rector said.

"But, my dear chap, you distinctly told me—"

"'Have an audience of the Pope' implies that the Pope's going to do all the talking and I'm going to do all the listening. Well, that's not going to be so at all."

"No," said the Major meditatively. "Come to think of it, I dare say it isn't."

"I'm not going to kiss His Holiness's ring, either," said the Rector, "(a) because it's idolatrous, and (b) because it's unhygienic—you never can tell who kissed it last—might have had yellow fever or something. But Woppie says the Pope won't mind, so considering all the circumstances, I shall go."

(In practice, as the Major wrote gleefully to Fen several weeks later, the interview had developed unexpectedly well, both men of God spending most of their time bemoaning not so much the Laodiceanism of their laymen as the follies of their clergy. "Not a bad chap at all," was the Rector's verdict on his return, "if only you could hammer some sense about Christian doctrine into his noddle.")

Now he said, "And your book, Fen: will you be going on with it when you get back to Oxford?"

"No, I shan't," said Fen, and explained about his publishers' voluntary liquidation. "Now that there's not likely to be any money, nothing would induce me to go on with it."

"But wouldn't some other publisher take it?"

"I dare say. But it's not really my line, you know. I was only doing it to fill in time."

"All those books that you've been reading," said the Major. "That must have been fun, anyway."

"Up to a point, Lord Copper."

"What *will* you do, then?"

"I shall write my own novel."

"Oh, good."

"It will be called *A Manx Ca.*"

"A what?"

"*A Manx Ca.* And once I get back to Oxford," said Fen, "I shall really be able to get down to it—in, as you might say, detail."